RACHEL L. SCHADE

Broken Kingdom

SILENT KINGDOM SERIES
BOOK 3

RACHEL L. SCHADE

Broken Kingdom

SILENT KINGDOM SERIES
BOOK 3

DRAGON SHADOW PUBLISHING

For my brothers, my reason to keep going.

And for my husband, who keeps me laughing.

NESTRED RUNES

CONDEMNED

DAUGHTER OF THE DEAD

ALONE

MAD KING

POWERLESS

INADEQUATE

PRONUNCIATION GUIDE

Characters

Halia (HAY-lee-uh)
Gillen (GILL-in)
Narek (NAIR-ek)
Velaire (Vuhl-AIR)
Avrik (Â-vrik)
Lyanna (LIE-ann-uh)
Elena (ELL-in-uh)
Captain Luiken (LOO-kin)
Haed (HAYd)
Iyleth (Î-leth)
Reylinn (RAY-lin)
Ilett (ELL-let)

Creatures

Sedwa (Sed-wuh)
Ichgor (ICK-gor)

Nestred (NESS-tred),
nestrae (Ness-TRAY)
Vilspen (Vill-spin)

Locations/Other

Misroth (MIZ-roth),
Misrothian (Miz-ROW-thee-
un)
Toryn (TOR-in)
Alrenor (AL-ren-or),
Alrenian (Al-REN-ee-un)
Vorvinia (Vor-vin-YUH),
Vorvinian Mountains (Vor-
vin-YUN)
Calidar (KAL-i-dar)
Vehgar (VAY-gar)
Nesrelle (NEZ-rell)
Elhalin (Ell-HAY-lin)

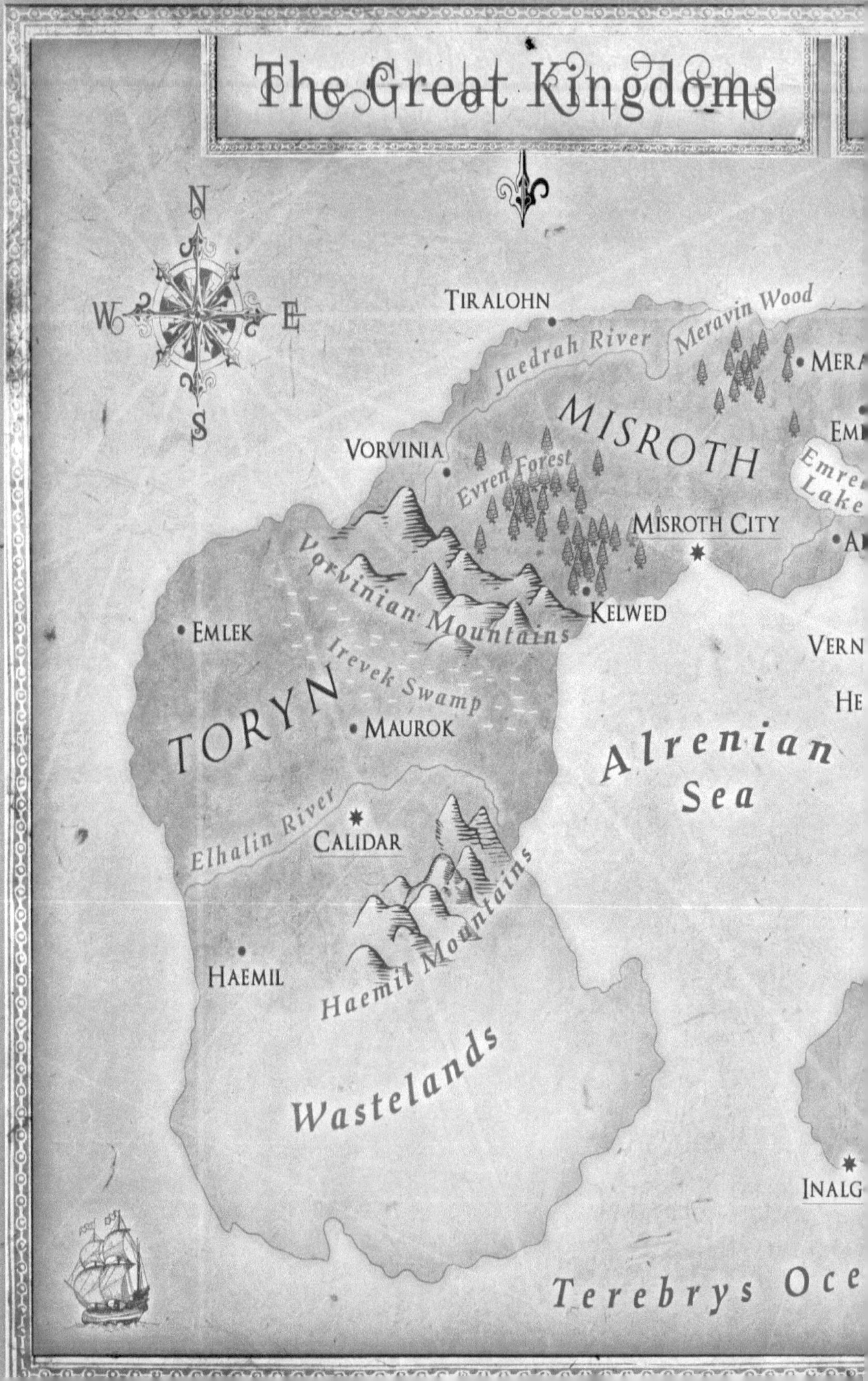

The Great Kingdoms
N
W
E
S
TIRALOHN
Jaedrah River
Meravin Wood
MERA
MISROTH
VORVINIA
Evren Forest
EM
Emre
Lake
MISROTH CITY
A
Vorvinian Mountains
KELWED
EMLEK
VERN
Irevek Swamp
HE
TORYN
MAUROK
Alrenian
Sea
Elhalin River
CALIDAR
Haemil Mountains
HAEMIL
Wastelands
INALG
Terebrys Oce

e Lesser Kingdoms
Hült Mountains
HÜLTEN
Shüldi River
BREVINN
Brevi Mountains
ell River
ok River
Brema Wood
Great Sea
Wild Lands
ENOR
ARAMITH
Brema River
est
Aramith
Mountains
Silondrian
Mountains
RHAEDA
FORWYTH
TERAMYL
VICIDOR
Maelvoc Forest
Xelrios River
Tuiros River

CHAPTER ONE

MY WORLD IS ENDING. THE horror of this realization made my mind reel. Smoke hovered over Evren like a living thing, twisting past Wanderer's Rest, past the shops along the streets, and into the hills and fields beyond, pressing toward the villagers' homes. Evren Garden was on fire, flames crackling and snapping at tree branches and devouring flowers. Rev and Lyanna were running, screaming, enveloped in thick black smoke as the flames leapt around them, licking at their backs. Consuming them.

I woke screaming. Tears clung to my eyelashes and blurred my vision. Hard earth pressed against my cheek and the scent of smoke stung my nose. Yards away, the nestrae were roasting meat over the dozens of fires scattered about their camp, but I lay in the dirt, stomach clenching from hunger and grief.

Maybe they were done with me now; I'd served their purpose by helping them break the barrier. Or maybe they would continue to keep me alive to torture me with the horrors they would unleash on my kingdom, all so they could sacrifice my grief to their goddess Nesrelle.

Chains clanked as I lifted my shackled hands to clutch at the pendants I wore about my neck: my mother's diamond star, Gare's gold circle, Jennah's diamond-studded silver constellation of Shyla, and the white and yellow gold rendering of Vehgar set with diamonds

Gillen had worn in memory of his father. I wore them like a record of the people I had lost. As I felt the cool metal against my fingertips, their physical presence brought me comfort.

Nearby, Narek shifted uncomfortably against his shackles. "You considered breaking it yourself, didn't you?" His voice was hard as he spoke of the barrier, now broken because of me. "They never would have seen your vision if you hadn't let yourself entertain the idea—if you hadn't let your emotions overwhelm you…"

Slowly, I forced myself to a sitting position, the world rolling and rocking around me like the tumultuous sea. Too many days of torture, of little water and food, of fear and worry, had me weak. I turned my head to find him staring at me, but for all the hardness in his tone, his gaze was broken and lost. My mouth was dry as dust, so I licked my lips.

"I had a different vision, before they brought us to the barrier," I explained slowly. "My aunt was pleading, praying…it was a *true* vision, not a nestred trick. I'm sure of it." My voice cracked. "Gillen…he cannot die. Misroth needs him."

"Your kingdom will fall," Narek said. His dark eyes were like bottomless pools of grief, reminding me of all the loss and horror he'd survived. "All the loved ones you left behind are in danger. The towns and cities will burn. The nestrae will be chanting to Nesrelle about all their sacrifices before year's end."

"Do you think I don't *know?*" I dug my hands into the dirt, squeezing it between my fingers, watching it slip away like everything else in my life was. My shackles cut into my wrists, a sharp bite of pain that kept my senses keen. "I have seen their visions in my head, slaughtering Lyanna and Rev, all of my friends, my aunt, my people, a hundred times since they broke the barrier. They've shown me how they will burn my home, how they'll torture and destroy everything and everyone I love." I swallowed to push the tears back, far back, before I fell apart.

Narek shook his head slowly. "I'm sorry. I didn't mean to—I

know," he said softly. "The nestrae played a cruel trick with an unfair advantage, pushing you to have that vision. It isn't you I'm angry with. I can't blame you. If I'd only had a barrier to protect my people…if the nestrae weren't so powerful with their ability to see into and manipulate thoughts…" His voice faded away. "I'd only hoped you would be able to control your visions when the time came, but how could you when they were threatening your cousin like that?"

At his mention of Gillen, I squeezed my eyes shut, trying to block out the memory of how they'd tortured him in front of me earlier that day. Naturally, they hadn't let me see him since. For all I knew, he was already dead.

"Isn't this what you wanted all along?" I asked bitterly. "For the barrier to be broken? Won't this save your people?"

He hung his head and closed his eyes. "How will the destruction of one kingdom save another?" His voice was ragged. "Who will come to Toryn's aid if the nestrae invade and burn every other kingdom? If these demons overtake our world?"

I studied him, realizing how much damage the nestred torture had done to us both. He looked how I imagined I must appear: face smudged with grime, onyx eyes shadowed from sleepless nights, body thinned from days without food, and his tattered clothing offering glimpses of ugly red burns and claw marks. How many times had he been visited by the ghost of Reylinn, the girl he'd loved, stalking his cell? How many times had he been forced to witness her terrible death? How many lost dreams had been paraded before him, only to be ripped away again when his harsh reality returned?

"We have to get away from them," I whispered. "We have to help Misroth before it's overrun."

Narek shifted beside me to survey the nestred camp sprawling around us. Tents and bedrolls lay everywhere, and fires dotted the nighttime landscape where our enemies clustered together, eating and conversing amongst themselves in their strange clicking and hissing tongue. The relaxed nestrae had removed their helmets and even from a distance I could see their dark, shell-like skin and the yellow fangs protruding from their maws. Patrols paced along the lines of other groups of prisoners, but Narek and I were set apart from them all.

My stomach ached with hunger at the scent of food. How could we escape, weak as we were? And how could we find and rescue Gillen in his wounded state?

Narek's face was grim. "We're heading toward the sea," he said at last.

I blinked, my despairing thoughts abruptly cutting off. "What?"

"All day we traveled eastward," he said, "toward the Alrenian."

I nodded slowly.

"That means they must have a way to travel by sea. They've prepared for this attack."

"I thought you said the nestrae hated water."

"I'm sure they're willing to face it in order to find another kingdom to raid. If there is any way we *can* escape, we'll need a ship. Even then, unless you know how to sail a ship, without a crew, it'd be useless to us and we'd never outpace them…"

My voice was firm. "We'll find a way. If they're taking us with them aboard their ships, we'll let them transport us to Misroth and then escape when we get there."

Narek nodded, his mouth tight with worry. He knew as well as I did that as much as we might speak about escape, it would do little to save my people. They'd already be overrun by enemies before we even had a chance to warn them and prepare. If only we could get a message to them.

I squeezed my eyes shut, hating how helpless I felt.

The night passed slowly and uneasily. After an exhausting day of being shoved along the nestred army's path, I'd hoped to be exhausted enough to find some relief in sleep. However, sleep proved to be nearly impossible. As Narek and I huddled together, shivering in the open air, frequent groans and shrieks from our fellow captives made the night a waking nightmare. At times, an ichgor's distant form would shroud the stars and I'd shudder at the sound of its wings beating steadily against the wind or its eerie cry echoing across the countryside. But for whatever reason—whether the nestrae and ichgor held a sort of alliance or the nestrae had a power over the bat-like beasts—the nestred patrols never seemed uneasy and none of the ichgor ever ventured near the camp. Whenever I did manage to drift off, frequent nightmares interrupted my sleep, and I found myself adding to the chorus of screams around us.

Finally, the first rays of dawn glittered on the horizon, melting the darkness into a mild grey sky. Stars winked out and wispy clouds turned pink and gold around the edges. The camp awoke swiftly, countless nestrae shoving away their bedrolls or stomping out of tents, some already wearing their weapons strapped at their sides.

As one stirred the embers in the firepit nearest to us, it tossed a glance over its shoulder as if sensing my gaze. For a breathless moment, it stared at me with black eyes as deep and emotionless as an abyss. Then it hissed and spun back toward the growing flames.

I snapped my gaze upward to see the nestred leader hovering over us. It lifted a sack full of food. "Eat," it snarled, dropping two hunks of crusty bread and two small chunks of mysterious meat on the ground. Though it would have once appeared unappetizing to someone who'd dined on royal fare or Lyanna's comforting meals, to someone half-starved, it smelled heavenly and tantalizingly rich.

Narek and I struggled against our manacles to grab our small portions of food. I reached for the meat first. My mouth watered as its gamey flavor burst across my tongue. When I lifted the bread, it took everything in me not to devour it in one bite, or to give in to a frantic animal instinct and rip some bread from Narek's hands as well.

My mouth was so dry it almost caught in my throat as I studied the nestred leader's face through the visor of its helmet. "Where are you holding Gillen?" I demanded, my voice sounding gravelly through my parched lips.

The leader held out a canteen of water. Scared it was a trick, I snatched it from it and drank greedily until I thought my stomach would burst. Narek, stirred and his chains rattled. With a start, I forced myself to stop drinking and passed the canteen to him, who finished gulping down the rest. I wiped at the water dripping from my chin and sucked the droplets off my hand, already desperate for more.

"Away from you," the leader said with an irritating smirk. It shoved another canteen toward me, one full of a bitter liquid I was already familiar with, one the nestrae claimed was a medicine to help with our wounds. One of their ways of ensuring their captives didn't die before they wanted them to. I choked half of it down, then passed the rest to Narek.

"Finish your food quickly," the leader continued, snatching the canteens back. "We leave soon and any prisoners who dawdle will be left behind to rot." It marched away.

Two more nestrae were already approaching with gauze and a bucket to clean our wounds and apply fresh bandages. I hated these false kindnesses almost more than I hated the ways they tortured us.

"Gillen already served his purpose for them," I murmured, staring after the nestred leader, trying to steady my breathing to stay off my panic. "They'll kill him."

Narek nudged my shoulder with his. "No," he said. "They've kept us alive. Why would they kill him now when they can torment him more by letting him watch his kingdom fall?"

It was such a miserable and futile hope it was hardly a hope at all, but I clung to it.

The nestred chants were an endless echo in my ears as Narek and I stumbled along the army's path, tripping and falling countless times in our weakened state. *Worthless, worthless,* came the whispers in my mind, even though I knew they did not speak a language I understood—that even my ability to understand their leader was probably only by another strange mind influence they held over me. I collapsed in the dirt, landing on my manacles. They slammed the air from my chest, the impact shuddering painfully through my entire body and making my eyes sting. *Condemned. Worthless.* The words reminded me of the nestred rune still stinging my back.

Beside me, Narek grimaced. "This is a trick—you're not real—*stop!*" I imagined he saw Reylinn again, or some other lost loved one. I thought of all the loved ones I, too, had lost. My friend Gare with his booming laughter and easy smile, with his storytelling gift that had enchanted and encouraged us, with his wife and son at home waiting in vain for him. My friend Layk, my Captain of the Royal Guard, full of integrity and loyalty, prepared to give anything to serve his kingdom and give his younger siblings a better life after the three of them had been orphaned. Then there were the two that I feared were dead. My friend Jennah, with her fiery courage and heart for her family, who had unquestioningly followed me on my mission, never hesitating, never faltering. And Avrik, with his light-hearted confidence and easy smile, who had known me like no one else had, whom I'd lost before we'd found a way to mend the rift between us, before I'd told him I loved him…

I shook the pain away before it overwhelmed me. There were still too many left to lose if I did not find a way to escape and help my kingdom. Gillen somewhere amidst the seemingly endless sea of marching nestrae and captives; Lyanna and Rev and my friends in Evren; my aunt Velaire and the remaining rebels and their families in the capital; and all the Misrothian people I'd been raised to serve and protect.

My armband felt constricting around my bicep, a reminder of so many more I'd lost since I'd left Misroth, making the haunting memories of my mother more distant yet somehow even more painful. The vision I'd had of her in the ruins of Delgoth came back to me: she'd been brushing my hair after my uncle's death, murmuring words of comfort and strength to me. *You will not be so easily broken.* It was a powerful reminder that drowned out the taunting nestred whispers in my mind. I was *not* worthless.

I'd almost broken all those years ago, when I'd been a timid thirteen-year-old longing for my parents' love. When I'd been quick to obey, quick to do whatever it took to please them. When my father had tried to murder me and everything I'd believed as a child had proven to be a lie. When I had run away to hide from my fears, from who I was. The kingdom had suffered too long because of my years of silence, weakness, and brokenness.

I pushed myself to my feet for the dozenth time, and reached out to shake Narek until he snapped out of his vision.

I would not break now.

Our long journey brought us close to the Haemil Mountains, until we were in their shadow, surrounded by grassy hills that marched toward the range. The mountains themselves were like rugged teeth of grass and tree, dirt and rock, with only their precipices dusted with snow. A stream burbled at the foot of the mountains, clean and clear as only water fed from mountains could be. Trees, now with fresh spring leaves coloring their low-hanging branches, bowed over the stream like thirsty old men reaching for a drink.

But it was impossible to admire the beauty around us. The sun quickly warmed the air until sweat beaded on my forehead and my hair clung limply to the back of my neck. Even the breeze was too soft and warm to afford much relief. My parched throat longed for just a taste of the water, but the nestrae gave the stream a wide berth.

We traveled all that day and into the next. The nestrae rarely stopped for rest, and when they did, they only gave Narek and me sips of water, enough to keep us moving—barely.

On the third day, as the shadows lengthened and the sun lowered, coloring the mountains we had left far behind, my weary legs began to tremble with each step.

Narek sensed as I faltered and reached for me, but his chains clanked and the manacles bit into his wrists, pulling taut before he could touch my shoulder. "Keep going," he murmured. "Just a little more." But his own legs were just as unsteady, and he'd fallen at least as many times as I had. All we could do was keep trying to encourage each other.

At last a breeze caught my hair and I smelled the sea. I blinked, something in my spirit rising at the same time my old aversion to the water curled nauseatingly in my gut. Eyes widening, I turned to Narek. "You were ri—"

"Keep going or you can make this place your grave," a nestred growled, shoving me hard between the shoulder blades.

The force dropped me easily, my arm twisting painfully beneath my body. Every inch of my body ached. Groaning, I spat out hair and dirt as nestrae around me chuckled cruelly and marched past.

I glared after their feet, longing for my strength again, for free hands and a weapon. I would make them pay for what they had done to my friends, to Avrik, to Gillen, to me. I would stop them before they killed everyone I loved. For one blinding moment my helplessness and loss and anger were overwhelming, like a windstorm tearing at me from within.

Then Narek laid a hand on my shoulder. "We will find a way."

I swallowed my emotions and focused on surviving what was in front of me.

With Narek's help, I fought to my feet and we trudged onward. The countryside had changed, becoming flatter and more open to the sky as we left the mountains behind. We climbed one last slope and stared down at a rocky beach running down to the Alrenian, calm and grey in the approaching twilight. But more breathtaking than the sea or the nestred army flooding the beach was the harbor there. Whether the nestrae had built it all or simply stolen from the Toryn, there were docks filled with ships, all swarming with nestrae. When I turned northward, I could see buildings tucked along the low-lying land hugging the beach and leading to another towering fortress set upon a hill overlooking the sea. A plain black flag with a forked tail fluttered over it: the nestred flag.

A chill ran over my skin. "They have a fleet. And there are so many," I whispered. "They've been preparing for this…for the barrier to break…" Tears collected in my eyes and I turned away. "We *cannot* fail."

Before Narek could respond, more nestrae snapped at our arms with their claws, half-pulling, half-dragging us down the slope. As night drew near, the beach was eerily devoid of wildlife: no gulls swooped through the air, no birds darting along the sand, hunting for food. Only the nestrae filled the space, plodding along in endless numbers or moving about the ships, preparing for their voyage.

The nestrae hurried us along unceremoniously, shoving us along the beach toward the village and the fortress overshadowing it. Soon more joined us: the leader flanked by some of its warriors. We left the sand behind to climb a dirt lane winding past weathered stone buildings, all that remained of what looked to have once been a Toryn village. The clang of metal on metal rang out from the smithies, smoke billowing freely from their furnaces out toward the Alrenian. Underneath the familiar tang of the sea, everything smelled of steel and flame, smoke and stone—the harsh scents of a rising army. Nestrae in the streets wore their helmets, heavy weapons strapped to their backs or attached to their belts. A steady stream of nestrae marched uphill toward the fortress, as if reporting for duty, while still more, laden with packs or leading mules burdened with food, tools, rope, and weapons, wound their way toward the docks. Everywhere there were signs of impending war, as if the enemy settled here had already known that other nestrae were bringing their armies.

And why wouldn't they? I thought. *This close to the sea they would have known soon after the barrier was broken that their people had succeeded. They've been waiting for this moment.* I shivered. They had been waiting for *me*, knowing I would be the one to break the barrier so they could overrun my kingdom.

"Condemned…" Nestrae hissed at us as we passed through the streets. They fixed their blank dark stares on us until I turned away, too unnerved to meet their gazes. Beside me, Narek's stance was rigid, his expression veiled. I wondered what word he was hearing the nestrae repeat in his head.

At last we climbed the hill and stood in the shadow of the fortress, made of weatherworn grey stone that had surely stood there since before the nestrae had invaded Toryn. Guards on either side nodded at the nestred leader and allowed us to pass without question through the open gates. The interior was dimly lit by flickering torches set in sconces along the walls. Nestrae hovered in the shadows, some passing through the halls, others posted as guards along the way. Ahead of us, the nestred leader wound its way through long, echoing passages, now and then passing closed doors, until we arrived in a small chamber where several nestrae were clustered around a table covered in maps and papers.

As we entered, one of the nestrae gathered at the table turned to the nestred leader and gave a curt nod. The leader bowed and gestured toward Narek and me, hissing and clicking in their language.

"Commander," the leader said in words I could understand, "we have come as quickly as we could to join you and your army."

The commander grinned at me, showing off its yellow, rodent-like fangs. "Princess Halia. You have brought a great victory to my people," it said. "Long have we prepared and waited for this day, ever since Nesrelle gave us a call to war. When your cousin failed us, she said you were our hope, and you have not disappointed."

Body rigid, I wanted to scream at all the demons grinning at me. At my elbow, Narek slipped his fingers around my arm, squeezing it in a silent reminder: the nestrae wanted to see me break. They wanted me to rage against them. I held my tongue.

"We will sail for Misroth City," the commander continued,

stepping toward me, "so you can watch us overtake your kingdom. Nesrelle has shown us that it is already weak from your father's rule, and the long years of peace beforehand have made your armies complacent. An invasion will be enough to topple your leadership and leave the people in chaos. Our visions will set them against one another." It grinned slowly, horribly. "But don't worry yourself, little princess. We'll give you plenty of time to watch us put our pieces into place, and Nesrelle is nothing if not merciful. We won't start killing your people or taking the capital until your birthday." His smirk widened. "Until then, they'll feel our presence when we arrive, but they won't know we're there."

Merciful? She only wants to draw it all out, let us all suffer more. Heighten our fear. Drain as much fear and despair as she can from all of her victims before her demons kill them. She wants to taunt me with the illusion of a chance to stop them, I scoffed inwardly, at the same time my heart slammed into my chest. *My birthday.* It was difficult to track time between nestred visions and the pain, but I knew spring was well underway. My birthday was in the heat of summer—far too soon.

I looked away, refusing to meet the commander's gaze. Refusing to let the nestrae see my anger and fear.

"We took over one hundred years to reduce Toryn to the rubble and terrified remnant of survivors you witnessed." The commander chuckled. "We can have just as much patience with Misroth."

Even though I kept my face impassive, I was sure the nestrae could feel my emotions anyway. Perhaps they were even reading my thoughts, just as they had when they'd tricked me into showing them how to break the barrier. I curled my hands into fists.

The commander turned to the nestred leader and clicked some orders. With final bows from the leader and its companions, Narek and I were dragged from the fortress, through the town, and back toward the docks. Without ceremony we were shoved up the gangplank of one of the ships, through the crowds of nestrae on deck, and down two sets of steps to a cramped area below. With a hissing cackle, one snatched a ring of keys from the wall and shoved us into a musty, damp cell. It stank of mud and viler things that made me want to gag. I slammed into Narek and fell to the slimy floor, where he collapsed next to me in a heap. With a grunt, I pulled myself up just as the nestred slammed the door shut. With a hiss, it turned to its comrade and they stomped away, back up the steps.

For a moment I stared into the darkness, listening to the faint sounds on deck and searching for any sign of other cells or other captives nearby. But there was nothing but Narek's breathing and the clink of our chains. Wherever Gillen was, he did not appear to be aboard this ship. My stomach dropped.

I tried to swipe some of the filth from my face onto my sleeve before glancing at Narek. "Another prison."

Narek laughed mirthlessly. "What's another prison to us now?" he asked, but as I slumped against the bars of our cell and listened to the sounds of our captors overhead, all I could think about was everything I loved, slipping away from me.

"When is your birthday?" he asked after a long, heavy moment.

"The last day of Ilae," I whispered.

Then he shook his head, just as much at a loss as I was. "What month is it now?"

I did some fast calculations in my head. If the nestred had invaded Calidar in Mareth, the first month of spring, it could easily be Varra by now, or even Kelah. That meant we could have as little as two months before my birthday.

Two months before the nestrae destroyed my kingdom and everyone within it.

CHAPTER TWO

Avrik

IT WAS AVRIK'S MOTHER WHO had instilled such unrelenting hope in him. Even when she'd grown too ill and feeble to do much more than stay in bed or sit huddled in her chair by the fire, she had pulled him close and told him stories about the afterlife, where no one grew sick or weak or tired and families were reunited, whole and happy again.

"And so that means that no matter what happens, dearest, it will not be goodbye. When my time comes to go to the afterlife, you must not lose hope. I will still be with you, in your heart, until you cross over and we are reunited." He'd been so young and small and alone then, even with his mother's words of encouragement. She squeezed him tight and wiped away his tears. "No matter how dark it becomes," she murmured, "there will always be light. Shadows are only a sign that the sun is near."

He was so like his mother and yet so unlike her, taking after his father mostly in form, but sharing his mother's charming personality. Just like her, he had made friends effortlessly. Just like her, he was an optimist. But he couldn't help but feel he had fallen so short of the courage and grace she had shown, even in her final days.

Her words echoed in his ears now, as the groans and panicked shrieks of his fellow captives filled his ears. The ship's steady rocking reminded him that he was no longer in the nestred stronghold, but no less a prisoner, still haunted by both nightmarish visions and reality.

It also reminded him that he hadn't seen Halia since the nestred attack in the Toryn capital of Calidar—an attack that could have happened months or years ago, for all he knew. Time held no meaning here, especially when nestred visions convoluted everything until the line between reality and lies blurred. His chest ached at the thought of her. Was she alive? Was she a prisoner too? The nestrae would never answer his questions about her and only taunted him with visions of her instead.

I was such a fool, he thought. He'd let himself give into his feelings of betrayal and his grief for his father, and he'd pushed Halia away when he should have reconciled with her, drawn her close. The regret threatened to tear him apart, and he couldn't afford to fall apart.

He had to escape. He had to find her.

Avrik's eyes fluttered open and he wished he hadn't looked. As much as he tried so desperately to hold on to the hope that his mother had taught him, it was hard when he stared into the unnerving voids that were the nestrae's stares. He liked to mask his fear with bravado and smiles, but the farce was only for him. The nestrae could feel his fear; they relished it, thrived on it, fed on it like the monsters they were.

"Up," one snarled. Only one of the nestrae aboard this ship seemed to speak anything other than the hissing, clicking nestred language, even though they all seemed to be able to understand his thoughts enough to exploit his fears with the visions they gave him.

"Well good morning to you too," Avrik said as two more nestred stepped into his cell and yanked him roughly to his feet. Every muscle and bone in his body ached and he was weak from hunger and thirst, but he smiled anyway. Of course, it was too dark in the brig to tell the time of day, but the nestrae had begun moving above him not long ago and the lanterns that had been out for hours had just been relit. Even demons had to sleep sometimes.

The nestrae's claws sliced into his arms, reopening wounds. He hissed through clenched teeth, refusing to cry out. The first nestred, the one that had spoken, pressed a cup to his lips and ordered him to drink. He knew now that the bitter liquid inside was medicinal. Then they set to work cleaning and binding his wounds, an action that never ceased to make Avrik smile bitterly at the irony. The nestrae healed only so they could hurt again.

"Who am I, that you keep me alive?" he'd asked once, but now he knew that any lowly prisoner of theirs was valuable, as long as the demons could continue to collect their tithes of fear and pain. And as much as Avrik tried to pretend otherwise, there was plenty of fear and pain swirling inside him for them to sacrifice to their goddess.

But he also couldn't ignore the way the nestrae had singled him out. There were at least five prisoners in every other cell he could see. As far as he could tell, he was the only one who had a cell to himself.

In one of the nearby cells, Avrik could hear another captive crying out in anguish. "No! Analeth, stop! Please, no!" His shouts turned into sobs, the sound so desolate and despairing that Avrik couldn't contain his grimace.

When he turned his head back, he found that the nestred not tending to his wounds was staring at him with its empty eyes. "What makes you harder to break than the others?" It nodded toward the sobs still emanating from the cell behind Avrik. "Than him?" it said, its voice low and hoarse.

Avrik's skin crawled, but he forced himself to meet the nestred's gaze without flinching.

"We know some of the things that haunt you," it continued, its stare flicking to the marks that crawled up Avrik's right arm, concealed beneath the fresh bandages the nestrae were wrapping around his skin. He grit his teeth, thinking of the strange markings they'd cut into his flesh, the ones that seemed to draw their haunting words to the forefront of his mind. *Powerless.* "But I'm not sure you are truly afraid yet."

Avrik smirked. "So what you're saying is you're failing your job of finding all my fears and weaknesses? Maybe you hate to see me suffer, because you just can't resist my smile…"

The nestred slammed its hand around his throat, shoving him back against the cell bars and jolting the other nestrae away from his arms. Avrik's head swam and spots danced across his vision as he choked for air. The tips of the nestred's claws dug into his neck until a trickle of blood dripped down his back. "You fool no one," it snarled. "I can taste your fear, even if it is buried deep. You think you have nothing left to lose that we can steal, but you are wrong." It released his neck and he gasped, his lungs burning. The nestred towered over him. "What is your gift?"

Avrik stared at him. "I—I don't have a gift," he rasped. He thought of Halia and her truth gift granted by the Life-Giver. Could these demons sense gifts like that?

The nestred growled. "You lie."

With a careless shrug, Avrik said, "I thought you were supposed to be able to read my mind."

"You won't be so smug when we overrun your kingdom."

He feigned nonchalance and shrugged again. "You won't be the first army to attack Misroth. It didn't work for Alrenor in the past. I doubt it will for you either."

This time, the nestrae worked together, two yanking him down to the floor while the third dug its claws into his back, tearing some of the fresh bandages. Warm blood trickled down his skin, and Avrik grit his teeth against the pain. He thought dimly about how all their work was already wasted.

But worse was the vision that dipped him back into the horror of his last day in Evren. Shouts tore through the night, mingling with ear-piercing screams. Animal snarls echoed in his ears while all he could see was a spreading pool of blood. *The sedwa!* came the shouts, and then, to his horror, Avrik heard his best friend Bren crying out. *Help!*

Avrik fought against the vision with everything he had. Hope was his shield, and though it didn't block out the nestred visions completely, it did make them less vivid. He knew they were nothing but memories, and they were ones he'd already been learning to cope with. They were another battle he'd fought countless times before in an endless war. And though it never felt like he won any of the battles, he had learned to survive. He knew each trick to keep the churning emotions from drowning him.

Lying facedown, the ship swaying and creaking beneath him, he wanted to scream in anger or smash his fist into a nestred's face. But he was too weak with hunger and thirst, and that was what the nestrae wanted, anyway. Any reaction other than the one Avrik always gave.

Catching his breath, Avrik lifted his head slowly, painfully, and smiled.

CHAPTER THREE

AS THE SHIP ROCKED, MY stomach seemed to rock with it. I curled into a ball against the slick floorboards and groaned, squeezing my eyes tight against the swaying lantern light flashing across the walls. The salty tang of the sea filled my nostrils while my insides churned in fear. I listened to the waves crash relentlessly against the ship's sides and the nestrae hiss and chatter overhead. When I closed my eyes, the smells and sounds overwhelmed me, until I was convinced I was drowning in the Alrenian again, the deep closing in about me.

It disgusted me how the nestrae didn't even have to use a vision or torture against me to turn me into a shaking ball of fear.

The passage of time was difficult to track. At some point, whether hours or days later, the ship had clearly begun its trek across the Alrenian waters. Occasionally the nestrae had let us out to relieve ourselves, or entered our cell to apply fresh bandages, give us medicine, or leave us small rations of food and water. Each time I'd been far too nauseous to do more than nibble and sip. At some point in the endless stretch of dimness and rocking since the ship had set sail, the nestrae had unlocked our manacles and shackles, laughing in their eerie voices as they slammed our cell door shut again. There was no need for them in our cell and I had the distinct impression that our freedom of movement, creating the illusion we could easily find a way to escape our prison, was a new form of torment for us and amusement for them.

Now my lack of chains made little difference, for I was so sick and weak I could scarcely move. My mouth was gravelly and tasted foul. Another wave slapped against the ship's side and I cringed.

Nearby, Narek leaned against the bars of our cell, his face pale and drawn. Through the tears in his shirt I could see the nestred rune scarring his chest, marking the skin over his heart with jagged lines. They swirled outward in a spiral, like the legs of an ugly, spindly spider or the ripples of a consuming whirlpool. It was pale and raised, like he had been marked with it long before we'd been captured in the stronghold, and I wondered when and how he had been inflicted with it. What did it mean?

But Narek didn't notice my gaze. His eyes stared ahead, unseeing. I knew he was in the clutches of another of the nestrae's terrible visions. "Stay away!" he shouted suddenly, scrambling weakly to his feet and reaching for his sword, only to grasp empty air. His boots skidded on the slick floor and he reached out blindly to catch himself, his hand slamming into the cell bars.

Slowly, painfully, I clutched one of the bars and yanked myself to my knees. The world swayed and sparks danced across my vision. My limbs were like lead weights when I attempted to push myself up to stand. *We might very well starve to death before we ever reach Misroth,* I thought drolly. I crawled toward Narek, who had collapsed and slumped back against the ship's side with his face crumpled in defeat.

I hovered over him, sympathy shredding my heart. I knew his pain.

His eyes scanned my face as if studying me, but I knew it was someone else he was seeing. "Iyleth?" his voice was a whisper, full of something so close to hope it hurt.

I wasn't surprised to hear him say Iyleth's name. She was gentle and kind and full of relentless hope, the sort of bright presence that drew countless people to her. When we'd stayed in the underground refuge of Calidar, I'd noticed the way Narek watched her. He had been just as unhappy as me when she had chosen to shower Avrik with attention. I'd known then that he cared for her, and it made sense that he'd be worrying about her now.

For a moment, I wondered if she and the other Toryn survivors had made it to Haemil. I wondered if any of them were still alive.

"No," I said. My voice was hoarse and broken sounding. "Not Iyleth. Halia."

He squeezed his eyes shut, shoving the vision away, and when he opened them again, they shone with unshed tears. Cringing, he covered his face, and in that moment, the man I'd spent years fearing as my enemy, the companion who had baffled me with his dark humor and vague hints, the former Captain of the Guard who had commanded ruthless men and cut down a ruthless king—that man wept. The sight made something in me crumble. He wrapped his arms around me, desperate for human comfort, and I did not pull away.

As he wept, I lay my head on his chest and cried too. I cried for all he had lost, all I had lost, and all we still had left to lose. I cried for Rev and Lyanna, so far away, for the mother and father I'd once thought I'd had, before my gift had shown me what they truly were. I cried for the friends who had loyally followed me into darkness and given their lives, and I cried for their families, now left behind. I cried for Avrik and the friendship we'd once shared and the love we would never have.

When our tears were spent and Narek and I huddled close together in our cell, lost in a strangely companionable silence, I knew I had one more loyal friend, one who would give anything to stop the darkness that had stolen so much from us.

At last, I sat up and broke the silence. "What was Reylinn like?"

Narek smiled softly. "She and I both trained from an early age with Toryn's talented warriors, the Zare'forith. She was spirited, with a fire in her soul that could have rivaled the nestrae's flames." He laughed. "Like me, she'd lost much, but not her hope."

Hugging my legs, I was quiet for a long moment, staring down at my boots. "Is Iyleth much like her?"

"She is more of a leader than Reylinn ever was. But she carries that same fire inside of her. She just knows how to light it for others as well." He shrugged. "I don't even know if any of them made it. If the nestred visions are true at all…" He hesitated. "My people might all be dead."

I stared at him for a long time, unsure what to say. How could you respond to something like that? To the thought that you might be the last survivor of an entire people?

"Iyleth was the first person since Reylinn that…" Narek shook his head, stopping himself. "Reylinn was my anchor for years, my one bright spot in all the darkness consuming Calidar then. It is a hard thing, to lose the one who brings you the most joy."

I nodded, thinking of Avrik.

"You can't be sure he is really gone," Narek said, seeing the tears burning my eyes. "Any visions of him dying could have been fed to you by the nestrae."

Wiping the tears away, I shook my head. "How can I hope? We haven't seen a sign of him or Jennah among the nestred prisoners and…" I swallowed. "In the stories I read in Evren, people could feel when absent loved ones were gone, or still alive." My laughter was mirthless. "I feel nothing. Not even hope."

Narek studied the beams overhead. "I felt nothing when my parents died. They were members of the Zare'forith as well. They left one day to help aboveground survivors travel to Calidar." He shrugged. "They just never returned. I never imagined…" He shook his head. "At seven years old, I thought my parents were invincible and it never crossed my mind they might not make it. I think *feeling* that something is amiss the moment a loved one dies miles away from you—I think that is nothing but fuel for fictional tales. I had no idea until the rest of the soldiers returned and told me."

"I think what scares me most," I confessed at last, my voice a whisper, "is that I have not seen any visions of him. Not even of him…dying. After so many visions of seeing him tortured, I have seen nothing. I'm afraid that, after seeing so much of him, the reason I don't now is because…there is nothing left to see."

Narek only squeezed my arm, because what was there to say?

Nestrae pounded down the steps to the brig and flung open our cell door. "Up," the nestred leader said gruffly.

Before Narek and I could pull ourselves to our feet, two nestrae stepped forward and hauled us up. I cringed as their claws tore through my bandages and reopened old wounds. Blood beaded along my arms. They led us roughly out of the cell, up the steps to the nestred sleeping quarters, and then up more steps, leading us to the deck. The sunlight made my eyes burn and water. Even though the nestrae had dragged me more than I had walked, I struggled to catch my breath and my legs trembled from the exertion.

After the dank, rancid scent of old filth permeating our cell, the air smelled impossibly fresh and sweet. It was a bright, warm afternoon, the sun high in the sky and glaring brilliantly on calm waves. The sea stretched endlessly in every direction, only broken by the other ships in the fleet surrounding us. The ship undulated beneath my boots and sent another bout of queasiness through me.

"We draw close to the northern waters of the Alrenian," the nestred leader taunted.

The nestrae holding me shoved me closer to the ship's railing, where I could see the foam swirling about the ship's prow and feel the spray of saltwater on my face. Even as they and their comrades shoved Narek and me closer, I noticed how they all stayed back. Apparently their distaste for water had not disappeared in their need to cross the sea.

"Soon your people will be giving their sacrifices of pain and fear to almighty Nesrelle," the leader hissed.

"Condemned," voices all around me whispered, like phantoms closing about from all sides. I stiffened and looked around, but all the other nestrae seemed busy working the ship or polishing black blades and axe heads for their approaching war. Drawing in a shaky breath, I ignored the chills running down my arms, despite the warm sun.

"I'm afraid there's a flaw in your plan."

I turned in surprise at Narek's voice, sounding out far stronger and steadier than he looked. Like a mask, his usual inscrutable expression had returned.

"Have you not heard?" he continued. "The Misrothians are empire-breakers and dragon-slayers. Pain and fear do not come naturally to them. Your sacrifices to your demon queen will be insufficient and she will laugh at your efforts."

I couldn't hold back my smile, warmth from Narek's loyal words burning inside me.

With a snarl, the nestred leader slammed its clawed hand against Narek's cheek, drawing blood and leaving an angry red welt. Narek hardly even flinched, his gaze seeming to dare the demon to strike again. The nestred stared back with its emotionless eyes, and in that instant I was certain it would rip Narek to shreds.

Heart thundering, I shoved myself between them. Adrenaline fed the energy I needed to my body, and when the ship lurched, I held steady.

"It seems the lady still has much to lose." The nestred leader's smile made bumps rise along my arms.

"It seems you only brought us here to give empty threats," I retorted. "All you have are vague messages to instill fear, but are you sure a kingdom as strong as Misroth will fall so easily?" My words held more bravado than I felt. Somehow I doubted anything Narek or I said would truly discourage these demons, but I couldn't resist trying.

"We have already captured Misroth's heirs to the throne. Your king hovers between life and death and you no longer trust your visions." Its smirk was terrible. "We are patient. If it takes years to drive your people into madness and despair, we will wait years. Nesrelle told us: your kingdom is ours."

With an eerie chuckle, it motioned for the nestrae to lead us away. They pushed us back down the steps and returned us to the darkness of our cell. After their footsteps faded, Narek and I sat in silence for some time. Voices whispered at me once more, repeating "condemned" until I clamped my hands over my ears. The rune marring my back burned. Finally, I turned to Narek, desperate to block out the taunting words.

"Do you hear their voices too?" I asked. I sounded a little mad, even to my own ears.

He nodded slowly.

"What do you hear? What does your rune mean?" I whispered.

He studied me quietly for a moment. Black hair fell across his brow, the longest and most unruly it had ever been for the disciplined former captain. A muscle in his jaw worked and for a moment I thought he would refuse to answer after all. "Alone," he said simply. "And it's the truth, even truer now than when I was first marked with it. It's how it has been for almost as long as I can remember. First everyone near to me perished, then I served your father, living among people I hated. I hated myself too. I told myself it was justified, to save my people from their suffering. But I don't belong among the Toryn anymore either. That much is clear now."

I stared out at one of the lanterns swaying from the ceiling and watched it cast light that danced amid the shadows. "You're not alone," I said softly.

"I helped torture your friends under your father's orders," he said. "I sent men to hunt for you when you were only a girl and stood by when your father tried to execute you. And I refused to warn you that the barrier was real, or to dissuade you from a mission that has slain your friends and endangered your kingdom." He stared at the mud encrusting his boots and laughed softly, mirthlessly. "We both know it was I who should have died, not Gare, when the first ichgor attacked.

Or when the nestrae overwhelmed Calidar and killed Layk, it should have been me instead. They should have taken and slain me in their fortress, not Jennah and Avrik."

I shook my head fiercely. "You fought alongside us when Gare died, and there was nothing you could do for Layk." I blinked away the tears that threatened to form at the thought of my friends. "And you went with me to try to save Jennah and Avrik. It's not your fault they're gone." I bowed my head. "I knew the dangers of this mission, I knew there could be a barrier that would leave us in Toryn, and you told me about the dangers there. I didn't let that stop me and I couldn't dissuade my friends from joining me. Perhaps it is my fault they're gone, just like it's my fault the barrier is gone, and just like it was my fault that my father was able to deceive so many of my people for so long." I swallowed. "We've both made terrible mistakes. You're *not* alone, Narek."

He offered me a bitter smile and laid a hand over his scarred chest. "But you know in the middle of grief, when I only have the ghosts of everyone I've lost for company, there is a lot of truth to this rune."

I nodded. "I know. I often feel the same."

"What word did they mark you with?"

I watched him for a beat. The word tasted like bile on my tongue, only because it carried so much truth. It crushed me like a heavy weight, one I could not ignore, because my gift—sometimes my curse—would not let me lie. "Condemned."

Narek reached out his hand. I hesitated before taking it, finding his skin warm and calloused. He squeezed my hand and said, "Well, if we are both alone and condemned, let's do everything we can to change our fates and make the nestrae liars."

"As soon as this ship makes port in Misroth," I said when he dropped my hand, "we need to escape and find my aunt. We'll rally Misroth and do as much as we can to prepare for battle before the nestrae begin their attack."

Narek nodded. "Likely some of the nestrae will go ashore

immediately, and we can take advantage of their smaller numbers."

"And they love to taunt us, so I'm sure once we arrive, they'll take us on deck to see Misroth for ourselves," I mused. I drew a deep breath and mustered my confidence. "I'm going to concentrate on my gift. I'll learn to tell the difference between nestred visions and the truth."

We fell into making plans, turning our minds to what we would do once we arrived in Misroth City. Telling ourselves we could assemble an army before my birthday. Clinging to hope and ignoring the nestred voices always hissing in our minds.

Condemned. Alone.

Liars, I thought back fiercely, and something within me warmed at the response. My truth gift, reminding me that what I said was true. Hope, reminding me I hadn't broken.

CHAPTER FOUR

THIS TIME AVRIK KNEW IT was a vision because of its utter impossibility, but that didn't extinguish its power. Halia was dressed in the long, glittering dress she had worn to the festival in the underground Toryn temple. Her wavy hair was arranged to set off her face, and there was a hint of shimmery powder brushed along her eyelids that made her green eyes flash even more. She had always been beautiful, but that night she'd looked painfully, overwhelmingly like royalty. Every glance had hurt and reminded him of the countless reasons she should not, could not be his, of all the ways the rift had grown between them. That night, it was undoubtedly *Halia* he kept stealing glances at—not Elena. Was this princess still the same girl who had teased him for his clumsy feet when they danced together in Evren, who could toss a challenge or a playful jibe his way during an archery competition with a single smile or arch of her brow?

Now, in this dank cell with the sea churning outside, tossing the ship up and down in sickening motions, Halia opened his locked door easily and stepped inside with the grace and fluidity of a queen. She moved too gracefully—because she wasn't real. Avrik knew that.

He wanted to squeeze his eyes shut, to make her disappear. It hurt to look at even a vision of her. At the same time, he longed to see her again, to say everything he had held back, and he couldn't look away.

"I'm sorry," he whispered, as if this false Halia could pass his message across the miles to the real one.

She crossed her arms and stared stonily at him, refusing to come closer. There was no forgiveness in her eyes. "You left me to face my father alone," she snapped. "I was sentenced to death while you hunkered down in Evren like a coward, refusing to believe the truth about your father. I nearly *died*, and your last words to me were about how you trusted your father over me. Your lying, murdering father!"

Every word was like a knife to his chest. His guilt had been overwhelming, far greater than the mistrust or anger or hurt had ever been. At first, he had feared that she was someone entirely different than she'd seemed. He had felt betrayed by this girl who had withheld her identity from him for four years and then suddenly revealed an ability to speak, to accuse his father just like others had. All that time he had been drawn to Elena and how genuine and honest she had been, especially compared to the other Evren girls who had batted their lashes and preened, who had lied to his face about how great they thought his father was, or how they would love to shoot or build a fire or set a trap.

But when he'd met her again on her mission to Toryn, he had mostly avoided Halia because he knew he could not measure up. She was royalty; he was no one. She was a rebel leader who had overthrown a tyrant and chosen to lead her kingdom despite her fear. He had forsaken her to try—and fail—to save a man who, in the end, had sold a town's safety for his son's comfort. Halia made sacrifices like a ruler, while he made impulsive decisions with this foolish hope he had. When she had needed him, he had doubted and betrayed her. He had put his trust in his father over her, and his father had quickly shown him how wrong he had been. In the end, Avrik had kept his distance from Halia because a part of him had wanted her to hate him.

All these thoughts swirled through Avrik's mind now, refusing to be ignored when this vision threw them back in his face. He lowered his eyes, not wanting to see the hatred burning in this false Halia's gaze. "You're right. I deserve your hatred," he whispered. "I left you when you needed me, in order to save…him." He grimaced.

When he dared to lift his head again, his father sat across from him.

"Not you again," Avrik said. He squeezed his eyes shut, ignoring the sound of his father's footsteps, his slow pacing across the length of his cell. *It's not him. He's dead,* Avrik told himself. The anger, the shame, the regret, the grief—it all still engulfed him. Every time.

"I did it for you, son," Kyrin was saying, his voice urgent. "Please believe me. Don't leave your father to die here. We can leave this nothing town behind—you deserve more than this. We both do. Your mother—"

Fury overcame his grief. "Do *not* bring her into this!" Avrik cried, his eyes flying open to stare into his father's. Kyrin was seated across from him, his expression desperate, pleading. Avrik's voice turned low, dark. "She would *never* have approved of what you did, no matter your reasoning. She would never have shed innocent blood to help me, as you claim. She would have found another way."

"Avrik—"

"You never helped me! You hurt me! You let people I knew and cared about die." His voice shook. "This is a lie! You're already dead, and I *cannot* regret that. I refuse to, no matter how much it hurts. You deserved everything that came to you!"

Avrik blinked and at last, his cell was empty. A heavy silence had settled. Somehow, maybe because it was so unusual with the other captives in his neighboring cells always groaning or screaming amidst visions or torture, the quiet was ominous.

He peered into the shadows, beyond the first few cells adjoining his, always hoping—and dreading—to find a familiar face. Layk. Jennah. Halia, he knew, was not among them, or he was sure by now the nestrae would have used her, rather than only visions of her, to try to break him. At this point, he thought even Narek would be a comforting sight. But he couldn't see much in the darkness, only flashes of filthy faces he didn't recognize.

Pounding footsteps jolted him from his thoughts. The nestrae were returning. At least a dozen entered the brig and began unlocking cells and yanking prisoners from them. Two entered Avrik's cell and dragged him out with the others.

Before he had a chance to search among the other captives' faces, he was shoved up two sets of steps, finally leaving the belly of the ship. Above, billowy clouds smothered the night sky and the sea was placid. Under moonlight it might have looked like polished glass, but in darkness it resembled the yawning void of a hungry creature's mouth, waiting to engulf him. On deck, the nestrae were not working or even speaking in their hissing, clicking language. Motionless and silent, a group of them knelt in a circle, facing a pyre erected on a stone table.

Sweat trickled down Avrik's back. Here it was, the moment they burned him alive because they couldn't pull any more fear from him. They'd sacrifice him to their goddess and let her feed on the horror of his last painful seconds.

Behind him, a girl sobbed. She sounded younger than him, maybe just a child. Fury lanced through him like a knife. He'd spent days feeling sorry for himself, feeding his anger over all the nestrae had done to him, but to imagine the torment they'd inflicted on a child was too much. Growling, he tugged against the nestrae's grip, trying futilely to break free.

A woman's sharp voice cut the silence. *"Garashni!* You kill our bodies but damn your own souls. If you even have any," she snarled.

Eyes widening, Avrik glanced over his shoulder. The hope he'd clung to, even when it had flickered and threatened to fade, flared bright again. There she was: dirty and burnt, scratches oozing blood down her arms, but with a fierce glint still in her eyes. She was a tall figure, with smooth brown and gold skin in a sea of pale faces. A spark of courage and defiance in a flood of despair. Her eyes met his, and a rush of strength flowed through him. "Jennah."

CHAPTER FIVE

FATHER SAT ACROSS FROM ME, his back propped against the cell bars.

"You've brought more death to our kingdom than I ever did, Halia. And now you think you can return to Misroth and lead them? That the people will turn to you with respect and hope?" He scoffed. "You're *nothing.*" He seized my arm, and to my horror, I felt the weight of his hand, ice cold and calloused.

With a cry I jolted back. Narek watched me with concern.

I pressed a hand to my racing heart and breathed deeply. "My…my father," I stammered.

He nodded. "I see him sometimes too."

When I turned back, my father had vanished, nothing but another nestred lie.

The next time I saw Father leering down at me, I glared straight back at him. Though a part of me knew he was dead, he was so real— from the sound of his footsteps creaking along the shipboards to the familiar scent of his soap, which had always reminded me of the scent of pine trees. I concentrated on reaching for the truth living inside of me, warm and reassuring. When I did, I could *feel* the difference in the reality I saw versus the nestred vision.

On one side, Narek frowned and called out to me. "Halia! It's not real. Snap out of it!" That felt right. True.

On the other, my father stalked across from me, repeating the same words he'd tried to haunt me with before. "You're *nothing*," he snarled. But he rippled now, like a vision on water. He didn't appear as solid, and the sound of his voice was distant, more like a memory than the real thing. Strongest of all, though, was the sensation that poured over me—icy cold and pulsing, almost like a warning bell. As if my gift were crying out to me: *This is not real.*

"You're a lie," I said through my teeth. "You're dead. You're not real." I lifted my hand to shove him away, and it dropped through empty air, my father disappearing like mist.

I drew in a sharp breath. "I did it," I whispered, turning to Narek. "I saw through a vision. I turned it away."

Before Narek could respond, nestred footsteps creaked down the steps and to our cell. They swung open our door and seized me, dragging me out alone. I tried to wrench myself away, but their claws dug deeper, slicing into my arms until I bit back a cry. Narek leapt to his feet and lunged for the open door, but before he could reach it, a nestred slammed the cell shut with a clang. The echo shuddered through my chest as my eyes met his wide, terrified ones.

"No!" Narek shouted, pounding on the bars as the nestrae pulled me toward the steps. "Take me instead!"

The nestrae hissed and chuckled, making bumps stand up along my arms.

"No!" I cried out, terrified the nestrae would listen to him and go for him next. I didn't even dare struggle against them for fear that they would change their minds and choose him. "Narek, stop! It's all right!"

Narek didn't stop, but neither did the nestrae as they dragged me toward the steps. "I'll throw your bodies to the waves and let the sharks devour you!" Narek cried out. "I'll tear you apart!"

He continued to yell empty threats, his cries fading away as we stepped out onto the deck. Starlight bathed the world in a silver glow. Everything was soft and unnaturally hushed—even the sea was nearly still, like a vast looking glass reflecting dozens of constellations along its glistening surface. I searched for a sign of Vehgar in the sky, any sight to bolster my courage, but with the changing season, the stars I'd grown so used to studying during our winter travels were nowhere to be seen.

When I scanned the deck, I was surprised to see the nestrae awake and gathered in a circle. They stood mute and motionless. A chill descended on my heart. Were they preparing to sacrifice me to their goddess? Or were they planning to torture me more?

We drew nearer to where the nestrae were grouped into two rows, all kneeling down to face a figure in the center. The nestred leader parted those blocking our path and shoved me toward the figure. What I saw made me halt and wait motionless, heart hammering in my temples.

Amidst the demons stood a woman, crimson curls tumbling nearly to her waist. The starlight made it look as if tiny silver gems glistened in her hair, giving the illusion of an ethereal crown gracing her head. She was weaponless, barefoot, and pristine, clothed in a shimmering, pale blue gown that trailed behind her. The bodice was embellished with diamonds and pearls and delicate embroidery, while the skirt was overlaid with lace. With its hood thrown back, a white silk cape hugged her shoulders. She turned to me and my heart stuttered when I was caught in her gaze: her eyes were the same icy blue as her gown, beautiful and piercing and terrifyingly cold.

When she moved, she walked like a creature from a dream, so smooth and swift it was like she was gliding. Her gown whispered along the deck behind her. My unconscious mind understood who she was before my waking mind caught up. Fear froze my insides and sweat broke out on my nape. It took all my willpower to hold my ground and meet her stare.

I realized it was my truth gift, warning me. She was real and dangerous. Someone it was wise to fear.

"Nesrelle," I whispered, my voice hushed, tremulous.

The demons' goddess of death and despair smiled softly, almost comfortingly. "I suppose I cannot fool Princess Halia, gifted with the truth," she said. Her voice was also like something from a dream: slow, breathy, and lilting. She studied my face intently. "How I've longed for the day my faithful followers would bring you before me."

I narrowed my eyes at her. "Are you here to kill me?"

She laughed, the sound like music, like an echo of the beautiful songs lifted up to the Giver of Life in the far-away Evren Garden. Her pale hand darted out to clutch my arm in a surprisingly tight, bony grip. I gasped. As her fingers squeezed, I could feel my blood go cold and my chest constrict painfully. My heartbeat raced and then slowed to a dull thud, slowing still more until my knees went weak, my breaths became shallow, and my vision blurred and darkened. Just when I thought I would collapse to the deck, chest heaving for air that would not come, or that my heart would burst, she pulled her hand away.

"Ah, no," she sighed, still standing so near I could have counted the freckles dusting her cheeks and nose. "Unfortunately, it is not within my power to decide when everyone lives or dies. My power allows me to drain the life from one soul every year, and I don't expect I will choose you. But who can tell, in your circumstances, how much longer you have left to live anyway?" Her cool hand caressed my cheek, and I repressed a shudder. "It is fascinating to meet someone who has felt my presence so often, yet who has *defied* me so many times." A hint of anger slipped into her tone. Her nails brushed along my jawbone and then pressed in, until a sharp pain blossomed along my skin. They weren't nails at her fingertips at all, but claws. Warm blood dripped down my neck. How had I not noticed the hideous features lurking beneath her beauty before?

As if a spell had broken with that shock of pain, I found I could move my limbs again and take a step back. Dozens of nestrae shifted and hissed at me, disturbing the quiet. "You want my kingdom to fall and my people to die."

Her smile was soft, but her gaze was hard. "I thrive on pain and fear. From you"—her smile widened—"as you watch everyone you care about suffer. And from them, as they face the death and destruction my followers will bring to them." She cast an almost motherly look on the bowing nestrae before shifting her eyes back to me. "I don't want your people to die as much as I want them to suffer terribly. At least, until they have no terror, no sorrow, nothing at all left for me to savor but their own deaths."

My fingers curled and anger burned through me. "It was the Life-Giver who defied you and saved my life," I snapped. "And he is why you don't have the power to kill me now, yourself. *Or* my people. Your power—and your demons' power—is nothing compared to his."

She snarled, her beautiful face contorting with rage. "How dare you speak that name to me! *Life!*" she screamed, her tone full of mockery. And suddenly the spell-binding hush was gone and the light went from her eyes until they looked as dark and fathomless as those of the nestrae. My blood glinted on her claw-like nails. Her teeth were long and glistening, like fangs. "You cry out to one who gives *life*, but you know that none die without his approval. He is the Giver of *Death* too! He gave death to your friends and he'll give death to you in the end!" She laughed cruelly, her teeth too white, her lips too full and red. Lifting her fingertips to her mouth, she licked my blood from them. "And if I cannot have you myself, not yet, then I will be near, feeding off your despair as all you love die around you and you cry, 'Life, life, life!'" Her voice rose to a shriek in my ears. "You cry in vain."

Then she drew a breath. As if recovering herself, she blinked and her eyes were bright blue again, her hands clean of blood, her face composed. Her fangs and claws were gone, as if they never were there. "You will see me again," she whispered.

I blinked and she was gone.

The nestrae around me shifted restlessly, those on their knees rising again. I drew a breath, suddenly recalling myself: I was surrounded by my enemy, whom I'd just angered by insulting and enraging their goddess. I was weaponless and weak; they were all armed and well-fed. My heart sounded unsteady in my ears.

"*Condemned One*," the leader hissed, gesturing to me with its claws.

Another nestred stepped forward, grabbing me roughly and leading me to its leader. "You are unwise to insult the Goddess of Death."

"There is nothing more she can do to me," I said as the two nestrae led me toward the brig.

"I would not be so sure of that," the leader said with a laugh.

Narek was still at the cell door, clinging to the bars. When the nestrae led me toward him, his eyes widened, taking in the blood still dripping down my neck. Opening the door, they shoved me inside and Narek caught me in his arms, holding me tight. I understood in that moment that he was terrified of losing me. *I'm just as terrified of losing him,* I thought as I hugged him back. In our prison, we had no one else. We were the only friends either of us had left.

"What happened?" he demanded, pulling back to look at me again. "They hurt you."

I reached up to wipe at the blood. "Just a scratch." I smiled grimly. "They are always hurting us."

His brow creased. "I heard nothing for a long time, and then shouting and screaming. But it didn't sound like you."

I tried not to shudder at the memory. "No. They took me to see their goddess."

"Nesrelle?" His eyes widened even more. "Did she do this to you?"

I nodded. "She only gave more threats. It was just another attempt to scare me." I shrugged, hoping he couldn't see how much her words really had shaken me.

His fingers, still gripping my shoulders, tightened, and I could feel them shaking. He looked down and grimaced. "I thought they were going to kill you."

"Me too." I drew a deep breath. "I've heard of…darker powers…but she…" I shivered. "Have you ever seen Nesrelle before?"

Narek pulled back and leaned against the side of the ship. "I stopped believing in the Alrenian gods and goddesses years ago. They were silent through all our hardship and loss, and I couldn't believe they truly cared or were doing anything to intervene." He shrugged. "But I hadn't believed in your Giver of Life either, when it's clear he has saved your life and gifted some of your people. Perhaps it is just my people he has forsaken." With a sigh, he ran his hand through his hair. "Probably because they have been beseeching the wrong gods."

"No," I said firmly. "I can't believe he would abandon anyone, not after what I have learned about him. I think there is a reason you and I are here together now—to work together to save Misroth *and* Toryn."

Narek watched me silently, then slid to a seat. I settled in beside him. "According to Toryn beliefs," he continued, "Nesrelle isn't a deity. She is what you have already called her: a demon queen. She is a deity to the nestrae and certainly more powerful than you or me, but not a true ruler. She despises all that is good, and she feeds on death and despair and fear."

"It was her that you heard screaming, when I mentioned the Giver of Life. She hates him."

Narek turned to look at me. "Then you have something to use against her."

"Yes," I said, leaning my head back against the side of the ship, feeling the ship rock beneath me. But Nesrelle's words left my heart unsettled, sticking like a barb I couldn't quite shake because they rang with a truth I could not ignore. The Life-Giver *had* let my friends die. He could have rescued them as he had rescued me, but he had not. I lifted my fingers again to the scratch Nesrelle had left along my jaw and felt unease creep over me. What if the one I'd been depending on to protect the ones I loved couldn't be trusted?

CHAPTER SIX

Avrik

WITH JENNAH IN THE CROWD, even if they were kept apart so they couldn't talk, Avrik felt less alone. Her gift of courage bolstered him even as he watched the pyre blaze and cast shadows along the captives' faces. The stone table looked more like an altar waiting for its unwilling sacrifices. The nestrae chanted and pushed some of the prisoners closer to the flames, eliciting shrieks and sobs.

If death was about to claim him, he wouldn't be afraid.

He thought of the girl he loved and of his best friend back in Evren. *I'm sorry, Halia. I'm sorry, Bren.* The list of people he'd failed was unending, but at the very least he could face the end with courage and hope.

In his mind's eye, he saw his mother smiling down at him. As a child, he'd often run too fast through the house, occasionally bumping into furniture and falling face first to the floor. Ever the picture of patience, she would shake her head at him, a soft smile playing about her lips. He'd always felt brave when she was there to hold out her hand and help him up. She'd always been there.

Now she was reaching out her hand again, and he wasn't afraid.

But when he looked up, none of the prisoners had been thrown into the pyre. No one was screaming or weeping, and the nestrae, still clinging to their captives, had fallen back to their knees. Stillness settled over the deck.

There was a new figure standing beside the pyre.

A chill snaked down Avrik's back, and he wondered if this was some new nestred trick. The figure was a woman, dressed in a violet gown sparkling with gems and a white cloak with its hood thrown back to show off her beauty. Her hair was long and red, curling in thick tendrils down her back. Aside from the freckles across her cheeks and nose, her skin was flawless, almost glowing, even in the cloudy night. She turned her gaze to him, tilting her head to the side as if she were as intrigued with him as he was with her. Her eyes were as cold and unforgiving as ice.

Stepping forward gracefully on bare feet, she drifted around the nestrae, not even sparing them a glance, and stopped directly in front of Avrik. "Avrik," she said breathily. "Why is it that my servants have found a way to leech hope from every heart here but yours?" She pressed a hand to his chest, and her skin was so cool he felt it through his shirt.

His mouth was dry. "Who are you?" he whispered.

A slow smile graced her lips. "I think you know."

"Nesrelle."

She nodded, her smile spreading. "Yes." Her gaze snapped briefly to Jennah before fastening back on him. "Even Jennah with her gift of courage can't ignore the pressing horror of leaving her husband and children behind. Wondering how the girls will feel, growing up motherless. Wondering how her husband will manage as a widower with two young girls to care for. But you…" Her eyes drifted closed and her nails dug in, piercing through fabric to draw droplets of blood from his skin. He could feel their warmth warring against the chill of her hand. "You have regrets. You have loved ones you would leave behind…oh, but you have loved ones you think wait for you in the afterlife, too."

She snapped her eyes open. Avrik felt like she could see into his soul.

"Is that part of the hope you cling to?" she murmured. "Does your mother wait for you? Maybe even—dare you hope for it?—your father?" She cupped his face with her hand, brushing his own blood across his cheek. "Or is there something else that isn't letting me relish your fear?" Her gaze turned searching. "You *are* afraid, I can sense it. And you're full of pain. So why can't we feed on all that emotion?" She paused. "What gift do you have, dearest?"

Avrik's mouth tasted sour. After all these years, he could hear his mother's voice the clearest he had in a long time. *Dearest. Avrik dearest.* Nesrelle was mocking him, trying to pull his pain to the forefront of his mind. Trying to feed off it. "Don't call me that," he snapped.

Nesrelle stepped back, looking him up and down as if to assess him. "Release him," she ordered the nestrae, still without sparing them a single look. "What will I do with you," she continued, staring into Avrik's eyes, "if I can't use your fear? What good are you to me then?"

For a moment that felt like an eternity, her eyes turned dark, almost as black as the nestrae's, and her expression hardened. Her dreamy, ethereal aura receded, leaving nothing but a sense of danger and death in their wake. The fear Avrik had been feeling in her presence turned to terror. This time he really was staring death in its beautiful, hideous face.

"Run," she snarled, and he swore that now her teeth looked more like fangs, her nails like claws. "Run!"

The threat in her tone was unmistakable, even before she lunged for him. He threw himself to the deck and rolled away from her grasp. He kept rolling until his feet were beneath him and he leapt to his feet. He was running on pure adrenaline, its wild energy rushing through him.

As soon as he was standing, he knew his mind was being manipulated again. He was still on the ship's deck beneath the cloudy night sky, but the pyre, nestrae, and prisoners had vanished. It was like he was alone in the middle of the black sea with death stalking him. The wind caressing his face was as cold as Nesrelle's fingers. There was nowhere to hide, not really, and Avrik didn't want to spend his last moments retreating from his enemy.

Perhaps even in this vision overlying his real world, he could find a nestred weapon and face the demon queen. He charged along the deck toward the ship's cabin, plowing up the steps and shoving open the door. Lines from the endless books about fighting techniques he'd read over the years darted through his head. He thought of moments in Evren Forest when he'd hunted the sedwa, foolishly slaying monsters as if he could have killed them all to save his people. To redeem his father and himself. To have revenge. He'd learned a lot then, even if he'd ultimately failed.

But now he was facing something supernatural.

Inside the cabin, he found two beds at one end of the room, with a desk and chairs on the other. A blade hung on the wall behind the desk. Not a black nestred blade, but a two-handed Toryn sword. He pulled it down and spun to face the door, knowing Nesrelle would not be far behind him.

He stepped back in surprise. One of the beds wasn't empty.

"Mother?" he whispered, his voice sounding too loud in the quiet. The ship rocked gently. Wind rustled through the open window. Had it been open before?

His mother looked as weary and weak as she had in her last days. Tangled, dirty hair framed her pale face. Once it had shone so gold that as a child, he'd wondered if maybe she was really an angel sent to care for his father and him. Now it was thin and dull. Her body looked small and frail, even frailer than he remembered, maybe because now he was taller and stronger than she'd ever been.

"Avrik?" Even her wide, dark eyes seemed dim.

Though he knew in his heart it was a trick, Avrik couldn't ignore how real it felt. That was *her* voice. Those were her eyes watching him.

Tears stung his eyes. Sword trembling in his grasp, he drew closer to the bed.

"Be brave, dearest. We'll see each other again," she whispered, the same words she'd told him countless times as death crept close.

He could see death's shadow over her, the way her breathing grew shallow and her eyes became less focused. "Avrik?" she said again, and this time, he detected fear in her voice.

This was wrong. His mother had been at peace, even in the end. He didn't know how she'd faced the pain, the ugliness of her body fading away, or the sorrow of being forced to leave her family behind too soon. But she had. Now tears sparkled in her eyes.

"What did you let your father do?" Her voice broke. "Why didn't you help him when he lost hope and fell into darkness?" A tear glistened on her cheek, running down to her chin. "And how could you let them…how could you let them kill him?"

Avrik felt frozen to the floor. All his guilt and pain rose to the surface of his mind, everything he'd feared his mother would wonder about if she could see him now.

"You f-failed. You've failed everyone." She wept. "You've failed me."

He stared down in horror, wanting to protest but too overcome to do so. After all, wasn't she right? He *had* failed. Images of Bren and his family screaming and grasping at him flashed through his mind. *Help us, help!* they'd screamed. A sedwa's snarls. A mother's horrified sobs. The judgmental glances from the townspeople, and Rev pulling him away from a street brawl: *Are you all right? Let us help you…* The noose waiting for his father. The moment he'd turned his back…

He blinked and the images were gone. Except they never were. They always haunted him, the ways he had failed. The things he could have changed and the things he couldn't have.

"Come here, Avrik," his mother pled. Tears glistened on her face, but maybe she could find it in her heart to forgive him.

He stepped closer, reaching for her outstretched hand. When she was there to lift him up, he didn't ever need to be afraid.

Avrik's fingers brushed her palm, and it was so cold, it was like she was already dead. *Fool, of course she's already dead. This isn't real.*

As if the thought banished the vision, the sight of his mother changed in an instant. She sat up in the bed—but now she was Nesrelle, her cold hand seizing his. Claws pierced his skin as she snarled, pulling him in.

He staggered back, and with his free hand, swung his sword at her. It was heavy and unwieldy in one hand, but the threat of the blade was enough for her to release her hold on him. He attacked again, gripping the sword in two hands and slicing for her neck. With unnatural speed, she darted from the bed and leapt for him. He stood his ground.

She growled, ducking and crawling away to avoid his blade, then moving in to slice his legs with her claws. He hissed as a swipe of her hand tore through fabric and drew blood. Stumbling back, he raised the sword again, trying to remember everything he'd learned and practiced. But Nesrelle was something entirely different from anything else he'd ever faced, and she'd already drawn an advantage by rattling him with the flood of emotions the sight of his mother brought.

Grinning, she stood and paced the floor like a wild cat waiting to pounce. He eyed her warily. "I can taste your fear and pain," she said, licking her lips. She looked like a beautiful woman again as she tossed her hair over her shoulder and stared up at him through her long lashes. "But something…something still holds me back…" She narrowed her eyes. "Your disgusting gift!" she snarled. "You really are of no use to me alive."

In the blink of an eye, she was directly in front of him. She pressed her hand against his chest. Pain shot through him, like a frozen dagger slicing through his heart and then spreading, the agony piercing every inch of his body. He was ice cold and immobile, unable to breathe, unable to scream, unable to fight back. Black spots danced along his vision. His heart was slowing…slowing… It stopped. Numbness spread over his body and his vision blacked out.

He crashed into nothingness.

CHAPTER SEVEN

DAYS PASSED. NAREK AND I discussed our plans for escaping, but we had nothing to act upon until we reached Misroth. I practiced seeing the lies in the nestred visions haunting me so I could discern between what was real and what was not, but the more I weakened, the harder it became.

A storm began, rocking the ship more violently than usual and showering it with the steady beat of rain. Now and then, cracks of thunder boomed so close that the ship shuddered. And as time passed, the storm only grew worse. Terrified of being overturned and thrown into the restless sea, I could scarcely sleep. Narek tried to distract me from my anxieties by talking long into the night, sharing stories of the Zare'forith, confessing sins he'd committed against my people, or worrying aloud about Iyleth and the other Toryn we'd left behind. When the nestrae came below deck, they appeared restless and uneasy, if the demons could truly feel such emotions.

On one of the long, stormy nights, I dreamed of Evren. A misty morning dawned, tinging the eastern sky hues of gold and orange, and Rev and Lyanna rose early in their small cottage. Rev lit a fire in the hearth while Lyanna prepared a breakfast of eggs, sugared bacon, and fresh berries from her garden. They ate at the table in a companionable silence, but with frequent glances toward the empty chair across from them.

Lyanna brushed her hair away from her face. It was considerably greyer than it had been the last time I'd seen her. She drew a deep breath, but tears still sparkled in her blue eyes. Rev looked at her and ran an agitated hand through his dark hair, spiking it in all sorts of directions until he would have looked almost comical if my heart was not aching to see them this way.

"She's not worth the trouble," Rev said at last, laying a hand over Lyanna's.

She dropped her fork with a clang against her plate and buried her face in her hands. "How could she have betrayed us like this?" she asked, her voice trembling. "Why did she never tell us who she was and leave us without a proper goodbye? Or leave Misroth on a fool's errand to find her cousin? How could she have let the nestrae invade the capital and overrun the kingdom? This could be our last meal—"

Distant pounding interrupted her. The whole house shuddered, shaking the table, and rattling the silverware and dishes. War drums. An army was marching toward them.

Rev and Lyanna stared at each other in horror.

"The demons are here!" Lyanna said.

Perhaps it was the thunder that woke me, or the roiling of the waves, which slapped against the ship's sides angrily. My dream, which I now knew was a nestred lie, gripped me with horror anyway, and my mouth tasted sour with fear and shame. What if Lyanna and Rev didn't survive? What if they couldn't forgive me?

The ship tilted, slamming me into the cell bars. Pain bit into my scalp. I grasped one of the bars to keep myself from rolling more, using my free hand to feel my head. It came away red with blood.

"Are you all right?" Narek asked from the other side of our cell, where he too clung unsteadily to the bars.

I nodded carefully, ignoring the way my head pounded and my

scalp smarted. "Yes."

We hung on as wave after wave rolled the ship. The storm was worse, much worse. I couldn't escape the fear lodged in my chest. I knew all too well the violence of the sea, all the times merchants had left the capital to cross the Alrenian or the Great Sea, never to return. If the waves became too great, our chances of survival were minimal anyway, but locked in this cage below deck would guarantee death.

I hadn't been awake long, struggling to keep myself from being tossed about in the cell, when nestrae swarmed the steps and approached our prison. The leader was foremost among them. With hisses and clicks, they unlocked the door and wrenched us both from our places. They led us up to the deck, into the full fury of the storm.

It was impossible to tell if it was day or night in the dark whirlwind around us. The scents of rainwater and saltwater filled the misty air and sprayed against my face. The tang of the sea stung my tongue. Rain pelted down so thickly I could scarcely see the hulking, shadowy forms of the nestrae aboard the ship. The clouds swirled and pulsated overhead like a living creature, occasionally flashing with jagged streaks of lightning so close that the air crackled and the thunder was almost deafening. Waves slammed into the ship and splashed over the railing, foaming along the deck before tumbling off again as more waves rocked us in the opposite direction. If not for the nestred claws clutching my arms, I wouldn't have been able to stay upright through the constant motion.

Terror clung to me like a dark shadow at the sight of the angry sea, rising up like a hungry animal prepared to consume us all.

"Take him to the edge!" the nestred leader shouted.

Held between two nestrae, blinking against the lashing of the rain and waves, Narek was dragged toward the ship's side.

A new fear gripped me, filling my insides with ice. "What are you doing?" I demanded.

"Sacrificing him," the nestred snarled. "Our fleet is in danger and has been thrown off course. We need to appease and strengthen

Nesrelle so she may calm the storm." It studied Narek and then me, and for once there was almost an expression in its eyes, like a glint of mirth tucked away in their blackness. "We will throw him into the sea. A just ending for your last remaining friend, don't you think, princess?"

I swallowed and turned to Narek, who was struggling fruitlessly against the nestrae.

"No! You can't kill him—you have to keep him alive—for more sacrifices," I said quickly, desperately. "Nesrelle said she didn't want anyone to die quickly, but to suffer."

"I think he has suffered much," the leader said, studying Narek again. "And I think to kill your remaining friend and leave you alone would be a great sacrifice to her." It sneered at us. "After all, how much more does this Narek have left to give when he has already lost everything?"

Lightning made the hairs on my arms stand up. Thunder blocked out all sound for one nightmarish second, consuming my protests. They couldn't take someone else from me; they couldn't condemn him to such a horrible fate.

"No! Narek!" I screamed, wrenching myself toward the sea, my earlier fears forgotten in my terror for my friend. Nestred claws bit into my arms, yanking me back.

The nestrae lifted Narek over the railing.

"Don't—stop! Please! I'll do anything!" I shrieked, as if the nestrae would listen to my pleas.

They tossed him overboard, into the roiling sea.

CHAPTER EIGHT

Avrik

AVRIK OPENED HIS EYES TO the sounds of screams and clanging weapons coming from the deck. He was sprawled out on his back. A dull ache throbbed through his body, annoying but tolerable compared to the agony that had gripped him before. A chill ran over him; he was terribly cold. The effects of Nesrelle's touch lingered, yet he wasn't dead. Though he was sure his heart had stopped beating earlier, he could feel it pounding steadily against his ribcage now.

Slowly, he sat up. The world swayed around him before righting itself. He was still in the cabin, but it was empty, with Nesrelle nowhere in sight. Stretching out his arm, he found the sword laying at his side and lifted it.

It took him several long moments to stand and stumble to the door. He paused to breathe and gather his strength. It was clear there was a fight happening on deck, but he had no idea what he would find. For all he knew, he was still caught up in visions from Nesrelle or her nestred servants. It could be that nothing he was seeing or hearing was real. Even if it was, he was probably only running to his death.

But better to run and face it than flee and cower from it.

Avrik shoved open the cabin door and charged down the steps.

In the middle of the deck, the pyre on the stone table blazed high and he could smell the sickening scent of burning flesh, but the nestred weren't kneeling around it anymore. Somehow the prisoners were fighting back. Some held nestred weapons, black-bladed axes or swords or daggers, while others attacked with flaming sticks they'd yanked from the fire. The fire had little effect on the nestrae, but it seemed to give the desperate captives some courage. There were bodies strewn across the deck, mostly human, though Avrik spotted a few nestrae.

Avrik found Jennah in the middle of the fray. She wielded a dagger—no, two—and fought with more strength than seemed possible after the nestrae's torture. It was clear her courage gift fueled her, and likely it was what drove the other captives as well. As he pushed toward a knot of nestrae, he felt her gift grasp him. Warmth overpowered the lingering coldness in his body, and strength rushed through his weary limbs. He severed a nestred head from its body and spun to face another enemy.

Hope had never abandoned him, but now that he was no longer defenseless, no longer forced to believe his death was imminent, joy flooded his veins. Laughter burbled out of him and he didn't even try to hold it back. He felt reckless, maybe a little too carefree. His body easily remembered the motions he'd practiced under an open Evren sky for years. Duck. Parry. Dodge. Slash. Cut.

Once he'd wallowed in guilt for shooting a man who'd attacked Elena—Halia. It hadn't been easy to take a human life, even to save a friend. But he didn't feel remorse for cutting down the demons who had tortured and slaughtered countless lives, who had bent and broken scores of people with their cruelty and lies.

He waded through his enemies, and then the bodies of his enemies, and he was amazed to meet Jennah's eye amid the battle and find her smiling too. Their fellow prisoners were falling and dying. They were both wounded and half-starved. They might not survive this fight. But they were fighting back.

Then Avrik's smile faltered. Behind Jennah, a nestred charged and swung its axe at her neck, faster than she could turn. Faster than she could take down the enemy in front of her and face a new one. Time stretched. Avrik was trapped in those seconds, watching his friend's death play out before his eyes. The blade sliced slowly through the air. Jennah plunged a dagger through the visor of the nestred in front of her. The axe drew closer.

No! Avrik thought.

Jennah moved in for the kill, unaware of the axe coming at her from behind. She drove her other dagger into the nestred's neck.

Behind her, the axe shuddered, as if the nestred wielding it had been struck. The blade's trajectory jerked and altered, swinging upward. It sliced over Jennah's head, just missing her.

Avrik stared in shock and relief. The axe-swinging nestred wasn't hurt. It had simply, astonishingly, missed its mark. But there was no time to wonder about it now.

Snarling in frustration, the nestred swung again, but this time Jennah heard it and ducked. She charged it with her daggers and Avrik leapt forward to help. Together, they slew the enemy and turned to see a handful of remaining prisoners cutting down three more nestrae.

Avrik blinked. There was no one else left standing. They'd outnumbered and overpowered their enemies, all because Jennah had filled them with the courage to resist.

But why hadn't nestred visions confused and stopped them?

In his mind's eye, Avrik saw the axe blade swinging at Jennah and missing. Perhaps there had been some supernatural help? He breathed a quiet thanks to the Life-Giver.

For a long moment he stood there, wiping the sweat from his forehead and trying to comprehend what had happened. The influence from Jennah's gift slipped away and weariness overtook him. His stomach ached with hunger and he shivered with cold. He felt grief and anger when he studied the mangled bodies of captives littering the ground, people he'd never known but who had suffered and bled alongside him. But tangled in that was relief and joy. He was alive. Jennah was alive.

He closed his eyes and dared to picture Halia, dared to imagine telling her what an idiot he'd been to try to push her away. Everything that had ever come between them felt so inconsequential now, and at last he might have a chance of seeing her again.

"Now what?" one of the surviving prisoners, a man not much older than Avrik, asked.

Jennah's gaze flicked to the pyre and back to the bodies. She swallowed. "We burn the bodies." Her voice was thick with emotion.

Together, they worked to feed the human bodies into the flames. The smell filled Avrik's nostrils until he thought he would be sick, until it seemed like burning flesh was all he'd ever smelled and all he'd ever smell again. Flames seared his vision until they danced before him even when he closed his eyes. Weak and wounded as they were, the task was exhausting. A few, including Jennah, wept openly, especially over the smaller bodies.

They tossed the nestred carcasses overboard for the sharks.

At long last, they were done, able to scour the ship for food and water, bandages and salve, and able to tend to their wounds and rest.

"Does anyone know how to sail a ship?" one of the women asked after a long time.

"Do we have enough people to sail?" a man asked.

"How long before the other ships in the fleet realize what's happened?" someone else asked.

They were quiet for a long time. There were eight of them in total, eight left out of what Avrik estimated had been sixty prisoners. After the few that had succumbed to their wounds or starvation during their voyage and the others the nestrae had burned tonight, he and the other survivors had tossed forty-four bodies to the flames. There had been thirty-five slain nestred.

Before anyone could begin to talk about a plan, the first flash of lightning tore across the sky. Even inside the kitchen area, the light flared through the window and across their startled faces. Seconds later, thunder rumbled and rain pelted against the side of the ship.

"This complicates matters," Avrik muttered.

The storm lasted days. They blended into one another, endless days of fear and cold. Avrik couldn't tell if the weather was to blame when he shivered, or if Nesrelle's icy touch continued to linger.

As the waves rose, battering the ship more each day, he and the other survivors began to worry they'd escaped their captors only to drown at sea. Unable to control the ship's course, they took turns wrestling with the sails and the helm as best as they knew how. In between turns abovedeck, they hunkered down below and prayed the storm would end soon.

In the meantime, they spent time trying to rest and determine what they should do next. Jennah spent the first night explaining how her gift worked in a way the other survivors could understand. Everyone was grateful she'd had the strength left to encourage them to fight back, although some of the Toryn sniffed a bit at what they called an "unnatural Alrenian gift."

After they'd had time to process the fact that they'd survived the nestrae, they tried to determine how to survive the storm. The ship had become like a prison all on its own. Even after the storm ended, would they be able to navigate wherever they needed to go? And where should they go next?

Avrik worried continuously about the threat the nestrae posed to Misroth, which was undoubtedly the fleet's destination. The nestrae had taunted him with this fact countless times during his imprisonment. Now that the barriers were down, no kingdom was safe from the demons.

"What does it mean for Halia if the barrier is broken?" Avrik asked Jennah one night. His voice was low and hoarse with his concern.

They were each sitting on their hammocks, trying to settle down to sleep. The ship rocked and swayed while thunder rumbled overhead.

As difficult as the storm made it to sleep, Avrik's fears made it far worse. He couldn't shake away the images from the last time he'd seen Halia, before the nestrae had taken him. She'd been screaming and pleading with someone for help as the nestrae held her down and dug their claws into her. He felt his own nestred scar flare with pain at the memory. What word haunted her? Maybe they had taken her captive and tortured her into submission, forcing her to break the barrier. Maybe she was even dead.

No, he told himself. *She can't be dead.* If they'd killed her, he was sure the nestrae would have shown him her body. They'd tortured him enough with visions that he couldn't imagine they would ignore an opportunity to present him with a real nightmare. But it was difficult to be sure about anything anymore.

"It means she needs our help to protect Misroth," Jennah whispered back. Her eyes were soft with sympathy. "She's strong, Avrik," she added, nudging his shoulder gently. "I'm sure if we can survive the nestrae, she can too. Her truth gift could help her see through their lies."

Avrik's throat was too tight to answer. He leaned back in his swaying hammock and closed his eyes, but that only emphasized the sickening motion and made the sight of Halia screaming even clearer in his mind.

He wouldn't fail her again.

The next night, as they gathered at one of the tables to eat some of the nestrae's store of cured meat and crusty bread, they went through a conversation they'd already had more than once. Above, it was Ryal's shift at the helm while the rest of them tried to relax.

"Thank the gods the demons eat edible food," Tyren muttered around a mouthful of meat. He was a young man with premature wrinkles and a dusting of white already shimmering in his black hair.

"Do we really know what this is? Maybe it's dried rat meat," Avrik said, grinning.

Zara, a young woman around Avrik's age, smirked back at him. Her long black hair had probably once been glossy, but now it looked dull and tangled, and framed a face drawn with weariness. Her dark eyes looked haunted, even when she smiled. Who knew what horrors she had seen in Toryn, even before the nestrae's torture?

Jayvok, an older man, sat with his shoulders slumped in exhaustion. He didn't even smile at Avrik's feeble attempt at humor. "We can't afford to be picky when we're half-starved. I'd eat live beetles now if I had to."

"So, if we can navigate to Toryn after this storm ends," Tyren began, "what awaits us there?"

Zara picked at her fingernails with the nestred knife she'd begun carrying with her everywhere. "Nothing," she said flatly.

"I know Toryn is your home, but the nestrae just left to attack *our* home," Jennah cut in, nodding toward Avrik, who sat beside her. "We need to return and fight."

The Toryn stared back at her darkly. Avrik supposed they were used to focusing on themselves and their own survival, and he knew they hated Misroth for abandoning them, but he hated how their first instinct was to flee. Find a haven. Forget the damage the nestrae were about to inflict on others.

"That's suicide," Aralinn whispered. At thirteen, she was the youngest survivor in their ragged band.

"She's right," Jayvok said. "We would arrive after Misorth was already under attack. How would eight people sail into the harbor without being seen and immediately overrun by the nestrae? It's impossible." He grunted. "Besides, what did Misroth ever do for us?"

"As a Misrothian, I'd like to point out how I helped save you pathetic wretches with my gift," Jennah snapped. In the candlelight, the gold in her eyes flashed.

"We can't abandon Misroth," Avrik agreed. He was seated at the table with a blanket bundled around him in a futile attempt to fight the constant chill he felt. He'd found it stowed in a chest near his hammock on the first night. It was threadbare and moth-eaten, and smelled terrible, but it helped a little. His body didn't seem feeble, only cold. So cold. He closed his eyes and tried to ignore the shadow he felt growing over his heart: the knowledge that something wasn't quite right.

He opened his eyes to see Jennah studying him, and he smiled. It didn't fool her.

"I don't think you have to abandon Misroth," Zara said after a long moment. "But you have to be cautious." She glanced around at her fellow Toryn. "After all, if Misroth falls, what hope does Toryn have to ever rebuild itself? And after the nestrae conquer Misroth, they will flood Alrenor, and perhaps move on to the kingdoms across the Great Sea. If they aren't stopped, there will be nowhere left for us to hide."

Slowly, Tyren nodded. A few others followed his lead.

Jayvok sighed. "We wouldn't be able to reach Misroth before the rest of the fleet. We don't even know how to sail this ship properly. By the time we reach shore, the nestrae will have overtaken Misroth and we'll be in just as much danger as before."

"Since when did Toryn just give up?" Zara slammed her knife into the table. Aralinn jumped.

They looked around at each other uneasily. The truth was that they were all weary and afraid. Nowhere was safe. No plan sounded secure. They ached with injuries that were only beginning to heal. They were half-starved and only starting to regain their strength from a few days of regular meals and troubled rest. They were each still haunted by nestred visions or their whispered chants echoing in their heads, as if the nestrae's ghosts lingered behind.

"We don't have another choice," Avrik said at last, breaking the heavy silence. "Let's show the nestrae they can't take our kingdoms without a fight."

CHAPTER NINE

SOMEWHERE MEN, WOMEN, AND CHILDREN were waiting and praying for loved ones that would never return. Somewhere the nestrae had possibly even scattered the ashes of the man I'd loved and deceived. Somewhere my people fought to rebuild our kingdom, not knowing an army of demons was about to overrun them. And somewhere Gillen lay beaten, perhaps dying, and Narek sank beneath the vicious Alrenian waves. All these thoughts taunted me as the storm shrieked through air and water, threatening the nestrae and captives alike, and I was unable to change any of it.

Or maybe that was wrong.

These demons won't determine my fate, I thought.

Tears burned my eyes. My screams had died as shock and rage sparked white-hot in my heart. Grief was a monster inside me, but perhaps not the sort of monster the demons wanted it to be. Instead of despair, I was full of anger and defiance. My sorrow was raw, blinding, and desperate for revenge.

There was much I couldn't change, but maybe there were some things I still could.

Though I couldn't pry free from the nestrae's grip myself, the storm made it easy. A wave crashed over the deck with enough force to knock even the sturdy nestrae over with me.

Here my speed was my strength. Gasping and spluttering as the ship tilted and the wave receded, I sat up and yanked a knife from a nestred's belt before it had recovered. Adrenaline rushing through my veins, I sprang to my feet and darted away. The leader let out a cry that was drowned out in the storm's roar. Most of the other nestrae were consumed with fighting against the storm, clutching the rigging or the rails for support and praying in their hissing whispers that their demon queen would accept their sacrifice and spare them.

Weak and tossed about by the storm, I barreled along the deck, pushing toward the railing. I didn't know how, but I had to find Narek. He *had* to be alive. My eyes scanned the waves, but I couldn't see him in the lashing wind and rain.

Unexpectedly, a single thought fluttered through my mind: *Find Gillen.*

Though it was physically painful to turn from the railing, I knew leaping from the ship would be foolish. And, if Gillen was aboard, it would mean abandoning him.

As the nestrae plowed across the deck toward me, I stumbled toward the ship's cabin. It was a flimsy hope but my only one: this was the only place I hadn't seen, the only place that might hold Gillen if he were aboard. And in my mind, it made sense: if I were the nestred leader with an important prisoner I wanted to keep under my watchful eye, I'd keep him as close to me as possible.

What I would do next I didn't yet know or care. I had to trust the Life-Giver wouldn't lead me astray. Just to find my cousin, to reassure myself he was alive even for a moment, was worth any risk.

I charged to the cabin, sometimes stumbling through waves, sometimes crawling, but never stopping. When I reached the entrance, another rock of the ship shoved me into the door, smashing my shoulder into the knob as I fell. I staggered to my feet and threw open the door to find a low-ceilinged room lined with shelves of books and maps, most scattered across the floor. Slamming the door shut behind me, I stepped over soggy pages and broken bindings toward a table and chairs, set close to windows overlooking the tumultuous sea. In an alcove on one side of the space was a small bed, its sheets unmade; I turned to see an identical one on the opposite side, this one occupied by a still, quiet figure. My heart leapt with a mixture of relief and pain. Gillen.

I scanned the room and found what I needed: a chair set near the desk. I dragged it toward the door and wedged it under the knob. It wouldn't be long before the nestrae arrived, but between this and the storm I could hope for a delay.

Running to him, I knelt beside the bed and called out his name. He lay sprawled across the covers, unrestrained, apparently too weak and wounded to be considered a threat. He looked even more broken than the last time I'd seen him. His face, beneath layers of grime, scratches, and bruises, was drawn in pain. His long golden hair was matted with dirt and old blood. Beneath rips in one of his shirt sleeves, between layers of bandages, I could see bright red burns disfiguring his skin. When I cried out his name, his blue eyes fluttered open, looking glazed and distant, like the sky dimmed by a haze of swirling grey clouds.

"Little Lia," he said, so softly that I could barely hear him over the roar of the storm. It sounded less fierce here, in the shelter of the cabin. A hint of a smile upturned his lips. "I'm not sure if I even have the strength to be angry at their tricks anymore. I've missed you so much."

My eyes filled with tears. "This is not a trick. I'm here."

He squeezed his eyes shut again. "I don't know what to believe anymore…"

"Gil, it's Halia."

"They cannot hurt you too…" He blinked, looking momentarily confused. His gaze settled again on me. *Do not break the barrier, Halia.* He snatched at my arm, his grip surprisingly strong. "Misroth is falling…already falling…"

"Gil," I cut in firmly. "We will stop it. We're going to escape."

He shook his head. "No one escapes. They drive everyone mad…

They kill all…"

His voice drifted away, and for the first time I no longer heard the shrieking wind outside. Everything was quiet. I ran to the windows to see the storm calming as suddenly as it had begun. The waves had shrunk, and patches of sunlight pierced through the clouds. The rain had turned to a thin drizzle, through which I spot a swell of green on the near horizon. Land.

Thudding footsteps outside the cabin jolted me back to the present problem. A nestred slammed into the door and the chair shivered. I dashed back to Gillen.

"You must find a little more strength, Gil, and I can save you. But I need your help."

I didn't wait for his reaction. Lifting another chair, I returned to the windows and swung. Glass shattered everywhere, raining into the sea below and grazing my arms. Mist swept through the broken window and wet my face with cold slime. I dropped the chair with a clatter and stepped back from the rush of wind tearing at my hair and clothes.

Returning to Gillen, I slid my hands beneath his shoulders and tugged him upright. He felt lighter than I'd expected, his frame slight from the long weeks as a nestred captive. At my touch, he cried out in pain and I realized with a jolt that one of his arms was hanging limply at his side, all but useless. I moved my hand and pulled on his good arm.

"You have to stand," I said, helping him swing his legs over the edge of the bed and slowly rise. He was meek and obedient, never questioning my words. He swayed on his feet, but he did not fall.

The pounding against the door came louder and faster now. Wood splintered, and I tugged more urgently on Gillen. With one arm wrapped around him, I guided him as he leaned against me. As we approached the broken windows, wind swept hair into our eyes and spat water on our cheeks. My blood thrummed in my veins and my knees went weak just looking down at the sea I'd feared for years. What if we never left its grasp once we leapt into its cold embrace? But the nestrae feared it too. This was our only chance.

I kicked off my boots and turned to my barefoot cousin, praying he had some strength left. Even if he could only keep himself afloat, I hoped we might have a chance. "We have to jump!" I clutched his hand tightly, but he only blinked in response. "Gil!"

He jerked at the sound of his name, his eyes clearing. Slowly, he nodded, and we stepped nearer to the broken window. As the door splintered, the chair fell, and a nestred forced its way into the cabin, we leapt together.

Cold wind whipped through my tattered clothes and raindrops pelted my skin. With a last gasp for air, I plunged into dark waves. I opened my eyes, and in one terrible instant I was back beneath the cliff at Misroth City, fighting against the ropes binding me and losing air. The weight of the sea pressed on me from all sides. I blinked when a shadow darted forward, then stretched toward me, pushing through the water. Something groped at my back.

I spun around to see fingers reaching and wide eyes staring back at me. My mouth opened in a silent scream: it was Gare, clawing at me with dead fingertips, watching me with unseeing eyes. More hands grasped at me from all sides—there was Mother with her pale, shocked face and Father with his piercing stare. I turned and faced Layk and Jennah. Unlike Gare, their eyes followed me, their expressions accusatory.

Then I saw Avrik. He held out his hand to me and waited, expectantly. Like he alone was living amongst the ghosts haunting me, and if I just dove deeper into the shadowy sea and grasped his hand, it would be warm and solid in mine and we would be together again. I held my hand out in response to him and my fingers brushed against his, finding them as warm and inviting as I'd imagined. My heart twisted inside me. *It's a nestred trick,* I told myself. *Let him go.*

But the pain was almost more than I could bear. Did this mean he truly was gone? He looked so real, so alive, that it felt like I would be abandoning him to death to swim away now. When I looked into his brown eyes, I felt at home again, like we were in Evren and all this pain and loss and death was nothing more than a nightmare. Together we could conquer anything. *We're survivors,* he'd told me. And we were. All I had to do was reach out and pull him to safety, yet he beckoned me closer. I started to forget why I wanted to swim to the surface, when Avrik was right here before me. My lungs burned, but in that moment I thought I would be content to drown here, to follow the one I loved into the afterlife.

Avrik's mouth twisted into his familiar grin, as if he could read the feelings of longing and hope darting across my face. Just like he had always been able to read me. His eyes were full of life, and maybe, just maybe, the same emotions I felt for him…

No! Swim away or you will drown, I thought fiercely. Though it felt like I was tearing part of my heart from my body, leaving it to sink to the bottom of the sea along with these visions of my lost loved ones, I pulled away and kicked toward the surface.

Retching up sea water, I emerged from the waves and began searching for Gillen. He was a few yards away, the Alrenian churning around him and pulling him under. He was barely resisting its pull. I plunged back beneath the water and grasped his waist, struggling to drag him back to the surface with me.

"Don't give up," I called when we broke the surface. Hair clung to my face and salt stung my eyes. One arm still wrapped around his middle, I used my free arm to tread water so I could look for the shore. "Lie on your back," I ordered Gillen once I had my bearings.

With my cousin floating the best he could, I was able to pull him along behind me while I swam. He kicked feebly now and then, but he was so silent and passive that it felt like trying to swim with a weight bound to me. Despair clawed at me. I wasn't sure I'd ever have the strength to get us both to land.

It hadn't looked too far away when we had been aboard the ship, but now it seemed impossibly distant. My arms burned and my chest heaved, all the while my muscles screamed against the demands I was giving them. Every scratch and burn the demons had marked upon my body, especially the rune on my back, smarted in the saltwater. At last, when I thought I couldn't swim another instant, I flipped over on my back and tried to make my body as light as possible, still clutching Gillen's hand and kicking to keep above the waves.

Every muscle in my body was taut and heavy. My head spun, my breaths were shallow, and my body was numb with cold. Maybe we would both descend to the bottom of the sea after all, and the depths that had opened wide for me years ago would claim me at last. Nesrelle must have been watching. Maybe her cold, greedy fingers were sweeping through the sea too, her claws ready to drain my blood.

Seconds or maybe hours later, we crested a tall wave that sent us tumbling backward into the water. Panic renewed my energy and I kicked frantically, reaching for Gillen, the surface, something. At first I was disoriented, but then I noticed it was brighter here, easier to see my cousin and the direction I needed to swim. Sunlight sparkled through the water and there—there was the sandy bottom, not too far away. We were entering shallow water. My heart leapt.

I paddled toward Gillen, caught his hand, and kicked upward. We'd barely caught our breath when another wave sent us rolling. The water was pushing us toward land. I kicked up, breathed deeply, and let another wave carry us forward. Breathe. Tumble. Kick. Breathe. The cycle continued again and again. I held Gillen's hand so tightly that it hurt, yet still I had to keep finding it in the churning water each time another wave struck. My lungs ached. I broke the surface, gasped a shallow breath, and was pushed under again. Fear tugged at the edges of my mind. Lights sparked along my vision. How ironic it would be to drown now, mere yards from the shore. Another shallow breath. My greedy lungs took in some water on the way down. We rolled, I swam, and I almost missed Gillen as the next wave came. Then another came far too soon; I reached in vain for him; I couldn't rise to catch air. Water swirled and pulled, pushing me down, down. Panic made it hard to think clearly. My back pressed against sand and I rolled some more. Water churned above me. *This could be my grave,* I thought.

I stretched out my arms and felt the sand around me. *Sand,* I thought, and then my brain cleared. I pushed myself to my hands and knees and my head cleared the surface. Coughing up the water I'd inhaled and gasping for air, I crawled until I found the strength to pull myself, wet and heavy, to my feet.

Gillen lay facedown nearby, floating motionless in the waves rolling up the beach. I ran to him and pulled him to shore, where I rolled him onto his back. His eyes were closed, but he coughed up water and took several deep, shuddering breaths. Then he lay still and quiet again, his chest rising and falling softly. Every breath seemed to hurt him.

I laughed, feeling a mixture of relief and fear. Standing, I took stock of our surroundings. The nestred fleet was nothing more than a series of distant black forms on a calm sea. A few shreds of grey clouds drifted across the clearing sky, the remnants of a rainbow melting into them as the warm sun dissipated the last of the storm's mist and darkness.

Turning, I studied the beach, its golden sand rising smoothly up to a deeply shaded forest. Fresh green leaves graced their boughs, reminding me that while I'd been trapped in darkness, spring had long since taken hold of the outside world. There was no sign of life nearby, nothing to indicate where we might be. With the Alrenian calm again, I could track the northward progress of the enemy fleet, which told me it was unlikely we were on Misrothian soil. I'd never found any islands on any maps of the Alrenian, but I'd learned enough of the world recently to know there was much Misroth did not know or had chosen to forget. It was possible we were somewhere in Alrenor, but I wasn't sure if that prospect was encouraging or not.

A form farther down the beach snagged my attention. I squinted against the sun, not sure I could believe my eyes.

"Narek?" I called out, my voice cracking. I almost didn't dare believe it.

Narek raced toward us, his soaked clothes dripping water. Tears pricking my eyes, I charged forward, throwing my arms around him and fighting back an embarrassing sob. His arms were warm, and his heart pounded steadily against my ear. Impossibly, wonderfully, he was here.

"You're alive!" I said, stepping back at last and wiping at a stubborn tear that had escaped.

To my surprise, Narek's own eyes were misty. His eyes darted over my shoulder to Gillen, and he turned back to me in shock. "What happened?" he asked, at the exact same time I asked him the same question.

We stared at one another for a moment before bursting into laughter. The first true laughter either of us had heard in days.

"Maybe the Life-Giver is on our side after all," Narek said once I'd explained to him how I'd found and rescued Gillen. "I cried out to him when I was fighting against the waves in that storm. And here we were, close to land all along."

"I think we're in Alrenor. I just hope it won't prove to be our curse instead of our salvation," I said softly, studying the ancient trees behind us. I shivered and stretched out on my back beside Gillen, enjoying the soft, warm bed of sand while the sun slowly dried my clothes.

Lying on Gillen's other side, Narek looked just as exhausted as I felt.

"Once we discover exactly where we are, we'll need passage or horses to return to Misroth," I muttered sleepily, my brain feeling foggy. For the first time, I was at peace, making the temptation to rest overwhelming. I closed my eyes, only for a moment. If Narek replied, I didn't even hear him.

I drifted into a dreamless sleep.

CHAPTER TEN

Avrik

IN THE END, THE CHOICE of what to do next was made for them. After days of floundering in the storm, the wind trapped them in shallow water along Alrenor's coast. Armed with weapons, rations, and medical supplies, they lowered one of the boats and rowed for shore.

As they approached land, the sun rose rapidly, turning the day hot and humid. Sweat gathered on Avrik's forehead as he rowed. The chill he'd felt for days was distant now, and he dared to hope whatever Nesrelle had done to him was passing.

He focused on the coast, trying to catch a glimpse of what they were headed toward. Beyond a stretch of golden sand, a thick forest rose. He couldn't see any buildings or other signs of civilization.

His companions were silent. Ryal, Zara, and Jennah were also rowing, while the others sat staring at the Alrenian landscape.

With each stroke of the oars, Avrik imagined the distance between Halia and himself growing greater and greater. He pictured her as a nestred captive, perhaps aboard a different ship in the fleet or in a different nestred fortress in Toryn. Or maybe she was a captive of the Toryn themselves, injured and alone. But maybe Layk was still with her to help, and surely Iyleth wouldn't let her people hurt Halia. Unless

Iyleth was dead.

They pulled the boat ashore and headed toward the forest. Before them stood trees as wide as three men and so high Avrik could have sworn the leaves brushed against the sky. Keeping their hands close to their weapons, the group stepped among the trees.

"This must be Lorin Forest," Jennah said thoughtfully as they pressed through the undergrowth.

The foliage was vibrant and alive in a way entirely different from the plant life in Misroth. Evren Garden didn't even contain flowers growing in such bright hues. Flaming red, orange, and yellow petals contrasted sharply with deep green leaves. Moss draped from thick branches like veils.

Avrik watched squirrels dart effortlessly up the climbing branches and a rabbit scurry into the underbrush, and he wondered what it would be like to hunt in this forest. To climb one of the towering trees and stretch out on a branch with his bow, waiting for game to creep into view. He breathed in the scent of last year's crushed leaves underfoot mingling with the fragrance of earth and flowers. For an instant, he let his mind take him back to his childhood, when his father had first taken him into Evren Forest—only ever in daylight—to teach him how to hunt. How to identify footprints and trails. How to set a trap. How to hide himself and then wait patiently for an animal to approach.

Then he opened his eyes. *He's dead,* Avrik reminded himself harshly, *and he deserves to be.*

"There's a path ahead," Tyren said, pointing.

Sure enough, they stepped out of the thick undergrowth onto a smooth dirt path, wide enough for four to walk beside each other. Zara, who refused to put her knife away even when she went to sleep, twirled her blade nervously in her fingers. At Avrik's side, Jennah shot him a reassuring smile, and he felt her courage gift seep into him, steeling his nerves.

That's when they noticed the iron gate, twisted into elaborate patterns of flowered vines. Six guards, dressed in gleaming silver armor and tunics that bore Alrenor's swirling sun insignia, stood stiffly on either side.

Jennah stepped forward, gesturing for everyone else to stay behind her. *"Dieni,"* she greeted the men, her voice loud and confident.

She spoke a few more words, quickly and lightly, but the guards' eyes narrowed. They flicked from her, to Avrik and the others, and back again. When one replied, his voice was gruff and heavy with a threat.

"Jennah…" Avrik began, concerned for his friend. His hand hovered near his sword hilt.

But Zara had already flown into action. With a cry of fear, she lifted her knife.

"Wait!" Avrik cried. "Put down your knife! Don't be rash—we can show them—"

Zara paid him no mind. Her face was pale and her entire body shook. Her eyes were wide and horrified, lost in the grip of some nestred nightmare. Despite the tremble in her hands, she didn't miss when she flung her knife at a guard's face. It lodged in his eye and he dropped instantly.

"What are you doing?" Jennah shouted, but it was too late.

The guards drew their weapons and attacked. Avrik's heart hammered as he watched Jayvok cut down. The next instant, another guard slit Zara's throat.

A guard swung his sword for Avrik's neck and he ducked, kicking at the man's knee to knock him off balance. The man tottered for just a moment, long enough for Avrik to slam the flat edge of his sword against his face. Nose streaming blood, he fell unconscious. Jennah dispatched another guard.

But Avrik could see that it was already hopeless. In seconds, Alrenor's trained guards had slain every one of their companions. Horror snaked through his stomach at the bloody sight of the Toryn survivors, all dead at his feet. Only he and Jennah were left.

Even with just three guards still standing, it was clear the Alrenians had the upper hand. In moments, they surrounded Avrik and Jennah. Avrik pressed his back to Jennah's and clutched his sword hilt tightly, letting Jennah's gift course through him.

The gates creaked as they flew open, drawing all eyes, Alrenian and Misrothian, to a new guard, running and shouting at the remaining three in their language.

The guards hesitated, their weapons still pointed toward Avrik and Jennah. Avrik's heart pounded as the fourth guard advanced toward the others, speaking in rapid Alrenian. Even though sweat clung to Avrik's back and the humid air swirled around him, his fingers felt like ice. A chill shuddered through him. He blinked against the darkness gathering along the corners of his vision. Apparently Nesrelle's influence hadn't vanished after all.

Avrik hazarded a glance over his shoulder at Jennah and registered hope on her face. What were the Alrenians saying?

At last, the three guards lowered their weapons as the fourth guard turned to Avrik and Jennah. "Drop your weapons," the man demanded.

He and Jennah complied, and all four men seized them, shoving them toward the gate.

"Because we're foreigners, the captain insisted we had to be kept alive for questioning," Jennah hissed, before one of the guards pushed her roughly.

"Shut up," he snarled in the New Language.

As the guards led them forward, Avrik was forced to step over the bodies of his companions. Fellow survivors of the nestrae, only to fall here to a new enemy. He and Jennah were alive for now, but as captives of the Alrenians, he wasn't sure their fate would be any better. The chill he'd felt grew stronger, making him shudder.

He remembered stories of fearless, cruel Alrenian warriors and couldn't help the growing knot in his stomach. He wondered if Alrenor would prove to be even more ruthless than Toryn.

CHAPTER ELEVEN

AS DARKNESS DESCENDED, I WOKE to the painful reminder that my stomach was empty and my body was weak, my muscles spent. Gillen stirred fitfully beside me, muttering something incoherent in his sleep. My clothes and hair were still uncomfortably damp, making me shiver in the cool breeze coming off the water. But when I laid a hand on Gillen's brow, he was hot and clammy.

We needed food and shelter desperately, but most of all, we needed a healer. It was likely some of Gillen's wounds were infected and I knew he had broken bones. His arm was certainly giving him pain. None of us were in any condition to travel far.

Narek sat up, his body rigid and his eyes alert as he searched the shadows around us.

Movement and the snapping of twigs and rustle of underbrush from the woods drew my attention. Heart pounding, I reached for the nestred knife in my belt. Narek tensed and reached for a weapon he didn't have.

"We are not enemies," came a woman's voice. She stepped from the trees, accompanied by several others, men and women alike. They were all dressed in ivory cloaks with the hoods pulled low to cast their faces in shadow. Their clothes and boots were plain and simple, all in shades of black, brown, or grey, and I didn't see any weapons at their sides. Some of them carried blankets, a welcome sight.

I hovered over Gillen, pulling my fingers away from my knife but remaining wary. "Who are you?"

"We are truth-gifted from the Aremakkin Temple near Hemlaen," the woman said. Beneath her hood, I could make out little of her face. "I am Meli. I had a vision of your arrival on our shores and we came to help." She hesitated, her gaze flicking from Gillen to Narek and back to me. "Will you let us help you? We'll take you back to the temple."

Hemlaen, I thought. We were in Alrenor.

I glanced at Narek, who frowned. *Other truth-gifted?* My heart accelerated with both hope and suspicion. *Can we trust them?*

Concentrating, I took a moment to call on my gift, pushing all of my thoughts and emotions into this one task. I saw flashes of Meli in an immaculate palace, speaking with a woman who, from her extravagant clothing, appeared to be the empress. The empress began shouting in anger, and next I saw a new scene. Meli was shrouded in a cloak and hood, fleeing the capital on horseback under cover of night. Lastly, I caught flashes of her working in a temple, smiling at a woman who gestured as if making a request; eating dinner at a table surrounded by men and women dressed in ivory cloaks; and kneeling in a sanctuary to pray to the Life-Giver. *I can trust these people,* I thought, the truth of it overwhelmingly reassuring, like a warm wave of comfort washing over me.

"It's all right," I whispered to Narek. "They speak the truth."

As a few young men and women approached, covering Gillen in warm blankets and lifting him from the sand, I studied Meli. Beneath each of these people's hoods, I caught the flash of Alrenian gold in their eyes and on their skin. "We're in Alrenor, but you speak the New Language…" I said in confusion.

"Yes, we know how to speak the Common Trade Language as well as Alrenian here." She grinned. "I'm sure you have as many questions for me as I have for you. But here," she tossed me an extra cloak from beneath the folds of her own, "you'll want this to keep you warm…and to conceal that." She nodded at my knife. "You cannot be seen with a weapon on you."

Before she could continue, I cut in desperately. "What month is it?" I had to know how much time Misroth had left. How much time I had to reach my kingdom and prepare to fight.

Meli's brow furrowed. "It's the tenth day of Kelah."

My heart slammed painfully against my chest. I hadn't been far off, but I'd hoped for better news. Narek and I had lost so much time in the nestred fortress. More than I'd realized. But time had had no meaning there… I swallowed back my panic and wrapped the cloak Meli had given me tightly about myself.

"We must hurry back to the temple," Meli continued. "Follow us."

Another woman handed Narek a cloak that matched mine. I swallowed back further questions and pulled my hood low. The group returned almost silently to the forest, some carrying Gillen while the others gestured for Narek and me to follow.

The shadows were deep and cool beneath the trees, which were wide and ancient-looking, stretching toward the sky and creating a thick ceiling far overhead. Their trunks looked rough and wrinkled as an old woman's skin. I breathed in the scents of bark and warm earth, and for one aching moment, I thought of Evren. Aside from the noise we made, the night's stillness was only broken by the rustling of wind through the leaves and the distant hooting of an owl. With the cloak tucked securely around me, I felt pleasantly warm, but my body ached with exhaustion and the twigs and roots underfoot scratched my bare feet.

Fortunately, we didn't have far to go. Soon the forest thinned until it revealed a hilly countryside with distant homes and farms, all nestled among the lowlands. Farther away, I could make out the city of Hemlaen on the horizon. Before us, right at the edge of the forest, rose a grassy knoll with an imposing temple at its summit. The temple's stone face, the same shade of ivory as the strangers' cloaks, was framed by massive pillars, and shone in the starlight. The steps leading up the slope to the ornately carved doors were wide and smooth. Everything about the temple appeared pristine and lovely.

As we ascended the steps, I studied the temple grounds, filled with lush flowers and shrubs. Intermingling scents of flowers and greenery drifted on the breeze. Somewhere out of sight a fountain bubbled peacefully, and close at hand was a plain horse stable, its door open. Another cloaked figure stood inside, stroking a dappled grey's nose.

Two more cloaked figures waited on either side of the temple doors. At our approach, they exchanged nods with Meli and swung the doors inward for us. Flickering torches ensconced on the walls lit the temple's interior and reflected in the polished stone floor, a deep black that contrasted sharply with the ivory walls. High windows afforded glimpses of the stars twinkling in the eastern sky.

We followed a narrow hallway past several closed doors and a winding staircase until we entered the temple's sanctuary, a vast room filled with rows of stone benches, engraved with scenes of nature, all facing an altar in the front. Vases of colorful, fragrant flowers—many I'd never seen before—lined the outer walls. Set in the center of the room, surrounded by still more benches, was a rushing fountain. The ceiling was high, with windows set within its center to offer a view of the sky.

"Welcome to the Aremakkin Temple," Meli said, spreading her arms wide in a warm gesture of welcome. Her voice echoed within the open space.

"It's beautiful."

"The rest is not quite as grand," Meli admitted. "Come, we'll take you to your rooms so you can rest."

Meli directed some of her companions to fetch food and then turned to me. "We'll take Gillen to our healers' rooms."

"Can I go with him?" I asked, hating the frantic note in my voice. After all I'd endured to find my cousin, it was physically painful to be parted from him now.

"The healers need time to work uninterrupted," Meli said, her brow scrunched in apology.

The trust I'd felt from my gift lingered like the gentle touch of a hand on my shoulder. I knew everything would be all right. Relenting, I swallowed and nodded.

"I'm sure they will let you in to see him soon," Meli reassured me as I watched two men carry him away. "Come, I'll show you to your room." She glanced at another figure close by. "Amek, please take Narek to his room."

I startled to hear Narek's name, when neither of us had shared our names with the strangers. Narek himself seemed a little surprised, his brow furrowed as he cast one more uncertain glance my way before he left with the stranger.

Meli led me to a small room on an upper level that overlooked the gardens. It contained a bed, a rug woven with Alrenor's swirling sun insignia, and a chest of drawers holding a basin of water, with a mirror above it. Overall, it was clean, simple, and the most comforting sight I'd seen in a long time.

A cloaked woman entered bearing a tray laden with stew, brown bread, cheese, and a cup of water. She laid it on the bed for me and departed, but Meli stayed, bidding me to sit down and eat. She leaned against the wall and crossed her arms, studying me thoughtfully while I sat on the bed and ate, forcing myself to go slowly despite my painfully hollow stomach.

When I had nearly finished, she spoke.

"In my vision, you came from Toryn."

I cringed at the mention of Toryn and the memories of all I'd suffered and lost there. I set my spoon down, staring at the remnants of beef and potatoes in my bowl. I didn't trust my voice, so I merely nodded.

"You were captives of…strange creatures with claws and armored skin…" She frowned. "I've never seen the like in recent memory, but I think I've heard tales of them."

"Nestrae," I whispered. "Demons." Memories of torture in their Toryn fortress jolted through my brain. Their visions haunting me. Gillen's screams keeping me company each night. Flames flickering along my flesh. Claws pressing into skin, drawing blood. I glanced down at my arms, a ruin of ugly burns and claw marks. I could still hear the nestrae's hissing whispers in my mind, infiltrating my thoughts even when I tried to block them out. *"Condemned. Hopeless… All you love will be taken. Everyone you love will die."*

"They are invading Misroth?" Meli asked, interrupting my dark thoughts.

I nodded.

"The barrier is gone at last," she mused aloud, "but only to bring new curses upon us." She closed her eyes. "You are Halia, princess of Misroth, and you brought your king, Gillen, to us." Her eyes snapped open, her gaze intense. "The plight of your people must be desperate, to take you both into Toryn's darkness and bring you to us in this state."

My chest constricted. I didn't like that she knew both immediate heirs to the Misrothian throne were under her roof, even though my gift told me to trust her. All of the old Misrothian stories about Alrenor spoke not only of Alrenian strength and courage, but also of Alrenian greed and lust for power. My instinct was to consider her an enemy.

But Meli didn't seem to notice my misgivings. "Will they turn their eyes on Alrenor once they have conquered Misroth?"

I didn't like the way she phrased the question, as if Misroth's defeat was certain. But I knew her gift didn't allow her to see the future any more than mine did. "Anything and anyone they can destroy, they will." I hesitated. "Would Alrenor consider an alliance if both our kingdoms are in danger?"

Calling on her gift, Meli concentrated only a moment before she spoke crisply. "It's unlikely the empress would be helpful toward Misroth."

I blinked, trying to conceal my surprise. This woman's visions came to her so seamlessly, it was hard to believe we had the same gift. She gleaned information she wanted with impressive ease and speed.

"The empress doesn't…appreciate our gift much," Meli explained. "The Aremakkin Temple is far from the capital, but here we live in fear of the day she might put out our voices forever." She shifted on her feet. "But all of that is a story I can share another time." She turned to the chest and opened a drawer, removing a neatly folded linen dress and underclothes. "If you think these will fit you, I'll show you to the bathing room and then let the healers look at you too."

I imagined the nestrae sailing even now toward my people and my heart filled with dread.

"First, I need to send a message to Misroth," I said. "Then I'd like to see Gillen as soon as possible."

Meli nodded. "I understand. Come with me."

She led me down the hall to another room at the far end, which I assumed was hers. It was as simply furnished as mine, but with the stacks of books on a shelf and the scattered papers, pens, and inkpots on a desk, it was clearly lived in. She gestured to the desk, offering me a blank sheet of paper and envelope.

"Write your message tonight, and tomorrow we will take it to Hemlaen and pay a messenger to deliver it."

"My aunt could pay him once he delivered it," I offered, but Meli smiled gently and shook her head.

"I will cover the cost," Meli insisted.

Thanking her, I turned to the paper while Meli stepped back to let me write undisturbed. She shifted toward the shelves near her bed and skimmed idly through a book while I dipped a pen into an inkwell. I stared at the blank sheet for a long moment before I found the words.

My dearest aunt, I began, and proceeded to explain Misroth's danger to her. I knew the biggest challenge wouldn't be convincing her to prepare for war. It would be convincing the Royal Council. Those old skeptics would hate listening to her orders and plans as much as they'd loathed heeding mine. I also told her about Gillen and my fear that it would take some time for him to heal, delaying our return.

After I'd slipped the letter into an envelope and labeled it, I tucked it into my pocket. Silently, I prayed the message would do its job in helping my kingdom.

"Come," Meli said gently. "Let's get you cleaned up, and by then the healers might be ready to let you see your cousin."

She guided me downstairs to a long room with a stone bench along one wall and several enclosures hidden by curtains along the other. From a cabinet in the corner, she withdrew a towel and handed it to me. She gestured to the nearest enclosure. "Please forgive us for not drawing you a warm bath tonight."

When she left me alone, I drew back the curtain to enter a small space with another bench at one end and a stone spout and lever on the far wall. There was a drain in the middle of the floor. I stripped off my torn and dirty tunic and leggings, wincing when the fabric pulled against the cuts and burns marring my skin. When I moved the lever, cool water spilled from the spout. I stood beneath it like I was bathing in a fountain. Though a hot bath would have been more comforting, the coolness was refreshing and did not sting my wounds too much. I found bars of soap on a shelf along the wall and set to work washing away the layers of grime, sweat, and dried blood.

As I watched the filth darken the water and swirl down the drain, I wished I could wash away my loss and guilt just as easily. The scars from the nestred rune on my lower back burned like the nestrae had set a permanent fire beneath my skin.

And in the seclusion of the bathing room, I finally found tears for my grief. Every friend I'd let accompany me to rescue Gillen was gone now, and Gillen himself was badly wounded. As the water rushed over me, I could hear the nestrae's voices in my mind. *"Tyg kurik vouren. Condemned One, Bereaved One, you are ours."* I shuddered. After all those days as their captive, and now bearing their mark, I wondered if their words were true. Even this far from their lying visions and torture, their presence was like a shadow in my mind, a weight on my back.

Maybe I truly was theirs.

When I exited the bathing room, Meli was waiting for me. Her eyes snagged on my belt, which I'd strapped around the dress, and then the naked blade I'd tucked into it.

"You'll want to hide that," she said.

I snatched at it defensively. "I've been a captive for days," I said. "The last thing I want to do is surrender my only weapon."

"The empress confiscated all weapons belonging to anyone but soldiers, guards, and Dragon Keepers years ago. If you were found with a weapon on you, the penalty would be severe. You can choose to take that risk, but you can't wear it openly." She crossed her arms. "Especially not in my temple."

Raising my eyebrows, I removed the knife from my belt and tucked it into my boot. Never had I imagined a world where I couldn't carry a simple knife at my side. Knowing that I wasn't supposed to arm myself here made me feel vulnerable, at the mercy of this strange new land. "What sort of kingdom confiscates its people's means of defense?" I asked.

Meli set her jaw. "A broken one."

She led me to the healers' rooms, where an older man with wispy grey hair and a short beard squinted at me with his watery brown and gold eyes. He gestured for me to sit on a bed while Meli watched from the doorway. While the healer worked, I studied my surroundings.

He gathered jars filled with ointments and bandages from an assortment of shelves and cabinets throughout the room. A heavy scent of mingled herbs wafted through the air as something bubbled in a pot over the warm hearth. The room was cozy and crowded, but large enough for the healer to assist more than one person comfortably, for there was another bed set against the wall across from mine, and doors led to adjoining rooms that I assumed were also reserved for the healers and their patients. Two windows on the far wall were open to a fresh breeze that carried the sound of the gurgling fountain and the fragrance of grass and flowers.

Meli stayed with the healer and me while I stripped down to my underclothes. The man worked with a methodical eye and swift pace, soothing injuries along my legs, shoulders, back, and stomach with a clear ointment for my cuts and a darker ointment with a heavy, pungent scent for my burns. Then he began wrapping the worst wounds with bandages. When he reached the rune on my lower back, he hesitated.

"I've never seen something like this in person until today, on you and your cousin," he murmured. "But there are ancient accounts…before the barrier separated Alrenor from the outside world…"

"It's a nestred rune," I said. "They like to mark their victims as they torture them." My skin crawled as their voices hissed in my head: *"Condemned One."*

"The accounts say they are not ordinary scars, but cursed. They supposedly don't ever fade, and let the demons continue to hurt you…" He stopped, his hands twitching nervously. "I'm sorry." He sighed. "Some wounds never leave us."

I dipped my head in acknowledgment and studied another ugly scar: the mark above my navel where a sword had once pierced me through, the day my father had tried to publicly execute me. A reminder that, as Nesrelle said, I had defied death. That was one scar I didn't mind carrying with me. It showed me what I could survive.

At last the healer finished and Meli approached him with a smile. "Thank you, Veykan," she said. I expressed my gratitude as well and then asked about Gillen.

"Come," Meli said. She escorted me to an adjoining room where two other healers hovered around Gillen. This room was nearly identical to the previous one. My cousin lay still in one of the beds.

I approached slowly, watching the healers step aside, their faces taut with worry. "We've done all we can for now," one of them murmured to Meli. The healer was a blonde, freckled girl who was at least two years younger than me. "He had cuts, burns, and broken bones, and he was half-starved. But what concerns us most is the infection. Many of his deep wounds were poorly stitched together…"

Everything else faded to the background as I studied my cousin. It was as if the world were shrinking around me until only this one moment existed, repeating in my head with only slight changes. First it had been in my uncle's chambers in the Misrothian castle, with his pale form in the bed. Now, years and miles apart, I looked down on the pale form of his son.

It was as if my father had never died, not truly. He still cast a shadow over my family's life. He'd already taken much from us, and he was still taking too much. It was because of him that Gillen had entered Toryn in the first place. I drew in air and tried to shake the feeling that my father was watching and breathing down my neck.

You didn't win before and you won't win now, I thought viciously.

Gillen's chest rose in shallow breaths beneath the blanket, but his bandaged arms were exposed at his sides. I touched his cheek and smoothed back his hair, now clean and brushed. The healers had cleaned and trimmed the blond beard shadowing his face, which reminded me of the years that had passed since I'd last seen him. While I'd hid in Evren, he'd grown from a boy into a man. A king.

"Don't give up," I whispered.

Little Lia, he'd called me, my nickname from a childhood that felt so distant it seemed disconnected from me, like it belonged to another girl. Little Lia did not exist anymore, but neither did Elena, the girl who had run rather than face the truth. Rather than save her cousin in time. Tears stung my eyes.

"Please forgive me." I placed my hand over his. "I won't be weak and fail you ever again."

"We should let him rest," Meli said gently, from where she stood at my side. I hadn't noticed her approach. "And you need rest too…"

I shook my head. "Let me stay."

Meli hesitated, turning to the healers, but after a few moments of whispered conversation, they relented. Meli bid us goodnight while the girl brought me a chair. For a time, both the healers stayed near, monitoring Gillen or moving to a table to crush and mix herbs. Occasionally I watched them work, but mostly I studied Gillen's face and monitored his breathing, reassuring myself with this sign of life. Sometimes one of the healers would sit beside me and offer me a cup of water or another tray of food. As consumed with emotions as I was, I was still hungry, and ate every bit of bread, soup, berries, and nuts they brought me throughout the night.

Slowly, the temple fell quiet around me. The fire burned low and the healers took turns sleeping, one retiring to his bedroom, which adjoined the healing rooms, and the other finding a chair and sitting silently nearby. She did not speak, as if sensing I had no desire to talk, and when, hours later, Veykan entered the room to take her place, whispering, "Goodnight, Kaelet," he remained quiet as well. Outside, the night deepened, the breeze growing hushed and cool until it was only a whisper breathing through the room.

It was difficult to process the passing of time. I felt numb, but not too numb to forget my fear. My eyes frequently darted to the window, listening for a sound that could rise over the noises of the bubbling fountain and the breath of wind, that could find me even here, far from their clutches. The whispers of nestrae. When I closed my eyes, I could still see their empty stares. Still feel their fire against my skin. Their claws digging, cutting, tracing ugly lines along my body to mark me as theirs. When I searched the shadowy corners of the room, I almost expected to see them watching me.

Lies. All of that is in the past.

Concentrating on my truth gift, I pushed those thoughts away and held Gillen's hand, willing him to fight. Throughout the night, one of the healers filled a basin from a small spout in the room, like the one in the bathing room, and dipped the cloth into the cool water to lay across his clammy forehead. Occasionally Gillen murmured in his sleep, stirring slightly, but I could never make out his words.

Guilt and worry made my throat tight. My body ached with exhaustion, but not with the type sleep would cure. In fact, I felt as if I could remain like that forever, just existing in this dream-like state, surviving only on the energy from the emotions pumping through my veins.

As the shadows grew, fear became the only thing that made sense in my head anymore. It was so thick in the air it was a physical presence beside me. It was the wind whispering across my skin. It was the darkness shrouding me. There was fear for Gillen and fear even for myself, that I could not escape the nestrae's influence on my body or mind. I could dismiss it with my gift, but it was an ongoing, exhausting battle. The scars they'd left weren't only physical. I'd have to fight against memories for a long time to come, perhaps the rest of my life.

But I won't break. I won't give in to the lies, I told myself fiercely.

Other fears gripped me too. What if Gillen didn't survive? Or if he lived, what if he could never forgive me? And of course, there was the ever-present fear for my kingdom, already breaking and thoroughly unprepared for the demon fleet sailing toward it.

Two months. Two months to return to Misroth and prepare it for the greatest war it had ever faced.

Would Aunt Velaire receive my message in time? Would my warning make any difference for my kingdom?

As grey light seeped into the sky, Gillen settled, no longer moving or talking in his sleep. He lay quiet, his breathing even. Though sweaty, his brow felt cooler to the touch and he looked more peaceful than he had all night.

Veykan laid a hand on Gillen's brow and smiled at me. "His fever has broken," he said, the first words spoken in the room for hours. "You can rest easy now. Perhaps you should try to get some sleep?"

His words were gentle but firm, more of an order than a question. I smiled and stood, my heart relieved but my mind still restless.

I gave Gillen's hand a squeeze and crept to the hallway, listening to the stillness of the temple. I longed to see the sanctuary again, to study the stars before they vanished. Even though I feared Nesrelle was right and the Life-Giver was only preparing to give death, I hoped that maybe, if I asked him, he would return to me and explain. Maybe he would untangle the twisted thoughts in my brain. Maybe he would heal Gillen.

I wound a path through shadowy halls and down narrow staircases, skin prickling at the memory of everything the shadows had contained when I'd been a captive. Eventually the sanctuary fountain burbled nearby, and rounding one last corner, I found myself at the entrance to the expansive room.

The entire sanctuary was bathed in a silvery glow from the starlight streaming through the overhead window. I looked up to see that the constellations were still clear and bright. Without any torches burning at this hour, the shadows around the room's edges were deep. At a bench near the fountain, head bowed and brow furrowed in concentration, sat Meli.

I hesitated at the entrance, unsure if I wanted to speak with anyone right now. But going to sleep seemed impossible. I stepped forward, the long linen dress Meli had given me whispering along the stone floor.

Meli lifted her head, her gaze meeting mine. "I take it your cousin is doing better."

"His fever has broken and he's resting," I said. "But I cannot." After the words were out, I wondered if she could see the shadows that seemed to follow me everywhere I went. If she knew, by my admission, what sort of thoughts kept me awake tonight. But if she did, her expression did not show it. "I see you couldn't sleep either," I added.

Her mouth quirked up in a half-smile. She no longer wore her cloak, making it easier for me to study her face and see her expressions. Her gold-tinted skin was dark, but a shade lighter than Jennah's. Her blue, gold-flecked eyes reminded me strongly of my lost friend in that moment, even though Jennah's had been warm and brown. Perhaps it was because Meli watched me with such a sense of comradery that I could not help but think of my friend, or maybe because the long night had given me far too much time to think about everyone I missed. My throat constricted with emotion. Jennah would have loved to see Alrenor, to speak with natives of her mother land.

"I come here often to pray or call upon my visions, when it is quiet," Meli said. "It seems especially important in these days, when so much is at stake for those of us gifted with the truth."

I nodded in understanding, recalling the dangers this gift had brought me.

"Was your gift revered in your kingdom?" she asked, watching me thoughtfully.

With a small laugh, I shook my head. "Not many understand gifts in Misroth. The priests do not teach about them. And no, my gift was not appreciated. I was almost killed for it."

Meli stood and stared down at the fountain's clear water, studying the stars' reflections in the places where the water lay tranquil. Her dark hair hung in a tight braid down her back. In that moment, she reminded me of a painting of a Toryn goddess I'd seen in the ruins of Delgoth. The painting in a ruined temple amidst the carnage of the city... The same melancholy atmosphere I'd felt there was present here, in the Aremakkin Temple. "Mine nearly killed me too. It might still kill me," Meli said slowly.

"What happened?"

Meli sighed. "To truly understand, you probably need to know some Alrenian history. Cut off from the world as we have been, I don't know how much Misroth knows about us anymore."

I seated myself on the edge of a nearby bench. "Honestly, many of us seem to know very little of our own history."

"Well," she began, "I believe the Life-Giver blessed Alrenor, in the beginning, giving us fertile land, numerous resources, abundant crops, and great wealth. We had strong ties to many kingdoms across the Great Sea, and trade brought ever more wealth and luxuries from around the world. Alrenor was committed to pursuing greater understanding and skill in the gifts the Life-Giver gave to everyone. The Alrenians built temples throughout the kingdom dedicated to many of the various gifts, places that served as schools for the gifted to grow in knowledge as well as sanctuaries for all to worship and learn about the gift the temple had been dedicated to. Often people would seek the services of someone with a particular gift they needed."

Meli paused and stared up through the overhead window, where the stars were beginning to fade. "I believe we are all given gifts. Especially those who serve the Giver of Life, but even those who do not. Sometimes I think they are his way of drawing people to him, to learn about him. But who is to say? I've known and heard of many who have misused their gifts and brought death rather than life."

I thought of my father and his uncanny ability to persuade others to serve him or to charm a crowd. He had manipulated my mother and had made me long to please him. He'd always had a way of getting what he wanted, of making everyone around him believe and love him, even as they feared him. Had he possessed a gift? Was it only because of my gift of truth that I'd ever been able to see him as he really was?

"However," Meli continued, "the Alrenians of old cherished some gifts above others—otherwise I think today we would have as many different temples as there are stars in the sky." She laughed. "That is how countless the gifts are."

"What other sorts of gifts are there—that you know about?" I asked.

"There is the healing gift, which our healers here at the temple possess," she said with a smile. "And there is the gift of joy, being able to find light in any circumstance and spread that hope to others. Some I believe have a gift for telling stories to pass history from one generation to the next. And, of course, some are gifted in arts, like song or dance or painting or poetry. I think all serve their purpose and all are important, even if not all are recognized or deeply admired."

She sighed. "Much of the favoritism toward certain gifts was due to Alrenian desire for conquest and power. Over time, our rulers grew greedy and turned their eyes toward other kingdoms. They taught the people to admire the courage- and war-gifted most of all. They built up the Alrenian army and formed elite regiments of highly respected Dragon Keepers. The emperors and empresses started to grant their best warriors titles of nobility and other lavish gifts."

Meli reached out a hand toward the fountain, letting the clear water play over her gold-tinted fingers. "And that is when the Alrenians created a reputation for being fearless and fearsome warriors. Everything in our kingdom centered around lust for power and conquest, strength and bravery. Other gifts were no longer as admired or desirable. Soon even those who were not gifted in courage, war, or any superior finesse or strength were trained in the ways of war and pushed to find conquerors' spirits within themselves.

"Alrenor began conquering the continent, until all of the Great Kingdoms were part of the new Alrenian Empire. Alrenian emperors and empresses were notoriously greedy and cruel. They enslaved many of the people of Forwyth, oppressed and heavily taxed Misroth, and encouraged disunity and chaos among the tribes of Toryn, hoping their people would depend on Alrenor for guidance and protection."

I nodded, recognizing this part of the story she was telling. The evils of the old Alrenian Empire were well-known among Misrothians.

Meli shook her head. "When, two hundred years ago, our people discovered the barrier locking us within our kingdom, not much changed. Even with a shattered empire, we remained under imperial rule. But the only people left to tax and tyrannize were the Alrenian people themselves, along with the Forwyn slaves here on the mainland, and the unfortunate merchants and diplomats from other kingdoms who became trapped here." She shook her head sadly. "No one from an outside kingdom has come to our shores for many years, not after those kingdoms realized no travelers ever returned to them. The only reason we still learn the Trade Language, other than in hope we will someday be accessible to the outside world again, is because the Forwyn slaves do not know Alrenian; all this time they have clung to their native tongue. The Trade Language is the only way their masters could speak to them." Her brow furrowed and for a moment she was lost in thought, or perhaps as she closed her eyes she was seeing a vision about her people's slaves. Blinking, she returned to the present. "But now here you are, with the barrier broken…"

She shrugged. "I once was an advisor to the empress. Generations of my family have been blessed with the gift of truth and have advised empresses and emperors for many years. However, Empress Karye generally disregarded my words. The truth holds no sway over her, even with the convicting power our words usually have. But eventually she grew tired of my words condemning our practices of slavery and her tendency toward ruthlessness and bloodshed. She called for my death. It was only because of a vision I had, seeing her make her decision, that I was able to flee here, to the other side of the kingdom. Practicing our gift is dangerous because the empress does not love it, but it has not been outlawed. Still…we only have eight other truth-gifted who live and learn here, aside from myself. Not many claim the gift these days."

I nodded my understanding. I knew both the power and danger the truth could carry.

"My hope is to continue to help prepare and strengthen as many of those with the gift as I can," she said, her voice thick with passion. "If enough of us have the courage to use our voices and share the truth, maybe we will finally be heard. Maybe enough Alrenians will want to change our kingdom to make a difference." She bowed her head. "It is ironic…the kingdom known for its bravery is enslaved by its own ruler."

I studied her thoughtfully. "Have you taught many?"

She smiled. "I am still young and learning much myself, but as a former advisor, I was recognized for my skill with my gift. I do what I can to help here at the temple."

"We'll only stay until Gillen is well enough to travel, as long as we're welcome, of course."

Meli laughed lightly. "Of course you're welcome."

"Then while we're your guests," I continued hesitantly, "could you teach me also?"

She grinned. "Yes, I'll teach you. We spend time on little else here at the temple, especially in these days. Very rarely does anyone come here to seek our help or to worship in the sanctuary with us—Hemlaen fears to associate too much with us for fear we will endanger them, now that we are out of the empress's favor." She glanced back up at the sky, where the first light of dawn was making the clouds blush. "But for now, I'm going to try to sleep."

When she bid me goodnight, I rose and walked slowly back toward my room. Rest did not come easily. As golden rays of sunlight flooded through the window, I curled up in the bed and prayed for Gillen, for my people, and for myself.

CHAPTER TWELVE

O N OUR SECOND DAY AT the temple, Meli gave me a fresh ivory cloak to shroud myself in, despite the humid, hot Alrenian weather, and we walked to Hemlaen. We didn't even set foot past the city gates, but paused at a stable on its outskirts, where a small, unassuming building stood. Within, a gruff man lounged with his boots on a table, picking at his teeth and staring out the window.

"We have an urgent message to deliver to Misroth," Meli said in a low tone, "and before you object about possible dangers, we're willing to pay extra. Even more if you guarantee discretion and speed."

The man sat up immediately, eyes widening. "Misroth?" he exclaimed.

When Meli extended her open palm to show off her handful of gold coins, the man's jaw dropped. Clearly, the empress had once paid Meli handsomely for her services as an advisor.

Slowly, the man smiled and took the money. "Well then. I know someone who will take your job." He chuckled softly. "And for that price, if you want me to be discreet, I'll ask no questions," he added, accepting the letter from me.

His eyebrows raised again when he saw my address. "The Misrothian castle? Will they welcome an Alrenian messenger?"

"Have your messenger tell anyone who stops him that it's an urgent message from Halia," I said quietly.

"I'll fetch my rider now," the man said, springing from his seat.

As soon as we returned to the temple, I checked on Gillen, but he continued to sleep. With nothing left to do but wait and pray, Narek and I began training with the temple dwellers.

"Why am I training with truth-gifted?" Narek asked in amusement when I led him outside to where Meli and many others waited.

I shrugged. "What else do you have to do?" Then I added, "Meli thinks everyone is gifted, so perhaps they can help you discover your gift?"

Narek simply smiled, but I could see the doubt in his eyes. Still, he humored me.

In the garden, Meli introduced Narek and me to a young woman named Nakita, whose smooth olive skin spoke of Teramese blood somewhere in her lineage; a shy redheaded boy just younger than me named Amek; the wrinkled, soft-spoken Seera; and the elderly yet strong Lirem.

"Many of you know that your thoughts and emotions control where your visions take you," Meli said, raising an eyebrow at me.

Uncomfortable under her scrutiny, I rubbed my shoulder—right where my armband was. Somehow the leather band had survived the nestrae's torture. Perhaps they'd relished this physical reminder I had of my grief. I grit my teeth at the intrusive memory of the nestrae, and turned my face to the sun, warm and bright in a clear sky. There were no shadows in the garden at this hour.

"If I concentrate my thoughts and emotions on what I want to see, can I call on any vision I need?" I asked. "Know anything?"

I was starting to feel like her ability was limitless and she expected the same of me.

Meli smiled and plucked one of the blue embyth flowers growing nearby, twirling it between her fingers. "Not always. We aren't meant to know everything. Even when you do your best to control your emotions, visions can sometimes surprise you, and other times you can focus precisely on whatever you hope to know, and still find nothing."

I sighed.

Nakita laughed at my frustration. "If we were given all knowledge, we would go mad. It is a difficult gift already—being burdened to know and share the truth, no matter how difficult or dangerous it may be. Being burdened to never be able to tell a lie, no matter how desperate we may be to hide the truth."

Meli tugged the embyth petals from their stem one by one, dropping them carelessly. Her face was solemn as she studied me. "I know controlling your emotions is difficult right now, given everything you have suffered. I've seen some of it." There was genuine fear in her eyes. "There are true horrors in your past. Much loss. But trying to push your feelings away and pretend they aren't there…that won't help you either."

"If I let myself feel, I'll be overwhelmed by those visions and show everyone around me how…" I swallowed, stopping myself. *How weak I am.* I sounded like my father. There they were again: his handprints, always marking me as his. His influence still clung to me. *Tears are for the weak,* he'd said. *Never let anyone see an heir of Eldon looking undignified and weak with tears in her eyes, no matter what you are feeling.*

"The only way you will be able to control those emotions is to face them," Meli said gently. "You'll have to face the horror and the pain if you ever want to replace those feelings with courage and strength." She reached out and squeezed my shoulder. "Do not misunderstand me. You already have the courage and strength you need. But you are going to have to remind yourself of that."

I frowned, twining my fingers together. "Why does a gift concerning the truth rely on fickle emotions?" I couldn't keep my impatience out of my tone.

Meli watched me steadily. "Because the mind takes us where the heart wants it to go." She smiled. "Even the visions that take you by surprise will be about something that has been on your heart, whether at its forefront or buried somewhere, where you have tried to hide it. That is why control comes more easily when you allow yourself to recognize your emotions and claim them all, rather than push them away."

I sighed. "So first, I will have to let myself see the painful visions."

Meli's smile was bittersweet. "Truth is painful. How could we expect a gift in truth to be anything less?"

I squeezed my eyes shut for a moment to gather my strength. I knew the easiest visions to conjure right now would be ones about the nestrae.

As a blessedly cool breeze cooled the gathering sweat from my brow, Meli instructed everyone to practice summoning a vision about someone else, present or otherwise. Discomfort settled over me when I noticed more than one pair of eyes dart my way—naturally everyone would be most curious about *my* past. Pushing everything away, I concentrated on Meli, directing all my thoughts and emotions toward her and her past with Empress Karye.

Karye.

It was she who filled the images that fluttered through my mind: her fierce, proud face. Hair streaming a gold as pure as the dragon scale armor that glittered on the men and women flanking her. Blue eyes as bright and cruel as Nesrelle's. I saw her walking through a garden, talking with the armored people surrounding her. Then she was lounging, eating pastries, and complaining of boredom, or riding a breathtaking dragon with a small girl seated before her on the saddle. Next I saw Karye training in a weapons hall within the palace, slicing through a dummy with her curved Alrenian dagger. Then came images of her with Forwyn slaves. Those were haunting: the spurt of blood across the plush carpet of Karye's bedchamber when a woman spoke and the empress angrily cut off her hand. The gurgling, choked sound of a man as Karye sliced his throat before an audience in her throne room, and then, with a look of disgust, kicked his body away.

Before I could pull myself from the images, my vision changed, focusing on one scene. Karye lay curled up in a luxurious bed, gossamer curtains hanging from its posts. Beside her lay a little girl, the same one that had been riding the dragon with her. Now that I could study the girl, I realized she looked like Karye, with her golden hair, bright eyes, and freckled nose. It was clear she was Karye's daughter.

"They started a line of dragons that remains strong to this day, one that is tied to the empire's strength," Karye was saying, as if she were finishing a story.

Starlight sparked in the girl's eyes as she smiled up at her mother and said the next words in tandem with her: "Whoever controls Alrenor's dragons, controls Alrenor."

When I opened my eyes, Narek was studying my face intently. "Not a pleasant vision?" he asked softly. I glanced around, but most of the others were still concentrating, drawing on their own visions.

"It was about Empress Karye," I whispered back. "Her daughter and her dragons. If only she'd help us against the nestrae…" I let my words trail off longingly, knowing that was unlikely. It was clear from everything I'd seen that Karye was a ruthless woman.

I couldn't help but wonder what Alrenian dragons, with their massive claws and razor-sharp teeth, could do against the nestrae.

Every day, I scratched another tally onto the front page of a journal Meli had given to me. *The twelfth day of Kelah. The thirteenth. The fourteenth…*

Every day, I stumbled over the words as I tried to pray to the Life-Giver for Misroth, and for Gillen, who remained unconscious.

Every day, I woke up sweating and trembling from vivid visions, some marked with the falsehoods of the nestrae, others true. In my sleep, I could still discern the difference between true visions and ones filled with lies, but it didn't remove their nightmarish power over me. I sat up in bed with my heart racing, listening to the sounds streaming in through my open window: birds chirping, the fountain bubbling, the breeze rustling through leaves and grass.

As I waited for Gillen to recover, my own injuries recovered at a rapid pace under Veykan's care. His and the other healers' gifts allowed them to speed the recovery process for nearly any injury, all with the mere touch of a hand. In a few short days, my scars and burns began to fade. Regular meals and sleep helped my strength return.

With little to do but wait and our worry driving us wild, Narek and I threw ourselves into anything we could do in the meantime. We ran through the temple grounds and sparred with sticks in the mornings to rebuild our strength and finesse, though I longed most for the feel of a bow in my hands. We helped the healers collect and mix herbs, tended to the horses in the temple stable, gathered fruits and vegetables from the gardens, or helped with other daily chores around the temple, such as preparing meals.

I tended to Gillen whenever I could, sometimes sitting him up to spoon feed him broth or force water into his mouth. He had yet to fully wake, but occasionally he regained enough consciousness to mutter incoherently and swallow what we gave to sustain him. The healers were optimistic. Veykan told me that Gillen's infected wounds and bones were healing.

Most of all, Narek and I threw ourselves into the training Meli and the other gifted provided us.

"Even without the truth gift, there are ways you can experience it," Meli explained to Narek one day as we stood with her in the sanctuary. She glanced to me. "Anyone with a truth gift can share a vision with someone else."

Reaching out, she touched Narek's and my arms, and I was overcome in a vision. It was nighttime in a city beside the sea, where moonlight glistened on its foaming waves. Meli pulled a cloak tightly about herself and slipped through a shadowy street, pausing in the darkness when a patrolling guard dressed in shimmering silver armor passed by.

When Meli lifted her hand from my arm, the vision faded. My eyes took in the sanctuary as warm daylight flooded the room.

I drew a breath. "That's amazing."

Meli smiled gently. "Be careful, though. Anyone who knows how—even if they aren't gifted with the truth—can also steal visions from you. I mean, you won't lose the vision, but they can pull it from your mind and see it too." She turned to Narek again. "Focus on something you want to know about me."

Narek frowned. "Are you sure?"

Meli laughed lightly. "Yes. Put all your thoughts and emotions into it." She held out her hand, palm up, for him to take.

When Narek clasped her hand, he closed his eyes. A frown furrowed his brow and I knew he was seeing something.

Then it was my turn. I concentrated again on Meli, but when I laid my hand on Meli's, it was Empress Karye who dominated the vision.

"You're vile and worthless!" Karye shouted at Meli, stalking toward the truth-gifted woman with a terrifying shimmer in her eyes. Bloodlust. "I didn't appoint you to the position of advisor to belt out anything and everything you thought. I need you to tell me what I *ask* of you—nothing more." Her hand groped at the hilt of the dagger slung at her side. "Or there will be consequences."

When I pulled away, Meli's smile had turned strained, her lips thin.

"Do you see what we see when we…steal a vision?" I asked.

Meli nodded. "Karye was not a pleasant empress to serve," she said quietly, lifting her arm up higher so that the loose sleeve of her linen dress fell back to reveal more of her skin. An ugly scar traced its way from her wrist to her inner elbow. "This is my reminder that I'm never truly safe in her land. None of us are, not even her own people if we displease her. Not even here at the temple."

Forcing a smile, Meli continued. "Now, if someone tries to steal a vision from you, Halia, you can fight back. But it isn't easy. It takes a lot of concentration, and if someone takes you by surprise, that's extremely difficult to master. Still, let's practice."

The twenty-third day of Kelah. The twenty-fourth…

The nestrae were in Misroth. I'd been seeing it in their haunting visions for days now, when my rune burned and their hissing voices whispered in my head. *Condemned.* Misrothians were blinded to their presence through the nestrae's powerful visions, but they weren't spared their influence. Without knowing why, Misrothians throughout the capital were plagued with fearful nightmares, waking and sleeping. They broke down weeping or started when they saw a friend. Some snapped at one another or cursed each other like enemies.

Meanwhile, to my great frustration, I was unable to conjure a vision of my aunt. Had she received my letter?

"She has," Meli said one day when I asked her, opening her eyes and grinning at me.

"Why can't I see her?" I asked, unable to conceal the tremor in my voice.

"Your fear for your people is starting to consume all your thoughts. It would be hard for anyone to focus on specific visions with the weight you carry," Meli explained, resting a calming hand on my shoulder. "But have hope. Your aunt received your warning. And Gillen should be strong enough to travel soon."

Please let that be so, I thought toward the Life-Giver, even though he was maddeningly silent. Why couldn't he appear and speak with me as he had in Misroth and Toryn?

Today, Meli followed Narek and me outside, and while he and I went through our usual sparring matches, she gathered herbs and vegetables from the temple garden.

I'd lost soundly to Narek—for the second time in a row—when Meli set down her basket and approached us.

"You're war-gifted," she said, awe filling her tone as she studied Narek.

He blinked at her. "What?"

"You have a gift that has vanished from Alrenor. It makes sense. Everything Halia and you have said—every vision I've had about you.

Your natural ability. Your clear head in times of stress. The fact that you were able to survive those bloody battles in Toryn when so many around you…" She cut off her words quickly as a shadow passed over Narek's face. "Even at a young age, your trainers in the Zare'forith marveled at how naturally you picked up the skills they taught. You are war-gifted, I'm sure of it."

As Narek and I continued to spar, Meli stayed with us, answering questions and explaining everything she'd learned about the war gift.

"You've been using it most of your life without realizing it," Meli told him.

"Can it be shared, like the other gifts?" I asked, ducking one of Narek's swings and scrambling to block the next.

"Yes, you can help others to fight," Meli told Narek.

Narek paused, and I took that moment to wipe the sweat from my brow and catch my breath. "I can?" he asked.

"Yes, from what I've read in different accounts about the gift. If you concentrate, it's almost as if you can transfer your skills to others around you, controlling their movements so they fight more fiercely in battle."

"Control them?" Narek cocked a brow at her.

"Only a limited number, and at cost to you," Meli said slowly. "Your use of the gift will weaken the more you project it to others. Sharing it with one person might not affect your ability to fight much, but sharing it with several would begin to take its toll. It'll wear you down faster, make you slower. And, obviously," she finished with a laugh, "it'll take a lot of focus away from your own fight if you're using it in battle."

I couldn't help the mischievous grin that flitted across my mouth. "Can it be *stolen*, like the truth gift?"

Meli winked at me.

Before Narek could step out of my way, I seized his arm and concentrated. He swung his stick, but I ducked away and then launched my own attacks. His gift flowed through me, warm and intoxicating, guiding my movements almost without me having to think about them. I struck with precision, grace, and speed like I'd never had before, until I'd landed Narek panting on his back.

"Ridiculous," he huffed out, but he was smiling. "Unfortunately, it's temporary."

And of course, he was right. The warmth had already vanished, and when Narek sprang to his feet again, I was left to my own devices as I parried and sidestepped his flurry of attacks.

"If Narek were to *surrender* his gift to you, it wouldn't be temporary," Meli called out over the clacking sounds of our sticks slamming into each other.

"What do you mean?" Narek grunted as I managed to strike his leg.

"Anyone with a gift must choose their gift. If they don't, they can repress it, usually with unfortunate consequences."

My brain flitted back to the days when I'd fled from my father as a girl, terrified of both him and my own gift. I'd prayed for it to disappear, and it had—but so had my ability to speak.

"But someone who doesn't want their gift, or wants someone else to use it, can surrender it to that person," Meli explained. "Permanently."

As we finished our match, ending with me landing on the ground like usual, Narek's face grew thoughtful. "Would someone be able to pass their gift on when they were dying?"

He held out a hand to help me up, but I stuck out my tongue and ignored it as I stood.

"Unfortunately, no. Even surrendered, someone's gift only lives on as long as they do," Meli sighed. "The only case I know of in which there was an exception was that of Eldon and his barrier. He was powerful enough in his protection gift that when he built the barrier, he asked the Life-Giver to let it live on, only to be broken by his descendants." She flashed me a smile. "I've seen it all in visions." Then her smile faded. "But no other aspects of his gift lived on in his children. And no one else in history, no matter the gift they possessed, has managed to successfully keep it alive beyond their deaths. It would be a nice way to ensure posterity had our gifts, wouldn't it? But for the most part, we don't get to choose our gifts. They're given to us."

Narek's brow crinkled. "I didn't think a Toryn who didn't serve your Giver of Life could be granted a gift."

Meli had already turned back toward the temple, her basket on her arm. Tossing a grin over her shoulder, she said, "I think he's gifted many people, but not many realize it."

Narek kept up his spirits throughout the day as he practiced with his gift, managing to share it with some of the other temple dwellers. But I could tell there were thoughts churning through his mind. His eyes grew darker and more troubled as the day wore on, and he often drew away, lost in thought.

"This is a strange feeling," Amek laughed as his hand swung through the air at an imaginary opponent, all under Narek's influence. "No wonder our ancestors loved this gift so much—an Alrenian general could have controlled portions of his armies this way." His eyes widened at the thought.

Amek's hand dropped and he frowned down at it before turning to Narek, who blinked.

"What?" Narek asked, before drawing himself up and clearing his throat. "Sorry, I lost my focus. Let me try again."

I shot Narek a look, but he ignored it.

After dinner, however, Narek sought me out in my room. "Can you try to summon a vision for me?" he asked, his tone dangerously close to tremulous. Pleading.

My heart lurched.

"What's wrong?" I asked, turning away from my journal, where I'd been obsessively marking down everything I knew of the nestrae's movements, based on my visions.

"I need to know how the Toryn are," he said quietly. The dark circles under his eyes reminded me of the haunted way I felt. A jolt of guilt shot up my spine.

He's just as worried about his own people as you are for yours, but all this time you've only thought about Misroth and Gillen.

"How…Iyleth is," Narek finished.

I reached out to take his hand. "Of course," I whispered. "Do you…want to see it with me?"

When Narek nodded, wrapping his fingers around mine, I closed my eyes and focused on Toryn. On Iyleth.

Immediately, I saw Iyleth kneeling in a cavern, torchlight flashing in her dark hair. Instead of a dress of shifting colors and soft slippers like she had worn during our stay in Calidar, she was clothed in a plain black sleeveless shirt, trousers, and boots. Shadows played along her pale face and bare arms, at intervals concealing and emphasizing the matching jagged scars on her biceps. They were nestred runes, forever taunting her with their meaning: *Daughter of the Dead.*

She held out her hands as if in supplication, fulfilling her responsibility as the Intercessor to the Toryn gods for her people. Her jaw was taut, her brow crinkled. When she lifted her face toward the torchlight, her blue eyes swam with angry tears.

"I know now that if you are listening, you do not care." Her voice trembled with fury. "And I'm tired of waiting for help that never comes."

She stormed from the small cavern, pressing through shadowy tunnels and winding her way around people who blinked and stared at her unusually livid expression. She swept into another chamber, this one larger and filled with men sitting or standing around a table covered in maps and papers. Her brother Haed was at the far side of the room, pacing, but when Iyleth walked in, he froze. Everyone at the table looked up and stared.

"Wh—what is the meaning of this intrusion?" a gruff-looking

middle-aged man demanded, watching Iyleth as if she were a madwoman. "You were not invited to this council…"

"Have you heard from the gods?" another man asked, this one younger. His voice was low, full of awe, and his gaze was far more respectful.

Iyleth set her shoulders, watching the men in silence.

"Haed," the first man grumbled, "this is absurd. She cannot interrupt meetings whenever she wants because she is an Intercessor or because she is your sister."

Haed nodded. "I understand, Velnik." He glared at Iyleth. "This is unlike her." He crossed his arms over his chest. "Why are you here, Iyleth?" He frowned.

She waved her brother away carelessly, before settling her gaze on the man who'd asked about the gods. "The gods have not spoken to me." Her voice hardened as she looked at Velnik and then her brother. "They have *never* spoken to me. They are not listening to my pleas for help, or perhaps they don't care or do not exist at all."

One of the men shifted uncomfortably.

"Why are we hiding away in the dirt, pleading with gods who are letting us die off, instead of taking action?" She strode forward, jabbing a finger at a map of Toryn spread out on the table. "How long will it take before the nestrae find us here too? Before they slaughter every last one of us while we bide our time, waiting for them to come to our door? What kind of *life* is this?" She stared at Haed. "Survival is not living. Survival has not helped us preserve our way of life or our kingdom. Where are the Zare'forith? Where are the twelve warrior-tribes of our forefathers? Does the same courage and fortitude that the old stories speak of still run in our veins?" She drew a breath, as if steeling herself. "I'm going to look for our people, the ones the nestrae took hostage."

Velnik scoffed. "You are no warrior."

"At least I'll die with the sun on my face!" Iyleth burst out.

Haed sighed. "Iyleth is right." His eyes were dark as he scanned the room, studying the men gathered there. "We've never heard from the gods. They've all abandoned us. Except for Nesrelle." He closed his eyes, as if pained. "The only thing that we know is death, from a goddess we have never honored. One we've considered an enemy. What if we have it all wrong? What if we've been calling on the wrong deities?"

Iyleth's eyes widened as she stepped back. "Wh-what are you saying?"

Velnik stared at the map of Toryn spread out before him. "He's right," he whispered. "How could we expect anything better than death if we've spent years angering the Goddess of Death?"

"You can't be considering this," Iyleth said in horror. "Think about what you're saying."

Haed stepped closer to Iyleth. His gaze was still haunted, just as it had been ever since he'd been tricked by the nestrae into killing their father, but now it was lit with a frenetic hope. "Intercede for us, Iyleth," he said. "Speak with Nesrelle."

Horrified, I snapped out of the vision.

Narek bowed his head and sighed.

"Maybe the nestrae are influencing their minds, to consider something so mad," I said.

"Or maybe they're just that desperate." Narek shook his head. "Feeling forsaken. Lost. Hopeless." He sank his head in his hands. "I'm afraid for my people, that soon there will be nothing left of them." He hesitated. "And for Iyleth," he admitted.

I hesitated for a long moment, wrestling with a selfish part of me that wanted to hold back. When I spoke, I kept my voice low and couldn't meet Narek's eyes. "You could leave, you know. You don't owe any allegiance to me or my people. You've fought so hard for Toryn. I know Haed threatened you when we left to save Avrik and Jennah, and I'm forever grateful for all your help. But I know his threats wouldn't hold you back. The distance wouldn't hold you back. I know you could find your way to them and fight at their sides." I drew a deep breath and finally raised my chin to meet his gaze. Brow furrowed, he stared at me, a muscle flexing in his jaw. "I know if I were in your place…if it were my people and Avrik back there, suffering, it would kill me to be apart from them."

Narek clenched his hands into fists and stared down at them, unseeing. "It does," he confessed. "It's haunted me endlessly." He glanced up at me. "But I haven't lived in Toryn for years," he went on. "Misroth was never home, but I feel I owe your people as much as I owe my own now."

"And Iyleth?" I asked quietly.

He squeezed his eyes shut. "I can't believe her brother has failed her like that," he said, his voice strained. When he opened his eyes again, Narek seemed as torn as before. "There was always a saying among the Zare'forith: *Don't leave another warrior to fight his battles alone.* We have fought and bled together, Halia. You're my fellow warrior, my friend." He swallowed back the tremor building in his words to continue. His unusual display of emotion made my eyes burn, tears threatening. "You're the closest thing to family I have left."

Gently, I placed my hands over his fisted ones. "It's because I feel the same that I have to say this," I told him. "You've fulfilled all the promises you made to me. You led me through Toryn and helped me find Gillen. Even if we failed to find…" I couldn't finish my sentence. Speaking Jennah's and Avrik's names aloud was too painful. "You did everything you said you would. You don't owe me anything. There would be no disgrace if you left now, and I would never think badly of you for it."

Slowly, a grim smile crossed Narek's face. A determined spark lit his dark eyes. "There is one promise I haven't yet fulfilled—one I made to myself years ago. To destroy the nestrae as they've destroyed Toryn." He drew a deep breath. "I can't leave you. I must see this through. If we can defeat the demons in Misroth, we have hope to send them back to the Wastelands and save my people too."

I couldn't deny the relief that spread through me, invigorating and powerful. I'd have my friend with me, helping me see this mission through to the end. "Iyleth is strong," I said, hoping my words were reassuring.

Narek nodded, even though his expression was pained. "I trust in her and her strength. I ..." he hesitated. "I have to believe I'll see her again."

Squeezing his hands, I nodded. I tried to ignore the pang piercing my heart. I wished I could promise myself I'd see Avrik again.

CHAPTER THIRTEEN

Avrik

THOUGH THE AIR WAS WARM and muggy, even in the shadowy confines of his cell, Avrik still felt Nesrelle's unnatural chill coursing through him. The cold spread through his blood and lingered over his heart, as if he were slowly freezing from the inside out. It made him think of moonless winter nights, or the cool flesh of his mother's hand after all life and warmth had fled her. It made him think of the life leaving his Toryn companions' eyes when Zara had succumbed to the nestred vision and attacked the Alrenian guards.

There was still blood splattered on his torn and dirty clothes. He swallowed a lump in his throat and tried to block out the horror of the memories. No matter how much suffering and bloodshed he had witnessed at the hands of the nestrae, death could never become commonplace.

He sighed and stared up at the huge expanse of tree roots that were pushing through the dirt ceiling and winding about the underground space. When the guards had led Jennah and him to the building that housed these cells, they had entered a circular space built around a huge tree trunk, with holes in the floor and ceiling cut out to accommodate the tree. It was beautiful and unique, something Avrik would have enjoyed experiencing if he had traveled here of his own accord, in friendly circumstances, with Halia at his side.

Now he was separated from Jennah, each of them crammed into cells far apart from one another in the dungeon, but not so far apart that he couldn't hear Jennah when she screamed. The Alrenians had decided to start questioning her first. As soon as he'd heard her, Avrik had shouted and pounded against his cell wall, trying everything from taunting to begging the Alrenians to speak to him instead. No one had approached.

After a long while, silence settled. Avrik prayed Jennah was all right. And as always, his mind wandered to Halia and his concern for her.

He settled on the cell floor and closed his eyes, willing Halia's face to appear in his mind's eye. He was struggling to convince himself that she was safe. The simple fact that the barrier was broken meant that something was very wrong, because if he knew anything about Halia, it was that she never gave up. She would have never agreed to break the barrier and endanger her people, not unless something truly terrible had happened.

An image of her lifeless eyes staring back at him flickered in his mind, haunting and horrible. What would become of Misroth without her? What would become of him without her?

No, he told himself. *I can't believe she's dead.* When he steadied himself and pushed aside the cold fear crawling through him, he could still find the familiar hope he'd clung to for so long, the way his mother had taught him.

Footsteps made him lift his head to see an approaching guard. It was his turn now.

The guard stopped outside his cell door and leveled a glare at him through the grate. He was a burly man with a wide brow and a fierce glare in his gold-flecked eyes, one that reminded Avrik strongly of the Alrenians' ferocious reputation.

"Your friend is brave, but she sang like a bird once I started breaking bones," the man said with a sneer.

He didn't bring any weapons with him, but he didn't need to. Avrik's hands had already been shackled to the wall earlier, so he had nowhere to go and few ways to resist.

Instead, Avrik pulled himself to his feet and shot the guard a careless smirk. He wouldn't let the man know the way his stomach was roiling as he pictured brave Jennah with broken bones, screaming and hurting. "You're not fooling anyone. Neither of us have anything to sing about."

The man responded with his own fearsome smile. "Fine, choose to be difficult. It makes my job so much more entertaining."

Seizing a stool from the hallway outside, the guard unlocked the cell door, dragged the stool to the middle of the floor, and sat down. Crossing his arms over his chest, he smiled contently. "What is your name and where are you from?"

Avrik raised his eyebrows. "Avrik," he said with a shrug, his chains clanking around him. "And you've already guessed where I'm from—Misroth."

"But you traveled with some Toryn."

Avrik nodded. "We came from Toryn. We were prisoners of the nestrae before we escaped their ship and landed in Alrenor. Thanks for the warm welcome, by the way."

The guard frowned at him, drumming his fingers on his own arm. "What were you doing in Toryn?"

Avrik explained their mission to find the rightful king of Misroth.

"What do you know about the barrier?"

There was no need to lie, so Avrik told him the little he knew.

"Who broke it?"

Avrik hesitated. "I'm not sure."

"Why are you in Alrenor?" the man continued.

"I already answered that," Avrik said, rolling his eyes. "Our ship—"

The guard stood, looming over him menacingly. He reached out, seizing Avrik's wrist. "The truth, and I might spare you."

Avrik scoffed. "Might," he repeated in a mocking tone, while inwardly, his defenses shot up. His heart pulsed in his ears as he prepared himself for more pain. Mentally, he reminded himself of the battle he'd fought with the nestrae, and he grit his teeth.

Do your worst, Avrik thought. *You won't see me beg or break down.*

Snarling, the man twisted his wrist roughly—and nothing happened.

For a long moment, the guard and Avrik both stared. Every effort from the Alrenian was met with invisible resistance, as if something were stopping the guard's hand before he could break Avrik's wrist.

"What *are* you?" the man demanded, eyes wide. He looked almost…frightened.

Avrik's mind spun. He was just as much at a loss as the guard was.

A chill snaked through him again, reminding him of Nesrelle and her hatred toward him.

What *was* he?

As much as Avrik tried to resist, that first mysterious incident with the guard didn't always repeat itself. While the days blended together, characterized by two scant meals each and interspersed with Jennah's screams of pain, various Alrenian guards entered Avrik's cell to ask the same endless questions. Weariness weighed on his mind, shaking his concentration from the hope and confidence he tried to project. His stomach ached and his head pounded. His lips cracked and his throat turned dry as dust, while the shackles bit into his wrists until they bled.

Once the guards were able to begin breaking his finger bones, the interrogations became unbearable. The Alrenians took pleasure in breaking each bone, one by one, and then carefully resetting them only so they could break them again during their next questioning session. Avrik's fingers seemed forever swollen, forever painful. And still, the guards were relentless.

No matter what Avrik said, even when he began to tell outrageous lies, they were never satisfied. They believed he and Jennah were Misrothian spies, enemies of their people sent to scout them out for a war effort, and so nothing short of that admission would satisfy them.

And then, at last, something changed.

The guard from the first day clambered down into the dungeon, accompanied by another man. Together, they unlocked Avrik's cell, released him from his shackles, and led him wordlessly through the dungeon. They paused outside of Jennah's cell, where she sat hunched, her own bleeding wrists fastened to the wall. When she saw Avrik and the two guards, hope sparked in her brown and gold eyes. Two more guards were already inside Jennah's cell, unlocking her shackles.

As soon as the guards led Jennah from her cell, all four men filed Avrik and Jennah through the dungeon corridors side by side, toward a set of crude wooden stairs leading to an upper level. One guard shoved open the door, and a flood of daylight poured forth. Avrik squinted. They entered a circular room with a low ceiling. The massive trunk of the tree whose roots graced their underground prison filled the middle of the room, stretching from the hole in the floor toward one in the ceiling. Its bark was rough and gnarled, marked with countless initials, names, dates, and Alrenian words Avrik couldn't read, but assumed had crude meanings.

Several other guards lounged around the room at small, round tables scattered about the space or in chairs pushed near the hearth. Some ate or drank, while others leafed through books or papers. A few hovered near the fire, chatting and laughing together in their language.

As soon as Avrik and Jennah entered with the guard, the men fell silent and all eyes turned toward them. Rather than let his discomfort show, Avrik squared his shoulders and threw a bold grin at anyone who met his gaze. Despite his outward show, the weight of their angry glares felt like the press of a blade against his neck.

A man clothed from head to toe in gleaming gold dragon scale armor waited across the room, tapping his boot impatiently on the floor. As soon as the guards drew near, the armored man assessed Avrik and Jennah with deep brown eyes flecked with Alrenian gold. "Why didn't you contact the empress immediately, Kiyev?" the man demanded of one of the guards.

Kiyev swallowed. "They were our prisoners—we didn't want to trouble Her Imperial Majesty with something we could handle—"

"This is a job for her Dragon Keepers," the man interrupted. His eyes flicked to Jennah, then Avrik. "They are already in a sorry state," he said, shaking his head as if disappointed. He laid a hand on the sword hilt at his side. "I can't believe you didn't break and kill them on the first day."

Avrik glared at the man, silently daring him to do his worst. Perhaps it was Jennah's courage gift flowing through him. Or maybe he knew the only way to meet the threat of death was head-on, with an impudent grin and a bold heart.

"Come," the Keeper told the guards, spinning on his heel. "Bring the prisoners so my men and I can transport them to Inalgoth."

CHAPTER FOURTEEN

"H E'S BEEN STIRRING MORE TODAY," Veykan announced when Narek and I entered the healers' rooms.

Seating myself beside my cousin, I reached out and brushed his hair back from his face. "Come on, Gil," I whispered.

Narek leaned against the wall. "Are you sure after all of this, he'll be prepared to step into his role as king and face a war?" he asked me in a low voice.

My eyes snapped to him, an angry retort already on my lips before I hesitated. *Would* Gillen be ready? "I'll be beside him to help."

I could feel Narek's gaze on me for a moment afterward, as if he were unconvinced, but he merely shrugged and looked away.

"Look!" Kaelet said, touching my shoulder.

Gillen moved in the bed, his even breathing turning into a sigh. His lips moved, but at first I couldn't hear him. Then he raised his voice: "Flesh and bones to ash…to earth…flesh and bones… No one survives!"

He jerked as if in pain. Blinking, he opened his eyes and stared about the room, his gaze wide and distant, as if he saw something else entirely. "No. One!" He screamed and began thrashing, one arm smacking hard against my cheek, the other slamming into the wall.

"Back!" Veykan cried, shoving me away. I was surprised by the old man's strength. He and Kaelet sprang forward, grasping Gillen's arms and legs to restrain him. When Narek stepped forward to help, Veykan waved him back and shouted, "Jerik!"

A younger male healer was already running from an adjoining room. Together, the three settled my cousin while I watched helplessly. Narek dashed to my side and tried to inspect my cheek, but I brushed him away.

"Will he be all right?" I demanded of Veykan, my voice shaking.

Between Jerik and Veykan, I caught a glimpse of Gillen sitting up in bed, tears wetting his cheeks. He blinked sorrowfully up at the elderly healer. "Father, don't leave me. Hold on. It's not your time yet. It's not your time! *Lia.*" I startled at the sound of my name, but he wasn't even looking at me. 'Don't give up! It's not your time…"

I folded my arms against myself to keep a chill at bay, yet the room was warm. "What is wrong with him?" I asked.

Veykan was quiet.

Fear clawed at me, and I almost shouted my words. "Did you expect this?"

"Like I said before, there is a cursed rune on him too," the healer said in a low voice, not turning away from Gillen. "Carved into his upper back. There are old stories that say that the runes…they let the nestrae influence you even when you are not near them. You know this already."

"Narek and I aren't screaming and beating everyone in sight," I said. "How is it different for him?"

"The nestrae prey on the mind—the emotions," Veykan stammered, sitting beside Gillen and checking his brow. The other healers had released Gillen but hovered nearby, watching him carefully. My cousin laid his head back on his pillow and surveyed all around him in silence, his forehead furrowed in confusion. "Their influence over enough time—it would be enough—bad enough to drive anyone mad," Veykan continued. "Torn between reality and nightmarish visions…the confusion…" He shook his head. "It is said if the nestrae keep a prisoner for a long enough period of time, they can interfere with that person's reality…deeply. Too much time in darkness will leave its mark."

My feet seemed frozen to the floor. The world around me was shrinking. "Please. Speak clearly! What are you saying?"

Veykan turned to me. "You and your friend might hear the nestrae speaking into your thoughts occasionally," he said. "But Gillen—it will be almost as if he never left the nestrae. Their connection with him is strong. They can torture him with visions at any time, as often as they want. And he is the rightful Misrothian *king*. They will want to torture him often." He hung his head. "When they are not torturing him, I'm not sure he will be fully right in the head any longer…anyway. The strain…the… I'm not quite sure what to expect, but the old accounts are not promising. I'm sorry. I had hoped…well, that maybe those stories were only stories. Or that he hadn't been under their influence for long." He ran a weary hand across his brow. "Your cousin's mind is no longer his own. Not fully. He'll be forever muddled between reality and their lies. Their visions and whispers and the world around him." He drew a deep breath. "There may be times he's fully lucid, from what I've read. But he'll never be fully predictable or entirely himself again."

I drew a breath. "Would he…act on their orders? Hurt his own people?"

Veykan shook his head. "No, I don't believe it is anything like that. But their influence, their visions, their words inside his head—they will all make him a captive in his own mind."

I sat motionless beside the fountain in the sanctuary, staring up through the window at the fading light outside. Normally the bubbling water would have been a soothing sound, but now I scarcely noticed it. The temple inhabitants had given me a wide berth all afternoon, allowing me to retreat to my room and avoid them at the noon meal and again at dinner. Instead, some of the women had brought food to me. Each time I'd picked at it, my appetite feeble. I'd imagined them all, truth-gifted and healing-gifted alike, sitting with Narek somberly in their cozy kitchen, gathered at the long stone table lined with benches. They'd murmur about Gillen and shake their heads. Maybe, wrapped up in their thoughts and emotions about me, the other truth-gifted would even see visions about my past: Gillen and me playing as children, laughing together, racing through the castle halls, practicing archery on the grounds, swimming in the Alrenian. It felt intrusive, but I knew from my own experience that visions such as those couldn't always be avoided.

Let them see. Let them know. After fighting and losing so much to rescue Gillen, I'd lost him too. No—I'd never rescued him at all. He was still as much a captive of the nestrae as before. Could he ever be the same again? Could he ever heal?

I clutched the chains hanging about my neck, running my fingers along the pendants I wore. I'd placed Gillen's pendant around his neck days ago, while he slept, but now I found myself missing it.

"I'm sorry," Narek said behind me. I hadn't heard him enter the sanctuary.

"I don't want or need comfort." I knew my words were callous after all we had suffered together, when he was my only friend, my only fellow survivor in a foreign land. But it was difficult to care about how my words sounded anymore.

"I know." He sat on the bench across from mine, forcing me to look at him. "But I figured it was the expected thing to say."

For a moment I studied him curiously, thinking of all the loss he had endured. Perhaps he did understand better than most.

"You're afraid this means you'll be queen," he said.

I shifted uncomfortably under his gaze. "That is a selfish fear, and not my greatest one."

He nodded once, slowly. "You're already a leader. You would be a strong queen."

I bowed my head to stare at my hands, because I didn't want him to see the doubt that lurked in my eyes. Or my selfishness. I didn't *want* to be queen.

Narek was unfazed by my silence. "You're afraid he can never fully be present or understand what is happening. That you have lost the cousin you remembered. Or that even if he someday recovers, after this endless nightmare he has suffered, he will never forgive you."

My head snapped up, and I searched my friend's dark eyes. "How do you know this?"

Narek laughed, a bitter sound that echoed hollowly in the vast sanctuary. "You know how familiar I am with guilt. It makes it easy to see it in others."

"It's another selfish reason for me to be afraid."

Narek shrugged. "It is a reason."

"How do you bear it?" I asked quietly.

He smirked. "With a great deal of indifference."

I frowned, not amused.

Narek reached for his belt, as if expecting a weapon he could fidget with, but finding nothing, let his hand drop. "I distract myself. In Misroth City, I would spend my free nights in pubs and bars, and my free days training even more. I'd run. Spar other guards. They hated me." Grinning wryly, he glanced down at his hand like he was imagining a blade there. "In quieter moments, I would practice instruments, play Toryn songs to remember home and why I was in Misroth, serving your father and carrying out his cruel orders. Or I would write down memories of my family or my friends, or Reylinn. The memories were painful but also comforting, and they angered me enough to help me justify what I did to your people for my people's sake." He shifted a little, looking uncomfortable.

"Now?" Narek continued, turning his gaze back to me. "I hope the choices I make can help atone, even a little, for the suffering I caused. That hope keeps the guilt at bay...a little."

I smiled half-heartedly. "I suppose *a little* is all we can have right now."

That night, my visions were especially vivid.

I watched Gillen and myself sitting at a table in the castle library, attempting to study under our tutors' watchful eyes. But whenever our tutors were distracted for even a moment, Gillen would slip me a note, his blue eyes sparkling with mischief. *Eryk is wearing the crumbs from his breakfast in his beard again,* one said. And later: *Does he call that a mustache? It looks like he bewitched a caterpillar to perch on his lip. I think I just saw it wriggle…*

I pressed a hand to my mouth at each of his jokes, trying to contain my laughter.

Then the vision shifted, and it was Avrik by my side, complaining about how tiresome the Evren schoolgirls were. We were walking back from a trip to town to purchase a few schoolbooks. At fifteen, he was a head taller than me and nearly as broad-shouldered as his father Kyrin.

"Jayn tosses her hair and flutters her lashes at me every day, like I give a pile of manure about what she looks like," he said. "Have you seen how she always tries to sit near me at lunch and talk?" He rolled his eyes. "So dull."

I stared down at my boots as I walked, kicking at pebbles. Of course I had noticed. I'd also noticed that as much as he might complain, he still enjoyed the attention. *Hasn't Avrik realized this conversation of his is equally uninteresting?* I wanted to smack him for bragging about the attention he received every day.

"And the worst part is," he growled, "that I've overheard all the girls talking about me when they think I'm not near enough to hear. They say how gruff and withdrawn my father is, how much he is disliked because he hates everything about this town. They say they hope he does not make me like himself, because they think

I'm…well…" He shrugged, his cheeks reddening, before he scowled again. "No one knows Father like I do. Everyone else hates him." With a sigh, he paused to pass a hand over his face, as if he could scrub away his frustrations.

Autumn was fading into winter and the breeze had a bite to it. Twilight came fast now, limiting the hours we spent outdoors after school. Kyrin was away to trade some pelts and dried meat again, leaving Avrik alone to do as he wished, but Rev and Lyanna would expect me home soon.

He hesitated, stepping closer, grasping my shoulder gently. He slipped his other hand in mine, and to my annoyance, my stomach fluttered in response. "Why are we waiting to leave Evren and see the world? My father comes back tomorrow. I could convince him to let us skip school. We could ask him to take us to see Misroth City! I've always wanted to see the capital…"

My heart pounded at the mention of the capital, where my father's men prowled every street and would surely recognize me. Stepping back, I broke away from him.

Flinching, Avrik let his hands fall to his sides and took a step away. He cleared his throat as silence stretched between us. Without him by my side, I noticed the wind's chill more. "Of course. Lyanna and Rev wouldn't approve of you missing school…"

Chest still tight, I noticed he wasn't meeting my gaze, his eyes scanning the distant hills. "I'll walk you home," he said shortly.

His shoulders slumped as he bid me goodnight, keeping his distance.

My vision changed again. I was in the Alrenian once more, sinking deep after escaping the nestred ship. My friends' dead hands clawed at me. But this time, their mouths opened and they spoke. "You condemned us to death! You led us to our deaths. Our blood is on your hands."

This isn't a memory; it's a nightmare, I thought. I must have fallen asleep, but now I couldn't wake.

Avrik reached out his hand and I clasped it, like it was an anchor holding me still in the surrounding chaos. But it was also pulling me down, down…

His eyes met mine, warm and pleading. He stretched out his free arm to brush my cheek, and his fingers were warm, gentle. "Don't let go."

But I had to. I had to let go.

At last I woke with a start, my heart beating an erratic rhythm against my chest, a discordant song of loss. The air felt heavy, my lungs full of fire.

Please forgive me, Avrik. I failed you. I have to concentrate on those I can still help. I squeezed my eyes shut. *And if by some miracle you are alive, come back to me. Please.*

When I sat up, I bowed my head. "Giver of Life, you know what I've lost," I whispered into the darkness. "But you know there's still so much left to lose. Please, I believe my aunt when she says Misroth needs Gillen. *I* need him. Don't let him be lost to the darkness forever."

Outside, crickets chirped. The wind stirred as the moonlight played on the foliage growing beyond my window.

"I need to get back to Misroth, and I need your help to save my people. We can't waste more time. Gillen needs to be well enough to travel." I paused again, aching. "I need your help for Misroth. Please, speak to me. Please! Where are you?"

When I lifted my head, a figure stood in the corner of the room, its form wrapped in shadow. But something was off, though I couldn't quite explain to myself why. It must have been my gift that made my neck prickle with fear rather than relief.

Stretching my fingers beneath my pillow, I felt the comforting solidness of my nestred knife.

"Who are you?" I demanded, holding the blade out in front of me and studying the stranger warily.

The figure stepped forward. Light from the open window touched her flame-red hair and glittered in her icy eyes. Nesrelle.

Despite my fear, I kept my expression carefully neutral.

"Do you think your Life-Giver is listening to you?" Nesrelle asked, red lips curved in a smirk. "He might be silent, but *I* hear you."

Instead of approaching my bed, she crossed to the empty fireplace in my room and gazed down at the ashes within. "You worry for your kingdom, but you're forced to linger in Alrenor," she said, her voice soft. Almost as if she were concerned. "How upsetting for you."

I glared at her. "Gillen suffers, thanks to your demons."

Nesrelle's lips curled into another grin. Leaning back against the mantle, she turned to face me and laughed, the sound ringing out like bells.

"What are you doing here?" I growled.

"I'm wherever there is despair and death," Nesrelle said lightly. "Those are my tributes, and those who offer them up to me are my faithful followers. Toryn pays them, Alrenor pays them. Even Misroth paid great tributes, especially during your father's short reign. All of that blood..." She sighed and licked her lips.

I tightened my grip on the knife, still aiming it steadily at Nesrelle. Though I suspected it was pointless, I longed to hurl it at her face.

Reaching down, she smoothed out her dress, as orange as a flame and so bright it hurt my eyes. She stared into my face, and her eyes looked like empty pools of nothing. "I also wanted to tell you not to worry. I promise you'll be back in Misroth in time to watch your kingdom fall," she whispered.

Standing, I grit my teeth in anger as I stepped closer to her, my knife steady in my hand. "We'll fight back. Misroth won't fall."

She laughed again. Stooping down by the hearth, she reached in to stir the ashes with her fingers and flames flared up, curling about her hand. She stood, lifting her palm for me to see the fire dancing and twisting around her fingertips, her skin still pure white and unharmed. Her eyes held an unearthly glow as she stared into the flame. "Do you think you can stop demons who can burn your city to the ground as they march through it, unfazed? Do you think you can slay *me*, an immortal?"

I thought of my truth gift and Narek's war gift, of Meli's belief that most people were gifted and simply didn't know it yet. "We have powers you can't touch."

Nesrelle closed her hand into a fist and the fire went out. "Is that true?"

Before I could cry out or swing the knife at her, she launched herself at me. Her icy hands clamped down on my shoulders and her nails curled, digging like claws into my skin. I could feel blood oozing out, warmth to counter her coldness. A jolt shuddered through my entire body and I gasped. Every muscle felt like it was melting into water, a growing weakness that made me shake and shiver. Sweat sprouted along my forehead and the back of my neck. I wanted to throw myself at Nesrelle and try to choke the life from her, but I didn't have the strength to fight back. The knife slipped from my grasp and clattered to the floor.

Nesrelle stepped back and I gasped for air, desperately filling my burning lungs. I didn't know what had happened, but I could feel something spreading throughout my being. An emptiness. A void as vast as the pits that were Nesrelle's cruel eyes. It was as if she'd torn something vital from me, making me feel lesser.

"What did you do?" I rasped, even as understanding rushed over me. Strength was returning to my limbs and the pain had faded, but the emptiness remained.

Nesrelle's smirk widened, revealing her sharp teeth. "Who are you, Princess Halia, without your precious truth gift?" she demanded. "Now we'll find out. Try to fight my nestrae now, little one. See how powerful you feel."

And with that, she was gone.

My whole body shook. How could she have taken my gift? Now, when Meli had taught me so much? When I knew how to discern nestred lies from the truth?

The sweat dried on my face and my body grew steady again, my pulse even, but I felt crippled. It was almost strange, to realize how accustomed I'd become to a gift I'd once considered a curse and repressed.

Even with the windows thrown open, the temple air was too stifling. I had to get outside to clear my mind. Tugging on my boots and a brown linen dress, I tied a sash tightly about my waist and swept the ivory cloak Meli had given me over my shoulders. I tucked my knife into my boot.

I slipped through the temple, tiptoeing past closed doors and down steps until I pushed through a side door that opened to the garden.

Here the air was like a warm embrace, gentle and reassuring. I seated myself in the grass and inhaled the flowers' perfume, trying to distract myself from my thoughts.

"Lia?" His voice was hesitant, unsure.

I started to my feet and turned to face Gillen. Standing beside the fountain, he was motionless, staring back at me. How had he managed to leave the temple without the healers noticing? They must have all been exhausted from their constant vigil over him.

"Gil." My throat was tight, making my voice hoarse. "What are you doing here?"

His pale eyes were wide and shadowed by circles so dark they looked like bruises. "I cannot sleep. The voices…" He searched the shadows with an anxious glance while he combed his hand through his hair. "Are they here too?" He met my stare, his expression looking lucid at last. "Did we truly escape, or is this a lie?" He waved his hand around at the garden as if it could vanish in an instant. "Lia, is it *really* you? Are you truly alive?" The tears in his eyes made them look icy, almost silver.

"Yes." I ran to him and embraced him. He did not pull away, but he didn't hug me back either.

"Where are we?" he demanded.

"Alrenor." I pulled back, studying his furrowed brow, drinking in his familiar face.

"But…Father…no." He pressed a hand to his head and cringed. "He's dead, isn't he? There was a war…your father…" His eyes froze on something behind me, just over my shoulder, and he clutched my arm. "*Halia.*"

"It's all right," came Narek's voice. I hadn't heard his approaching footsteps in the grass. "It's only the other former prisoner who also cannot sleep." He smiled as he stopped beside me, studying Gillen.

"Captain," Gillen said, recognition in his eyes. He turned back to me. "We are at war with Alrenor, Halia. Why are we *here?* Unarmed? Why did *you* come to rescue me? Where are your father's—my men?"

I swallowed, trying to find the words to describe everything my father had done, everything that had happened in the long years my cousin and I had been apart.

But an earth-shuddering shriek split the sky, dropping all three of us to our knees. I scanned the horizon. Four huge winged shapes were approaching rapidly from the south.

"Ichgor," Gillen breathed. When I turned to him, his pupils were dilated in terror, his expression lost, as if he were trapped in another world entirely. "Blood…death… Stop, no!" he screamed.

I reached for him, clinging to his arm and murmuring soothing words, hoping I could reassure and quiet him. His entire body shook, and when I grasped his hand, it was clammy and cold in mine.

Before the dragons drew close enough to be anything more than dark shapes on the horizon, they dove low, disappearing into the countryside surrounding the temple. Their wing beats were like distant thunder, and my pulse echoed with the sound.

Dragons. The Dragon Keepers had come.

My thoughts flew to the visions I'd seen of Meli fleeing from the palace in the dead of night. Had the empress sent the Keepers to the temple—because of Meli's past? Every muscle in my body coiled as tightly as a wire.

I launched myself toward the temple, Narek and Gillen close on my heels. As we entered its cool interior, I heard echoing footsteps and a rallying cry as the people within began to stir. "Dragon Keepers!"

On our way, we encountered Meli and Nakita already in the sanctuary. Kneeling, Meli was pulling up a piece of stonework from the floor, revealing a wide hole filled with…weapons. I stared at the pile of dusty leather sheaths holding curved Alrenian blades, their hilts glittering in the moonlight.

Before I could speak, Meli turned to me.

"I had a vision," Meli said breathlessly. "The empress *does* have another truth-gifted advisor, and she knows you're here. She's sent the Dragon Keepers to search the temple for foreigners she considers spies. You must run—take our horses and return to Misroth. Help your people." She pressed one of the blades into my hands.

"What about you?" I asked as I fastened the sheathed sword to the sash around my dress. It wasn't as secure as a belt, but it would do.

Meli passed Narek and Gillen each a sword. "We'll fight and hold them off. If you leave now, you could be far from the temple before they reach it on horseback. They had horses waiting for them, so they left their dragons to try to catch us unawares. But they will miss you if you're fast enough."

As the other temple dwellers flooded into the sanctuary, Meli began tossing them each weapons. She shot me a fierce look. "Go!" she urged.

Narek tugged my arm.

Heart hammering, I grasped Gillen's hand and the three of us charged back through the hall and out the side door. We emerged into the garden, the inky blackness of the surrounding shadows consuming my vision for an instant. A horse whinnied in the darkness.

Several horses galloped toward the temple, slowing at the bottom of the hill. Two figures swung from their saddles, throwing the reins to their companions, and crept up through the garden on our side. The others led their horses toward the front of the temple.

I dipped down behind some shrubbery, Gillen and Narek crouching low on either side of me. The two Dragon Keepers ascended the hill with breathless speed, their limbs moving with grace and precision as they crept silently through the plants. Their dragon scale armor gleamed like flames in the moonlight. The foremost Dragon Keeper was a woman, the gold specks in her grey eyes sparkling with bloodlust, while the Keeper behind her was a man, dark eyes cruel and intent.

"*Iyg kurick vouren,*" Gillen breathed, his voice tremulous. "Careful, Lia. Don't let them take you." I squeezed his hand tighter, willing him to be all right. Willing him not to lose himself entirely to a nightmarish vision from the nestrae and cry out—not now. His fingers shook in mine.

"More filthy Misrothians," the woman Dragon Keeper spat in Alrenian, her fingers clasped over her sword hilt as she slunk toward the temple's side entrance. "I'm weary of questioning the other two." Then she said something else I couldn't quite translate, but I did understand one word: *amara*, which meant *empress*.

More? I wondered. *How could there be more Misrothians in Alrenor?*

The man responded in their Trade Language, pitching his voice high and ridiculous in a mocking imitation. "We're not spies! We were captives in Toryn." He shook his head and finished in Alrenian, "Pathetic."

My lungs seized; my heart stilled. There were no other Misrothians who'd travelled to Toryn, who had become captives, who might have been on nestred ships that went off course in the storm. *Avrik. Jennah.* I hardly dared to even think their names, let alone imagine them to be alive.

The woman silenced the man with a sharp gesture. They'd passed us now and were nearing the temple entrance. It took everything in me to remain motionless, to let the two Keepers slip soundlessly into the temple, looking for Misrothians but clearly prepared to kill. And what they'd just said...

My mind whirled. I'd wondered what sort of leader I was to have allowed the nestrae to even tempt me to break the barrier in order to save my cousin's life. Now the same dilemma stared me in the face. Did I travel deeper into Alrenor to rescue two Misrothian prisoners, likely my friends, and spend more time away from my kingdom? *Two months until the nestrae stop feeding on Misroth's fear and my people start dying.*

But could I leave two Misrothians behind to die in an enemy kingdom?

I curled my fingers into fists. I refused to believe I had to choose between individual lives and my kingdom, between saving friends and saving all of my people. *Two months to rescue the prisoners and return to Misroth. We can do that.*

Tugging Gillen to stand with me, I leapt from behind the bushes and sprinted toward the stables. Narek followed. There was no sign of the Keepers' horses, which I assumed they'd hidden among the trees, or the Keepers themselves, who must have already infiltrated the temple. As we drew near the stable, my thoughts were confirmed. Screams erupted from within the temple, bouncing off the stone interior and mingling with the clangs of steel on steel.

Fear threatened as I thought of encouraging Meli, of wise Veykan, of sweet Kaelet, of the bravery of all the truth-gifted and healing-gifted in the temple. Of all their kindness and how they had welcomed us as old friends. Of the way they had unquestionably, unwaveringly served the Life-Giver and followed their callings. They had willingly chosen to draw illegal weapons and distract the Dragon Keepers to let us flee. My instincts screamed at me to turn back, not to let anyone put their lives at risk because of me. But I knew that I had to respect their choice and to trust that they would be strong enough to survive it.

When we threw open the stable door, the hoses within stomped and whinnied nervously. Narek and I fumbled for saddles, and I was relieved to see Gillen comprehend our urgency and follow suit. We each prepared and mounted the geldings: my cousin's a dappled grey, Narek's a chestnut, and mine with a coat as deep as midnight.

The night air felt much cooler as we galloped through the open door, my hair tumbling into my eyes. Without hesitation, I steered my mount southward, sweeping through the grass and then over the hilly countryside skirting Hemlaen. I hugged the forest on our west to keep far from wherever the Keepers' dragons waited, and to steer us toward the beach as soon as our path cleared. Though I knew questions had to be tumbling through Narek's mind, both he and my cousin kept pace with me.

No provisions. No plan. No gift. I squeezed the reins until my fingers went numb. *Two months.*

Two months to save everyone and everything I loved, or watch it all burn in demon fire.

CHAPTER FIFTEEN

ONCE WE LED OUR MOUNTS into the shallows of the Alrenian, sea foam swirling about their legs and salt spray stinging my face, I relaxed my horse into a trot. It had been a while since I'd ridden at such a frantic pace, and I was already saddle sore. I hoped our path was far enough from the one the Dragon Keepers would take back to their dragons that they would never notice the hoofprints. Never think to follow us. And if they did, I prayed this detour into the water would help shake any would-be trackers off our trail.

For an instant, the tang of the sea, the soothing rhythm of the waves, and the warmth of the gelding's back against my legs conjured vivid memories. I drew a deep breath, banishing thoughts of Gillen and I racing along the beach at home in happier times. Instead, I cast a quick glance over my shoulder. For now, my cousin seemed almost like himself, sitting up straight in his saddle as he scanned the moonlit sea, his gaze distant but not troubled.

Narek pulled his gelding up beside mine, his gaze cutting into me. "Where are you going?" he demanded. "If we travel north, we could be in Argelon within the week."

"The Dragon Keepers *were* searching for us, like Meli suspected," I said. "But the two we hid from in the garden spoke of two other Misrothians they're holding captive."

Narek's brow cleared. "That's what the man meant about spies and Toryn captives." His eyes widened. "It would have to be…Jennah and Avrik. How is that possible?"

I shook my head. "I don't know, but we still have two months before…" I let my voice drift off, not wanting memories of my visions to flash before my eyes. The haunted expressions on my people's faces as the nestrae, still hidden to their deceived eyes, terrorized them and fed off their fear. "We *can't* leave them here in Alrenor, not if there's a chance to save them and help Misroth before time runs out."

Narek didn't question me. "Of course," he said. *"Don't leave another warrior to fight his battles alone."*

When we felt we'd traveled a sufficient distance in the water to avoid being tracked, we steered our horses back to land. The shoreline grew rougher and rockier the further we went, gradually rising until we were riding along a cliffside overlooking waves at least a hundred feet below us. At first boulders riddled the grassy expanse before us, and then, as we went farther, they started to form a clear row on our eastern side, like a stone fence, or landmarks indicating a path.

As the moon set over the Alrenian, drawing the night to a close, we approached what the old path had been leading toward: an abandoned temple overlooking the beach below. Overgrown with moss and darkened with age, much of the temple's stonework was defaced and crumbling. Some stones had collapsed into heaps. Within its shadow grew ancient trees, wild plants, and weeds, the remnants of what had once probably been a garden as beautiful as the one at the Aremakkin Temple.

The possibility of shelter was appealing, but we faced many other problems. We had no food or water, with little hope of finding any out here. If we did come across a sign of civilization, we wouldn't have much choice but to risk venturing into it. I doubted other Alrenians would be as welcoming of us as the temple dwellers had been.

Pain stabbed my chest when I thought of them. Had they survived? Had they been captured? Would I ever know?

"We should rest here, while we have some shelter," Narek said. I followed his gaze to Gillen, who looked pale, his shoulders hunched from weariness. He was wheezing, probably against the pain of his newly healed ribs. I cringed to think of how much pain he was in.

When I met his eyes, Gillen blinked at me dully before comprehension settled in his gaze. His brow cleared, as if the sight of me chased away a hundred nightmares.

"Lia," he said. "They were chanting for their fear sacrifice. I try not to be afraid but…" –he squeezed his eyes shut— "…the worms were squirming; the flies were everywhere…bones and blood and—" He cut himself off, his expression horrified. "He was too strong to burn, to be devoured. How could he crumble? They were gnawing on him…"

"Gil. Everything is all right. That wasn't real."

He shook himself, passing a weary hand over his face. "Of course not." When his eyes met mine again, they looked dimmer than before. "It's so hard to tell what's real and what's not anymore, Lia."

I was at a loss for words, so I pressed my horse onward, toward our shelter.

The temple entrance was bordered by two enormous pillars, both still standing and carved with symbols of nature: a sun, moon, and stars, water and trees, flowers and thorns, dragons and sheep and foxes and dozens of other animals. It made me wonder if the scenes were merely decorative or held some meaning for whatever gift this temple was dedicated to. When Narek and I dismounted to do a brief exploration of the interior, we found it to be empty, only a series of corridors and rooms with blank stone floors, walls, and ceilings. The entire building smelled strongly of mildew and dirt, and in some places, moss and vines grew on the walls or weeds pushed through cracks in the floors. If there had ever even been glass set within any of the windows, it was all long gone.

After rubbing down our horses and tying them to a tree where they could graze, the three of us huddled uncomfortably in one of the temple's smaller rooms. "I'll take first watch," Narek said, and I didn't argue.

I gave Gillen my cloak to use as a pillow, then removed my sash and folded it until it almost resembled a pillow for me. Gillen huddled close, his breathing rhythmic. I was grateful he was finding rest from the nestrae's influence. Stretching out my hand, I found his and squeezed it tightly. Without a word, he squeezed back.

"Goodnight, Gil," I whispered, but he had already fallen asleep.

When Narek woke me, his brow was pinched in concern. "Something's wrong," he said.

Golden light filtered in through the lone window, strong enough that I guessed it was far into the afternoon.

I sat up, my body aching from sleeping on unforgiving stone and my stomach growling with emptiness. Gillen was awake, the cloak draped about him like a blanket.

"What do you—" I began, but then I heard them: footsteps approaching the temple from three sides, beating out a steady rhythm. They weren't even trying to be stealthy.

The back of my neck prickled. Dragon Keepers. My fingers strayed to my sword hilt.

Narek frowned. "I should have noticed them tracking us sooner."

From what I understood of the imperial Dragon Keepers, they were some of Alrenor's most elite fighters. With Gillen in his unpredictable state, I wasn't sure what that would mean for us to face three of them at once.

Narek crouched at my side, and I could tell by his intent expression that he was thinking fast. "Listen," he whispered. "We'll slip deeper into the temple and force them to follow. Then we might be able to strike when they're walking through one of the narrow corridors. In close quarters they can't all attack at once and we'll have an advantage."

My heart hammered in my head, the blood rushing so loudly in my ears it almost drowned out his voice. I hated how vulnerable I felt without my truth gift or the familiar sensation of a bow in my hands. I couldn't reach to see what the Keepers were planning, and I couldn't shoot them from a distance.

I grasped Gillen's arm and whispered, "Gil, we have to stay quiet. You have to follow us."

He blinked at me, looking dazed, and for a moment I was afraid he wouldn't see me but some horror the nestrae wanted him to see. That he would recoil and cry out in fear or fight against my hold, running toward our enemies. But his vision cleared, focusing on my face until he smiled and nodded.

"Eryk and Meeryn would hear us and make us finish our work," he whispered, referring to the childhood tutors we'd occasionally slipped away from to escape our lessons.

I ignored the twinge of pain I felt and stepped forward, quietly drawing my sword before gesturing toward Gillen to follow. I glanced at Narek, who already had his blade drawn, and he took the rear.

Behind me, Gillen hadn't drawn his sword, and I wasn't sure I wanted him to. I couldn't stop thinking about the nestred attack in Toryn, when they'd trapped Haed in a vision that had convinced him to kill his own father.

Creeping forward, I strained to hear our enemies' approach. I assumed the layout of this temple was similar to that of the Aremakkin Temple, with a wide-open sanctuary somewhere near the middle of the ground floor and doors on every side. That meant the Dragon Keepers could each enter from different sides of the temple and continue to surround us.

We crept through the narrow hall and approached the doorway to a small kitchen. Remembering the kitchen door leading to the garden in the Aremakkin Temple, I clutched Gillen's arm and pulled him back at the last moment. I leaned forward just enough to see the cramped space: a fireplace on one wall, some of its stones collapsed into a heap on its hearth. It was surrounded by dusty shelves, some still holding recipe books warped from weather and age. In the middle of the room, a three-legged table lay on its side, splintered and rotting, a few chairs scattered on the floor around it. Across from us, just as I expected, was a closed door. Nearby, two windows were set high in the ceiling, open to the warm summer air. Sunlight streaming through them exposed inches of dust and dirt on the floor, dotted with grass and blooming weeds growing through numerous cracks. Everything was empty and silent, but that made me warier.

Behind me, Narek tapped my shoulder and gestured that he would go first. I nodded once. Narek pressed into the room, and I nudged Gillen forward so I could take the rear. Our boots crunched on splinters and bits of stone from the crumbling walls and fireplace. Outside a bird chirped; another answered. Any moment I expected the door to fly open and swords to be shoved in our faces.

Near the hearth, Narek lifted one of the largest stones and squeezed it in his fist as he approached the door. In his other hand, he held his sword aloft, ready to swing. His eyes darted everywhere—to the windows, where only sky and grass were visible, to the door, and once, over his shoulder, to the hall behind Gillen and me.

I looked back toward the shadowy hall too, unable to shake the feeling that the Dragon Keepers could already be right behind us, ready to strike. My sword hilt was slick in my palm. It seemed as if we'd been in this kitchen forever, and all along, I could hear nothing but the sigh of the summer wind outside, of the distant crash of waves, of the chirping birds.

Face pale, Gillen froze in the middle of the kitchen. Did he know the danger we were in, or was he having a vision of nestrae closing in on him?

Narek paused beside the door and glanced back at me before he opened it. As if the thought hadn't darted through my mind at least a dozen times already, he mouthed, *It could be a trap.*

Tense and alert as I was, nothing prepared me for the gold figure that hurtled out from behind me. Unnaturally quiet, he sprang from the hall with grace that was more feral than human. Narek threw his stone at the man's face, but it clanged off his helmet.

The next instant I was beneath my attacker. As he crashed into me, the back of my head slammed against the floor and sparks flashed across my vision. My sword flew from my hand, skidding across the floor and out of reach. His hot breath brushed my cheeks as I felt the cold metal of his curved sword press against my throat. The man's blade cut into my skin, drawing a trail of blood.

Narek swung his sword at the man in one clean move, but the Alrenian was fast. He rolled off me and struck with his own blade, twisting Narek's sword from his grasp. It flew across the room in a clatter. Without hesitating, Narek lunged, slamming his shoulder into the man's armored chest and seizing his arm. He twisted until the Alrenian's blade fell from his hand.

Weaponless, they grappled one another, falling in a fierce heap on the ground, ragged breaths and clinking armor the only sounds in the heavy stillness. The air was thick with sweat and adrenaline. My mouth tasted of blood.

Where are the others? I thought suspiciously.

Blinking, my eyes landed on my sword a few feet away. I leapt to my feet and dashed toward it.

Narek was still on top of the man, but the Alrenian had his hands around Narek's throat, squeezing, crushing. Red-faced and gasping in vain, Narek tried and failed to rip the man's hands away. Instead, he lifted his fist and slammed it against his enemy's face—once, twice, three times, until his hand came away soaked in blood. Narek struck again, and the man's fingers jerked and released him.

By the time I reached Narek, sword raised, the Alrenian man already lay still, sprawled out on his back. His face was a bloody pulp, and I averted my eyes. Narek stood, grimacing against the pain as he rubbed at his bruising neck. He reached for the sword he'd lost, only inches from where the dead man lay.

Footsteps echoed in the hall and two more fighters poured through the entrance, their movements fluid and lethal. Their curved swords flashed wickedly, and their gold dragon scale armor was blinding in the sunlight. Narek and I didn't even have a chance to cut them off at the doorway. As swiftly as the first Keeper had, they sprang at us, one soaring toward Narek while the other charged for me.

I lifted my sword just in time, managing to stop the first strike.

"*Filkni* Misrothian!" the fighter spat. She was a woman, tall and slender, her grey, gold-flecked eyes flashing with disdain. It was the same warrior from the temple who had spoken so contemptuously of their Misrothian captives.

She launched into a swift attack, each movement efficient, effortless, and deadly.

I couldn't use my speed to an advantage with her, because she was clearly much faster. Spinning, she swung her sword in a flurry of strikes toward my neck, my feet, and my side. Each time I parried in time, but just barely. I had the horrible sense that she was toying with me, only letting me defend myself to prolong the fight for her entertainment. She slammed her blade into mine one last time, twisting in an expert maneuver that forced my sword from my hand. It flew to the floor in an echoing clank that made my heart sink.

Sweat dribbled in my eyes, my breath heaving in labored gasps. This woman had likely trained all her life for this, and I knew I wasn't a match for her.

"*Val re holna*," she snarled.

Weak. She thought I was weak.

The woman laughed, low and throaty. She reached her sword out almost gently, carving a shallow cut into my shoulder. Blood trickled down my arm as I watched her, trying to mask my wariness as I studied her for any weaknesses, any openings.

I knew what to do the moment Narek's influence stirred inside me. Whereas my missing gift had left a cold void inside me, Narek's gift washed over me, warm and reassuring. Without even having to think about it, I reached for the nestred knife in my boot and my limbs sprang forward, ducking easily beneath the woman's sword as she swung. I plunged my knife into a weak point in her armor, right above her kneecap, and she roared with pain.

Tearing my knife out of the woman's leg, I hopped out of her reach, but Narek's focus on his gift faltered. I felt it leech out of me, the shock almost painful, making my body numb. My weary feet stumbled, and I fell. The Keeper raised her blade, gleaming sharp and deadly in the sunlight.

Steel struck steel as a sword met hers before she could make the fatal strike. I blinked to find Gillen standing between the woman and me. Though his face appeared pale with pain, his jaw was set, his eyes intense and furious.

"Stay away from her," he growled, staring the Alrenian down fiercely.

The woman's lips twisted in a smile. "Drop your weapon and maybe, if you answer our questions, I will spare both of you," she said in the Trade Language.

Her blade dripped red with my blood, staining the tip of Gillen's sword. He glared at her, their swords crossed between them, both refusing to lower their weapons.

I knew she meant it. It was clear from what she'd said outside the Aremakkin Temple that the empress wanted us alive for questioning.

"We're not fools," Gillen snapped. "You wouldn't keep us alive after we answered your questions."

The woman sheathed her blade and stalked closer, leering over us both. I'd known that the Alrenians were a tall, brutal race, but it was still startling to see this woman tower several inches taller than my cousin. Gillen hesitated, unwilling to strike an unarmed opponent. He lowered his blade a little, my blood running down its tip.

And then—a swift shadow and choked gasps. I looked up to see Narek tightening his fingers around the woman's neck. Her eyes bulged in rage and shock as she clawed at his hands and kicked at his legs, but his grip didn't loosen.

Horror seized me. "Narek—"

In one smooth motion, he snapped her neck and she crumpled to the floor, her armor clattering as dust clouded the air.

I couldn't tear my gaze from the body in front of me. Glassy and bloodshot, the warrior's eyes stared back at me. When I glanced up, my eyes latched onto the bodies of the men Narek had slain. I avoided looking at the first man's disfigured face, only to find the second was lying facedown in a pool of his own blood.

"She'd sheathed her weapon," Gillen said, his taut expression mirroring what I felt.

Narek didn't meet my eyes as I stood. Perhaps I'd forgotten he had been trained with the Zare'forith since he was a boy, and, in a world where survival was the primary aim, taught to be ruthless. Since we had forged our friendship, faced common enemies and torture together, and fought to save our friends and kingdoms, I'd nearly forgotten how I had once feared and hated him.

Narek laughed mirthlessly. "That's because she'd already made the fatal cut." Drawing the woman's sword, he tilted its broad edge back and forth in the light so I could study it more clearly. Its curve was elegant, the blade itself forged with complex designs and Alrenian words scrolling along its surface: *O j'eh y'vonu.* I translated it in my head: *I will not bow to fear.* My blood trickled along the sword's surface, mingling with a liquid that was thick and almost clear, but for a faint green tinge.

I frowned. "Poison?"

Narek nodded once in disgust and tossed the blade away. "Come," he said, "they probably left their packs outside. If they poison their blades with kruvla, they'll have the antidote too."

Exchanging shocked looks, Gillen and I followed Narek as he strode out the door and into the overgrown temple grounds.

We found the warriors' packs piled at the foot of one of the old trees. Narek riffled through one quickly, stopping when he found a sack filled with vials. He plucked one out and held it up to study the liquid inside, which was a soft amber shade. Pulling the stopper, he sniffed the contents and smiled. "Vylae."

A chill slithered down my back. "You said that was the poisonous plant my father brought from Toryn to kill my uncle." I cut a glance toward Gillen, but he didn't seem to be listening anymore. He'd sheathed his sword and was scrubbing his hand over his eyes, as if trying to push away an oncoming vision.

"Yes," Narek said, "vylae is used as both a poison…and as an antidote to certain poisons, like the kruvla you were cut with."

I hesitated, staring at him.

"Alrenor learned about poisons and antidotes from Toryn. The vylae and others are native to Toryn, transported to Alrenor during the Age of the Empire. The Zare'forith were still required to learn about poisons and cures in my time, even if excursions to the surface to find such plants were rare. Now," he finished, holding out the vial, "unless you want to start dying a painful death by nightfall, drink this."

I took the vial from him slowly, staring at its amber contents, thinking of my uncle and Narek's role in his death. Tipping it back, I swallowed the liquid in one gulp. It tasted bitter but felt cool slipping down my throat.

"The clear liquid extracted from vylae roots is deadly," Narek explained, still not meeting my eyes. "The leaves and stems can be crushed and boiled to create this—an antidote to several other known poisons."

"Is it an antidote…to itself?" I asked quietly.

"No," Narek said slowly, staring down at his empty hands. "There is no known cure for vylae poison."

Afterward, we worked in silence. We found our horses untouched, still tethered where we'd left them, along with the Dragon Keepers' steeds, which we released. Narek and I sorted through the contents of the Dragon Keepers' packs, eagerly making a meal of the dried fruit, jerky, cheese, and crackers we found. The three of us drank from the Keepers' canteens but rationed the water a bit more carefully.

Finally, Narek spoke. "We should take their armor."

I had been watching Gillen as he reached toward a yellow butterfly fluttering near his fingers. In nature, he seemed at peace, like himself again. It reminded me of his gentleness when he'd nursed an injured bird back to health, or the rapt way he'd drink in a sunrise and attempt to capture it in his paintings. I snapped my gaze to Narek, unable to conceal my disgust.

Narek hesitated and looked away. "It could help us rescue your friends. And we could pass as Alrenian warriors in towns along the way. No other Dragon Keepers would be searching for us dressed in their own armor."

"You're right," I said. "We'll need them if we want any chance of getting into the palace. But as for wearing them into towns…" I hesitated. "We would be discovered as imposters by anyone we spoke to," I said uneasily. "I don't speak fluent Alrenian, and my accent is terrible."

"Did Jennah teach you enough to be able to purchase food?" He held up a money pouch he'd found in one of the packs, the coins inside clinking together.

"I think so," I admitted. "But it would be risky."

Narek shrugged. "Pretend to be an arrogant warrior, better than anyone else you meet. Speak little, and grunt and point whenever possible."

We set to work on the grim task of stripping all three corpses. Narek helped Gillen into his armor, then we each found some privacy to slip into our own. I was surprised to find it light and comfortable, not at all like the heavy ceremonial armor the Misrothian guards and soldiers occasionally wore. The bottom portion was like a pair of leggings overlaid with lightweight golden scales that flexed easily when I moved. They were a little long since the woman had been so tall, but I was grateful that they were a close fit at all. The upper pieces were a sleeveless tunic, gloves that stretched past the elbows, and a mantle. Her boots were supple leather overlaid with more scales. Lastly, I strapped the belt, her scabbard, and several wickedly curved daggers to my waist. I carried the helmet and sword back with me to the garden.

Narek was already dressed, seated beside Gillen, their helmets laid at their feet for later. Once the helmets covered our faces, none of our skin would show, and we would be able to conceal the fact that we did not have Alrenian gold-tinted skin. Only our eyes would be visible, and if we kept those downcast, we could hide the lack of gold in them, unless someone drew uncomfortably near.

We stowed all our old clothes in the packs. Narek helped me scrub the woman warrior's blade clean of blood and poison before I sheathed it.

"We should travel inland and search for a town," Narek said quietly.

Tension hung thickly in the air. I was unable to quell the emotions I'd felt when I'd watched the effortless way he'd killed, and he could tell. He was keeping his distance, speaking and making eye contact as infrequently as possible.

"Narek—"

"Let's not waste time," he said, strapping his pack to his saddle and mounting his horse. He slid his helmet on as he rode, transforming into an Alrenian warrior, his posture sure and graceful.

I climbed into my own saddle and waited for Gillen. We each placed our helmets on our heads, and I was not surprised this time to find that mine was comfortable and cool, just like everything else. Maybe there was a quality to the dragon scales that kept the bearer cool as well as flame-resistant.

As we rode, I wondered who I was to feel uncomfortable about the blood on Narek's hands. I'd killed to survive and to save my friends too. I'd made choices that haunted me. He and I weren't that different at all.

But I couldn't quite say the words to Narek, not yet, not when I thought about his knowledge of the poison that had killed my uncle. His role in Reylon's death made my grief wash over me afresh. It was easy to remember now that Narek had been my enemy not long ago. The same ruthlessness he'd shown toward the Alrenian warriors, he had once shown toward my people, my friends, and even me.

As the summer day grew hot and humid, the dragon scale armor continued to keep me cool. With our recent meal and our supply of water, we had renewed strength to travel farther and faster than before. When we drew further inland, the landscape gave way to rolling hills, the grass thick with wildflowers. Occasional copses of trees rose on the hilltops or huddled close at their feet. The sky was wide and open, reminding me of the view in Evren and making me ache with homesickness. Rabbits and squirrels scurried out of our path, and once we came upon a few does feeding mere yards away. Beside me, Gillen inhaled softly, his eyes wide at the peaceful scene. The deer stared back at him, but let him draw his gelding cautiously nearer, so near he could almost reach out and stroke the fur of the closest one, until Narek pushed his horse forward impatiently and all three deer bolted.

As the sun sank lower, we came upon a clear stream burbling and winding its way through the hills. We set up camp and gathered firewood from the cluster of trees spreading their roots along the stream's bank. Narek and I took turns walking a short distance away from our camp to bathe in the water.

"I can bathe too," Gillen said when I returned, picking through my hair with a wooden comb I'd found in my pack. I met his gaze and knew he understood Narek's and my unspoken fear: that he would have another vision alone in the stream and drown. Was he offended? Or maybe he was a little afraid too. Did he already feel like he was drowning in his own thoughts, or was he too confused to even know he was losing his mind?

"I'll stay near with my back turned," I said, and Gillen didn't object.

When we reached the stream, I settled with my back against a tree and returned to combing my hair.

"Does Father know?" Gillen's voice drifted to me calmly, like he was asking about the weather. "Does he know how the nestrae drive their prisoners mad? Will he expect me to be crazy?"

My stomach clenched. Somehow, Gillen had forgotten what had happened to his father again. Should I remind him his father had been dead nearly five years? Could I be the one to bring grief upon Gillen again? Would he even remember this conversation tomorrow, or would it be tangled up in a series of new nestred visions?

"No," I rasped. I wondered if I could lie without my gift, but the very idea of lying to my cousin made my throat burn. Instead, I could withhold the truth to spare him, so I didn't elaborate.

"Why did he send you and the Captain of the Guard to rescue me?" he demanded. "Why risk your safety?"

"Gil…" I hesitated. "Do you remember why you were in Toryn?"

There was another long pause. "No," he said at last.

How could I ever apologize to him if he couldn't even remember what was happening half the time?

"Misroth is in danger," I said. "Some people…they betrayed our kingdom and left it weak when it needs to be prepared for war."

"Against the nestrae," he muttered, as if to himself. "Will we return in time to help?"

I pulled my damp hair back and tied it up with a piece of string. "Let's pray we do," I said.

We dared to indulge in a fire that night. Narek used a few of the Alrenian throwing knives stowed on the belt he wore to bring down a squirrel and a rabbit for dinner. The roasted meat tasted especially delicious after going without food, and I burnt my fingers in my eagerness to eat my portion, relishing its savory flavor. Gillen ate in fits and starts, flinching at every sound and shadow. As darkness settled, he grew more and more withdrawn, constantly muttering to himself. At one point, he stood and shouted into the night, drawing his sword.

"Come fight me! Face me, you cowards!" he shouted.

Narek sprang gently to his feet before grappling the weapon from my cousin's hand. Gillen spun toward him, and without warning, punched him in the face. Before he swung again, he froze, staring up at Narek, who was rubbing his reddened jaw.

"Captain?" he asked, blinking in confusion. "I—I'm sorry." He shook his head, brushing at his eyes. "I thought…" He turned to me, his expression afraid and apologetic. "I could have hurt you."

I shook my head hurriedly. "No, it's all right. Come, Gil, let's go to bed."

When we lay out our bedrolls, I tried to engage my cousin in a cheerful conversation. "Look," I murmured, sitting beside him. I pointed to one of the many constellations we'd studied as children. "There's Kaegen, wrestling the Bear." The summer sky didn't contain Shyla and Vehgar, the winter constellations, and I felt a little lost without them. Those symbols of Misrothian fortitude had been comforting to see when I'd first left Misroth, a time that now felt ages ago.

Unseeing, Gillen blinked up at the sky. "Lia? Is that really you?" he whispered.

I reached out to hold his hand and swallowed against the tightness in my throat. "Yes, Gil. It really is. This time, I'm not going anywhere."

We sat like that until Gillen sighed, seemingly at peace again, and lay down to sleep. Narek, who had attached Gillen's sword to his own belt, offered to take first watch. Agreeing, I curled up in my bedroll.

In my dream, I was a girl in the Misrothian castle again. I stood outside the door to Gillen's chambers, watching two servants leave, hands covering their mouths to stifle their giggles. One curtsied and held the door open for me.

I found Gillen in his bedchamber and immediately understood the servants' amusement. He was in one of his flurried creative moods again. He had silver paint splattered on his cheeks and blue flecked on his arms, nearly up to his elbows. His hair was pulled back in a low ponytail, the only neat thing about him. With his wrinkled trousers, crumpled shirt with its sleeves rolled up crookedly, and bare feet, he hardly looked like a crown prince.

He'd abandoned a half-painted canvas to attack the wall itself with his paintbrush. He'd shoved his chest of drawers aside to give himself enough space to work. Resting on a nearby chair was a tray holding a plate of untouched food and a cold mug of tea.

"Gil?" I asked, quirking my eyebrow.

He spun around, his blue eyes sparkling in excitement. "Look at this, Lia!" He gestured to the wall, where he'd begun painting constellations in shimmering silver and white on a midnight blue background. "I can paint all the constellations we've studied, right here in my room, where we can stargaze whenever we wish! It won't matter if we can't get away or the weather is poor." He gestured to another wall. "The summer constellations will go there."

I stepped closer, studying his renditions of Vehgar and Shyla, prominently displayed across his wall. "It's beautiful," I breathed. I never ceased to be amazed at the creativity, skill, and vitality my cousin possessed.

Rather than let the rigidity of court life and royal training drain him or dictate how he lived, he found moments like these to fill his life with vibrancy and color. He urged me to escape to the tower rooftops to stargaze when our lessons ran long, or to slip away with him to the beach, where he'd taught me to swim, despite my father's arguments that it was unladylike. In his free time, he painted beautiful landscapes that looked more mystic than real, or renditions of legendary beasts—all supposedly impractical things his tutor insisted shouldn't consume the energy and time of a future king. Even kind and gentle Uncle Reylon said Gillen's efforts to nurse injured birds or to tend plants that attracted butterflies and hummingbirds outside his bedroom window weren't always the best uses of his time.

I spent the rest of that day laughing with Gillen as I tried, and failed, to help him paint more stars. Instead, I ended up covering my fingers in paint and then sitting and waiting for it to dry while I watched him fix my mistakes.

It had been a beautiful day, one of the last before Uncle Reylon began showing symptoms.

Then my dream changed, and I saw Aunt Velaire sitting in one of the castle studies, the window open to a breeze coming in off the Alrenian. A shadow passed over the sun and she looked to see the nestred fleet flooding into the harbor. I knew this wasn't true—the nestrae had concealed themselves from my people's sight, but that didn't change the icy chill that crept over me, even in sleep.

The dream shifted again to show me Lyanna and Rev fleeing from nestrae as the demons burned Evren homes and fields. Flames filled the blue sky with smoke, blotting out the sun, until ashes fell like snow. Finally, my dream showed me Jennah and Avrik. Nestrae shoved them through a crowd of prisoners, who were being thrown one by one into a pyre. The nestrae pushed my friends into the flames and I awoke with a start, tears streaming down my face.

My heart felt carved hollow, emptied by everything I'd lost and everything I still could lose. I buried my face in my arms. I felt broken, and in breaking, I was weak. I'd given into the weakness my father had despised and worked so hard to train out of me. Where was the strength I'd learned from him, that my mother had admired in me? *You will not be easily broken,* she'd said.

This is weakness, I thought. *This is breaking.*

I didn't hear Narek until he was sitting beside me.

"Bad dreams?" he asked.

Slowly lifting my head, I nodded. Silence settled over us for a long moment. Wind rustled through the leaves and whispered in the grass. A chorus of crickets sang to the stars. Shadows from the clouds glided across the ground.

"Why are you ashamed?" he asked finally. He still didn't meet my eyes, and I thought I might ask him the same question.

"A leader can't be weak," I muttered. Father's words.

"Jennah wept when Gare died. Why can't you weep for your friends too?"

I hesitated.

"Was she weak?" he pressed.

Jennah had always radiated resilience and courage, and Narek knew that. I didn't have to consider, so I shook my head.

"Then why does doing the same make you weak?"

I thought of the fierce way Jennah had embraced her emotions, how it had never caused me to question her strength or stop respecting her. My father's disdain for so-called "displays of weakness" had taken root so deeply in my heart that I'd let his ghost, that part of him that unfortunately still lived in me, tell me I was weak and broken. But Narek was right. I let his words settle over me. I let Jennah's courage comfort me.

"I don't think a weak leader could have made it this far," Narek said.

Staring up at the stars, I let myself smile through my tears. My friends, living and dead, deserved to be honored through tears that showed they were remembered and missed. "Thank you," I whispered.

To myself, I told the echo of my father's words and teachings to flee. *I'm freeing myself of you,* I thought grimly.

"Narek?" I asked at last.

He inclined his head toward me.

"The things you did…when you served my father." I turned to face him. "I hope you know I've already forgiven you."

He dropped his gaze. "I hurt your people…your friends…even you." He paused. "Your father might have never even killed your uncle without my help."

My chest tightened with grief, but I pressed on. "He would have managed without you. He was stubborn and used to getting his way. And I know you were trying to help your people. I can understand that, especially now."

Narek worked a muscle in his jaw. "At first, it was only about survival. Your father offered to take me from Toryn in exchange for my services. Everyone I cared about was dead and I'd barely survived myself. I didn't think I had anything to return to, and I'd seen…so much death…" A shadow passed over his face. "I was desperate to escape." His shoulders slumped with shame. "It was later, when guilt overwhelmed me, that I said I would stay in his service only if he agreed to help my people."

"And he did?"

"I think he saw a chance to rule a frightened, weakened kingdom, so he implied he would help them eventually. Later, I pressed him for a greater commitment, insisting that he would have to vow to break the barrier around Toryn and wage war against the nestrae. The bolder I grew in my demands, the more he must have realized Toryn wasn't worth it. It didn't take me long to see your father had lost interest in our agreement and was lying to me."

After a beat, I dared to voice the question that had haunted me longer than I wanted to admit. "I know this is something you couldn't have known for sure, but maybe you saw things…" I squeezed my hands tightly together in my lap. It was like steeling myself for a physical blow, with every muscle in my body coiled. "Did my father care at all? Did my parents ever grieve for me?" The rest of my sentence went unspoken: …*as I have grieved for them.*

Narek hesitated. "He'd hoped to raise a strong heir who would continue his legacy once he was gone. I think…there were times the grief he showed, when he discussed your absence and supposed kidnapping with the Council, when he ordered us guards to search for you, or when he finally held a memorial service for you… There were times I think his grief wasn't only for show. I think he did feel some loss. He cared for you, in his own way."

"He was angry I didn't blindly obey and follow him," I said bitterly.

"I think he was also disappointed that the strength he'd wanted you to show all along only came when you stood against him. And your mother…she mourned for you. Your father convinced her you attacked him when he went to speak with you in your rooms the night you accused him. He cut himself and went to her bleeding and looking frantic. He claimed you were half-mad with grief and dangerous, and that he was forced to exile you to Ivannah with a host of guards."

Anger boiled within me. Ivannah was a convent for women who devoted their lives to serving the Giver of Life, and it was on the opposite side of the kingdom, along the northern coast. My mother would have thought I was far away and lost to her forever, but she wouldn't have ever imagined I was in danger—and from her husband, no less.

"She could have loved me more," I whispered. "She could have been stronger, braver. She could have seen through my father's lies and manipulation and fought for me."

Narek didn't argue.

Somehow, that made it easier to let the pain go.

Both unable to sleep, we spent the night going over plans: how to best enter the capital while impersonating Dragon Keepers and how to infiltrate a palace we'd never seen. Without my truth gift, I couldn't rely on visions to give us more information, but I did have memories of past visions that had shown me portions of the palace. In the dirt, I drew as much of the palace layout as I could remember with a stick. We discussed where the dungeons would most likely be located and how we could find them. As long as no one saw through our disguises, we could pretend to be Keepers on our way to question the captives, but if it was obvious we weren't familiar with the palace, we'd give ourselves away immediately.

"We'll have to observe the palace routines," Narek mused. He drummed his fingers on his leg. "We have time to perfect our plans," he reassured me. "First, we have to reach Inalgoth."

"Without wasting the little time we have and returning to Misroth too late," I said, holding back a dark laugh.

Narek smirked. "Well, we enjoy a challenge, don't we?"

CHAPTER SIXTEEN

THE STOLEN ARMOR AND WEAPONS proved to be a burden as well as our security. I didn't want to risk posing as Dragon Keepers until it was necessary, when we needed to enter the capital. For days, we'd traveled as invisibly as possible, even resorting to stealing simple homespun clothes and cloaks from an empty farmhouse to cover our armor so we could venture toward homes and markets unnoticed. There, we committed petty theft: a loaf of bread here, a handful of apples there.

But when we found ourselves nearing a more populated area with no clear route to avoid it, I agreed that the armor was our best defense. No one would dare draw near enough to see we weren't Alrenian. We removed our cloaks, pulled on our helmets, and rode the winding road leading past orchards, farms, and houses growing closer together.

The air was thick with humidity, the sun a bright eye glaring down from a blazing blue sky. With each step, mud squelched beneath our horses' hooves, left from last night's rain and the early morning's mist. Here and there, the occasional copse of trees overshadowed the road and gave us relief. Even the trees were different here, an ever-increasing reminder that we were in a strange land, among a foreign people. Now they were mostly palm trees, their fronds waving invitingly in the breezes that came all-too infrequently and failed to bring cooler air.

Uncertainty gripped me each time travelers passed us on the road.

Shoulders squared, head held high, I hoped my demeanor fooled them. They seemed intimidated; most averted their eyes or tried to pretend they weren't staring. Despite the heat, men and women alike drew their hoods low to conceal their faces in our presence. Even without dragons, it was clear the Dragon Keepers were respected and feared.

Over the days we'd traveled further south, I'd noticed other changes in the landscape besides the different trees. Even the grass was unfamiliar here: each blade was thicker, darker, and rougher to the touch. Brown and green lizards darted over rocks or scurried up trees. The flowers were larger, their colors more vibrant.

Now, as we drew closer to the town of Lorin, we rode along a winding dirt road bordered by thick hedges and flowers in shades of orange and yellow. We passed orchards of citrus trees fragrant with fruits that were considered delicacies back home. Nestled amongst towering palms were stone houses several stories high, all built around courtyards filled with lush plants and trees. Birdsong filled the air, a soothing chorus. Overhead, despite the hot sun, the gathering clouds were thick with the promise of coming rain. I could smell its approach as it mingled with the perfume of flowers, citrus, and sunbaked earth.

At last, as the grey clouds clustered over the sun and gave us a slight reprieve from the heat, we drew close to a stone wall. Set within one side was a plaque, marked with Alrenor's swirling sun insignia and declaring the beginning of Lorin's boundaries. The road wound toward the gates, which were wide open for the many travelers, on foot and horseback and in wagons, coursing in and out of the town.

Guards on either side, dressed in simple leather armor, caught sight of us and their eyes widened. They stiffened and saluted according to Alrenian custom: spreading their hands, palms open, before them. It looked like a supplicating gesture, one that, as I remembered from my history lessons, had come about as both a way to show respect and a way to prove one wasn't holding a weapon.

Rather than be caught acting strangely, I turned away before I gazed at them for too long. A haughty Alrenian in direct service to the empress surely wouldn't salute back, or even acknowledge others if she didn't have to.

I had to conceal my awe as we rode through the gateway. Stone buildings adorned with columns lined the wide cobblestone roads, and fountains featuring past rulers, famous warriors, or fierce dragons graced every square. Citizens rode in carriages or walked the sidewalks, peering into the front windows of shops, bakeries, smithies, and inns. Everything rose in a gradual sweep toward a hill on the far side of the town, where a temple stood alone on its crest.

The citizens were dressed in vivid colors. Women wore linen dresses adorned with sashes or tassels, while the men wore loose linen trousers and shirts overlaid with brightly colored vests. Even here, outside of the capital city, the women wore an abundance of jewelry—all except, of course, the slaves.

There was no mistaking the slaves, with their dark Forwyn skin, their worn, patched clothing, and downcast eyes. Men and women alike had shorn hair. I remembered from my studies about Forwyth culture how women wore their hair in braids woven with ribbons as a religious custom. The short hair was clearly a way to degrade them and alienate them from their own religion and culture. The thought made my stomach sour.

Aside from the occasional guard patrolling the street, there were no weapons to be seen on anyone. It was a glaring absence for me, when in Misroth it was commonplace to see someone with a knife strapped to their belt or a bow slung on their back. Even in our cities, one came across hunters, traders, or travelers who'd needed protection on the road, or citizens who were wary of alley thugs and thieves. Here, the guards held all the weapons and therefore all the power, which meant they had probably been approved by the empress herself and the citizens were at their mercy.

At last, we came to the hill's summit, where we circled around the temple, with wide stone columns and arches. More fragrant scents of floral and citrus wafted on the breeze as we rode beyond the grounds toward the streets on the far side.

Here, we came to the town marketplace, a wide, bustling street in the shadow of Lorin Forest. Beneath bright tents, vendors waved toward the wares spread out in beautiful displays on their tables and shouted at passersby.

Squaring my shoulders haughtily, I pushed my mount ahead of Narek's and Gillen's and led the way down the road. The vendors clamped their mouths shut at the sight of my companions and me. Even the handful of guards patrolling the marketplace avoided eye contact and gave us a wide berth.

I drank in the scenes greedily. Once I'd dreamed of traveling to other kingdoms to experience their cultures, see new sights, taste new foods, and hear new sounds. I'd imagined adventures of a different kind, with Avrik by my side, rather than the uncertain quest I was on now. But despite the heavy weight on my heart, I couldn't help the thrill rushing through me. I could imagine Avrik's smile, how he would have tugged me along to purchase candies or oranges, or to chat with some of the local traders. Thinking about it made him feel closer and further away all at once.

Beneath striped tents of blue and silver, red and orange, or purple and gold, sat displays of fresh vegetables and fruits. My mouth watered at the scents of oranges, lemons, and peaches. Other tents contained candies or sugared almonds in sacks that purchasers could eat from as they shopped. Under solid tents of shimmering gold or silver were assortments of jewelry, pottery, woven blankets and rugs featuring beautiful colors and designs, or bright clothing.

Everywhere I looked the market was packed with cheerful colors and laughing faces, and the air was teeming with intoxicating smells. The scent of roasted meat drifted toward me and made my stomach growl. I thought of the coins in my bag and wondered if I dared to try interacting with an Alrenian. Despite how much I'd studied Alrenor under my royal tutor, there were still many customs I didn't know, and many things that had likely changed in the two centuries our kingdoms had been separated. Certainly I'd raise suspicions when I wasn't even familiar with the Alrenian coins I'd need to pay with.

As I hesitated, trying to decide which vendor I felt most comfortable approaching, Gillen gasped. Pulling my horse alongside his, I clutched his arm and searched his face. He flinched at the chaos of sounds and smells surrounding us.

"Gil," I whispered fiercely, "it's all right. You're safe."

His eyes looked distant, wide with fright yet burning with anger. I saw him reach for his missing sword, his fingers drifting futilely through air, and I found myself thankful Narek still carried Gillen's weapon.

"It's not real—" I continued.

"What is this?" one of the guards called out in Alrenian. Stopping a few yards in front of us, he studied us warily. He seemed hesitant to speak to a Dragon Keeper directly, yet I noted the suspicion pulling his eyebrows taut. One wrong move and we were doomed. "Are you all right?" he ventured.

Scrambling for the Alrenian words I knew, I answered him gruffly. "Yes. Move on."

The guard lowered his eyes swiftly, nodding once and striding away.

Beside me, Gillen's eyes cleared, and I let out a breath of relief. On my other side, Narek's hands relaxed away from his weapons.

"Go to the edge of the market with Gil," I directed Narek quietly. "I'll purchase food and then we need to get out of here—fast." I tossed Narek my reins and dismounted.

Narek gestured to Gillen, and, leading my horse, the two of them rode away. Keeping my eyes averted and praying no one noticed they weren't Alrenian, I approached a vendor selling an array of traveling food: apples, dried cheeses, and jerky. Pulling the coins from my bag, I gathered my own food and shoved it into one of the sacks the vendor kept on hand before he could assist me. The elderly vendor, his hair white and thinning, opened his mouth as if to protest before thinking better of it and snapping it shut.

I slammed a pile of gold coins onto the table, and from the way the man's jaw dropped open, I knew I'd overpaid. At least he wouldn't fuss. Without a word, I shouldered the sack and sauntered away.

"I'm sorry," Gillen whispered. Knees pulled to his chest, head bowed, he looked utterly defeated, so different from the lively cousin I'd once had. Light from our fire flickered across his face and made his golden hair shine. "I almost lost control and gave us away."

Though I was relieved that Gillen was back in the present and seemed to understand the plan Narek and I had outlined to him over dinner, my heart still hurt. These moments were fleeting and unpredictable.

"Gil, it's not your fault," I said.

He lifted his head to search my eyes. "It is." He stared down at his hands, at his trembling fingers. "I *am* mad. It's so hard to tell what's real and what's not anymore… And—and when the vendors were shouting, it started to sound like screaming, and I—I could hear the nestrae torturing people again." He swallowed. "Burning and sacrificing them. I could see it, *smell* it…" He shuddered.

I squeezed my eyes shut as my own memories threatened to overtake me. The trouble with the torture we'd survived was that it hadn't ended once we'd escaped. Maybe it never would. "I'm so sorry."

"You're not alone," Narek cut in. His gaze on my cousin was steady, his voice firm but reassuring. "It's normal to be haunted by nestred visions after…being affected by them. Or to relive horrible experiences."

I nodded. "I still hear them too." My hand went to my lower back, where the nestred rune marked me.

Gillen shook his head sadly. "My mind doesn't feel like my own." He grimaced. "And I have this place between my shoulder blades where they cut into me. It burns all the time, and I think it means…" He sighed. "I hear their voices taunting me and calling me the Mad King. I think that's what they marked me with, on my back."

I considered telling him about my own nestred rune and that he wasn't alone, but I didn't think focusing on what the nestrae had done to all of us was what Gillen needed. Instead, I moved from the rock I'd perched on and settled into the dirt beside my cousin, closer to the fire. Wrapping my arms around him, I laid my head on his shoulder. "Do you remember when we used to pretend we were warriors of old, fighting the Alrenian empress with Eldon? Or fighting off the sedwa in Evren Forest?" Back then, I'd thought that battles were glorious and noble, not the bloody, horrifying chaos they really were. And I'd thought the monstrous sedwa were only a myth. I'd never dreamed that they and even worse monsters might actually exist.

Gillen smiled faintly, his hands finding mine and clasping them tightly. "I was always healing you of a grievous wound or finding an antidote when you were fooled into drinking poison." He laughed, just a little. "I always wanted to play the hero."

"And I always wanted you to be the hero," I said. "Because you have always been my hero."

"I'm not fit to be a hero," Gillen muttered. "Much less a king. I'm haunted by shadows in the dark, and most of the time my brain is muddled and confused. I get lost in their visions until it's hard to tell what is real and what isn't. I…" His voice trembled. "Sometimes it's hard to know where I am, or even *who* I am anymore."

I shook my head firmly. "No, you *are* fit to be king. I believe in you. I always have. Everyone who knows you has always loved and respected you. You're gentle and kind and wise and just. You've always known what is right and what must be done. For me. For Misroth." I forced myself to smile. "You're a teacher: you taught me to swim when Father refused my lessons. You've always been a natural leader, and you were the more eloquent speaker of the two of us when Eryk and Meeryn made us practice. You—you have always been strong-willed and passionate and creative and persuasive…" My voice wobbled and fell away. I was overwhelmed with an image of the lively, laughing cousin I'd once had, someone so bright and full of life. Now that same boy had shoulders stooped with weariness and defeat, and he looked at me with haunted eyes.

"Lia," Gillen said quietly, "I think *you* are the one meant to lead. Who cares if you weren't trained for the role? What matters is what you've already achieved. You defied your own father and overthrew him. You led…" He hesitated, gesturing to Narek. "You led an enemy to your side, gained his loyalty and trust. The nestrae didn't break you, like they've done to me, and in the end, you escaped them. You rescued me." He smiled mirthlessly. "Meanwhile, I led my men to their deaths in Toryn, and without you, I would have died too. Lia, *you* are my hero. And you are more fit to rule than I have ever been. Heir or not, the people won't want me. I'd do better surrendering the throne to you. What will the history books call me?" He scoffed. "The Mad King?"

Selfish tears clouded my vision. All I wanted was to save Misroth and then return to the old life I'd left behind, the simple life I'd led as Elena. In my mind's eye, I saw Rev and Lyanna and their cottage. Home. But if I became queen of Misroth, it wouldn't ever be my home again.

But there were also overwhelming doubts about what Gillen had said. My throat felt tight with grief and fear. Did he realize that I'd known my father had murdered his years ago? That I had fled and lived in hiding, leaving Gillen to his fate? I wouldn't have ever needed to rescue him if I hadn't left him behind in the first place.

I considered confessing this now, but the thought felt like ice water coursing through my veins. What if he couldn't forgive me?

Gillen didn't know all the ways I'd failed as a leader. He didn't know that it was my weakness that had left him to his fate, that had doomed Misroth to suffer under my father's oppression for years, and that had broken the barrier.

He worried about what the history books would call him—but

what would they call *me*? The Condemned Queen? My rune smarted painfully. The Bloody Queen? The Broken Queen?

"I'm not sure I believe that," I said instead, my words coming out slowly. "Your mother knew... I had a vision in which she said you were the only one who could save Misroth. And my visions don't lie to me. Besides, you don't know what could happen. Don't give up on yourself so soon. Just because you're struggling and feel like you're losing your mind now, doesn't mean you will always be this way." I squeezed his hand tighter. "Don't renounce the crown to me yet."

Doubt flickered in his eyes, and Gillen shook his head sadly. "Your vision and what I said can both be true at the same time." His smile was wistful. "Believe it, cousin. I need you. Misroth needs you."

I didn't try to argue with him this time. The sorrow in his eyes was almost too much for me to bear. "Then hold on for me, because I need you too."

CHAPTER SEVENTEEN

Avrik

THE DRAGONS THAT FLEW JENNAH and Avrik to Inalgoth were stunning creatures that made his boyish daydreams and wishes come to life: all the times he'd imagined what it would be like to ride a dragon, or the moments when he'd pretended to slay one. He'd played Eldon, luring the great dragon Raklov away from Empress Ilett until the beast was loyal to him, and then he'd ridden Raklov into battle, winning the Misrothian people their freedom. Later, he'd dreamed of exploring Alrenor with Halia, back when she was still Elena, and how they would gain the Alrenians' friendship and trust until they were permitted to ride the dragons.

Now it was just Jennah and him, each strapped into huge leather saddles behind silent Keepers. Jennah was perched upon a dragon the rippling, varying shades of water, while Avrik rode one the colors of flame: deepest red and fierce orange shimmering with hints of gold.

Avrik drank in the landscape excitedly. When Inalgoth stretched before them in all its beauty, he couldn't hold back his smile, and when he caught Jennah's eye, he found she felt the same. This was the Land of the Sun, as stunningly beautiful as it was brutally violent.

The Dragon Keepers landed at the Keep and took them on a winding path toward the palace, and then through the palace grounds.

Each courtyard and hall, each statue and painting, was more breathtaking than the last. Avrik remembered the stories Gare had told, especially the one in which Empress Ilett had shown Eldon all the wonders of the Alrenian palace. The stories did not exaggerate.

Of course, the wonder of it all faded when the Keepers led Jennah and him into the dungeons and threw them into separate cells. Once again, they were trapped, at the mercy of the ruthless Alrenians and their torturous methods of interrogation. Once again, they'd merely gone from one set of captors to another.

Avrik jerked awake as the guards stormed into his cell, their boots thudding heavily on the filthy stone floor. After being imprisoned for days, his body ached at the thought of another round of questioning, of the Alrenians taunting and jeering at him as they broke bones. Each time, they summoned a gifted healer to his cell, summoning power Avrik had never witnessed before to mend his injuries. The process was painful but surprisingly quick. Quick enough that the very next day, the Dragon Keepers could return to break his newly healed bones.

But as he blinked away the bleariness gathering across his sight, his mind caught up to his eyes. These were Royal Guards standing before him, not Dragon Keepers. One of the men bore a ring of keys that he held toward the shackles attaching Avrik to the wall. As the guard unlocked the shackles, Avrik's chains clanked together.

Avrik bit back a groan when he pulled his arms down to his sides. The blood rushed back painfully through his veins as he rubbed at his smarting wrists. Fresh blood welled at the cuts the shackles had dug into his skin.

"The empress would like to see you," one of the guards said, smirking cruelly at him.

The men dragged Avrik out into the light of the sun, where they joined other guards leading Jennah. When Avrik met her gaze, he saw her familiar indomitable spirit shimmering in the fire in her eyes. Flashing her a grin, he welcomed the comforting sensation of her courage gift flowing through his veins.

The guards led them down the last hallway toward a set of double doors, through which was the throne room, magnificent and glowing in the afternoon sunshine streaming through the glass ceiling. Avrik's eyes burned as they adjusted. He drank in the vibrant colors on the gathered nobility, the imposing architecture of the carved columns filling the room, and the huge throne overtaking the wall on the far end.

Empress Karye lounged upon a throne of ivory and gold, picking at her fingernails with an Alrenian dagger: golden, curved, and wrought with beautiful Alrenian words he couldn't read. Though her slumped posture and sigh of boredom were anything but intimidating, Avrik knew immediately not to underestimate her. She was clothed in a dress decorated with dragon scales, and leather boots that looked more fit for a soldier than an empress. Instead of glimmering with diamonds and gemstones, she shone with weapons: daggers on her legs and at her waist. She wore no crown, instead wearing her long, golden hair loose in a waterfall down her back.

"Her Imperial Majesty Karye, daughter of Verilae, ruler of the Empire of Alrenor, Guardian of the Dragon Army, Captain of the Dragon Keepers, and Blessed Chosen One of the Giver of Life and Death," a man standing in the shadows of her throne called out, his voice echoing in the vast space.

"Kneel," the guard standing behind Avrik snarled.

He landed a blow to Avrik's head before he could respond, sending sparks skittering across his vision. A chill snaked up his belly and into his ribcage. For a moment, his fingertips were numb with cold. Again, he wondered what Nesrelle had done to him.

He and Jennah dropped to their knees and bowed their heads. Avrik stared down at the marble floor, listening to the empress approach.

"These are the Misrothians who infiltrated our kingdom and slew *my* people?" a cold voice demanded. As she spoke the New Language, Empress Karye's Alrenian accent made her voice sound sharp.

"Each time we question them, they insist they're not spies, but came from Toryn," one of the guards spoke up.

"Then why are you here?" Karye snapped, this time addressing Avrik and Jennah. "Stand and show yourselves."

Pulling himself to his feet, Avrik faced the empress, studying the cold light in her eyes as she assessed them. She scanned him from head to toe and lust simmered in her gaze. Avrik swallowed back his disgust. He was used to being noticed by young women, but being ogled by an older empress was a new experience.

"Two Misrothians, in the company of Toryn men and women, enter Brema Wood and attack the first Alrenians they encounter," Karye murmured, circling them slowly. Her stare was dangerous, like a predator considering its next meal. "And it happens so soon after my informants told me that the barrier is down. Was it a failed attempt to spy on my empire?" She cocked her head, a wicked light dancing in her eyes. "A foolish declaration of war? Did Misroth ally itself with Toryn? Your comrades are dead, and you are my prisoners. The only reason you are not dead already is because you're useful to me." She smiled slowly, and Avrik's blood ran even colder than before.

Her eyes flicked to Jennah. "And you," she growled, "are an abomination of an Alrenian. A stinking, cowardly, pathetic descendant from our line of powerful warriors. We are the gifted, chosen people of the Life-Giver, and yet you are tainted with the blood of Forwyn heretics and Misrothian traitors. You disgust me."

Jennah's nostrils flared almost imperceptibly, but Avrik caught it. And then the fury drained from her and an impertinent smile flitted across her lips. She bit back her response just in time, but Avrik recognized it in her eyes: *You do too.*

He wanted to laugh aloud. *Go ahead. Threaten us. Torture us. Give us your worst. Nothing you can do can compare to what has already been done to us.*

Sensing how unafraid they were, Karye's eyes narrowed. "It's almost a shame we've tortured you," she murmured, stepping forward and stroking Avrik's chin. Avrik tensed, but held himself still, refusing to recoil or let his disgust show on his face. *Give her nothing.* "But my Dragon Keepers grow bored," she whispered. "I needed a way to entertain them."

"We're here for your *entertainment?*" Avrik said. "Do you even believe we're spies?"

Karye laughed. "It became quite clear early on that you're both far too pathetic and underprepared to be spies." She smirked. "So, yes, I need to keep my people busy. And of course you're in the capital to receive your sentence for killing my people. But that won't happen until you've outlived your usefulness."

Fear curdled in Avrik's stomach. *Usefulness for what?* he wondered. *Entertaining your sick Dragon Keepers?*

Karye waved at her guards lazily. "Take them away."

"Wait, we can tell you about the nestrae—" Jennah began, and Avrik noted the tremor she tried to hide in her voice. They truly were backed into a corner now.

"If you have anything of use to say, scum, talk to my guards before I choose how I'll kill you," Karye said, striding back to her throne, dagger twirling in her hand. "I have my own informant."

As the guards dragged them away, Jennah hung her head. "I'm sorry. I failed."

"No," Avrik murmured. "You can't bargain with a bloodthirsty madwoman like her. You didn't fail. We'll find a way."

CHAPTER EIGHTEEN

O N THE EVENING OF THE second day of the month of Raehn, fifty-two days before my birthday, we passed through the gates of Inalgoth, Alrenor's capital city. As usual, our armor protected us from searching glances. Both the crowd entering with us and the saluting guards monitoring the gate gave us a wide berth and averted their eyes.

Before we'd entered Inalgoth, we'd agreed it would be easiest to scout unseen without worrying about our horses. We'd released them into the countryside, hoping they'd find their way back home. Hoping they had masters to return to. I'd breathed a prayer for Meli and the other temple dwellers as I'd watched our retreating geldings, their manes streaming behind them.

Now we walked, but with everyone scurrying to make a path for us, we were able to move at a fast clip. The city was breathtaking. Encircled by towering, pearlescent stone walls, the buildings and streets gradually rose toward the palace and Dragon's Keep, a shining, sprawling mass of buildings and gardens. Below, Inalgoth was a huge maze of streets and alleys churning with people, carriages, and wagons; bustling marketplaces full of brilliant color; towering, columned buildings rising toward the sky; and lush courtyards bursting with vibrant plants, palm trees, and fountains.

It was all too much for me to take in at once. I was constantly turning my head, catching everything in bright glimpses and flashes: the crowds dressed in their flowing attire of bright whites and vivid colors, the guards in gold and silver armor, the towering architecture, the gracefully arching bridges placed over rushing streams and crashing waterfalls, presumably created from water redirected from the nearby seas. The entire city shone white and gold, both because numerous buildings were draped in the white and gold Alrenian flag or painted with emblems of its spiraling sun, and because the setting sun tinged the shimmering white stone of the buildings fiery shades of yellow. Everywhere that water flowed—in avenues beneath the bridges, fountains, and waterfalls—the sun set it aflame.

Inalgoth was so bright and beautiful it hurt to look at. Despite the reason I was here, despite the weight of my people's danger and the danger my friends and I were in now, my heart soared. If I was in the Land of the Sun, I would drink in the experience while I could. For Avrik. For Jennah. For a long-gone girl that had once lived and dreamed in Evren.

As we drew deeper into the city, we caught glimpses between buildings of the deep blue Alrenian flashing under the westering sun. On the opposite side, I had my first glance at the Great Sea. My heart expanded at the sight, once again reminded of how big the world was, a world I had longed to explore for most of my life. Here, on the Alrenian coast, the Great Sea glistened like a gem, bright blue and astonishingly clear.

Overhead, dragons leapt from the cliffside near the palace and soared through the air, stealing my breath with their beauty and power. The citizens, as familiar with the dragons as they were, often paused and stared in awe and fear when one of the dragons' shadows passed over the streets. The dragons' scales flashed every color imaginable in the setting sun, from burnished gold to deepest midnight to a vast array of glittering colors like a rainbow spread across the beast's body. The Dragon Keepers, strapped into saddles on the creatures' backs, swooped low over the streets and then ascended high into the sky until they were mere specks above us. With wings beating like thunder and stretching longer than several men, the dragons were as terrifying as they were stunning, yet I couldn't ignore the thrill swelling inside me.

I wanted to be like those Keepers. I wanted to be diving and soaring through the air, the wind rushing in my ears and the world laid out before me in all its wonder and beauty. Each time a dragon dove low enough that I could see its eyes, gold or green or richest black, I wasn't afraid. Perhaps Gare's stories of King Eldon taming a dragon had taken a hold of me, but I didn't feel like potential prey, only an equal.

Eventually, the dragons returned to the Keep, and I had to focus my mind not on dreams but the task ahead of us.

Just as with the city itself, it wasn't difficult to enter the palace grounds. As usual, the guards—dressed in traditional gold armor, beautifully crafted but without dragon scales—recognized our dragon scale armor immediately, saluted, and opened the gates without question. A trickle of uneasiness washed down my spine as we entered the lush gardens surrounding the palace. It all seemed almost *too* easy. For what felt like the thousandth time, I reached for my truth gift, longing to conjure up a scene that would tell me what the empress and her truth advisor knew, but I found only emptiness. My stomach dropped and I was filled with an overwhelming sense of loss.

Like everything else, the palace gardens were stunning, filled with palms and citrus trees, shrubs and vines, ponds and fountains, and both familiar and foreign flowers. The grounds overlooked the surrounding city and a small harbor off the Great Sea, though I noted that the docks held no more than fishing boats and small sailboats. Why build and maintain ships when the barrier prevented the Alrenians from venturing far to sea?

The high palace walls were inlaid with metalwork depicting the swirling sun insignia and former Alrenian emperors and empresses, conquerors and warriors, priests and priestesses. Beyond the walls, the palace was not a single huge building, but a sprawling mass of many buildings, towers, and courtyards, all arrayed with colonnades and arches, all climbing to a circular building at the hill's pinnacle.

We wandered within the vast, interlacing garden paths, biding our time as the sun set and dodging the patrolling guards. Once the shadows lengthened and the first stars glittered in the eastern sky, we found a clump of shrubbery with a good view of the back of the palace and lingered there, studying the patterns of the guards' patrols and shift changes. As the night darkened, we were able to draw close enough to the palace to peer into the windows set below ground level. Most opened to rooms for the slaves. I grit my teeth at the sight of the Forwyn men and women's downcast eyes and the women's shorn hair, sharp reminders of Alrenian cruelty.

At last, we found a window that allowed us to peer into a dim room occupied by a handful of guards. Most sat around a table set close to an unlit hearth, playing a card game. On one wall were rings of keys, while at the far end, away from the men playing cards, was a heavy, barred door.

"We've found the entrance to the dungeons," Narek said with a grim smile as he studied the guards' movements carefully. "Are you ready?" he asked me.

Over the past few days, I'd rehashed as much of the lessons Jennah had given as I could, practicing various words and phrases over and over. Drawing a fortifying breath, I nodded.

"Can we find this room once we've entered the palace?" Gillen asked, quirking a brow at Narek.

"The slaves will lead us there," I said. "They won't dare be suspicious of us or tell us no."

"I don't think the trouble is getting into the dungeons," Narek said, "but getting out again."

There wasn't any time to waste, however. Palace guards and slaves might not dare to ask any questions when they saw us, but if we encountered any other Dragon Keepers, they certainly would. And although we'd observed the outside guards long enough to avoid encountering them in the gardens, the longer we lingered, the likelier someone would find us slinking about. Even a palace guard would surely be suspicious of that.

We had to make our move tonight, taking the information and plans we had and trusting we could fill in the gaps as we went.

Narek returned Gillen's sword to him, and my cousin carefully attached it to his belt, his expression pale and taut, as if he feared what he might accidentally do with it. We stowed our bags behind some bushes near the stables after removing two of the worn, ragged cloaks we'd stolen on our travels. Slipping off my armored tunic, I tied the cloaks around my shirt before replacing the tunic.

Intentionally making our footsteps loud and confident, we traced our way toward the palace. We marched up a stairway leading to a set of doors, carved with symbols of waves and flowers and the swirling sun, and again were welcomed by guards, who swung the doors inward for us.

Above, the arched ceiling was painted in vibrant scenes of Alrenians being blessed by what I assumed was their representation of the Giver of Life, who, unsurprisingly, had tanned skin shimmering with Alrenian gold. I wondered how scandalized they would be to know that he had dark Forwyn skin, without any Alrenian gold at all. In the paintings, men and women kneeled before him in a garden pulsating with color and life. Other scenes were depictions of the gifts he gave. Truth-gifted in ivory cloaks stood before crowds as if they were sharing news or giving speeches. Warrior-gifted slew enemies in battle, enemies that looked like they could have been Misrothian and Toryn rebels. Other gifts were harder to recognize, but the one that gave me chills was a scene of what must have been a courage-gifted woman, staring unafraid into the eyes of the Queen of Death. The black and grey curls framing her face were wrong, but the queen's sharp blue eyes reminded me of my encounters with Nesrelle, and I had to look away.

Afterward, we passed through numerous other wide halls, some indoors like the entryway, while others were columned pavilions, with rooftops to protect from the weather and gauzy fabric hung between the columns to keep out insects. At last, when I was certain we were drawing close to the dungeons, I saw a Forwyn boy creeping down our hallway. Shoulders hunched, eyes downcast, he walked in the opposite direction. He shrank against the wall as if he were willing himself to vanish into the shadows, to become a part of the palace and disappear before our eyes.

Horror and disgust burned the back of my throat. But I had a part to play.

"You," I barked at the boy. Since I knew the Alrenians didn't encourage their slaves to learn their language, I knew it was safe to use my own here—the merchant tongue every Alrenian used to address him.

The poor boy flinched, freezing in place before collapsing to his knees before us. His too-thin body shook as he forced himself to stretch out, facedown, on the floor.

Beside me, Gillen cringed visibly, but thankfully we were the only ones in the hall. The boy never once dared to lift his eyes to our faces.

"Take us to the dungeons," I continued.

With the smallest nod, the boy scurried to his feet and darted down the hall, only daring to cast one look over his shoulder to ensure we were following.

He led us to a heavy door monitored by a single guard, who glared at the boy until she noticed our approach. Then she stiffened and saluted, dropping her eyes to the floor. I didn't even have to order her to open the door, because she was in so much haste to swing it open and avoid our anger.

The boy scurried away, bowing and backing up as he went, but I didn't watch him. That would be too suspicious. Instead, I stepped through the doorway, ignoring the pounding in my heart. My tongue clung to the roof of my mouth and the cloaks tied about my waist suddenly felt constricting, shortening my breath.

You can do this, I told myself. I knew what to say, and I knew if I behaved confidently and arrogantly enough, my refusal to look the guards in the eye wouldn't be considered strange. The Alrenians' fear and respect for the Dragon Keepers would be my armor.

"Take us to the Misrothian prisoners," I snapped at the nearest guard, who had been leaning back lazily in his seat, cards clasped in one hand and a mug of ale in the other.

When he heard my voice, he startled and burst from the chair, cards spilling across the floor and ale sloshing over his mug. He slammed the glass down and saluted, clearing his throat as his neck flushed red. All around him, the other guards rose, some stumbling over their chairs as they scraped them back from the table.

If I hadn't been forcing my brain to remember exactly the correct way to pronounce the Alrenian words I needed, the scene would have made me want to laugh.

"The empress wishes to see them," I continued, remembering to enunciate each consonant until my voice was as sharp as a knife's edge. The Alrenian language was full of contradictions, from its soft edges to its harsh sounds. For an arrogant Dragon Keeper, making my voice rough and low seemed the best way to cover any possible slips.

This time, the foremost guard glanced up sharply, his eyes blinking uncertainly, hands twitching nervously. "Do you—have a paper from her?"

I stared straight past him, toward the barred door behind which Avrik and Jennah might be trapped. The blood in my veins rushed with intermingling hope and fear.

Make them fear you.

Instead of answering the man's question, I pretended it was absurd. Beneath me. "She's *waiting*," I said, keeping my gaze trained impatiently on the door. My fingers strayed toward the hilt at my side, as if I were cold enough to cut a fellow Alrenian down if he were in my way.

Eyes widening in horror, the man dipped his head in another bow and nearly leapt toward the rows of keys hanging on the wall. Lifting a ring, he spun on his heel and strode toward the door.

A new voice made him halt in his tracks, mid-reach for the door's lock. My blood froze in my veins.

"You made it farther than I anticipated," the male voice said, speaking in the New Language.

Seizing my sword hilt, I spun around. Narek and Gillen inched closer to me, their hands on their weapons. In the doorway, flanked by two Dragon Keepers, stood a cloaked man, his hood pulled low to keep his face in shadow.

"Advisor Vionn," one of the guards breathed as they all crumpled to the floor in exaggerated bows.

The truth-gifted advisor to the empress. My stomach clenched. I'd been a fool to hope that our plans could have gone unnoticed by them all this time.

"Come," said Vionn, and from the way he stretched out his words, he seemed to speak through a smile. "Her Imperial Majesty has requested your presence."

CHAPTER NINETEEN

Surrounded and outnumbered, there was nothing else to do but lay down our stolen weapons. We threw down the Alrenian swords and throwing knives, but I kept the nestred knife I'd hidden in my boot. The two Keepers seized Narek and me by the arms, while another guard grabbed Gillen.

Trailing the advisor, they pulled us roughly from the room and back through the series of halls we'd already traversed. We exited the building we were in and approached a larger one protected by heavily armed guards. As they saluted the advisor and Dragon Keepers, we ascended the marble steps leading to tall, arched doors.

The guards pushed them open and we stepped into a vast, circular room lined with towering columns reaching toward…glass. The columns ended just below a smooth glass ceiling, offering a perfect view of air-brushed clouds gathering about the silver moon. Torches lined the walls, bathing the entire throne room in an eerie, dancing glow that elongated each shadow, making the darkness seem as alive as the light. Arranged amongst the columns were lounging nobles, stiff-backed guards, and a handful of abject-looking slaves. At the far side of the room, a woman descended a gold and ivory throne, stalking toward us with the air of a predator.

"Empress Karye." The advisor kneeled, and before I could react, the Alrenians behind us shoved Narek, Gillen, and me down with rough blows to our backs. Our knees struck the floor with audible thuds. Bowing my head, I looked up through my lashes at the woman approaching us.

She was dressed as lavishly as I expected an Alrenian empress to be, her appearance even more intimidating in person than it had been in my visions. Rather than a full gown, she wore a short dress of shimmering white silk that reached mid-thigh and was drenched in gold chains and dragon scales. The neckline of the dress itself was so heavy with scales that it looked like the Dragon Keepers' armor, and she even wore scaled pauldrons on each shoulder. Her leather boots laced up to her knees, and the sash about her waist was not cloth, but mail woven of black scales. She wore daggers at her thighs and waist, as if she were dressed for battle rather than court.

Kneeling as I was, I couldn't make out her features, but her stance was lethal. She circled us with the soft-footed grace of a great cat, and I was reminded of the sedwa stalking their prey through the forest.

"Stand," the empress commanded.

The advisor, guard, and Keepers stood as one, their backs rigid, hands balled into fists, eyes staring straight ahead. I dared a glance toward the empress and caught a flash of blonde hair and a sneering face.

"What's this? Misrothians that don't know their place?" The empress's accent was thicker than anyone's I'd heard yet, probably because she rarely deigned to speak the lowly merchant tongue. Her vowels stretched long, but the rest of her words were sharp, clipped. A violent voice for a violent woman.

"Stand, prisoners," Karye snarled, and we obeyed.

The empress halted in front of me, a full head taller. Her lithe, muscular body reminded me of Jennah's build, but otherwise, she was nothing like my friend. Karye had long golden hair plaited in several braids down her back, as if she were mocking the Forwyn slaves in attendance who couldn't wear theirs in their traditional style. A headpiece of gold and silver dragon scales wove through her hair and hung across her brow. Ice blue, gold-flecked eyes flashed at me, sharp as the daggers on her hips, and her fair skin shimmered with the gold tone of Alrenor. The only break in her smooth complexion was the freckles dotting her nose.

It was no surprise the Alrenians had been described as such a fearsome people when they'd conquered Misroth and the other kingdoms. They stood taller than most, wore weapons like others wore jewelry, and shone golden like gods. They were proud and convinced they were blessed by the Giver of Life, and no wonder they thought so.

Still, I thought of Gare's stories of Eldon, of the old histories I'd studied about our war for freedom. I remembered the way Misroth had defied Alrenor and won, and I felt a smile flicker over my lips. *We are the Dragon-Hearted,* Gare had said proudly, and that thought bolstered me.

What had the Alrenian sword I'd stolen from the Dragon Keeper said? *I will not bow to fear.* And I vowed that I would not, either.

I stood tall and stared the empress in the face, unflinching.

"So you are the Misrothians and Toryn who murdered my Dragon Keepers, impersonated them, and infiltrated my palace," Karye said, her piercing eyes dancing with an emotion I couldn't identify. Bloodlust? Amusement? A threat? Her gaze flicked to her advisor briefly, and as if answering an unspoken summons, Vionn stepped forward to stand beside her. "Who are you and what are you doing trespassing in my empire?"

Was this a test? I was sure that, with Vionn to provide her with information about us, the empress already knew the answers to her questions.

Behind me, Gillen shifted on his feet. I wondered where his mind was: lost in nestred-inflicted torment or here in the present. I wondered what the empress would do if he began screaming right there in her throne room.

I drew myself up to my full height. "This is my cousin Gillen, descendant of Eldon and heir to the Misrothian throne, and I am Princess Halia."

Before I could introduce Narek, Karye interrupted me. "*He* is your king?" she scoffed. She stepped past me and I glanced over my shoulder, watching her warily. Gillen met her gaze with a fierce glare, but his eyes were shadowed and dim. With his tangled hair and the scars tracing his face, I could see that he didn't cut the formidable figure Karye expected from a ruler. Not like her, certainly.

When the empress stood before Gillen, they were the same height, though with his slumped shoulders, she appeared taller. She placed a hand beneath his chin and jerked his face toward her. "Well, he is handsome, I suppose," she said, as if he weren't present. She'd lowered her voice to a dangerously sultry tone, making my skin crawl. I wanted to slap her hand away, to gouge out her eyes rather than let her even look at my cousin or speak about him as if he weren't there. "For a Misrothian. I see the Alrenian skin tone was lost in Eldon's bloodline." She snorted. "How…degrading."

Spinning on her heel, she stalked back toward me. "But Misroth bred enough with Teramyl to keep passing on Teramese features." She cast a significant look toward me, taking in my dark waves of hair and the bright green eyes I'd inherited from my mother. Teramese features from her half-forgotten ancestors.

Karye frowned. "And you two are Misrothian *royalty*?" She sneered at me. "Do you speak for your king then, Princess Halia? Or does he have a voice?"

Gillen's voice rang out, firm and clear. "She is my representative."

Karye quirked a brow in his direction before seemingly losing interest. "And who is he?" she asked me, tossing an appraising glance in Narek's direction.

"The Captain of the Royal Guard," I said coolly. I felt Narek glance in my direction, but I didn't pull my gaze from the empress. I could hear my father's voice in my head, and strangely enough, it was giving me courage. *Show no weakness.*

Karye scoffed. "Misroth sent its royalty to spy? To fight my warriors and then impersonate them, like a pack of cowards too spineless to even face me as you are?"

"We are not spies," I said firmly.

"Oh?" she asked, a dangerous smile playing about her mouth. "Then what *are* you doing in Alrenor, with such a small, secretive band? Why did you break the barrier? Why didn't you make yourselves known right away?" Her eyes narrowed to slits. "Why hide with a runaway criminal in her temple?"

I grit my teeth. Again, I wondered how many of her questions came from a need for information, and how many were only a test or a game.

"You have a truth-gifted advisor, *and* you have two of my friends captive in your dungeons, being questioned by your Dragon Keepers," I bit out. "Surely you already know the truth. You know we came from Toryn and that the nestrae are invading our kingdom. You know that they'll come for you next. You know the horrors they are capable of committing against your people."

Vionn stiffened, as if my words recalled horrific visions about the nestrae he'd seen many times. But Karye's sharp laughter echoed throughout the throne room.

"Do you think Alrenor fears them? Who do you think we are?" She gestured to the Keepers surrounding my companions and me, and then to the guards and nobles at court. It was then I noticed that even the noblemen and noblewomen were armed. Outside of the Keepers, soldiers, and guards, they were probably the only Alrenians in the empire trusted and privileged enough to wear weapons. "You have seen my dragons. My Keepers. My guards. Me." A threat sparked in her eyes. "Do you think I need to be *warned* about threats from the likes of *you*?" Without warning, she slapped me across the face, setting my cheek aflame and making me bite into my tongue. "Bow down before me, prisoner. Cower. Beg for mercy. That is all you are worthy of. Why would I deign to listen to you, murderess?"

All around me, the other Alrenians burst into cruel laughter. My mouth filled with the taste of blood, and I realized with a jolt of nausea that this was indeed a game to Karye and her court. She was wasting my time, mocking my people and me, laughing at the terror already plaguing my land.

Had she sent her Dragon Keepers to find us, to fight Meli and the other temple dwellers—perhaps even kill them—all for her own *amusement?*

But instead of intimidating me, her words only spiked my ire. Made me want to fight back. Her insolence was sickening, and part of me hoped she would discover the dark danger of being invaded without warning by the nestrae. Let her feel their torment.

I stood taller than before, straightening my shoulders, lifting my chin. I stared back at her without fear, or without showing a hint of pain.

"You're a fool. The nestred demons will wipe you off the world's map."

Karye cocked her head, studying me intently. "Are you *threatening* Alrenor?" She laughed again, languidly, as if she had all the time in the world. As if she were lounging and sipping tea with friends, not dripping with weapons and staring down prisoners she wanted to execute.

"I know I'm not in a position to make threats," I said calmly, "but I demand to know what you want from us. Why did you send your Dragon Keepers to find us? Perhaps we can give you what you desire, in exchange for releasing us and your other Misrothian prisoners."

"You're not really in a position to bargain either," Karye said with a slow smile. "I mean…look at you." She surveyed Gillen, Narek, and me. "Quite the ragtag party. Who else did you bring? Where is your convoy, the rest of your guards?" Her eyes flared dangerously. "Oh, right…the only others you took into Toryn with you are dead. I don't think I have anything to fear from you."

It was true. Even with Narek's gift—which, to my knowledge, he'd only managed to share with two others at once so far—we were impossibly outnumbered. Every Alrenian present was armed.

"Maybe we're not in a position for you to fear us," I said, "but the nestrae's threat is something we should all fear. You might laugh at the threat now, but imagine the demons devastating *your* land and *your* people." A memory of one of my visions in the temple flashed through my mind: Karye with her daughter, telling her a story about the dragons. "Or your daughter," I added.

Karye's eyes flashed with anger, but I went on.

"Vionn has seen what the nestrae are capable of. Even if you insist Alrenor doesn't fear them, that with your warriors and your dragons you are strong and will win against them, you need to know that even a victory will come at a heavy price. Once they enter Alrenor, they will control your people with their deceitful visions. Those warriors you are so proud of will turn against you."

I slid the dragon scale gloves from my arms, tossing them to the floor, and held up my arms in the moonlight shimmering through the glass ceiling. Even with Veykan's miraculous healing work, white scars traced my arms, reminders of every cut, every burn. This time, the silence in the room was heavy as the Alrenians studied my scars. Were they starting to believe me? "They're merciless," I said. "Show her, Vionn."

Every inch of his skin was concealed by his long ivory cloak or the shadows cast by his hood, yet I could sense Vionn's fear. It radiated off him as he stepped forward, the hem of his cloak whispering along the floor behind him. Karye shot him a piercing glance, though she didn't stop him from approaching her. I couldn't tell if she was accusing him for listening to me or for not already sharing visions of the nestrae directly with her.

Vionn reached out, removing his gloved hands from beneath his cloak. I frowned, wondering what the man had to hide. The night was warm and humid, and surely he was sweating under all of his layers.

Before he could ask, Karye gave him a sharp nod of permission. Vionn laid a hand on her arm and her eyes fell shut.

It only took a few moments. When the empress opened her eyes and Vionn stepped back from her, a vein pulsed in her temple. Though she concealed it well, I saw the moment a shadow darted across her face.

"Misroth and Alrenor would be more powerful together, as allies, than as enemies," I went on. *Show no weakness,* I thought, praying the empress couldn't detect my desperation. "With our common enemy, we can't afford to be divided. But if we fight the nestrae together, if you sent forces with us into Misroth, we could stop the nestrae and prevent them from overtaking Misroth and ever entering Alrenor. We could save Misrothian and Alrenian lives. Your people wouldn't have to suffer as mine do now."

Karye smirked. "Is that so?" she murmured. "You would like me to tell you what I want from you, to form an alliance with your kingdom, and then to let you and my other prisoners go?" She strode toward me, staring at me with unreadable eyes. "It's true you've given me something to think over, little prisoner."

I refused to flinch at her words.

"But as of right now, you're at *my* mercy. My people have time to prepare for the nestrae while they ravage your kingdom. You have a gift I could use against them." Her eyes flicked to Narek, and dread unfurled in my stomach. *That* was why she wanted us. She wanted to use Narek's war gift, the powerful gift that Alrenor had long coveted and hadn't seen within its own borders for many years. Would she force him to surrender it to her? Torture the rest of us until he agreed to give in to her demands? "And I have something I know you want."

She signaled to some of her guards, who moved toward a set of doors to the left and swung them open. More guards' heavy footfalls approached through the open doors. They shoved two familiar prisoners before them.

As I'd hoped and feared, they were Jennah and Avrik. They both appeared dirty and exhausted, their hands restrained by shackles, but they scowled in defiance. Jennah's eyes flared with hope when they landed on me. She stood tall and proud, unafraid in the presence of the cruel Alrenians.

My gaze darted to Avrik, my heartbeat such a crashing crescendo that I could scarcely hear anything. I drank in his tousled hair, long enough that the stubborn lock that once fell across his forehead hung almost in his eyes. Instead of stubble dotting his jawline, he had the beginnings of a beard. His warm brown eyes were full of life, not the haunted, grieved expression he'd worn when we'd first entered Toryn together. Somewhere along the way, despite whatever hell he had survived, his familiar optimism had won out.

Our eyes met, and emotions flickered in his gaze: relief, joy, and something more. Something that made my pulse quicken with hope.

I longed to run and embrace them, or even weep for joy. Here were my friends, alive and whole and free. Against all odds.

Though I didn't move my eyes from my friends, I detected the smile in the empress's voice as she spoke. Cold fear washed down my back. Her words came as no surprise, yet to hear them so soon after finding Jennah and Avrik alive made them unbearable.

"I suppose I'll make a decision about your offer, Princess Halia, after your friends are executed. I'll summon you to announce their sentence tomorrow."

CHAPTER TWENTY

Avrik

FOR A MOMENT, THE SIGHT in front of Avrik didn't make sense. He'd seen Halia so many times in nestred-induced visions, in dreams, and in his own imagination whenever he closed his eyes. It didn't seem possible she could really be there now, in Alrenor.

But there she was: the girl who had put his world back together. The girl who had torn his world apart.

She stood unflinching before the empress, her hair cascading down her back in windswept waves. In the golden Dragon Keeper armor she wore, she looked like royalty, and more beautiful than ever. Maybe it was the way her expression hardened with courage, or maybe it was simply because she was there, the picture of strength, and wondrously, miraculously alive.

Narek and another man, probably Layk, flanked her. But Avrik couldn't tear his gaze from Halia. She'd turned and noticed him too, and for an instant, something softened in the rigid lines of her expression. She couldn't hide the relief in her eyes.

Karye was speaking, making Halia's face turn back to stone. The empress's tone was vicious, yet Avrik couldn't even feel threatened by her anymore. Couldn't take in whatever she was saying. All he could think about was how he wanted to pull free from the guards and take

Halia into his arms. To tell her what a fool he'd been and beg for her forgiveness, and then, maybe, just maybe, he could explain how he felt.

Instead, the guards wrenched him back. Others slammed the doors shut. Despite his and Jennah's cries of protest and their attempts to pull free, they were dragged back to their separate cells.

Soon he was alone again in the solitude of his thoughts, accompanied by nothing but the steady burning of the torches and the distant mutterings of other prisoners too far away to carry on a conversation with him. He sunk to the floor and lay his head in his hands, thinking.

Avrik had contemplated and discarded endless escape plans in the hours that followed his and Jennah's first meeting with the empress, but nothing had seemed viable. His apprehension grew until it felt like a tangible presence in his cell, a living shadow wrestling with the light that was his struggling hope. It would be like a punch to the gut, he thought, to survive the nestrae's terrors only to be executed here by the Alrenian empress.

He could feel death calling to him, almost as if Nesrelle were whispering threats into his ear.

It was another punch to the stomach each time he closed his eyes and imagined Halia's face. How could he die without telling her how he felt? How could he have squandered every other chance he'd had over the years?

Hope is a light in the darkness, he thought, remembering his mother's words.

But when he shut his eyes next, he saw nestred flame roaring, devouring. Their clicking, hissing language whispered through his mind as they damned him and everyone he loved. A chill swept through him, and he could have sworn he could feel their sharp claws slicing through the skin on his back.

Avrik opened his eyes, but there was nothing there. Only the shadows in the corners of his dim, windowless cell kept him company.

He couldn't die. He *wouldn't.* Not when he had so much left to say to Halia, so much left to experience with her. Not when he still needed to help his people and wash away the guilt of bloodshed his father had bequeathed to him. How could he die, when he still had so much life left to live?

You silly boy, a hauntingly familiar voice murmured. Avrik jerked his head up and studied the shadows, but he was alone. Coldness like a fist clutched at his heart while invisible, icy fingers caressed his face. He closed his eyes and saw Nesrelle's glittering blue eyes staring back at him, gloating and greedy. *I can already taste your death,* she continued, her words echoing in his mind. *Don't you feel the way I've claimed you?* The cold feeling grew, spreading throughout his limbs and making him shiver. *You're mine. I'm coming for you.*

CHAPTER TWENTY-ONE

WITH A MOCKING SMILE, KARYE insisted that for the time being, we were royal guests, her possible future allies, and so she commanded some of her slaves to escort us to the guest quarters.

But only after her Dragon Keepers searched us. They took us to a small, windowless space off the throne room, its stone walls dismal and dark but for the few torches lining them. There they stripped us of our stolen dragon scale armor and inspected us for weapons. When they found the nestred knife I'd tucked into my boot, they laughed at me. Before they shuffled us from the room, they gave us plain linen shifts to cover our undergarments, though they left little to the imagination. It was humiliating the way they sneered and taunted us, their eyes lingering on every one of our scars as if they were signs of weakness.

Three slaves, all younger than my friends and I, were waiting outside when we exited. The Dragon Keepers shoved us toward them.

"If you let them get away from you," one of the male Dragon Keepers said, his tone grating against my ears as he stared down at one of the trembling slave girls, "I'll gut you slowly, so you can study your own insides as you die."

Choking back a whimper, the girl nodded, and the slaves led us swiftly away. Inwardly, I seethed. *Disgusting, cruel, arrogant monsters*, I thought, wishing I could put them all in their place so they could never threaten another child again.

Though we'd been treated more like prisoners than guests, our quarters were indeed within the palace and not the dungeon. All three were on an upper level overlooking a courtyard, with mine between Gillen's and Narek's rooms. Guards were posted along the hall, making it clear that we were just prisoners in luxurious cells. I traded glances with Gillen and Narek as the slaves separated and led us each to our own rooms. Would the guards let me out to speak with them later, or would they keep us apart?

When I entered, I found my bedroom was spacious, with windowed doors opening onto a balcony, an enormous bed, and an adjoining washroom. All of the walls were decorated in colorful scenes depicting Alrenian history: the Life-Giver blessing an Alrenian emperor and empress; Toryn, Misrothian, and Forwyn leaders kneeling in submission before an Alrenian emperor; the Dragon Keepers and Alrenian soldiers training; and illustrations of some of the Alrenian temples and the gifted performing impressive feats.

An ornately carved wardrobe, already filled with Alrenian clothes, stood in a corner. On the opposite side of the room sat a side table, where another slave girl was setting out a tray of food. I glanced over my shoulder and realized the one who'd led me to my rooms had already departed, silent as a shadow.

Consumed as I was with worry, I was surprised when my stomach growled at the smell of food. "Thank you," I said.

The girl started, her head jerking up, her deep brown eyes wide with fear. Just as quickly, she dropped her gaze to the floor and tucked her hands into the folds of her oversized linen dress. It was stained and patched, the frayed hem trailing on the floor. Her too-thin body trembled in my presence as she bowed her shorn head and muttered words I couldn't catch. She couldn't have been much younger than me, although it was hard to guess her age when she was skinny as a knife-blade and frightened as a young child.

"I didn't mean to scare you," I continued uncertainly.

But the girl was already darting toward the door. For the briefest instant, as she pulled it open, she looked back over her shoulder. This time, the fear had melted from her face. In its place was a mingling expression of determination and hatred so intense that it took my breath away. And then she was gone, swift as a fleeing rabbit, and I wondered if I'd imagined her look. Did she hate me along with the Alrenians, since I was apparently a guest here, surrounded by Alrenor's finest luxuries? If only she knew the truth.

I turned back to the tray. My stomach growled again at the sight of freshly sliced oranges, cheese and crackers, chilled shrimp, salmon flavored with lemon and butter, and a salad of greens, tomatoes, and olives. Another plate held a selection of pastries and miniature cakes. A steaming pot of tea sat beside jars of cream and sugar. Filling an empty plate with food and making myself a cup of tea, I sat in a cushioned chair on the balcony as I ate and thought. Despite my hunger, knots of fear formed in my stomach, and every bite of the fine food tasted like dirt in my mouth.

Considering how to demand a meeting with Karye and convince her to spare Jennah and Avrik, I decided to bathe and change. After all, half of politics was ruled by appearance. If I could cut a more imposing figure, perhaps I could influence Karye more than I had earlier. Selecting a green linen dress with a gold sash and a pair of leather sandals from the wardrobe, I turned to the washroom. There I experienced the wonder of Alrenor's indoor plumbing again, only needing to turn a spout to fill the tub with freshly heated water. I scrubbed the filth from my skin and cleaned my hair before dressing.

Pulling my wet hair back into a knot, I drew a deep breath. It was infuriating to be this close to my friends and yet feel so helpless. But I vowed that I'd find a way, even if I had to sneak like a thief through the palace and break down the bars to my friends' cells with my bare hands. I would *not* let my vision of Avrik's and Jennah's deaths become reality. I refused to lose them again.

A knock sounded at my door, interrupting my thoughts.

"Come in," I said, and the door swung inward.

Narek and Gillen entered together, both clean, freshly shaved, and in new clothes. Face a rigid mask, Narek immediately crossed to my balcony, checking the doors were closed and secure. My cousin, meanwhile, seated himself beside me on my bed. Gillen's blond hair hung in wet strands to his shoulders and his eyes were bright and clear. Shadows still lent them a troubled look, but otherwise, he was almost himself. He wore a white and gold linen shirt and blue trousers.

His eyes swept the room with a half-smile. "I remember reading about the luxuries of Alrenor, but I never thought I'd experience them." The muscles in his jaw tensed as his smile fell. "No wonder the empire was so hated, taxing the conquered kingdoms nearly to starvation while the Alrenians lived so comfortably."

"I take it your rooms are as fine as mine?" I asked, my eyes darting over to where Narek stood, silent and frowning.

Gillen nodded absently.

"I'm guessing you've been thinking of a plan to help them already?" Narek asked, and I nodded.

Gillen turned to me. "Who are they? The ones Karye has sentenced to death?"

I swallowed. "Friends," I said in a tight voice. "They came to Toryn to help us rescue you."

"I'm so sorry," he said, pulling me into an embrace.

I leaned my head on his shoulder, relishing the familiar comfort of my cousin's presence. His *true* presence, fully here and in the moment. "They won't die," I said firmly. "Somehow, I'll stop her. When she summons us to announce their sentencing, I'll find a way to convince her."

When I sat back up, Gillen's smile was bright and hopeful. "I don't doubt it. That is why you'll make a good queen. You were brilliant out there. That was some quick thinking, cousin."

I drew a deep breath. "But in case I can't change her mind, we need another plan."

Together, the three of us swapped ideas, from how we could possibly threaten Karye into releasing our friends, to how we could slip past the guards posted outside our rooms and break Jennah and Avrik free. Perhaps with Narek's war gift, we could steal some of the guards' weapons and turn enough of them against one another to break past them and into the dungeons. But just as before, it would be getting *out* of the palace that would be the problem. Once a fight broke out, the noise would be heard by anyone passing.

I turned to Gillen. "Narek and I will stay behind to fight and hold off the guards, and you will take the keys and sneak inside. Try them all—do whatever you can to slip in and out as fast as possible."

Narek leaned back. "It's a plan where many things could go wrong, just like before," he said with a wry grin, "but I think we're experts in disaster now, aren't we?"

I huffed out a nervous laugh. "Yes, I suppose we are."

Narek's eyes darted to the eastern sky, still velvet-dark and glistening with stars. Dawn was hours away. "And now we wait for her summons."

Nodding, I murmured, "Now we wait."

Gillen shifted beside me. "It's courageous, even if I hate our backup plan," he said with a short laugh. "But I know I'm not as trustworthy in a fight, so I'll leave it to you brave warriors."

"I'm not as brave as you think," I said, my cheeks warming with shame. I could feel my heart thundering in my chest as I forced myself to keep speaking, to say the words that would show my cousin what a coward I'd been. How all his suffering was my fault. I felt the weight of Gillen's and Narek's eyes, heavy and piercing. "Gil, I—I ran away. The night of your father's funeral…I learned that my father had killed yours so he could be crowned regent. He ordered Narek to execute me, but I survived."

I shot Narek a glance to see he was staring down at his boots, cringing.

"I survived *thanks* to him, but I didn't know it at the time." I drew a deep breath and went on. "Instead of doing something, of telling everyone what a monster my father was, of helping you…I kept running. I left you and Aunt Velaire and my mother behind."

Gillen nodded. "I knew you were in danger, even when I didn't always understand why or from what. I… I called out to you. Or I tried to."

"What do you mean?"

He shook his head and shrugged. "At first I thought I was only having nightmares. They were vague and unclear, but always gave me this urgent sense that you were in danger and you needed to know you couldn't give up. The first time, I pled for your life and begged that you would hear my words. I didn't say anything all that important," he said with a sheepish laugh. "It was something simple, like *Don't give up…*"

I remembered the Alrenian closing in around me, my lungs burning as I kicked and struggled. Darkness. Terror. And then powerful words, seemingly voiceless, coming from somewhere outside of myself. "*You can do this,*" I finished for him in a whisper.

I remembered how encouraging words had come to me again when my father tried to execute me before a crowd of people and I'd finally used my gift to speak against him. And then a third time, other words had come to me when I'd first ventured into the nightmare that was Toryn, until they faded away, as if losing strength, and I no longer heard them again. All along, it had been my cousin, speaking to me across the distance, helping me when I needed it the most. Until the nestrae had pulled him too deeply into their darkness and he hadn't been able to reach out to me anymore.

"You…heard me?" Gillen asked, blinking in surprise.

"Yes," I said. "You helped me more than once, when I thought I was going to die."

Gillen brightened visibly. "The Life-Giver spoke to me once in Toryn," he said. "He was *there*, right in front of me! Can you believe it?"

I laughed, feeling the lightest I had in far too long. "Yes! He's spoken to me too."

"He told me I have a gift for intercession," Gillen continued. "I suppose he meant I could intercede for you in those moments. I'm not sure exactly everything I can do." He glanced at me expectantly, and I relayed what the Life-Giver had told me about my gift and how he'd encouraged me to finally wield it against my father.

"But this doesn't change what I did," I finished, when our excitement had finally waned, and I could turn the conversation back to how it had begun. "I didn't just run. I stayed away…for *years*, living in hiding even though I knew you and Aunt Velaire were…were with *him*."

"Lia…" Gillen began gently, but I interrupted him.

"Don't you see?" I asked, my voice shaking. "Everything that has happened to you…it's my fault. He wouldn't have sent you to Toryn if I'd gone back sooner. The nestrae wouldn't have…" The words drifted away from me, too bitter to say. I covered my face with my hands.

Gillen's hand on my shoulder was gentle, his voice soft. "It's not your fault. Your father's crimes aren't yours."

I pulled my hands back to study his face. There was nothing in his expression but love and comfort. As if *I* needed comforting when he was the one living in constant torment from the nestrae. The rune on my lower back burned. *Condemned,* I thought.

Gillen shook his head. "The only one to blame is Zarev himself. And the nestrae." He turned to me. "I forgive you, Lia," he said firmly. "And I love you. None of that will change, and it doesn't change how brave you were to stand against your father or to help Misroth. Or to go into Toryn with a man who once tried to kill you in order to save me." He hesitated, grinning slowly at Narek. "But can you explain why exactly you're our friend now?"

Laughing with Narek, I went back to the beginning, giving Gillen a short version of everything that had happened since that fateful night

I'd discovered the truth about my father—from my time in Evren to meeting the rebels in Misroth City, to our journey through Toryn and our time in Calidar, and finally the moment I'd realized Narek truly was on our side.

When I'd finished, Gillen smiled at me. "Everything you've faced to save Misroth and me proves you can rule. If I can't overcome this…" He paused, shaking his head as if he could just as easily toss the haunting nestred voices away. "I know Misroth will be safe in your hands."

Before I could say anything more, there was another knock on my door.

Two guards, a man and woman, stood outside. "Princess," the man said, his lips twisting into a mocking smirk. "Empress Karye said her royal guests should have a chance to say goodbye to her prisoners. If you would like, we'll lead you to them."

My blood boiled. Karye was reminding me that I was at her beck and call, and that I couldn't hold any threats over her head, not when she was about to murder my friends and take whatever she wanted from Narek.

It was easy to play the part of an angry royal who thought she truly was a guest and not a pampered prisoner. I barged through my doorway, pushing past him and the woman at his side. "If she wants an alliance," I snapped, "she'll reconsider what she's doing. Those prisoners are *my* people. You will take me to Karye immediately." I leveled a glare at him. Behind me, Narek and Gillen stood in the doorway, watching the proceedings with dark expressions.

The guards appeared unmoved. "The empress has retired to her chambers and will not see anyone she does not call for, princess," the woman said. My title sounded like a threat in her mouth. "She has generously given you a chance to say goodbye to her prisoners."

I crossed my arms over my chest. "*If* she wants an alliance—"

"They slew our people," the guard cut in. Her sharp tone reminded me that I commanded no respect from her, that she didn't view me as a superior in any way. "The empress said you might protest, but she assured me that, though you are a *guest* for now among us, you too have our blood on your hands. What they did—and what *you* did— are crimes punishable by death in the empire. You can come with me and say your goodbyes, or I can take you, your captain, and your king to your own cells."

I bit my tongue, reining in my frustration. *There's still time,* I told myself. *If she wasn't considering what we can do for her, we would be in her dungeon already.*

"I will come with you," I said in a low voice. I glanced back at Gillen and Narek. "Will you?" I asked.

Gillen shook his head. "They're your friends," he said quietly. "I think you need this time with them alone."

I almost asked Narek before remembering that Avrik and Jennah didn't know how he'd helped me. To them, he was still more of an enemy than an ally. When I looked at him, I could tell he was thinking the same thing.

"This is for you," he said.

"Lead the way," I told the guards.

The woman gestured down the hall. "You will see the prisoners one at a time, for a few minutes each."

They turned without another word, expecting me to follow. The palace was dim and quiet. Torches cast huge, dancing shadows along the walls, making the Alrenian paintings look eerily alive. Statues stood half in shadow and half in garish light. We passed only a few other guards on patrol. Otherwise, the halls were empty and quiet. At one point, we encountered a noble couple whispering in a shadowed alcove, and they turned pointed stares in my direction, their gold-flecked eyes burning with unmasked contempt.

At last, we stepped into a courtyard bordered by palms and flowers. A fountain carved into the shape of a white dragon, mouth open in a fierce roar, rested in its center. Surrounding the perimeter, guards stood straight-backed and still beneath the trees as they studied a solitary figure seated at the fountain. Starlight caught the burnished gold glistening in her dark skin, and my heart soared at the sight of my friend.

The guards leading me halted in the entrance to the courtyard, letting me run ahead. As soon as I closed the distance between us, Jennah rose and we threw our arms around each other. A strangled cry erupted from her throat.

"I was so afraid you were dead," I said. "It's so good to see you."

She smelled like fresh soap and citrus and her curls were damp, as if she had just bathed. Her dress was clearly Alrenian, pale violet with a plain white sash cinched at her waist. The empress was either making a show of treating her prisoners well, or she was planning something.

When Jennah pulled away, tears glistened in her eyes, making the gold flecks shine brighter, but her smile was as fierce as I remembered. "I could say the same of you," she said softly, squeezing my shoulders tightly. "We didn't know what to think when we found out the barrier was gone."

Shame unfurled in my stomach and I dropped my gaze. "Narek and I tried to save you, but the nestrae overwhelmed us. They—they tricked me into revealing how to break the barrier."

"You and Narek?" Jennah asked, a frown furrowing her brow. "I saw him with you, and…your cousin? Is King Gillen alive?"

I nodded, my throat tight with emotion. "Alive, but suffering from the nestrae's influence," I said softly.

Jennah hesitated, her voice low. She had to already suspect my answer. "Where is Layk?"

I shook my head, tears welling in my eyes.

She sat back down on the bench with a thud and dropped her face into her trembling hands. "May the Life-Giver carry him into peace," she whispered. "What will we tell his siblings?"

Wrapping my arms tightly about myself, I shook my head again, too overcome for words. Sharing the news was like losing Layk all over again. The grief felt sharp and new. Two of our friends had given their lives, and for what? To save not only their king, but their kingdom. And now Misroth was being invaded by demons and their king, though free in body, was still enslaved by them.

Jennah lifted her face, her tears making the scar on her cheek glitter, as if it were a mark of beauty rather than a reminder of pain. "The nestrae are invading Misroth, but I'm sure you already know. It's a long story, but after Avrik and I escaped the nestrae, we came ashore in Alrenor and were captured."

Before I could respond, two guards strode out from the shadows. "Your time is up," one growled, yanking Jennah away from me.

"Wait, Jennah—" I called, but the guards were already dragging her up the steps, back into the palace. Two more were leading another figure out into the courtyard.

Avrik.

Just like Jennah, he'd had an opportunity to clean up and change. He was clean-shaven and his unruly hair was trimmed and washed. His clothes were Alrenian: brown pants and a loose white shirt beneath a black and gold vest. Again, I wondered what Karye was planning.

Even when the guards released him, Avrik stood uncertainly, frozen in place. It was strange to see my confident friend at a loss. It was stranger still to stand only a few yards apart and yet feel as if a hundred miles stretched between us.

Words from out last conversation fluttered in my head like panicked birds, trapped and lost. *Elena was everything to me*, Avrik had said in Calidar, right before the nestrae invaded. *But now you are Halia…I don't know who to be around you anymore.*

Avrik approached slowly, hesitantly. I could tell by the way he searched my face that he was trying to read me, and I knew I wasn't making it easy for him. "When I said I was a fool, I meant it."

"You're not going to die," I blurted out, "so don't start talking like you will."

"I appreciate your confidence in my ability to not die," he said, a small, uncertain smile playing on his lips.

I hated how awkward things were between us. Our hasty apologies back in Toryn hadn't been enough, not when things had been so complicated and we'd been so unsure. But as much as I wanted to mend the rift now, I had to make sure Avrik would live another day first.

I bridged the gap between us in a few quick strides. With a sharp intake of breath, his gaze snapped back to me. His eyes looked darker than usual in the torchlight.

"Having her prisoners cleaned and dressed up before their execution? There's a reason she chose to do that," I said, lowering my voice.

A mischievous grin darted across his face, just for an instant. "Oh, there's a reason…"

"*Avrik.*"

Face hardening, he stopped.

Regret tasted bitter in my mouth. I knew his jokes were his effort at normalcy, his way to push aside his fear and pain. They were his mask as surely as my stony expressions were.

When he looked at me, I felt like he could see straight through me, yet somehow still missed what I longed for him to see. How could someone know my thoughts so well, yet miss my feelings?

"I'll demand to see Karye again," I went on, injecting confidence I didn't quite feel into my tone. "She's agreed to keep us as guests, which means she must be considering an alliance. I'll threaten to revoke the offer I made to her if…"

"You don't need to worry," Avrik said quietly, leaning closer to avoid the guards overhearing. So close, I wondered if he could hear my pounding heart. "Remember how the Life-Giver saved you when…back in Evren?" He stumbled over his words, the memory of how his father had left me to die still painfully vivid for both of us. "Well, he came to see me tonight."

I couldn't keep my surprise from showing on my face. It wasn't that I'd thought the Life-Giver only spoke to me—or had I?—but simply the fact that I hadn't heard from him in so long. Not even when I'd begged for help at the Aremakkin Temple.

"We have a plan," Avrik continued, talking fast. "He told me—"

"Time's up," a guard snapped, stalking toward us.

"Halia—" Avrik said, reaching for me.

Panic seized me as I tried to grab for him. Why hadn't I flung myself into his arms as soon as I'd seen him? Why hadn't I told him how I felt, or that I forgave him? What if this was the last time I saw him?

"One more minute!" I demanded, but the guards were already wrenching us apart. When we struggled, two men dragged me back while two others hauled Avrik up the steps, back toward the palace.

"Avrik!" I cried as he vanished into the shadows.

"You'll see him again soon enough," one of the guards said in my ear, his voice a vicious taunt.

Soon. For his execution.

CHAPTER TWENTY-TWO

I STORMED AHEAD OF THE guards, straight toward Narek's chambers, and pounded on his door. Both the man and woman trailing me and the guards posted in the hall studied me closely but didn't say a word.

When Narek opened his door, I didn't waste time. "Come with me. Now."

I spun on my heel to find the guards barring our path. "Take us to your empress," I demanded.

"The empress will see you when she calls for you," the female guard ground out, her hand on her sword.

Narek didn't hesitate. In a heartbeat, the second guard's sword was out and pointed at the woman's face. All around us, the other guards drew weapons, prepared to strike, but the woman didn't move. She merely raised her eyebrows in surprise. "So it *is* true. You're war-gifted." She studied Narek in fascination, a grudging respect in her gaze. "Fine, I'll take you to Karye."

The other guards shot looks in her direction, but she seemed confident in her choice.

She and the male guard at her side led us on a winding path through the palace until we once again entered the throne room. Apparently Karye hadn't retired to her rooms after all. Starlight shimmering through the glass ceiling bathed the space in a silver glow, but shadows cast by flickering torches filled the edges of the room. Karye was leaning against a column a few yards away from her throne, studying Narek and me intently as we entered. Beside her stood Vionn in his ivory cloak, hood still raised despite the warmth.

The guards bowed their heads as they pushed Narek and me to our knees.

"What are they doing here?" Karye snapped.

"Your Majesty," the female guard said, her tone demure. "The princess and her captain threatened the guards in the hall, and I didn't think you would want them to make a scene with his war gift."

The empress pondered this for a moment before nodding. "You're dismissed," she said with a careless wave of her hand.

The guards filed out, leaving Narek and me kneeling on the cold floor. Grinding my teeth to keep myself from blurting out something foolish, I lifted my face to stare back at Karye. She grinned at me.

"Stand," she said.

"If you want any hope of an alliance between our kingdoms, I think you know how foolish it would be to kill our friends," I said, letting my glare do the rest of the threatening.

Instead of responding to what I'd said, Karye smiled. "I still haven't decided if I want to accept your offer, Princess," she said smugly, stalking closer to me. "You're at my mercy, so you can threaten to revoke your offer all you want, but you have nothing else to bargain your way out of my empire and back to your kingdom."

I kept my face stony.

"You also murdered and impersonated some of my elite Dragon Keepers," she went on, "which, as you know, is punishable by death. The very fact that I'm even offering you a place in my palace and an ear to your requests shows how merciful I can be."

"They attacked us," I said, my voice steel. "It was defense."

Drawing a dagger, Karye stared at me, her gaze unfathomable and cold. "I hold a hundred threats over you, and you hold none over me."

I nodded at Narek. "I think we *do* hold a threat over you," I said, and though a cold chill washed through me, I continued, my voice harsh. "With only you and your advisor here against my war-gifted friend and me? You would be dead before you could cry for help."

Though he kept his expression masked, I noticed the way Narek's jaw tensed. *You are more like your father than you think*, he'd once told me, and now, suddenly, I believed it more than ever. Here I was, willing to use a friend as a pawn in a political game.

"Release our friends," I snapped.

Karye moved so quickly, I blinked in surprise. One instant she was near her throne, and the next she was leering over me, a blade to my throat. Narek tensed, and the next moment, Karye's limbs relaxed and her blade lowered. A vein throbbed at her temple as she dragged her furious gaze toward Narek.

"You're quick with your gift," she said to him with a sharp smile, but at a single gesture from her, half a dozen guards emerged from the shadows, their blades pointed toward us.

Karye twirled her dagger in her hand, studying us carefully. "It seems you are once again outnumbered." She waved her hand, as if gesturing to the citizens of Inalgoth spread out in their homes beneath the palace. "But I'll have you know that I *am* considering your offer. I care about my people, or at least the ones who matter, the ones who do not commit crimes against the throne, who are loyal to the empire." She drew a second dagger, swinging them both almost absentmindedly. "And because I care, I will *not* simply pardon your friends who slew my people in cold blood. You should consider it enough that I'm not imprisoning you two and your king for what you've done. *That* is my offer. Once your friends have served their sentence, we'll discuss the terms of an alliance further." Her eyes darted back to Narek. "And I'll decide if it's best for my people."

Vionn stepped forward, his face still concealed by his hood. "Don't try to trick us, either. I've seen the way you try to plan and save your friends, even now. But I also see your desperation to return to

Misroth. Know you never will if you go against the empress in this." This time, I could hear the smile growing in his voice as he drew nearer to me, close enough that I could feel his breath, a sickly-sweet stench of rot and blood. Yet I still couldn't see his face. "I know everything about you, Halia of Misroth," he said, his voice a low hiss. "I've seen the guilt you carry, the blood of your own people running from your hands. You are the reason the nestrae threaten your kingdom."

My heart pounded wildly, drowning out the sounds around me: the sputter of flame, the whisper of Vionn's cloak along the marble floor as he moved even closer. *Condemned,* the nestred voices hissed in my ear. My gaze flitted to the shadows in the room, half-expecting to see their hulking forms shrouded in the darkness, their claws gleaming in the torchlight. Beneath the Alrenian dress I wore, the nestred rune on my lower back burned as if the wound were fresh again.

Fight back, a sharp voice sounded in my ears. It wasn't like the voiceless thoughts from Gillen that had once spurred me on and kept me fighting when I'd been on the verge of death. This I recognized as my own thought—and yet, strangely enough, it came in my father's voice. His guilty blood ran in my veins, but he *had* passed on things of value to me: his determination and strength.

Straightening my spine, I narrowed my eyes at Vionn and seized his arm.

Though my ability to see visions had been stolen, taking them from another was as simple to me now as it had been when Meli had taught us. Shocked as he was, Vionn didn't even try to resist me, and so, fueled by my determination and churning emotions, I stole truth from him effortlessly. Closing my eyes, I saw the Life-Giver approaching a former emperor in this very throne room. The emperor hunkered down in his throne, his aged face twisted in fear. The Life-Giver's own face was lined with grief, but his eyes were dark with fury.

"I told you not to shed innocent blood," the Life-Giver said. "Not to enslave the Forwyn, my people. Day and night, I hear their screams echoing in my ears." His eyes narrowed, a fire flaring deep in his gaze, like a living light, immeasurably dangerous and deadly. *"I feel their pain. And I am weary of walking them into the afterworld before their rightful times have come."*

"I—I—" the emperor stammered.

The Life-Giver raised his hands, his cloak rippling about him. "You have abused the blessing I bestowed on you, and so now you and your empire will suffer my curse. No more will an Alrenian be gifted in war, courage, or protection."

I blinked and a new vision rose before my eyes. Vionn was hunched in his own quarters, staring out his window as the first light of dawn bathed Inalgoth in a warm glow.

"You were gifted to share the truth. *All* of the truth." This time I didn't see the Life-Giver in my vision, and I wasn't sure if he was even physically in the room. But his voice was, speaking for Vionn to hear. Vionn shuddered at the Life-Giver's anger, and the room seemed to quake. "My people scream for mercy, for deliverance, but you refuse to speak. The truths you hold back from the empress will eat away at you. They will be your end."

Only a moment had passed, but everything I'd seen gave me courage. As Meli had claimed, no one in Alrenor would have a gift like Narek did, which meant it truly did pose a threat. It really was something for Karye to covet. And Vionn, it seemed, was a weak coward. I opened my eyes and sneered. "You call yourself truth-gifted," I spat at Vionn, "but you are spineless." I snapped my gaze to Karye, then back to him. "You let your empress use you for her purposes. You hold back the truth."

Gasping, Vionn jerked back as if burned.

I spun to face the empress. "I'm not afraid of you," I said, my brain working furiously to think of another way out of this mess. It was true I couldn't afford to be trapped here, but I couldn't let Avrik and Jennah die. Avrik might have said he and the Life-Giver had a plan, but my anxious heart couldn't simply trust in that. I needed to know that I could keep them safe.

"Is that true?" With a slow smile, Karye beckoned to someone standing in the shadows—a slave boy I hadn't seen earlier. Cowering, he moved toward the empress noiselessly. He dipped his head and bowed low before her, but I didn't miss his quaking knees.

Karye moved slowly, gracefully. She reached out as if to caress the boy's face. Placing a gentle hand beneath his chin, she lifted his head to meet her eyes.

It was his strangled, choking sound that gave it away first—then I caught the glint of her dagger and the stream of blood. He teetered, grasping at his bleeding throat helplessly, but with a look of disgust, she kicked him to the floor. His body landed with a thud, where he writhed, gurgled, and stilled.

My body shook with horror and rage. "You're a monster!" I cried, lunging for the empress, but Narek was at my side, holding me back.

Wiping her bloody dagger on her dress, Karye sneered at me. "The Forwyn are *nothing*, princess. Disposable. Unworthy. Unholy. Most worship a false god. Some claim to believe in the Life-Giver, but they're blasphemers and say he appeared to them as a *Forwyn* man."

"He *is*—" I began, but she cut me off.

"Silence, you Teramese-eyed *kowra*!" she snapped. I didn't need to know that Alrenian word to guess its meaning. Her gold-flecked eyes gleamed in the torchlight with a fanatical light. "*Alrenians* are the Blessed. *We* are the Gifted, the Chosen. We are the glorious citizens of the Land of the Sun, the Bearers of his Strength." She pointed a finger at me. "And *you* Misrothians are impostors. You have an Alrenian truth gift? You don't even know how to use it to its full power. You know *nothing* about me, and I know *everything* about you." She gestured to the Forwyn boy's body, sprawled in his own blood on the throne room floor. "You are as significant to me as this slave was. You are *nothing*. Do you know why I'm keeping you alive? Why I haven't laughed in your face over your little alliance proposal and tossed you as food to my dragons?" Her grin was cruel. Wicked. "Because my people and me—we haven't seen any foreigners in hundreds of years. And it's a fun little game, seeing how pathetic the Misrothian rebels still are."

Narek's hands on my arms tightened, as if he too were struggling to hold himself back from this madwoman.

"I'm also keeping you alive," she went on, slowly, her voice lower and more composed, "because at least one of you has a gift that is rightfully Alrenian." Her eyes flicked to Narek. "And because you, princess, are a descendant of the traitor Eldon, who wielded one of the most powerful gifts known to Alrenor." She leveled a stare at me. "I am going to ensure none of you Misrothians ever erect a barrier again. And," she added, smirking, "I *do* have an offer for you." She stepped closer. "I'll agree to send help to your desperate, falling little kingdom, if you and your mad king submit your throne to *me*." She tapped her dagger casually against her leg. "Oh," she continued, as if she had just remembered something. As if none of this had been carefully premediated. "If you agree to this, *then* I might even reconsider your friends' sentence."

"That will never happen," I said, keeping my voice measured. This woman had to have a weakness, and I *had* to find it. "Misroth will never bow to Alrenor again."

She laughed. "You have seen that I *can* be merciful. I'm willing to help your pathetic kingdom and save your people's lives. I'm willing to let you and your companions stay as welcomed guests in my palace rather than as prisoners in my dungeons. And today, I will be giving your friends a chance to live."

I narrowed my eyes at her, and she laughed again.

"There will be a game," she said simply. "If your friends are as strong and worthy as you seem to think, they will prove it." She shrugged carelessly. "Maybe they'll survive even without your help."

She spun on her heel, Vionn flanking her. As guards stepped forward to lead Narek and me away, the empress's retreating voice rang in my ears.

"It's nearly dawn," she called. "My guards will escort you to our arena. Meanwhile, I hope you reconsider. Your kingdom is running out of time, and you know it. I know you've seen it."

211

CHAPTER TWENTY-THREE

Avrik

DESPITE THE GUARDS GRIPPING HIS arms, Avrik felt momentarily free. Standing on a rocky outcropping overlooking Inalgoth, he watched miniature shopkeepers trudge through the streets, vendors push their carts toward the marketplace, and slaves creep warily past patrol guards. Wind ruffled through his hair and brushed his face like a caress. From here he could see the Great Sea glittering beneath the rising sun, its foaming waves tinged pink and gold, while toward the west, the darker waters of the Alrenian were still plunged in shadow.

The guards holding his arms tugged him back, toward the flat expanse of rock that extended out from the dragons' cavern. Beyond this expanse, which Avrik had quickly learned was an arena of sorts, was a steep rock wall leading to the final peak of the cliff. Stone seats had been carved into the wall in rows, the top seats nearly reaching the rocky peak. In the lowest row of seats, closest to the arena, Alrenian nobles, guards, and Dragon Keepers clustered around the empress.

Avrik caught the empress's gaze and refused to flinch, despite the cold interest he found reflected in her blue eyes. Her yellow hair flashed in the rising sun and flew like a banner behind her, this time loose and long, making her look deceptively youthful and innocent.

When he closed his eyes, he could see Nesrelle staring back at him in triumph. He could hear her voice echoing in his mind: *You are mine.* Another icy chill swept through his body and made his heart skip a beat; for a moment, he felt his hands tremble and his knees weaken.

Then the moment passed. He opened his eyes and tried to ignore the cold. His strength returned to him.

"We can do this." Jennah's voice was steady. She laid a warm hand on his shoulder, and when he glanced back, she was smiling. Unafraid. Perhaps there was even a glimmer of excitement in her brown and gold eyes.

Avrik grinned back at her, even as he wondered if she could feel how cold he was. When she looked into his face, could she tell that the Queen of Death had claimed him?

Jennah laid a hand over her heart. "We are the Dragon-Hearted," she whispered, and for a moment her gaze held a faraway look as she remembered the words of her lost friend.

Not trusting himself to speak, Avrik nodded and pressed a fist to his own heart.

"Good luck," their guards sneered. Sunlight glinting off their armor, they stepped back and left Jennah and Avrik standing alone in the middle of the arena, facing the Dragon Keep.

For what felt like the hundredth time, Avrik turned to scan the gathering crowd. There were guards leading a dazed-looking Crown Prince Gillen to a seat near the empress. Not far away, Narek sat, flanked by two guards of his own. His face was grim, his posture rigid, and Avrik couldn't help but wonder if the man would secretly be glad to see him and Jennah die today. And then at last he saw her: surrounded by a crowd of Alrenian nobles who studied her with blatant looks of disgust and contempt, Halia stood tall and proud, refusing to sit. She tossed the Alrenians cool glances, making it clear their attitude unfazed her.

Avrik's breath caught in his chest. She was royal through-and-through. It should have been obvious to him from the beginning, he thought. Even in Evren, she'd always been poised and graceful in a way none of the other girls had been—even when she'd competed with him in archery or raced him across the open fields and hills. It wasn't all that surprising, in the end, when he'd learned she was the missing princess. But now, with her voice returned and new confidence and strength radiating from her, she looked queenly.

As if feeling his stare, she turned toward him, and their gazes met. Her eyes were like emeralds in the morning light, her face composed, even when he was sure she was raging and worried on the inside. As much of a mystery as she was sometimes, he could still read the thoughts she shared with him, just like when they were friends in Evren. Just like then, she could speak to him without a word. *Don't you dare die,* her expression said.

He grinned back at her. *Die?* his smile said. *I wouldn't dare go against your command.*

All the same, he wondered what she was feeling beneath the calm mask she wore. Did her heart race the same way his did when she saw him? It hurt to look at her and think of all the time he'd wasted, of all the things he wouldn't be able to say and share with her if he didn't survive.

Curse you, Nesrelle, he thought. *I'm not ready to die.*

The empress and a man in an ivory cloak stepped forward, surrounded by guards with weapons drawn. Karye turned to the crowd, her voice echoing off the stone around her, making her words ring out loud and clear. "My people!" Her voice turned smug. "And my esteemed Misrothian guests."

Avrik rolled his eyes while beside him, Jennah snorted.

"I welcome you today to witness one of our most sacred traditions: a game of courage, strength, skill, and wit!"

The Alrenians cheered, noblemen and noblewomen alike standing from their seats to lift their hands and raise their voices. Some stomped and laughed cruelly. Others began chanting, "Death to the prisoners!" The chorus mingled with others, many shouted in Alrenian words, their meaning lost to Avrik, but their sounds as sharp as a sword's edge.

Empress Karye held up her hands for quiet and the crowd's roar died to a low murmur. Wind rustled through her hair and rippled through the folds of her shimmering gold gown. She still looked as deadly as ever, with weapons strapped at her sides and on her back and dragon scales adorning her shoulders, chest, and arms. She gestured toward Avrik and Jennah, and Avrik threw her a careless grin in response.

See how you like your own arrogance tossed back in your face, he thought.

"These Misrothian prisoners are convicted of slaying some of the brave men and women who protect us," Karye cried out, "our valiant guards, honored protectors of our people and our empire!"

The people erupted into angry shouts.

"But despite the horror of their crime," the empress continued, her voice instantly silencing her subjects, "they will taste my mercy today." She smirked, a slow, terrifyingly cruel expression. The Alrenians burst into laughter, and she paused to let them indulge.

Off in the crowd, Avrik spotted Halia clenching her jaw, unable to fully conceal her anger. Narek was at her side, reaching out to calm her. What had happened to make them so comfortable and familiar with each other? A jolt of envy shot through Avrik's chest.

The guards surrounding Karye lifted weapons for her to choose from. She took them one by one and tossed them to the arena floor. Gold swords and curved Alrenian daggers clattered to the ground with a bow and a quiver full of arrows. "I give them their choice of weapons and a chance to prove themselves against one of our royal dragons." Her eyes gleamed with bloodlust. "Choose!" she shouted.

Avrik sprang forward and claimed the bow and quiver, then a knife that he slid into his belt. Jennah chose two long, curved daggers, similar to the ones she'd brought with her into Toryn. The weight of the bow felt comforting in Avrik's hand. He could tell at once it was sturdy and simple, a well-made piece that was exactly his style. Hope burned inside him, more brightly than it had before. This felt like a true chance, one in which the odds weren't impossible. Let the Alrenians mock and laugh and gloat in all their dragons' power. Here, he was in his element at last.

Laughing, Empress Karye flung her arms wide, as if to embrace all her people. "You know how this goes. I'll leave you in suspense no longer. Jennah and Avrik of Misroth will face my own beloved dragon, Reyva. Let the games begin!" She stepped back and flung herself into her seat, fingers drumming impatiently on her thigh. *Entertain me*, the cruel glint in her eyes seemed to say.

The crowd laughed with her, but Avrik ignored it and spun way. He drew an arrow from his quiver while Jennah twirled the daggers in her hands. His body thrummed with adrenaline, excitement, and a rush of courage he knew Jennah must have been sharing with him. In his head, he could still hear Gare's deep, resonant voice relating a tale of Eldon's feats against Empress Ilett and her famed dragon Raklov. He pictured Gare's smile, his ever-steady confidence in Misroth's ability to triumph over its foes with its people's strength, courage, and free-spirited nature. *Dragon-Hearted,* he thought. *I am a soldier, and I have the heart of a dragon. You won't have me yet, Nesrelle.*

Then—movement at the opening of the Keep. The steady beat of heavy footsteps thundered through the air and rumbled the ground beneath Avrik's feet. First came two slaves, a young boy and girl who stumbled as they clung to the chains attached to a collar around a dragon's neck. In the early morning sun, its scales shone like burnished gold and deepest ebony, flashing so brightly that Avrik had to squint at its approach. Black eyes dark as bottomless pits scanned the arena and fell on him and Jennah—its prey.

The dragon sniffed deeply, smoke curling from its nostrils, and erupted from the cave. Avrik hadn't realized a creature so large could move that swiftly.

The Forwyn boy fell, only to be trampled beneath one of the dragon's feet. His body lay still and mangled, a gruesome sight that told Avrik instantly he was dead. Trembling and shrieking in anger, the other slave, a young girl, released her chain and flew back toward the boy.

Her keening wail was the last sound Avrik heard before the dragon launched itself at Jennah and him, its fangs dripping saliva. Avrik dove and rolled away, scattering a few of his arrows across the arena floor. Just as he lifted his face to look, a blast of heat bloomed across the space where he'd stood only seconds before. Snarling, the dragon tossed its head and turned.

Again, it possessed speed and agility Avrik hadn't anticipated. But he had quick reflexes, borne from his years of trying to best Halia and the dark days in which he'd faced the sedwa of Evren Forest alone. He nocked an arrow and shot at the dragon's mouth mid-snarl. The creature snapped the arrow in half mid-air and lunged at Avrik. Thick fangs that made the ichgor's teeth look small snapped at his face.

Jennah used the dragon's distraction to make her move, shoving one of her daggers into its side, her blade sliding between its scales. The creature grunted and spun for her, forcing Avrik to stumble backward before its swinging tail could topple him.

Snorting smoke, the beast darted toward Jennah. Avrik nocked another arrow and closed in on it from behind. He crouched low, scanning its belly, finding row upon row of shimmering gold and black scales.

Find the weak spots, he told himself.

A few drops of blood from the wound Jennah had inflicted dripped to the ground, leaving a small trail, but it did nothing to slow the dragon down. To the creature, it was only a scratch. An irritation to anger it, not weaken it. Avrik needed to find a soft patch of flesh over a vital organ or artery.

Steel flashed as Jennah struck again, but this time, there was a clank of metal on metal as her blades bounced off the beast's scales. Unfazed, she darted back, her face confident, her lithe body poised and graceful, even in the violence of a fight.

The crowd was shouting and jeering, eager for the dragon to burn them to a crisp or draw blood. Avrik could smell their bloodlust like the acrid cloud of smoke lingering in the air from the dragon. He could see a shadowy shape at the corner of his vision, standing at the edge of the arena, beckoning him closer. Could feel death calling to him.

He shook his head. No, he must be losing his mind. When he glanced toward where he thought the shape had been, it was gone.

With a roar, the dragon unleashed another burst of flame, a tongue of fire lashing out in the blink of an eye, flying straight toward Jennah. Horror clawed up Avrik's throat. But Jennah was already tumbling away. The flames licked at the air harmlessly. Behind him, the crowd screamed its frustration and rage.

But Jennah had leapt back too far. Daggers flying from her hands, she landed with a hard thud and skidded across the smooth surface of the arena, sliding toward the edge. Her hands scrabbled for a hold, anything to stop her momentum. Avrik had a mere instant to catch his breath—to shout in vain, as if his cry could save her—before she disappeared over the cliff.

The roar from the crowd almost drowned out the ringing in his ears.

No! Not here, not now, he thought. Not another friend lost. Not another life gone. A chill swept through his body, like a winter storm bent on destruction. Cold claws grasped for his heart. Even with his eyes open, he could see Nesrelle's taunting face, her shining, too-beautiful eyes.

With a shout of fury, he strung another arrow and launched himself toward the dragon, diving beneath its belly and aiming for a soft patch of flesh where he imagined its heart should be. He landed on his back, rocks digging into his spine as he slid underneath the beast. Sweat stung his eyes and another chill made him shudder. He drew a breath and steadied his aim. *Later, witch,* he thought viciously at Nesrelle. *Your time with me will come later.*

His reflexes were as swift as a battle-hardened soldier, yet the dragon was faster. Sensing him beneath it, it turned to dart away as

Avrik released the bowstring. The arrow that would have flown true bounced harmlessly off scales and clattered to the ground. Avrik had just enough time to roll away before one of the dragon's clawed feet crashed down inches from where his head had been.

He yanked himself to his feet and the dragon whirled on him. For a long moment, they stared at each other, its black eyes like windows into a void. His hand shook as he reached for another arrow, but for the sake of the Alrenians watching him—and even, if he would admit it to himself—for the sake of Halia—he forced himself to smile.

Don't be afraid, his mother had murmured to him countless times as she'd faded away. She'd brush a lock of hair from his forehead and smile at him, despite the fear and pain in her eyes. Even as a child, he could tell something was terribly wrong, and that his mother was tremendously brave and strong. *Make fear afraid of you.*

A hush descended over the spectators, as if everyone held their breath. He was tempted to scan the crowd for Halia again, to meet her eyes. One last look, just in case. But he didn't dare lose his focus now.

"Is this it?" he shouted instead. His voice echoed off the rock, loud enough for all to hear. He laughed, and was relieved when it didn't come out forced. "This is your deadliest dragon?"

"You fool," Karye snarled, "you're staring your death in the face."

"I've already stared my death in the face," Avrik muttered.

The crowd drowned out his words, but it didn't matter. They shouted in their merchant tongue so Avrik could understand their words. Mingling with the thunder of their stomping feet and clapping hands, their voices rose as one in a raucous chant: "Death, death, death, death!"

A cool breeze ruffled through his hair and dried the sweat on the back of his neck. He could feel that icy hand reaching again, like the Queen of Death was toying with him, reminding him that his time was near and he had no control over when or how it would arrive. This time, he couldn't fool himself—he was shaken.

In his mind, he was a child again, reaching for his mother's cold, trembling hand as she lay back in bed. Shadows pooled beneath her eyes and wrinkles crinkled at the corners of her mouth. Her thinning hair clung, limp and damp, to her wan face. And yet still she smiled. Still she worried only for Father and him. "I will be all right, my dear one," she said, her voice raspy and thin. Like her once-rich, glossy brown hair. Like her now reed-thin body. "And so will you and Father."

Mother glanced out the window, where thick clouds threatened more rain. It had been many long days since they'd been graced with sunshine. Earlier, young Avrik had pouted, longing to play outside, tired of days trapped indoors while a cool wind blew and cooler rain pelted against the windows. That was before his mother had took a turn for the worse and stayed abed, scarcely strong enough to sit up against the pillows. Now playing didn't matter. His books about heroes—legendary and real—and his daydreams of being a soldier didn't matter. Nothing did anymore. "Don't fret for the sun," she whispered, just as she'd told him many times over this cold, wet spring. It was her way of reminding him the sun would always shine again. But that time, even his young mind understood she meant something more than the actual sun.

Now, smoke curled from the dragon's nostrils as it paced toward him. Maybe it was taking its time. Maybe it liked to play cruel games like its mistress.

He aimed for one of the empty black eyes and waited for the beast to come nearer. "Death has come for me many times," he said, his voice lost in the crowd's chant. But he wasn't speaking to them, not now. He was speaking to Nesrelle, the Goddess of Death who was waiting, biding her time. "Every time, I will always hold my ground."

Avrik shot the same instant the dragon unleashed another blast of fire. He threw himself to the arena floor, feeling the heat of the flames narrowly miss him. Arrows clattered from his quiver and he lost his grip on the bow as he rolled away.

Panting, he pulled himself back into a crouch, scanning the arena for his weapon. Tendrils of smoke curled away from the dragon's nostrils and rose from the spot where Avrik had been. Sweat collected on Avrik's brow and his lungs burned from the sickly-sweet scent. He caught sight of his bow several feet away, but the dragon was already lunging for him, fangs bared in a snarl. And the bow was in its path.

Avrik tensed his muscles, his mind screaming at him to remember everything he'd ever studied or practiced. Unbidden, a memory came to him of his father, teaching him to hunt.

Never be a fool about a hunt, he'd said from where he sat beside Avrik in the boughs of a tree in Evren Forest. *Never let yourself become the prey.*

But Kyrin was the one who'd made the entire town of Evren prey to the bloodthirsty sedwa. *Too late, Father,* he thought.

The dragon crushed the bow beneath one of its enormous clawed feet. It was time to do something completely mad.

Drawing a deep breath, Avrik drew his knife and lunged for the dragon, meeting it halfway. The Alrenians were roaring, their screams of *Death!* and *Slay the vesda!* so loud they drowned out the sound of Avrik's pulse pounding in his own ears. He didn't know what *vesda* meant, but the snarling way the Alrenians shouted the word made him assume it was some type of curse. Somewhere in the tumult, he thought Halia was calling out to him, but maybe it was only his imagination. *What are you doing?* her voice demanded.

He noticed a form at the edge of the arena, this time familiar and welcome. Jennah. There was just enough time for him to feel relieved before he came face to face with the dragon. Before it could attack, he dodged and leapt for its foreleg, clinging to it like it was one of the trees in Evren Forest he'd scaled countless times during the hunt. The beast snarled and tried to shake him off, but Avrik slammed his blade between two scales, plunging it hilt-deep so that he could hold on. He nearly lost his grip, until the dragon stopped shaking. Instead it turned its head toward him, snapping its fangs. But Avrik was already climbing again, clenching the knife between his teeth while hot blood dripped from the blade and onto his shirt.

When Avrik reached the dragon's neck, he plunged the blade in deep again, and the dragon roared. Avrik's arms trembled from the effort it took to grasp the dragon while it writhed under him, furious and desperate to throw him off. Sweat burned his eyes. He was vaguely aware of Jennah on the arena floor, dancing around the dragon's legs while she unleashed her own onslaught.

Avrik inched his way forward, toward one of the dragon's eyes. A coppery taste filled his mouth—at some point, he must have bitten his tongue. Smoke seethed from the dragon's nostrils, burning his throat and filling his mouth with the overpowering scent of flame and ash.

Panic seized him. The dragon was going to strike again, and this time, Jennah was too close to its mouth. There would be no chance for her to dodge out of the way, no miraculous survival. The Alrenians' chant thundered in his chest like a war drum, or like a battering ram bent on shattering his heart.

He didn't hesitate. Releasing his hold, he fell to the arena floor, knife flying from his hand and leaving a trail of blood on the ground. His hands and legs took the brunt of the fall, slamming into rock with a thud that made his arms ache.

Blinding light and searing heat blasted toward him, but he'd already spun and thrown his hands up. As if he could block the flames bursting from the dragon's maw with the sheer force of his will. As if his hands could command time to spin backward and give them a few extra precious moments to dart out of the way.

But the flames didn't touch him or Jennah. Staring between his shaking hands, he watched the fire lick at the air and then fall short, instead turning and curling about Jennah and him as if the flames had touched an invisible wall, one that encircled them and forced the danger away. He could feel the heat scorching the air in front of him, but only in a distant way. It couldn't touch him, couldn't hurt him, not through the wall that protected them.

As the flames died away and the dragon snarled its rage, quiet descended upon the crowd. There were no more screams for death.

No more shouts filled of victory and bloodlust.

One amazed thought consumed everything else: *The Life-Giver was right*. Avrik had barely dared to believe the man's words when he'd visited him in the dungeons the night before. But here was the proof.

He didn't lower his hands, instead staring in awe at the dragon. The creature, eyes dark and dangerous, stared back at him. It lowered its head and didn't even try to attack again, as if it could sense the power radiating from him and knew it didn't stand a chance against Avrik. Not now.

At last, Karye's voice rang out. "Take my dragon away." Her voice was low, without a hint of emotion. Heart pounding in his throat, Avrik didn't remove his eyes from her dragon. "The game has ended. Return home. I will speak with these Misrothians in my palace, alone."

CHAPTER TWENTY-FOUR

Y OU'VE KEPT ONE FASCINATING SECRET from us," Empress Karye snapped, as soon as the door had enclosed us in a small, private courtyard surrounded by the high walls of the palace. Even the guards had been ordered to stand watch outside, to be near only if they were needed and to keep prying eyes and listening ears away. Through the windows of the palace's upper levels, I caught glimpses of other guards on patrol, ensuring none of the servants or slaves could stare down at us through the glass.

Narek and Gillen flanked me, both hovering close as if I were the one who needed protection, as if I were the one under scrutiny. In the middle of the courtyard, where a fountain shaped like a dragon and its Keeper mid-flight bubbled cheerfully, Jennah stood with her arms crossed, glaring back at the empress and her truth-gifted advisor. She was bleeding from a cut on her forehead, but otherwise appeared unscathed.

At Jennah's side, Avrik kept a cocky grin plastered on his face. His hair was disheveled, his clothes covered in dust and dragon blood. He was unharmed and confident in the face of the Alrenian empress's rage, and I couldn't help the warmth that flooded me to see my old friend, so much like himself again.

And yet…also not. There was something different about him, something that was difficult to place. His aura radiated strength and power. Even his boyish charm, the dimple in his cheek and the light in his warm brown eyes, seemed fiercer somehow—if charm could be fierce. His smile was more like a weapon.

When I looked at him, I didn't only see Avrik. I was reminded of visions I'd had in the past of King Eldon, kneeling on the earth and pleading to the Life-Giver. I saw him defending his armies with a mere gesture, throwing up invisible barriers of protection. I saw him subduing Empress Ilett's dragon Raklov and turning the tides of the war, shaping the history of Misroth as a people dedicated to their freedom and brazen enough to stare an empire of dragons in the face and not turn away in fear. Those stories recalled to mind what had just happened in the arena, only minutes before, when Avrik had stared back at Karye's dragon and it had bowed its head before him. As if it, too, could feel the power radiating from him.

Avrik had the gift of protection, a gift so rare that the only other person in history recorded as possessing it was Eldon himself.

A gift that the Life-Giver had, according to the vision I'd stolen from Vionn, taken away from Alrenor.

I couldn't help but stare in wonder at Avrik as a hundred thoughts churned through my head. Had he known? And for how long? Had this been the plan he'd spoken of last night, the information the Life-Giver had shared with him?

I'd always known my friend was talented at swordplay and archery, but now I wondered if part of his talent, part of his ability to survive also had to do with his gift. It would explain how he'd lived while slaying the sedwa when he'd wandered Evren Forest alone, or how he'd managed to stay alive when thrown unarmed into the vilspen's pit, before I could help him. If only he'd been with me when the nestrae had tricked me into breaking the barrier. If only we'd *known*.

"Well?" Karye demanded. She spun toward her advisor. "How did we not know about this?"

Despite the warmth of the day, growing hotter by the moment as the sun climbed, Vionn was still draped in his ivory cloak, his hood concealing his face. He watched his empress pace back and forth while he sat at the fountain, gloved hands folded in his lap. Considering that he had failed to see Avrik's gift in any of his visions, he seemed remarkably calm. Did he know that the murderous gleam in his empress's eyes was directed only toward the foreigners, because he— a truth-gifted man who wouldn't share any truths she didn't want to hear—was too valuable to lose?

"My gift doesn't show me everything," Vionn said, shrugging carelessly. "Besides, Your Majesty, you must remember that once we learned about the Misrothians in our empire, you wanted me to focus on calling visions about the royal family or the war-gifted Toryn." His eyes darted to Gillen, Narek, and me.

Karye paused mid-pacing, her face scrunched up in anger. Even with her cheeks pink with rage, she was beautiful. Beautiful and cold and cruel. Just like her empire. She spun on Avrik.

"Fine," she said. "I see the game you're playing at." Her gaze flicked to me, her blue eyes dark with malice, the gold in them shimmering like flames. "You've let me think you're powerless, and then you play your hand." She smirked. "But you are still desperate, in the end. You still need my help to save Misroth."

Avrik didn't move, and I didn't respond. Better for her to imagine this had been my plan all along.

Karye paused, seeming to consider Avrik. "I confess I wouldn't be opposed to a marriage alliance, even to a Misrothian commoner like you. But it needn't be marriage. All you need to do is surrender your gift to me and stay in Alrenor." She reached out her hand to touch his cheek, and he stiffened and pulled back. Her eyes flickered with anger that she quickly masked with another smile.

"You're a fool, Karye," Avrik said. He stared into her face, unafraid of her power.

She stiffened when he addressed her by name, but she didn't retaliate. In a courtyard full of royalty, it was clear now who truly held the most power. In this way, I agreed with Avrik's father: he'd always been too good for a simple life in Evren. He'd always been meant for more.

"You know that with the gift of Eldon, I can rebuild the barrier," Avrik continued. "Your kingdom might have survived all these years on its own, but what are you without contact with the rest of the world? What is Alrenor without someone to conquer, without someone to recognize your glory? You and your so-called empire are *nothing*."

"And your kingdom will never survive without my help," Karye retorted. "Vionn has seen what the nestrae can do. What they have *already* done to your capital city. The torment they inflict, the destruction they have wrought. Nesrelle is growing stronger by the moment as she feeds off her victims in Misroth City. The nestrae may not have killed anyone yet or shown themselves, but they already own your capital. They control your people through fear, and soon enough they'll start sacrificing them."

A chill ran through me. I knew what she spoke of, for I'd seen the visions too. Misroth was running out of time.

Nearby, Jennah and Gillen were unable to hide their worry. Narek simply looked weary, probably already feeling the weight of watching another kingdom fall to his enemies. Another horrifying war, already lost from the start.

But I was angry.

"Your arrogance will be your downfall, Karye," I said. "What they do to us, they will do to you next. They've already ravaged Toryn; you're all that is left untouched on this continent. And any barrier Avrik placed around Alrenor wouldn't keep them out. It would trap you and your people in their hell. Do you think your powerful warriors and your dragons can really stop a demon army and the Queen of Death herself?"

Before Karye could speak, I shot her my most chilling smile, because I knew what she cared for most. What had truly frightened her last time we'd spoken about the nestrae. "What will it be like when you hear your daughter screaming for mercy when they torture her? When they bleed her of pain until she is so empty there is nothing left but a hollow, hopeless carcass to offer on their pyres?"

Karye's face darkened. "That will never happen. Alrenor will not fall. We are the Chosen Ones." She paused, thinking. "I will give you time to reconsider my offer, before it is gone for good. An alliance to save your people wouldn't be the worst fate, now, would it?" She studied Avrik carefully. "For now, you will *all* be my honored guests, and I will continue to show you my hospitality." She smiled, but it was unsettling. "But don't try my patience, or I'll find bloodier methods to subdue your power, and any hope for your kingdom will be lost. We could be married in a week's time, or I could make you an official advisor, and you could be living in luxury, resting easy knowing your kingdom would soon be safe. I'd send troops to help stop the nestrae in Misroth" –her eyes flicked to Narek– "and of course in return, I'd expect help from the Misrothian war-gifted whenever Alrenor needed it."

Avrik laughed, harsh and mocking. His smile had turned hard. "Yes, you would. And I'm sure I'd live in plenty of luxury indeed."

"Maybe I should just kill your friends to make you cooperate," Karye sneered.

Behind her, Vionn shifted on the bench uncomfortably, as if he wanted to say something but feared to do so.

Avrik wasn't fazed. "I can create a barrier around Alrenor in mere seconds. If you try to harm any of my friends, if you try to touch me, I won't hesitate. I'll use my power to protect us and then rebuild the barrier you hated so much." He shrugged. "Then you'll be trapped again, and all you'll ever be is the Empress of Nothing. What's the great Alrenian Empire with only slaves to rule over? What will Alrenor be like when the nestrae invade and there's nowhere left for you and your people to hide?"

Her eyes glittered with malice. "Your kingdom will die without mine. I can be patient. I know who will give in first."

Karye waved at Vionn. "Fetch the guards, tell them to lead all of our guests to their rooms. Tell them to keep careful watch over them. We wouldn't want anything to happen to them while they're here." She smirked. "Oh, and inform the servants we're having a ball in several days' time. We'll let the people meet our honored guests and give them a formal introduction. Maybe," she finished significantly, her eyes running over Avrik again, "we will have an announcement to make about a new alliance between Alrenor and Misroth by then."

The guards showed Jennah and Avrik to rooms close to my quarters. Apparently, the empress didn't feel threatened by the idea of her "guests" being near to one another or meeting together. I didn't linger long in my own room, and the guards didn't stop me this time when I stepped into the hall.

My heart pounded in my ears as I knocked on Avrik's door.

He swung it open immediately, still covered in dragon's blood, hair disheveled from the fight. As soon as he saw me, he grinned, the dimple in his cheek showing. Why did my breath always catch when he looked at me like that?

"Halia," he said, stepping back to let me enter and then shutting the door behind him.

Once again, he'd used my real name. Not *Your Majesty* or *Elena*, just Halia. No formality to ignore the familiarity of our past, and no false name to ignore who I truly was now. I couldn't deny the way it warmed me.

I strode toward the open doors leading to his balcony, overlooking the same courtyard as mine, and shut them. I didn't want to risk being overheard. "We need a plan," I said, trying to keep my voice level and full of business. "Agreeing to Karye's terms is unacceptable, but we need to get out of here. And I won't deny that Alrenian help would give us a better chance to defeat the nestrae."

When I turned back to him, his face was solemn. "Are you sure?"

He glanced down at his hands, as if his own gift shocked him as much as everyone else. "If this gift threatens Karye this much, maybe we can save Misroth on our own. I can hardly believe it," he added in a low voice, as if to himself.

"How long have you…known?" It was hard to look at him when I asked. Maybe I felt like a hypocrite for being hurt that he hadn't shared about his gift with me, when I had spent years hiding so much about myself from him.

"I hadn't. Not until last night."

"What?" I turned to see him looking thoughtfully out at the courtyard, where a few birds were flitting among the trees.

"The Life-Giver told me," he said, meeting my gaze. His eyes were wide, still full of wonder. "I'd fallen asleep in my cell, when he…showed up. Maybe it was a dream, I don't know, but he told me about my gift." He shrugged. "I still don't fully understand how to use it. I lied to Karye about being able to create a huge barrier. I haven't the faintest idea how that works."

I hated myself for the envy that jolted through me at the thought of the Giver of Life visiting Avrik. Why hadn't he visited me? It was difficult to feel ignored, especially now, when I needed his help so much.

"Karye knows the threat you pose, and only wants to use your gift for her own gain. If she married you or appointed you as a member of her court—it doesn't matter which—she could find ways to force you to use your gift for her, or even to surrender it completely to her." I closed my eyes, remembering what Meli had shared about gifts being stolen by others or even surrendered willingly. Avrik didn't know all these details about his gift, but the empress certainly did. "Agreeing to her terms would never help Misroth. We have to threaten her, force her hand. All she cares about is herself and her own power. And her daughter," I added. "But all that matters is that we give her a convincing threat, one that she will have to take seriously. We're running out of time. The nestrae said they would start killing

Misrothians on my birthday. Until then, they're torturing them with visions and feeding on their fear."

Avrik ran his hands through his hair. "Halia, I—I don't even know how I stopped the dragon's attack today." He glanced down at the blood staining his shirt.

"But you seemed so confident during the fight," I said, unable to hide my surprise. "How did you face the dragon like that if you didn't know what to do? When you could have died?"

Avrik's eyes met mine, and a shadow passed across his face. Almost as soon as it had appeared, it was gone, as if I'd only imagined it. "He told me I'd know what to do when the time came."

I nodded slowly. "It can't be a coincidence he gave you the same power that Eldon had. It's something you've had for years, maybe all of your life, but he would have known you'd need it eventually, when our kingdom went to war."

I'd expected excitement from Avrik—confident, adventure-loving Avrik, who had spent his childhood daydreaming of being a soldier, of facing impossible odds and saving his people. Of slaying dragons and defeating armies. But instead, he frowned. There was still an aura of power radiating from him, but it couldn't conceal his doubt—or the obvious weight in the slump of his shoulders.

"This power is like a horrible joke, Halia," he said, his voice low and broken.

Maybe we were finally crossing the divide between us, or maybe it was just old habit. Either way, it felt natural to cross the room and reach for him. It felt natural for him to take my hands in his and lean closer to me, until I could smell the dragon smoke lingering on his clothes. For a moment, his skin felt unusually cool against mine, but then, as if my touch helped warm him, I didn't notice it anymore.

"What do you mean?" I asked.

He stared down at our joined hands, hesitating. "I've failed to protect so many people, even the ones I care about the most," he said at last. "I abandoned you when you needed me, and…you almost died." His voice came out thick and hoarse. "I heard the stories about how your father tried to have you executed. And who did I leave you for? My *traitorous* father, who thought he was justified in trading the lives of the people in Evren for *me*, so I could live in comfort and safety away from a fictitious war. But—" he laughed mirthlessly. "That's not even the worst part. I left you only to realize too late what he was. Then I turned my back on him and failed to protect him too." His voice trembled. "No matter what he'd done, he was still my father, and some part of me wonders—wonders if I should have given him another chance. Saved him from death. Helped him make amends. Mother would have wanted…" His voice trailed off.

"Avrik," I interrupted, "I'm so sor—"

"I turned my back on him," Avrik pressed on, "because I failed to save *her*." His voice was a whisper now. "Because he let *her* die. I'd been too concerned with finding a way to save him to be there to protect her…"

A cold feeling clawed up my throat, and I had a feeling the hollow, haunted look in Avrik's face all those weeks in Toryn, the weight that crushed him, had a lot to do with this. A secret he had carried with him all this time, tucking it away from me when the rift between us had been greatest.

"Who?" I asked, terrified of the answer.

"Elysse," he whispered. "She's dead, Halia. A sedwa killed her outside her own house."

Bren's little sister. His best friend's little sister. For a moment, I couldn't breathe, couldn't think. Over my years in Evren, I'd spent most of my time with Avrik and his friends: Bren, Shilam, and Jaren. We'd shot together, ridden together, explored everything the village and surrounding countryside had to offer. We'd spent many days at one another's homes, eating dinner with each other's families or helping with chores. Bren had been a kind, protective older brother to his three sisters, but Elysse had been the baby of the family. When I'd left Evren, she'd been only eight years old, rosy-cheeked and with hair the color of sunshine. I'd watched Bren tickle and tease her, teach her to dance and, when she was little, help her as she learned to read. For him to lose her…

I squeezed my eyes shut. Death followed me everywhere these days, but it was especially terrible to think of its callous fingers stretching out and seizing quiet, peaceful Evren.

"Oh, Avrik," I whispered, because I couldn't find any other words to speak. My throat ached with unshed tears. His guilt had to be unbearable, even though, ultimately, it wasn't his fault. I understood what it was like to feel the blood your father had shed, staining your own hands.

He dropped my hands and pulled back. "If I can't even save the ones closest to me," he asked, his voice ragged, his eyes shining with tears, "how can I save an entire kingdom? I'm no protector."

"We'll come up with a plan," I said quickly. I sighed, rubbing a weary hand across my face. "I didn't mean to make it sound as if…as if it is all up to you."

Avrik watched me closely, his gaze soft and sympathetic, his eyes warm and kind. Just as I remembered. "It shouldn't be all up to you either. Princess or not, you shouldn't have to be alone."

Before I could respond, he dropped to his knees like a soldier pledging himself to his queen. "I once said I'd help you for Misroth's sake," he said, his expression earnest. The dragon blood on his shirt hadn't quite dried yet, and his eyes still shone with tears he refused to cry. "I know I've failed you in many ways, but I want you to know— for whatever it's worth—you have my loyalty, if you'll accept it. For *your* sake. I'll serve you until my last breath. I'll use my gift in your name, for Misroth."

His sincerity startled me, warming me to my core. Even if I wished he wouldn't be so formal, I knew this wasn't a vow he'd make lightly. "I'm—not queen. Yet," I said.

"But you might be," Avrik said quietly, and I wondered what he knew about Gillen. Had the Life-Giver told Avrik about Gillen's state and the fact that I might become queen?

With a shake of my head, I swallowed back my grief and doubt and managed a smile. "Stand up, Avrik. I don't need a soldier pledging his service to me. I need a friend."

Standing, he nodded, his eyes wide at that word. *Friend.* Who would have ever thought, back when we'd been inseparable in Evren, that that word would have been so startling to hear spoken between us?

As if thinking the same thing, he asked, "Do you ever wish we could just turn back time, back to Evren when everything was simpler?"

I frowned at the empty hearth, thinking of the ache in my heart for all I'd lost. My home with Lyanna and Rev, my simple, quiet life. The ease of my friendship with Avrik. But everything had been a farce, hadn't it? I'd squelched my power to the point of repressing my own voice, and I'd hidden like a coward while guilt and fear ate away at me.

"Not really," I said.

Avrik smiled, but it wasn't sad. "I knew you'd say that, no matter how much making the choice you did has cost you. If you were the type of person to say anything else, I don't think I would—" He caught himself and stopped suddenly. He studied my face closely, as if searching for something, an answer to an unspoken question. "I don't think I deserve your forgiveness," he said at last in a low voice. "When I said we couldn't be friends, it was in many ways because of that. And because I wanted someone to be angry at for my father's death and betrayal, and I foolishly thought I should be angry at you. Deep down, it was me I was truly angry with. I was so ashamed that I'd let you down…" His voice faded away. "But I want to earn your forgiveness. I'll spend…as long as it takes, however long it takes, to do so." His eyes were so intense my heart skipped a beat.

"You don't need to earn it," I said, shaking my head. "You already have it."

Despite the tears he had to blink away, despite the weight still clearly holding him down, his smile was beautiful and familiar. I hadn't understood just how much I'd missed it until that moment. Drawing me to him, his embrace almost crushed me, pressing my nose against his shirt that reeked of smoke and blood. But I didn't mind. His heartbeat was strong and steady beneath my palm.

"I've missed you," he said, his whisper soft yet fierce. "More than you could ever know."

When I returned to my quarters, the same slave girl who'd been there the day before had returned, bearing more food. As I entered, I noticed she was humming softly to herself as she arranged the tray on the table, but as soon as she heard me step inside, she stiffened and stopped.

Not wanting to scare her, I closed the door softly and then waited to step further into the room. "Thank you," I said.

Her brow furrowed, dark eyes darting to me uncertainly and then away again. They still smoldered with anger, and I couldn't blame her.

I waited a beat before speaking again. "What's your name? Do you…speak the New Language?"

The girl stared down at the table. She picked up a spoon and dipped it into the sugar bowl, then shuffled a napkin. Without meeting my eyes, she murmured, "Lo'laeni Nolanhou, *melhona*." Then she straightened her shoulders and lifted her chin, shooting me a dark look. "My family called me Lo. When I *had* family. And when I had a family, I was taught Alrenian, the merchant tongue—or your New Language, as you call it—*and* Forwyn. I am not an idiot."

"I didn't mean to imply you were," I answered carefully, feeling both encouraged and wary of her change in confidence.

She watched me carefully before demanding, "Why are the Misrothians here? What do you want in Alrenor, *melhona?*"

"To find a way to save my people from war." Cautiously, I shifted toward the table and began loading a plate with food and picking up my silverware. When she turned her back to pick up her empty tray, I tucked the steak knife into the sash at my waist until it was concealed beneath the folds of fabric.

"Maybe war is what your people deserve," Lo said darkly. When she tossed a glance over her shoulder, I took note of how proud and graceful she could be, when she wasn't hunched and cowering in obedience. She radiated strength, fueled by hatred that simmered in her eyes. How much of her fear was real, and how much was an act?

"I'd never been outside the borders of my kingdom until this year," I mused, "and so it wasn't until now that I've realized that everyone else seems to hate Misroth as much as they hate Alrenor."

Lo's gaze spat fire. "When your people rose up to free themselves from Alrenor, they only thought of themselves. They left my people behind. All the stories we share tell us that it became much worse for us after the barrier was formed. Alrenor had no one else to torment but the slaves left in their kingdom." She swallowed, her only sign of pain. Her voice remained steady, unwavering. "I blame Misroth for my brother's death, just as much as I blame Empress Karye."

Before I could say more, she stormed past me, the empty tray gripped in white-knuckled fingers. She slipped soundlessly out of my room, leaving me to stare at my door.

CHAPTER TWENTY-FIVE

Avrik

NESRELLE, QUEEN OF DEATH, WAS in Avrik's room, lounging by the fire and watching him sleep. She tossed an orange between her hands and smiled to herself.

Avrik sat up in bed, cold sweat beading on his forehead, his pulse pounding in his throat. He didn't know how long she'd been there before her presence finally startled him out of sleep. The idea of her sitting there, watching him breathe, biding her time, made his skin crawl.

"I can see why you charm so many girls," Nesrelle said, unfolding herself from the armchair and gathering her wispy, midnight blue skirts. They rustled as she released them and glided barefoot across the floor. Pausing at the foot of his bed, she cocked her head to the side, studying him as she peeled the orange with her long fingernails. The tangy, sweet scent of the fruit saturated the room.

"What do you want?" Avrik demanded, his voice rusty from sleep. After bathing, he'd fallen asleep in a pair of linen pants left in his bedroom wardrobe, and while he wasn't normally self-conscious, having his scarred chest bared before Nesrelle left him feeling vulnerable. Violated. Each mark, from the nestred rune marring his arm to the old burns puckering his skin, was a reminder of all her servants had done to him. A reminder of their whispered words in his ears. *Powerless.* As her piercing blue eyes slid over his form, he frowned.

Nesrelle laughed lightly, tossing pieces of orange peel to the floor. "I meant that you charm girls with more than the handsome package you come in, boy. You're full of strength and power, hope and...*life.* You want to experience every bit of life fully. Taste it all." She bit into the orange and juice dribbled down her bottom lip. "It's impressive to find someone as full of vitality as you are, even when you're haunted by death." She sighed breathily. "Your mother, your father, your friend's young sister..."

Quicker than he could blink, she darted to the head of the bed and laid a cold hand on his cheek.

The images were as vivid and sharp as if he were reliving the moments. His mother's soft voice lifted in a lullaby, but her voice cracked and trembled on the notes.

When shadows grow and the sun won't shine,
Place your weary head near mine...

She was weakening, her hands cold and shaky as she held him close, and even six-year-old Avrik knew everything was very, very wrong. He could taste the tears streaming down his face, salty and bitter. The room was dark and cold with the approaching night.

To Avrik, that night had been both endless and over in the blink of an eye, with his mother rocking in her bed and holding him, her arms comforting even as they weakened and struggled to keep him close. He was old enough that being held and sung to like that at any other time might have been embarrassing, but not then, not with his mother so sick. Not when he could feel Death lurking in the shadows. Father, weary from tending to Mother, had fallen asleep slumped in a chair by the bed, and Mother had told Avrik not to worry, not to wake him. Maybe she'd already said her goodbyes.

When stars fall and the mountains quake,
I'll hold your heart so it won't break...

Hours passed with Mother singing. Then whispering. Then simply holding him. He cried softly against her chest, not wanting to believe she was ill, that she was wasting away.

But finally, his tears dried. His mother had fallen asleep, and he was weary enough to want to curl up beside her. Pressing close against her side, he didn't wonder why she was so still, her skin even greyer and cooler than before.

In the morning, when he and his father awoke, he knew the truth: his mother was gone.

The vision only took moments to pass through his mind, but it left him breathless. He jerked back from Nesrelle's touch.

"How terrible to grow up with such heavy memories," Nesrelle said, her voice almost sympathetic sounding. "You were so young. Too young to be ashamed of your tears, as you are now."

Avrik blinked his burning eyes as his throat ached with grief. He wiped a hasty hand across his face, brushing away the tears before they could fall.

Nesrelle's face was solemn. "Her death was terrible. She was so ill, in so much pain, but all she ever did was worry about you. She poured the last of her energy into you…for what? So she could feel pain and misery in her last moments, while you felt a shred of comfort?"

Avrik's fury rose, twisting with guilt. He knew now the things his mother had sacrificed for his father and him during her long, wasting illness. The way she'd concealed her pain or pushed through it to tend to them and their grief. She'd never given into despair, so that she could fight off the demons that haunted her husband and son. But he'd been young and ignorant then, not knowing who else to lean on for comfort and hope. His father had been too consumed with his own sorrow to comfort Avrik the way he'd needed, and it was not until a long while after Mother had passed, taking her light and strength from them, that they had found how they could lean upon and strengthen one another.

His mother's final moments haunted Avrik all the time, visiting him in his nightmares with fresh grief and despair whenever he thought he had finally begun to push the memories back. Just when it seemed he would never lose himself to that darkness again, it returned in all its strength, surrounding him in its murky embrace. But those final moments of hers *were* over—however much he relived them, they held no more power over his mother. Deep down, Avrik knew she had passed on into the afterlife, that somewhere her soul was at peace.

It was time for his haunting memories of those moments to pass on too.

Avrik met Nesrelle's gaze steadfastly. "She's no longer living in those moments of pain," he said fiercely. "And neither am I."

Nesrelle shrugged, tossed the remnants of her orange over her shoulder, and clapped her hands on his shoulders. They were like icicles searing against his bare skin. And then—pain.

It struck him like a battering ram and sizzled through him like a bolt of lightning. Every ounce of his blood was on fire; every inch of his skin seemed pierced by daggers. His heart thundered in his chest and then slowed, slowed, slowed… Blackness seeped into his vision until he was lost in unending darkness and pain.

After the nestrae's torture, Avrik knew from experience not to give Nesrelle the satisfaction of crying out. He bit down on his tongue, reopening the cut he'd inflicted during his fight with the dragon, and blood flooded his mouth. There was nothing but pain, until Avrik thought he would pass out. Until he wondered if this was how he was to die, alone in bed, cornered by a demon goddess.

Then Nesrelle pulled back, and the pain receded. Avrik's pulse rattled in his chest again, his strangled breath catching in his throat and shuddering back into his lungs. He spat blood onto the floor and glared at the creature before him, who now looked more demon than woman. Her long fingernails were curled and darkened like claws, her blue eyes were black, deep as pits, and her sneering face showed teeth that hadn't been that sharp earlier.

"I've seen your death," she hissed.

"I thought you were here to finish the job of killing me now,"

Avrik managed. Part of him wondered if he was a fool for taunting her, but he wasn't about to give in and let her see his fear.

Nesrelle shook her head. "Not yet." She smirked. "But your time will come soon enough."

Avrik thought of the way she'd taunted him in his mind, the chill that had been growing steadily inside his body. Had she made him ill somehow? Would he die like his mother?

"Not ill," Nesrelle said, shaking her head, and with a jolt Avrik remembered how the nestrae had seemed to be able to see into his mind, to discover his deepest fears and sorrows and use them against him. Their goddess must have been able to read his thoughts as well. "I've claimed you for death. My powers are draining your life, and your aura bears my mark. Only I can see it…but you can feel it. I will lead you to your death soon enough."

Avrik frowned at her. "The Life-Giver leads us to the afterlife."

"Ignorant fool," Nesrelle snarled. "You look to your precious god to give you life, but where is he now when you face death? Where was he when your dear mother suffered and died, and you and your father prayed every day, asking him to save her?"

Avrik swallowed, unable to answer her.

"Your time is almost up. You're mine. Keep living fully while you can, Avrik, because you're dying." Satisfied, Nesrelle smirked again, offered him a mock bow, and backed away. When he blinked again, she was gone.

But the cold in his blood had deepened.

CHAPTER TWENTY-SIX

A S USUAL, THE NESTRAE FILLED my sleep with nightmares. Plumes of smoke consumed the night air as the nestrae seated themselves near fires in their camp, unseen and unheard by anyone in Misroth City. Instead, the people were lost in nestred visions that twisted their normal, everyday lives.

In one home, a woman screamed for help as she scratched at her skin until it bled. "Get them out, get them *out*!" she shouted, but her children ignored her, crying and leaping from the dinner table to hide under it from the "monsters." Her husband slammed his dinner knife into the table and clapped his hands over his ears. "Stop!" he shrieked.

Everywhere, normal routines were interrupted in the city by chaos. If I hadn't known better, I would have thought my entire kingdom had gone mad. Men and women, family, neighbors, friends, and even children, threatened each other as if they thought their fellow citizens were enemies. In the streets, men and women alike brawled viciously with one another. They snarled like rabid animals, or sobbed and wailed in fear and loss, trapped in whatever horrors the nestrae were showing them.

In the castle, Velaire paced back and forth, reading and rereading my letter, tears collecting in her eyes. Later, I saw her standing before the Royal Council, waving the letter and speaking muffled words the nestrae vision didn't let me catch. The Councilors muttered amongst themselves before rising from their seats and gesturing emphatically, clearly arguing with my aunt.

Meanwhile, the nestrae dared to stretch their army, sending troops to the coastal city of Kelwed to torment its citizens. Others marched on Argelon, setting up another camp to ravage that city with nightmares and incapacitate the Misrothian soldiers who trained there.

Nesrelle strode barefoot outside the city walls of Misroth City, several nestrae flanking her. "You've done well," she told them, studying the city with a smug expression. Dark clouds swirled overhead, and I couldn't tell if the gathering storm was real or part of their illusions. Nesrelle licked her lips. "Their fear is intoxicating."

I woke with a start. *Forty-nine days until my birthday.*

The nestrae might not have started directly killing Misrothians yet, but they were compelling my people to kill each other. Sweat drenched my nightclothes and snaked down my spine.

We must *get out of here.*

I stared at the ceiling, watching the morning light pour gradually into the room until it bathed everything in a golden glow. My chest ached with longing to be back in Misroth. Even if my kingdom's victory against the demon army was doubtful, at least I could fight alongside my people.

The only way was forward. Alliance or not, my friends and I would force Karye to release us, or we would find a way to escape.

Lo would return to my room soon to lay out breakfast and make my bed. Slipping the steak knife I'd stolen last night from beneath my pillow, I carried it with me as I gathered an outfit from the wardrobe and drew a bath. I laid it carefully on the bench in the washroom and then set the dress I'd chosen to wear on top of it. It scarcely counted as a weapon, but its presence reassured me, making me feel a little less helpless.

I was nearly finished with my bath when Lo entered my room and set down the breakfast tray. Instead of going straight to making the bed, she entered the washroom, a pile of dresses in her arms.

Lo didn't make eye contact as she murmured, "The empress told me to bring fresh clothes, *melhona*."

I narrowed my eyes. "Why?"

Lo shrugged wordlessly and started to move toward the bench, where I'd laid the other dress I'd chosen.

Thinking of my hidden knife, I snatched my towel from the bench and stepped out of the bath. Too late.

Lo lifted the dress and stared down at the knife. Slowly, she raised her head to meet my gaze. Her eyes were wide and unblinking, filled with a mix of terror and curiosity.

"Weapons are forbidden," she said at last, her voice a hoarse whisper. I knew what she was wondering: Would I slit her throat, as Karye would have done, for discovering my secret?

I set my jaw. One hand clutching the towel I'd wrapped around my torso, I stepped forward, dripping water across the tile floor. "Do you think your empress will reward you if you give me away?" I demanded, making my voice harsh.

Before Lo could react, I picked up the knife and held it out between us. She jerked back fearfully, but she didn't retreat. I watched her throat work as she swallowed and considered her next move. The only sound in the room was the steady dripping of water still leaking from the bathtub spout.

"No," Lo snapped. "She killed my brother without a thought, without even knowing his name or his past or his dreams. She would just as soon slit my throat as thanks for anything I told her." She hesitated before repeating her question from yesterday. "*Why* are you here?" When she finally lifted her eyes from the knife between us, they were no longer full of fear. They were bright with rage.

"I told you," I said levelly, "to save my people. They've lost loved ones, just like you. And more are being threatened with loss, even as we speak. Demons are invading my land—and they won't stop with Misroth."

"You think Alrenor will help you?" Despite her earlier fear, Lo laughed.

It was difficult to feel intimidating in a bath towel, my hair dripping wet, my only weapon a steak knife. Still, I didn't lower the knife, not yet. "Right now, I'm a prisoner in Alrenor as much as you," I replied. "It's a long story, but yes, I know a true alliance is unlikely. My friends and I need to either force her to let us go or find a way to escape. Misroth is running out of time before the nestrae start slaughtering my people."

"Nestrae," Lo repeated in a whisper. "*Hilvoku.* I have heard stories of them. My people say the Wastelands were once occupied by a great people, even greedier than the Alrenians, who traveled the Great Sea far and wide until they encountered the *hilvoku* in a distant land. The people gave their allegiance to the demons, and in return, the demons annihilated them and their land so completely, the people and their kingdom have long been forgotten." Her eyes darted to the scars tracing my bare skin in understanding. "Alrenor *should* fear the *hilvoku* too, but they share the same pride of that nameless people." She gestured toward the knife. "I'll admit it seems like you know what you're doing, *melhona*, so I won't laugh at you for trying to use a steak knife as a weapon. Even if I don't think that's what will help you escape."

I smiled slowly. "You're right."

Lo nodded, her stance gradually relaxing. The fire in her eyes appeared less intense, perhaps at last directed at a new target. "I could help you," she offered after a long moment. She gestured toward the knife. "If you train me."

Slowly, I lowered my knife. "Train you? Help me?" After navigating politics in the Misrothian court, after battling Karye with words, I hadn't expected a Forwyn slave to leave me speechless. For that matter, I'd never expected to be threatening her with a steak knife while wrapped in a towel, either.

Lo spoke quickly and eagerly, like a child afraid a parent would disagree before she could finish her argument. "You want to help your people. I've lived here, in the palace, all my life, *melhona*. I tend the dragons in the Keep. I know things. I can help you and your friends escape. And you want to stop the nestrae, who would kill my people and me along with the Alrenians, without a thought." She drew a deep breath. "I need a way to defend myself here—to fight back. Maybe, eventually, even to help free my people."

I watched her uncertainly, thinking of others who'd wanted to help me in the past, and what it had cost them. Gare. Layk. Jennah and Avrik. But Lo was already facing danger and death every day simply by existing in a land that hated her, by serving a bloodthirsty woman. She could just as easily die for tripping in the throne room. This, at least, gave her a purpose and a chance to defend herself.

"All right," I said at last. "I'm better with a bow, but I can teach you some tricks to stay alive."

Lo flashed me a surprisingly warm smile. "If you can threaten me with a steak knife, I think you'll be able to teach me what I need to know." She straightened. "I need to go before someone wonders what's taking so long. I'll be back later."

As she slipped out of my chambers, I finished drying off and studied the dresses Lo had brought to me per Karye's request. Most were typical Alrenian dresses in bright colors, adorned with shimmering jewels. Clothes the empress no doubt would want me to wear to the ridiculous ball she'd planned. But one stood out from all the others. It was a soft shade of violet with a lower neckline than I'd ever have worn in Misroth. Where the back should have been, there were golden chains decorated with shimmering dragon scales in flashing shades of gold and ivory and violet.

Was this another twisted game? A challenge? If I arrived wearing Karye's revered dragon scales, I would be sending a message. That I defied their laws and customs? That I didn't fear them or the consequences of wearing these scales?

Perhaps Karye hadn't selected the dress at all, and Lo had snuck it in with the others in her own act of defiance.

I couldn't hold back my smile as I ran my fingers along the dress's fabric and imagined what Karye's expression would be if she saw me wearing Alrenian dragon scales.

Despite the warmth of the night air, I wrapped myself in a thin shawl I'd found in the wardrobe and stared out at the gold, silver-veined flowers blooming just beneath my balcony. I couldn't remember what they were called, but I did know Alrenor was famous for them, these flowers that only bloomed by moonlight and shone like they were made of real gold and silver. They were beautiful, but not beautiful enough to block out the horrors I'd seen in my nightmares. Every time I blinked, all I could see were the nestrae attacking my people.

The luxury around me was an insult. I wanted to scream.

All day I'd been trapped in my quarters, weighing what moves to make against Karye, and wondering how Lo planned to help. The guards posted in the hall outside my door hadn't let me go to my friends. Any time I'd tried to open the door, they'd drawn their weapons on me and told me to step back or die.

I tend to the dragons in the Keep, Lo had said. The thought made hope bloom in my chest, hope I almost didn't dare examine too closely. When she'd brought lunch, I'd given her a quick lesson in fighting stances and how to break free from different holds. The lesson filled me with nostalgia, for days under the open Evren sky with Avrik teaching me how to stand, how to defend myself, and how to wield a blade. At dinnertime, Lo hadn't been able to linger, but promised to return later.

Now, to my surprise, the guards had finally let my friends enter my quarters. Had Karye given them different orders? Did she *want* us to meet with one another? Was it part of her twisted game, her desire for amusement, that she wanted us to be able to plot against her?

I reentered my rooms to sit with my friends, relieved to be together again. After Narek and I filled Jennah and Avrik in on everything that had happened to us in their absence, Jennah and Avrik told us how they'd been captured by the Alrenians. My cousin curled up in a chair in the corner of the room, his eyes faraway. Occasionally, he muttered to himself, but he was too quiet for me to make out his words.

When I explained to everyone how Nesrelle had stolen my gift, I burned with shame. Who let a demon goddess *steal* a gift their god had blessed them with?

Jennah's brow furrowed. "She can steal our gifts?" she asked, a rare trace of apprehension creeping into her tone.

"I didn't think anyone could permanently steal a gift—only borrow it briefly," Narek mused. I could tell he was thinking about the times we'd practiced at the Aremakkin Temple, how we'd viewed some of Meli's visions or how I'd used his war gift when sparring with him.

"I didn't think so either, but apparently she has even more power than we realized."

Avrik glanced away sharply, and I followed his gaze to a shadowy corner of the room, but there was nothing there. Wondering what was troubling him, I tried to meet his eyes, but he avoided my look.

"Maybe I could…steal my gift back," I added doubtfully, before changing the subject to finish telling Jennah and Avrik everything else that had happened since Narek, Gillen, and I had stayed at the temple.

When we'd finished sharing stories, Jennah's eyes darted to Gillen in concern. He'd ignored us the entire time, lost in his own world. "Is he…all right?" she asked hesitantly.

Grimacing inwardly, I explained what Veykan had told us about the lingering nestred influence on Gillen's mind. "He doesn't think he's fit to rule," I said quietly. "He wants to give the throne to me." I hesitated. "I told him he shouldn't give up yet."

We were all silent a long moment. When I caught Avrik's gaze, he looked like he wanted to say something, but he held himself back.

Finally, I told my friends about my earlier conversation with Lo.

"Dragons," Jennah said, a smile playing on her lips.

Avrik grinned too. "I'm already liking the sound of this escape plan."

I rose from my seat. "I'm going to try to use my gift," I announced, which was true, but I also desperately wanted a moment of solitude. My nightmares about Misroth haunted me, and having to discuss the loss of my gift with my friends only reminded me how crippled I felt. How helpless I was to save my people. I wouldn't even be able to see through the nestred visions and lies anymore.

For the second time that night, I stepped out onto my balcony, drinking in the night air. As before, when I tried to reach for my gift, I felt only emptiness and a painful reminder of what Nesrelle had done. Still, I couldn't give up. My gift couldn't just be *gone*.

Could it?

Low murmurs from within told me my friends were still discussing plans. I didn't feel quite ready to return and admit my continued failure to recover my gift. Not yet.

"Halia." Avrik's voice was quiet as he stepped out onto the balcony.

I leaned against the railing and pretended not to hear him. All I wanted was one more moment to be alone. A moment of weakness in which I could let the tears fall and the fear consume me.

"Do you want to talk about it?" he asked tentatively. I heard it in his voice—the weight of grief and guilt that he carried too. Maybe I didn't have to be alone.

"There's nothing to say," I whispered.

Memories of my nightmares about Misroth flashed through my mind. My people suffering, screaming, dying. Swallowing back my pain, I watched the fountain bubble, its water shining silver in the moonlight. It was ridiculously peaceful here, so far away from the war and death that was descending on Misroth.

Somehow Avrik knew, like he always seemed to know.

Wordlessly, he stood beside me at the railing, watching the light playing on the water and the flowers swaying in the breeze. Wordlessly, he reached out his hand, and I took it. We watched the night deepen as he shared the weight of my grief.

When we went back inside, Jennah, Narek, and Gillen were still sitting near the empty fireplace, their voices low murmurs. This time, Gillen seemed present, his eyes clear.

Lo had brought in a tray of tea, and was standing uncertainly with it in her hands, studying the group. When her eyes met mine, some of her fear faded away.

"*Melhona,*" she said quietly. "I brought you some tea." She dropped her gaze to the floor. Finding my friends in my quarters must have unnerved her. "I—I can fetch more cups."

"Thank you," I said softly as she set the tray on the side table. "They're my friends, Lo. You can be honest here."

Her eyes darted about the room again, landing on Jennah just as the woman rose from her seat. "Lo," Jennah said with a warm smile. "Halia mentioned you earlier." She came close, taking Lo's hands in her own and cradling them. "You have a courageous spirit about you," she continued, her voice low so the guards posted outside would not hear.

Lo raised an eyebrow. "You're a Misrothian with Alrenian and Forwyn ancestry?" she asked.

Jennah's smile was a little sad. "I grew up learning Alrenian and old Alrenian ways, from before they grew greedy for power and bloodshed. I was always proud of my Alrenian heritage, but being here…I wish I'd been taught more about Forwyth and its people and language."

Lo's face relaxed into a grin. "Our language is even better," she said with a proud tilt to her chin. Her eyes darted toward the door, from which we could hear footsteps. It was a shift change for the guards stationed in the hall. "I need to go now." And with a final glance toward me, she darted silently from the room.

"How does she plan to help?" Gillen asked skeptically from his chair by the hearth. He held an Alrenian book he'd found on my nightstand, even though he couldn't read it. "She's just a child."

Narek shrugged. "We sent children younger than her to battle in Toryn."

Jennah, who hadn't fully warmed to the idea of Narek being an ally, shot him a scathing glance. "Yes, I'm sure your people should rule us by example in all things."

"Think about it," I interrupted, before the tension in the room could mount. "Lo isn't in that different of a situation from the Toryn when they were fighting for survival. Her age doesn't matter to the empress. She's living in oppression and under threat of death every day. She already tends to the dragons, whether she's helping us or not. Why not give her a chance?"

"Are you trying to save the Forwyn slaves *and* Misroth?" Narek asked, crossing his arms. "Because you have to remember that we are struggling even to save ourselves. I might be able to move one guard against the empress, but I can't raise up an entire army of puppets."

"Thanks be to the Life-Giver," Jennah muttered under her breath, scratching her scarred cheek.

Narek nodded, his smile tight. "Exactly."

Gillen sighed, closing his book and running his fingers along the leather cover absentmindedly. "I'm afraid I have to agree with the capta—with Narek. We have to fight for Misroth first. We can't save everyone, Halia."

My throat burned. Memories came to me: ones of Gillen caring for a hurt bird, begging his father to let him visit and tend to his tutor Eryk when the man had fallen ill, or wiping away tears when he'd read stories about the way people suffered under the Alrenian Empire. I knew he'd been trained to think practically for the day he took the throne, but I also knew he had a tender heart.

"I know," I said, my voice hoarse. "But if there is a chance to help them in some small way, I want to."

Before anyone could say more, Lo returned with mugs. "Midnight tonight," she whispered to me, before rushing out again.

My friends lingered, sipping tea and discussing Karye's proposed alliance and Avrik's gift.

"Old Misrothian tales say there were different types of barriers King Eldon could form," Gillen mused. "I think, Avrik, you need to practice and master this gift, to see just what you can do. Right now, Karye sees you as weak and inexperienced. If she has a truth-gifted advisor, she will see through your threats soon, if she hasn't already. To her, you'll be like a child with a weapon. Someone to be manipulated and taken advantage of."

Avrik glanced down at his hands, looking for once in his life as if he were uncomfortable in his own body. "I wish I knew more about the gift and how it works."

"If I had my gift," I said wistfully, "I could look into the past and learn about yours."

"For now," Jennah said calmly, "we can play Karye's game while we plan to escape. Give her time to realize how little power she truly has over us. She can't force you to surrender your gift to her, Avrik."

"Are you sure?" Avrik asked, his tone bitter. "She'll use all of you against me. Threaten or torture or murder you one by one until I give in." There were shadows under his eyes, making him appear haunted. Powerful and powerless all at once.

"She views my gift as a threat too," Narek said. "We have more so-called Alrenian gifts than the Alrenians themselves have. She wouldn't be cooperating with us as much as she has if she didn't feel at least somewhat threatened by us—or at least by the idea of losing her chance to use our gifts. That's something."

I tried to still my shaking hands as I thought again of Misroth City and the horrors the nestrae were unleashing. "If our escape plan fails, we don't have much time to convince Karye to let us go. The nestrae are already harming people in Misroth. They might not be killing anyone directly, but you know what their visions can do to people."

Jennah nodded, tight-lipped. I could see the deep pain and fear swirling in her eyes, emotions she tried to conceal. Her family was in Misroth City, after all. "I know," she said quietly. "All I want is to be there." She steadied her voice, trying to keep it from breaking.

"We play Karye's game," I agreed at last. "We go to the ball and give her a show. Hopefully, that will be enough to distract her and her advisor, and Vionn won't see what we're planning. We'll let Karye's people see us looking powerful and unafraid." I set my shoulders. "And in the meantime, Lo will help us get out of here."

At midnight, Lo swung over my balcony railing and stood in the entrance to my quarters, shrouded in shadows. "Come with me," she said without preamble.

Armed only with my stolen steak knife, I followed her to the balcony. She made lowering herself from the railing and then climbing down the trellis look easy. Taking careful note of her movements, I copied her, cringing when I slipped and a splinter from the trellis bit into my thumb, and holding my breath when I missed a step and hung, for one heart-pounding instant, with the trellis nearly falling backward. From her position below, Lo grasped the trellis and pushed it back into place, allowing me to correct my position and finish climbing down.

When I joined her on the ground, I studied her curiously and a little warily. How had she become so talented at sneaking around the palace?

"The guard patrolling this spot will be here soon," Lo said. "Stay here in the shadows until I can distract him, then walk forty paces that way and wait for me." She pointed further into the gardens, in the direction I knew the Keep to be. My heart pounded with both fear and anticipation at the thought. *Dragons.*

It didn't take long for the guard to appear. As she scurried forward, hunched and trembling in a façade of terror, the guard grabbed for his sword hilt before sneering in disgust.

"What are *you* doing out here?" he demanded.

I didn't wait to listen. As I darted forward, clinging to the palace's shadow, I caught Lo stammer something about her duties at the Dragon Keep, and then I was out of hearing range. I paused, panting, and before my breathing had evened, Lo was at my side. Her cheek was bright red with a clear handprint impression.

When I frowned and opened my mouth, she shook her head fiercely, pressed a finger to her lips, and gestured for me to follow her. She led me on a winding route through the gardens, often straying from the path and ducking behind shrubbery to avoid another approaching guard. At last, we entered the arena and approached the Keep's entrance.

The entrance looked like a gaping maw, lit from within by torches that cast flickering orange light along the walls. There were no guards posted in front, reminding me that the Alrenians didn't need any. Anyone foolish enough to trespass inside would have deadly dragons to face.

I drew a deep breath and reminded myself of the old stories about Eldon. If he could tame an Alrenian empress's dragon for his people, so could I. Or so I hoped.

Lo entered with the ease of familiarity. As we stepped inside the cavern-like space, our footsteps echoed along the smooth rock walls. There was no sign of anyone—servant, guard or slave—but I could hear noises coming from deeper within the cave: the sounds of huge beasts shuffling, breathing…eating. Lambs' bleats rang out and then were abruptly cut short. The rich smell of earth mingled with the lingering scent of smoke and a tang of blood.

Sweat gathered on the back of my neck, but I picked up my pace before my fear could consume me. Instead, I focused on my goal: Save my people. Weighed against my fear for my loved ones, my fear of the dragons was nothing.

As we crept deeper within the cave, the path dipped down and other paths began to intersect it. We peered inside damp, dim rooms dedicated to gear for the Dragon Keepers: huge saddles hung from the walls, intermingled with spare pieces of dragon scale armor and weapons etched with the same Alrenian words I'd found on the blade of the Dragon Keeper who had tried to poison me: *O j'eh y'vonu.* Finding the first room empty, we darted inside so I could swap my steak knife for a curved Alrenian dagger. When we stepped toward the doorway, two Forwyn men were approaching from further down the passage, their footsteps slow and shuffling and their eyes downcast. My heart rate accelerated when I realized what they carried between them: a dirty sheet encasing the perfect outline of a body. The scent of charred flesh permeated the air, so jolting and sickening that inhaling it was a slap to the face.

Before the slaves lifted their eyes to notice us, Lo grasped my arm and tugged me back into the room. There we hid in the shadows as the men shuffled past silently, their shoulders slumped and their footsteps heavy. When I glanced over at Lo, her mouth was set in an angry line.

"They die all the time," she whispered, her tone full of venom. "The slaves forced to feed or help the sick or injured dragons."

"The Alrenian Keepers who tamed them are too afraid?" I asked, frowning. The Keepers had seemed confident of their control over the dragons when I'd seen them around the beasts.

Lo shook her head angrily. "Mostly they are too busy and too important to bother."

The next room we passed was a huge open space, larger than the throne room in the Alrenian palace. Damp air whispered through the opening, making me shiver. Despite the torches lining the walls, there was no one within this room either. With the high ceiling and stone benches encircling the smooth, open floor, I had the distinct impression this was used as another arena of sorts, perhaps where the

Keepers and their dragons trained. When I looked closer and noticed old blood stains darkening the floor, I knew I was right. Cringing, I turned away, and Lo and I pressed deeper into the passage.

It seemed almost too easy to infiltrate the Keep. Or at least, that was what I thought until the ground rumbled beneath me, and I remembered what lived in this cavern. I almost laughed aloud at my foolishness. Why would the Alrenians worry about intruders when any sane person would stay far away from here?

Before we reached the dragons, we came to a huge infirmary complete with cots and shelves lined with herbs, salves, pills, and liquids of all colors. One corner was dedicated to more pieces of dragon scale armor hanging on the wall, shelves filled with jars of clear liquid, and, on the floor, a basket of gloves. Ensuring the room was empty, Lo tugged me inside and strode straight for the corner, donning a pair of gloves.

"What is all this?" I asked as Lo lifted the tunic portion of some black scaled armor from the wall and reached for a jar of clear liquid.

Lo lifted the jar, letting the contents slosh around inside. In the shifting torchlight, the liquid looked golden. "Vylae," she said softly, naming the poison that my father had used to kill my uncle. "The Keepers coat their armor in a layer of it, careful not to let it touch their bare skin." She lifted a gloved hand. "We can't smell it, but the dragons can. It acts like a drug that calms them, makes them more manageable so the Keepers can control them."

I stared down at the vial for an uncomfortable moment before nodding.

Together, we coated two complete sets of armor in the vylae and let it dry before dressing. As we worked, Lo went over what she'd learned from helping in the Keep, as well as the basic Alrenian commands the Keepers used with the dragons. I hoped those would prove to be helpful, if I survived long enough to use them.

The passage was empty as we approached several intersecting tunnels, all leading to the rooms in which the dragons were held. It was impossible to mistake them for anything else, when they were all barred by heavy iron doors, all tall and wide enough to fit the beasts, and we could hear the snuffling and heavy movements of the dragons within. Where earlier the Keep had been damp and cool, the air was now hot and dry, the scent of ash and charred flesh growing stronger. As sweat gathered along the back of my neck, I thought of the body the two Forwyn men had carried from the Keep earlier. There was the barest breath of wind, telling me that there were vents somewhere within the Keep, allowing fresh air into the tunnels to clear out the stench of smoke and make the air breathable.

When we passed more slaves, shoulders slumped and eyes downcast as they led bleating goats further down the tunnels, they outright ignored us. I wasn't sure if they even looked closely enough to realize we were impostors in dragon scale armor, or if they simply didn't care.

It was easy to find the door I wanted, because the dragons' names were carved into the stone archways above the iron doors. *Reyva.* The empress's own dragon. I recalled the way Gare had once told the story of Eldon tricking Empress Ilett and taming her dragon. A smile curved my lips as Lo tugged the pulley that slid the iron door open with a creak.

"Good luck," Lo murmured when the door opened wide enough for me to slip through.

The space was huge, with starlight bathing the walls and floor from a hole high in the ceiling. Despite the fresh air, the tang of smoke settled on my tongue. Inside, Reyva moved restlessly, her wings curled against her back and her black and gold scales flashing brilliantly, even in the dim light. Every muscle in her body moved sinuously, strong and intimidating. Despite the open room for her to roam, there was nothing for the dragon to occupy itself, and I couldn't help but think of the horses in the royal stables back home, how they would stomp and snort in boredom and restless energy if no one had ridden them yet for the day.

Reyva was ready to fly.

I slipped forward soundlessly, clinging to the shadows at the edge of the room. Sweat dampened my palms, yet at the same time, my skin tingled in anticipation. The dragon circled the room, her back to me as I studied her on the threshold, waiting for her to turn and react to my presence. My blood rushed through my veins.

Tail swishing across the cavern floor and dislodging rocks, Reyva turned toward me. The instant her great black eye snagged on me, I froze. My pulse thundered in my ears, making it hard to hear anything but its frantic beat. Lo's whispered advice back in the infirmary ran through my mind: *The dragons admire confidence. Cower and run from them, and you will look like prey. Stand your ground and meet their gaze without flinching, and they will see someone that could be an equal. Put yourself in their line of sight. Stand tall.*

I straightened my shoulders and stared intently at Reyva. The beast held nearly as still as me, her sides rising and falling as she breathed steadily, her dark eyes unfathomable as she watched me.

Another awareness tugged at me, like a shadow of my truth gift trying to return. Something about the proud way this majestic creature carried herself made the vylae coating my armor seem like a crime. Reyva was restive, longing to taste freedom and spread her wings. Drugging her into submission and forcing her to follow my will seemed far more cruel and dangerous than earning this creature's respect and loyalty.

Fear made my fingers shake, but I trusted this feeling I had, whatever bare shred of my gift or strange instinct this was. Drawing a deep breath, I pulled the pieces of my armor off, one by one, throwing them back out into the passage behind me. I hesitated another moment before I tossed my dagger away with them, listening to its echoing clatter against the ground.

"What are you doing?" Lo hissed, peering around the door. I waved her away.

"Trust me," I said, stepping slowly toward the dragon.

For a long moment, the dragon and I stared at each other. I froze in the middle of the room, unsure if I should dare to step closer, to reach out and stroke Reyva's scales, or if I should wait for her to approach me. And then the dragon snorted, a curl of smoke drifting from one of her nostrils. Something glistened in the one eye I could see, like a distant glint of light at the bottom of a dark pool.

Without warning, she launched herself toward me, sprinting with impossible speed across the room.

Heart hammering, I grit my teeth to hold back my scream. Every muscle in my body coiled tightly as I hesitated. Did I stand my ground, or did I need to leap out of the way? Had I made a horrible mistake, throwing all my protection away?

My fingers longed for the reassuring grip of the dagger, lying uselessly in the tunnel behind me.

As abruptly as the dragon had charged, Reyva skidded to a stop, sending pebbles skittering across the cavern floor and dust clouding the air. She was directly in front of me, her sides heaving as she huffed smoke from her nostrils. Eyes wide, she tilted her head and studied me again, her tail twitching slowly behind her. Starlight reflected along her scales, making them glisten like jewels.

I stood tall and straight, keeping my stance confident as I lifted a tremulous hand to stroke the side of her face, just beneath her eye. Reyva's scales were warm and dry beneath my fingertips, as smooth and unyielding as polished stone.

"Are you tired of being a slave to the empress too?" I whispered.

For the next few days, the guards posted outside my room wouldn't let me out to see my friends. Perhaps the empress had changed her mind about letting us all spend time together. Instead, Lo visited to train with me.

I kept my stolen Alrenian dagger hidden under my pillow when I slept and in my boot when I was awake. I counted down the days left until my birthday. And I prayed that I could tame Reyva and create a successful plan—as long as Vionn didn't discover the truth. It was frustrating to be at the mercy of another truth-gifted person's knowledge while I was in the dark, feeling crippled without my own gift.

Each night, Lo led me to the Keep, where I eventually managed to slip onto Reyva's back. The dragon tossed me to the ground the first time. After that, I reminded myself to adjust my stance and conceal my fear. Using Alrenian commands Reyva was familiar with, I succeeded in getting her to cooperate when I climbed back on. Without one of the saddles the Alrenians had fashioned for dragon riding, I clung to her awkwardly as she paced about the room. The next night, I tried attaching a saddle, but it took most of our time together for Reyva to settle down and let me use it to ride her. By the fourth night, I dared to give her the command to fly—and Reyva didn't hesitate. We had little room to maneuver within her confined space, but she took me around in circles with the restless energy of a penned stallion. As she strained to brush the rocky ceiling and steal a breath of fresh air through the vent, a similar longing filled me, aching to be outside with the starlight filling my eyes and the wind in my hair.

Soon, I thought.

My success with Reyva made me bold. Together, Lo and I began to piece together a plan. As the days passed, Lo found moments to slip into my friends' quarters to share our plan with them, and then all that was left to do was prepare for Karye's ball.

CHAPTER TWENTY-SEVEN

FORTY-FOUR DAYS LEFT WAS my first waking thought.

As usual, my nightmarish visions had made my sleep restless. Once I'd even awoken to a strangely shaped shadow in the far corner of my bedroom, and I was sure I'd felt the demon queen's presence. But when I'd looked again, the shape was gone.

Now the breeze coming in through the open balcony doors was surprisingly cool, the light soft and golden. My visions of Misroth seemed distant, even if the guilt and horror were forever close, pressing on my heart. I sat at the vanity in my room, picking through a few tangles in my hair as Jennah, who'd been permitted to join me in my quarters to prepare for the ball, stood at my wardrobe.

The opulence surrounding me made me sick. My people were suffering and dying, and here I was, playing the empress's foolish games. Tonight, Karye was throwing her ball, an affair that promised to be as extravagant as any Alrenian ball or feast I'd heard about in tales and histories. No doubt she hoped, if not to announce a formal alliance with Misroth, to at least give her people the perception that we were cooperating. That Karye, in all her might and glory, was persuading the rebellious Misrothian kingdom to return to the empire's fold and submit to them once more.

Over the past few days, Lo had visited all my friends in their rooms, relaying our plan. That alone made my disgust over the ball pale compared to my growing sense of victory. As the days had passed without any interference, my confidence that Vionn was unaware of our actions had grown. Today, my hopes were high that we would succeed. Just like Eldon had done, we'd trick the empress with our own plan.

Jennah spun toward me, a dress in her arms. A mischievous grin flitted across her face. "If we must attend an imperial ball, then you will represent Misroth in the best light. I am going to make sure you look like a queen—that you outshine Karye herself."

I resisted the urge to roll my eyes. Jennah was right: sometimes the game of politics was all about appearances, like when she'd helped me don a patriotic-looking gown to reconvene the Misrothian Royal Council and put those old men in their places. Now it was time to show the Alrenians that Misroth wasn't as weak and ripe for conquering as they thought. After two hundred years of peace, our army might be too meager to defeat the nestrae, but politically, we could hold our own among the Alrenians. My friends and I would make sure of that.

Jennah brought me the dragon scale dress Lo had given me to wear to the ball. When I put it on, I found the violet fabric fell in loose folds, comfortable and light in the summer heat. A gold belt adorned the waist, while the bodice shimmered with gold beads I hadn't noticed before. The shoulders were detailed with delicate gold chains that fell loose down the arms. As I'd seen before, the open back was draped with more chains and violet, ivory, and gold dragon scales.

I knew immediately that this was what I'd wear. It sent Karye the perfect message: I would not be weak.

"We'll play her game and win," Jennah said, grinning so widely the scar on her cheek stretched.

"Thank you," I said as she helped me find sandals to strap on my feet and pushed me into a chair so she could arrange my hair.

Jennah chuckled as she experimented with a hair cream stored with the other toiletries in my quarters. "Well, this is new. You've never thanked me for helping you dress like a royal before," she teased. "You always hated it."

"You know it's more than that," I said. "You help me find my confidence. You've been an advisor and a friend…" I hesitated before continuing. "After everything you've suffered because of me, you don't doubt me." I dropped my gaze to my hands, folded carefully in my lap. So properly my mother would have been proud. "Surviving Toryn was a nightmare, and we lost good friends."

Jennah clenched her jaw. "It wasn't your fault. What we do now, we do in their honor. They died for their kingdom, Halia. They chose that."

I squeezed my eyes shut. "I know," I said, keeping my voice steady. "But letting myself be weak enough for the nestrae to discover how to destroy the barrier…I'll never be able to forgive myself for that." I repressed a shudder. "Do you know what I've seen? Do the nestrae show it to you too?"

A shadow passed over Jennah's face, dimming the light in her brown and gold eyes. "All the time," she said, her voice low. "I have a rune too, on my upper thigh." She lifted the linen shift she wore so I could see the jagged scars tracing a circular shape along her right leg. "It means…*Inadequate*. Not good enough." She sighed. "I'm constantly questioning my choices. Was I a good mother to leave my girls behind?" Tears burned her eyes. "I thought I was leaving to face dangers so my family wouldn't have to suffer, but now it feels like I've abandoned them to darkness and horror."

Heart aching, I reached out to wrap my fingers around Jennah's. Like me, she bore endless burdens, guilt, and questions. Doubts about her abilities. Her choices. As a mother. A wife. A daughter. Had she made the right decision?

"But," Jennah continued before I could even try to find words to comfort her, "we *will* find a way to push the nestrae out of Misroth." She flashed me a confident smile. "I believe in you, even if I'm struggling to believe in myself. Don't let doubt cause you to falter."

Dressed in a royal blue vest with black embroidered detailing, white shirt, and dark trousers, Gillen looked kinglier than ever. The dark colors set off his bright eyes, and his hair, sleek and neatly tied back, shone golden in the torchlight. His smile seemed sincere and warm, the shadows under his eyes almost concealed with its radiance. In the Alrenian attire, most of his scars were hidden. Only a few on his hands and a small, fading cut on his cheek were visible, and those perhaps only added to his charm.

More than one pair of eyes followed him with begrudging interest as, arm-in-arm, we stepped into the ballroom. It wasn't like the Misrothian space, which was enclosed within the castle. This was a huge pavilion, with a high ceiling supported by great columns and its sides open to the palace gardens. Though the sun burned bright and hot during the day in Alrenor, it had set quickly over the sea tonight, dipping the land swiftly into an inky evening.

The night air was warm and mild. Stars glistened like jewels overhead, despite the gathering clouds, and the scent of citrus intermingled with flowers and food from the side tables.

"Careful," I murmured to Gillen as we swept by a pair of guards patrolling the area and sidestepped a cluster of nobles, who looked at us with a mixture of derision and curiosity. "The empress may want to speak with you tonight, or insist you speak on behalf of Misroth."

Gillen shook his head. "I said that you are my representative, remember?" His smile looked a little more forced now. "She's seen me…not fully under control. She knows to only address you."

On my other side, Narek kept his voice low. "We should stay close together." His entire posture was stiff, all his training as a warrior in the Toryn Zare'forith and the Misrothian Royal Guard guiding his actions. Though he wore a loose black shirt with silver buttons and a bright green vest, he managed to make the clothes—formal yet comfortable—look like they were constricting him. He kept his mouth in a thin line and his face an inscrutable mask. "Remember," he went on, "she may disguise this as a party and hope you dance and chat and feast the night away, but anything could happen."

I rolled my eyes. "Narek, you're beginning to sound like Layk." As soon as I said his name, the words tasted sour in my mouth. My friends' absences were a void.

Jennah stood close behind me, giving my free arm a comforting squeeze. "Well, both he and Narek would be right to advise caution, but I think you're already prepared for this battle." I glanced over my shoulder at her in time to see her wink.

She was dressed in a flowing, sleeveless gold dress that flattered her dark, gold-tinted skin. When flickering light from the torches reached her, I could see scars near her collarbone and along her arms. She wore a gauzy shawl over her shoulders that covered her upper arms, but I didn't think she did it to hide any of her old wounds, especially when the jagged scar along her cheek was clearly visible. No matter what, she exuded confidence, and I imagined she embraced each of the scars as reminders of what she had survived and proof that she could endure still more. They made her look beautiful and formidable, the exact sort of message we wanted to send to the Alrenians.

"Is Avrik ready for this battle?" Narek cast a glance in my direction.

Jennah nudged me playfully. "You should probably find him," she said, not even trying to hide the suggestion in her tone.

"Karye will probably force him to spend all his time with her," I said.

Gillen turned to me, a question on his lips, but then he seemed to think better of it. I hadn't told him that my feelings for Avrik went deeper than friendship, but when my cousin searched my face, he seemed to see right through me. "Go, Lia," he said. "If we want to be successful, we'll have to at least pretend we're enjoying ourselves."

Avrik was the only one who hadn't joined us. The guards who'd escorted us to the event had informed us that he'd been summoned to the party early, by Karye.

I tried to push deeper into the crowd, past a group of noblewomen chatting and sipping from wine glasses, but one of the women stepped in front of me, eyeing me with a narrow gaze. Her brown, gold-flecked eyes were heavily lined with kohl, and the cherry red color on her lips looked overdone. Perhaps that was her intention—to look like she'd been drinking blood. "This is the Misrothian princess?" she sneered, speaking as if she were studying my likeness rather than approaching me in person. "The Mad King's representative?"

My blood turned cold. Rumors about Gillen were already spreading throughout the city. I hated that he'd be subjected to the Alrenians' hateful words tonight.

"Rebellious Misroth returned," she crooned, "coming to beg for our help when things grow difficult, like a spoiled child." She giggled and slurped at her wine, spilling a little so that it dribbled onto her pale, rose-colored dress.

"But I'm not the one behaving like one," I muttered, pushing past her easily. If she heard me, she reacted too late, because I was soon far past her.

As I scanned the crowd, I circled around a group of Dragon Keepers, arrayed in their glistening armor, each in shades of gold, silver, black, or emerald green. They wore their weapons openly and proudly. I longed for the comfort of a bow or even a sword at my hip, but all I had was the dagger I'd stolen, tucked within an inside pocket of my dress. Clustered by the side tables, the Keepers crossed their arms and scorned me as I slipped past them.

"—never stoop to helping them—"

"—ungrateful arrogance, thinking we need them as much as they need us—"

Their talk shifted when they studied me and my dress, turning to outraged mutters about my dragon scales.

"Surely Empress Karye did not approve…"

"The *gall* of that filthy Misrothian *kowra*!"

Keeping my chin held high, I ignored their words.

Finally, I spotted Avrik on the opposite side of the pavilion, chatting with a group of young noblewomen as if he'd been attending Alrenian parties all his life. He was dressed in a deep red shirt and black vest, transforming him from a commoner the Alrenians would have sneered at to someone who looked the part he was supposed to play: the willing and charismatic man soon-to-be betrothed to their empress. Grinning his most enchanting smile, he appeared to be mid-joke. The girls around him were covering their mouths, trying to hold back their laughter.

I wound my way toward him. "Avrik," I said, my voice level, but giving him a pointed look. "I was looking for you."

"Forgive me," Avrik said, offering them a winning smile. One of the girls giggled outright. "You'll have to excuse me."

The girls continued to blush.

What idiots, I thought, trying to keep myself from glowering at everyone around me as I led Avrik away. "Maybe," I said over my shoulder once we were no longer in earshot, "you wouldn't have to worry about so many unwelcome marriage proposals if you didn't work so hard to flirt with everyone."

Catching up to me, Avrik shrugged, his expression careful, measured. "Do you think I enjoy talking to them? I thought our goal was to play Karye's game and be amiable tonight."

A retort was on the tip of my tongue when the empress entered the pavilion, flanked by her advisor and a cluster of Dragon Keepers, all dressed in gold and ivory armor. Karye herself wore a vivid blue and silver dress with a v-neckline that plunged audaciously low and side slits in the skirt that revealed her thighs. On each leg, she wore decorative knives with jeweled hilts and sheaths traced with gold filigree. In place of a necklace, she'd draped a black dragon scale mantle over her shoulders so that it hung in decorative chains across her collarbone and down her back. Her arms shimmered with armbands forged of silver dragon scales. More silver scales flashed in her golden hair, which draped nearly to her waist, and the effect was reminiscent of a crown. Her blue eyes glittered with a cruel light as they fell upon Avrik and me.

"Princess Halia. Avrik," she said, her lips curling in a fierce smile. "I hope you are enjoying my hospitality."

Avrik dipped his head to nod briefly. "Thank you, *amara*," he said, using the Alrenian title for empress.

Jaw tightening, I forced myself to smile as well. Avrik might have been able to charm and lie his way through anything, but even without my gift, I knew I couldn't be quite that convincing.

Karye's gaze turned sharper as her eyes swept over the length of my dress, snagging on the dragon scales gleaming in the torchlight. "I see you are enjoying Alrenian fashion too, princess."

If smiles could kill, mine would have. "Very much so." I paused, a beat too long to be considered courteous. "*Amara.*"

"If you don't mind," Karye continued with false politeness, her gaze flitting over me, "I request your friend's presence."

Thankfully, she didn't wait for me to speak. Taking hold of Avrik's arm as if they truly were lovers, she led him toward the center of the pavilion. The crowd parted for her and her Dragon Keeper guards, giving her a wide berth when she stood to face them all. She spoke in Alrenian, so I could only translate a few of her words, but it was clear she was making an announcement, her way to officially begin the evening. I heard her say *Misrothian*, nodding to me, and Avrik's name. The Alrenians offered a smattering of applause when she finished, forcing themselves to demonstrate necessary respect toward their empress without displaying enthusiasm for the supposed alliance. Or, for all I knew, she'd already announced her betrothal. For his part, Avrik smiled cheerfully by her side, looking thoroughly unshaken.

At Karye's cue, the musicians seated throughout the garden began to play a more upbeat tune, drumbeats rolling like distant thunder, while the sweet notes of stringed instruments complemented the sound, turning the song into a cheerful melody. She spun Avrik into a dance, one that started fast with the music and then slowed. Other Alrenians paired up around them and joined in, twirling and spinning and then slowing to move in graceful, simpler steps as they held one another in their arms. Ever the clumsy dancer, especially in this new, unfamiliar dance, Avrik stumbled noticeably more than once, but Karye caught him and guided his steps. When the song slowed, she drew him closer. With a repressed shudder, I turned away.

I found Narek and Gillen at one of the round tables along the edges of the pavilion, eating and watching the festivities with wary eyes. "Pretend you're having a good time," I muttered as I passed them.

"How much longer?" Gillen asked softly. His eyes looked distant, and for a terrible moment, I feared he was having one of his visions again. But when he turned to me, he only looked sad.

I cast a discreet look around the party, scanning the slaves serving the food, but there was no sign of Lo yet. "I'm not sure."

Approaching one of the side tables, I claimed a plate and filled it with an assortment of meats, cheeses, and roasted vegetables. There were some sugared berries and pastries I decided to try as well, and I couldn't resist picking up an orange.

Pretend it's a party in Evren, I told myself firmly, plastering a smile on my face as I passed clusters of laughing or dancing Alrenians.

I found an isolated spot at the edge of the pavilion overlooking the grounds. Sitting on some steps descending toward a garden path, I ate in silence, ignoring the music and chatter around me. When I'd finished, I abandoned my plate and followed the path along its winding route. It was lined with torches that lit my way, chasing the deepening shadows away. Cricket song soothed my ears, growing stronger the further from the party I drifted. I passed a blanket of sun-yellow flowers each smaller than my thumbnail, blood-red roses, and delicate blossoms that looked like black velvet. They filled the air with their fragrant aroma, peaceful and relaxing even as it reminded me painfully of sitting with Lyanna in her garden and plucking weeds. Palm trees towered overhead, their fronds waving in the breeze, and citrus trees grew at perfectly spaced intervals. Here and there I arrived at a fountain. At last, I stopped when the path opened onto a wide, circular space surrounded by benches and points where several paths diverged. In the center, a fountain made to look like a woman pouring a pitcher towered over me. Somehow I'd wandered closer to the pavilion, because I was almost immersed in the sounds of the party again—music, laughter, the clinking of plates and glasses, and the incessant buzz of idle conversation. I was about to turn around, to seek a quieter spot, when a voice stopped me.

"I think the point of a ball is to socialize."

Nearby, Avrik leaned against the trunk of a palm tree. He didn't look like the fate of his kingdom—or his own future—was crushing him with worry. Instead he slid his hands into his pockets and gave me his boyish smile, letting his dimple show. Torchlight flickered across his face and reflected in his eyes.

"You escaped her clutches fast. Doesn't the empress 'require your presence?'" I asked, stretching my vowels and biting out my consonants to mimic her Alrenian accent.

He smirked. "I may have stepped on her toes once or twice, and it may or may not have been mostly on purpose. I think I embarrassed her enough for the evening. She told me to go pester someone else." He raised his eyebrows and looked at me significantly.

I suppressed a laugh. "If that is your way of asking me to dance…"

Avrik drew away from the tree and came to stand beside me. "Come on, it'll be like old times. And I have to do something to pass the time, or I'll go mad."

I couldn't keep the smile off my face as I turned to him. "And what will be worse?" I asked. "My bruised toes or your bruised pride?"

Instead of answering, he just laughed and placed a hand on my shoulder. His fingers slid along the chains strung across my arm all the way to my bare skin, and I stifled a shiver at his touch. I held my breath and prayed he hadn't noticed the way I'd reacted to him. Thankfully, he was distracted by my outfit. "You're wearing their dragon scales?" he murmured. "Daring."

"I had to send the right message tonight."

Avrik grinned. "Well, you certainly have." He slid his other hand to my waist and, listening to the beat of a new song, made a valiant attempt at leading us in the first few steps of a slow, supposedly graceful Misrothian dance.

I laughed when he nearly stepped on my foot. "No, it's like this," I said, leading him through the steps again. "How can you be graceful in a sword fight but so clumsy in a dance?"

Avrik shrugged. "I never thought of the two as similar."

I shot him a playful grin. "Well, this is like a swordfight." I twisted away from him. "A duel. Or," I added as I stepped closer to him, letting him take my arm and draw me nearer, "you can think of it as another competition." I tossed my hair over my shoulder, just like I'd used to do in Evren whenever I'd wanted to mock haughty Jayn from school. "One I'll win like usual, of course."

Avrik scoffed but rose to the bait. "I think we were pretty equal as far as our shooting competitions went." His eyes were more intent now, his steps more precise. I knew the comparison would help: when he thought about the movements as steps in a complicated fight, he could concentrate and his confidence grew.

As others from the party spilled out from the pavilion into the gardens, dancing or talking or laughing together, we let the thrill of another competition and the familiarity of our old friendly rivalry take over. For a little while, I didn't have to pretend I was enjoying myself. I didn't have to anxiously scan for Lo as I wondered if she'd been delayed. I didn't have to worry about if Avrik had truly forgiven me. We simply settled into what was natural for us, and spent the dance adding extra flourishes to our movements and teasing one another good-naturedly.

I noticed a flash of light overhead and glanced up: the clouds in the south had grown thicker and darker, blotting out the stars. A distant storm had settled over the Great Sea, and though we couldn't hear its thunder yet, the flashes of lightning were intense. The breeze grew stronger, more restless, rustling through the leaves on the trees and plants around us. I wondered how much longer it would be before the storm reached us.

As the song ended, I spun away from Avrik and shot him a victory smile. "I win," I declared.

He raised an eyebrow. "How do you figure that? How do I know if you made any mistakes?"

"That's the point." I laughed, stepping closer. "You don't even know enough about dancing to know which dance is which or which steps fit where."

"All right," he said, looking amused. "I concede."

The grins faded from our faces as we realized how close we stood. Every inch of my body tingled. Either the breeze or the dancing had pulled a lock of my hair free from the pins holding it back, and he reached up to brush it away from my cheek. Just as he used to touch me sometimes in Evren, in a way that seemed friendly, almost absentminded. *Friends,* I told myself, even as my breath caught in my throat. But his eyes, dark and intent, told a different story. Elena would have blushed under that gaze, but I didn't. Maybe I wasn't imagining the desire on his face. Maybe he felt the same way, his pulse pounding in his ears until he was as light-headed with the thrill of hope as I was. All the words I wanted to say tumbled around wildly in my mind.

But he was already pulling away and dropping his hand from mine. I blinked, confusion flooding through me. My tongue tasted bitter.

"Halia," Avrik said quickly, his eyes darting over my shoulder. His body was stiff, his jaw tight.

A chill shot through me—something was terribly wrong.

When I turned, Karye glared at us, with Lo caught fast in her grip.

"Are you playing me for a fool?" the empress demanded, her voice low and dangerous.

CHAPTER TWENTY-EIGHT

Avrik

KARYE'S GAZE FLITTED PAST HALIA, straight toward Avrik. With a careless wave of her free hand, she snapped, "Leave us, princess. My business is with him first."

Halia curled her hands into fists, but she kept her voice level. "Your business is with *Misroth.*"

Karye's eyes flashed. "Your best interest is to let me speak with him, *alone*, while your kingdom still has a chance to come to an agreement with Alrenor and you and your friends still have a chance of not being gutted right here, right now."

Squirming in Karye's clutches, Lo met Halia's eyes and mouthed, *Go.* Her eyes were wide and pleading, but Avrik didn't think the slave girl looked afraid—not for herself, anyway.

Avrik could tell by the way Halia stood, posture stiff and unyielding, that she was furious, but otherwise, she seemed calm when she strode back toward the pavilion. Only once, at a turn in the garden path, did she pause to look back over her shoulder and meet his eyes. He offered her a single nod—*It's all right*—and she disappeared.

Despite the threat in Karye's blade-sharp voice, in her cold eyes, and in her predatory walk, Avrik's gaze latched onto Halia's retreating form. He could still see Halia staring back at him, the lightning shining in her emerald green eyes. He could still feel the rush of hope when he'd held her in his arms. His pulse was erratic in his ears, and nothing seemed terrifying anymore. Not Nesrelle and her threats that death was coming for him, or the coldness in his veins, or the fierce stare Karye was giving him now.

"Are you playing games with me when your people's lives are at stake?" the empress demanded. She shoved Lo toward one of her guards standing in the shadows ringing the garden path. When she approached Avrik, she hovered dangerously close, her gaze tracing his face. The possessive look in her eyes made his stomach turn. "You pretend to cooperate and work toward an alliance while plotting behind my back? Last night, my guards caught that slave sneaking into your rooms. Tonight, she was stealing from my kitchens."

Avrik shrugged and smiled insolently. He rolled his shoulders back in a lazy shrug and gestured toward the swell of music coming from the pavilion. "The risk to your own people's lives certainly hasn't kept you from playing games with us."

Karye's eyes narrowed. "When you live here in Alrenor," she bit out, "I will teach you to show me respect." She stretched out her fingers to touch his face, but Avrik lifted his hand and hers slammed to a stop mid-air, as if hitting an invisible wall. Growling, she pulled her hand back, hiding her grimace and shaking her hand out to stop the pain.

"You'll never win my respect," Avrik countered, stepping close so he was staring down into her eyes, mere inches from her. She was tall, almost as tall as him, but in this instant, she seemed smaller than before. Her breathing hitched. Her gaze faltered. He didn't move away. "Because you'll never hold any power over me."

Quick as the lightning blazing above, Karye drew her dagger and drove it toward his stomach, but Avrik warded it off easily. This part of his gift, he realized, he'd already practiced often. In the thick of battle, when he was most alert, self-preservation came almost as effortlessly as breathing. In two clean moves he'd twisted the blade from her grasp and spun it so its point was inches from her face. Karye ducked, drawing her other dagger, and threw it at him, but her aim was wild. Avrik dodged it.

Thunder rumbled and the first drops of rain splattered around them. People in the pavilion exclaimed and ran through the gardens to seek shelter from the storm. They rushed toward the palace, taking their plates of food and their goblets of wine as if planning to continue the festivities inside. No one noticed Avrik and Karye in the darkness.

Avrik wondered when Karye's guards would choose to intervene. Surely if he cornered her, they would stop him before he could kill her. Adrenaline thrummed in his veins, and he had an overwhelming urge to end the political games then and there. Slit her throat and save his people, trading one evil life for countless innocent ones. He could do it. He wouldn't hesitate or flinch away when it meant saving his friends and his kingdom.

In the darkness, with only the flashes of lightning to brighten the night, the gold flecks in Karye's eyes glowed, making her look like a wild beast. He advanced on her again, but she snarled and gestured to her guards, hiding in the shadows.

When they charged him, Avrik lost his grip on his gift. It was like waking from a vivid dream, only to try to grasp for details as he regained consciousness and have it all flutter away. When his life was threatened, the barrier had come easily, but now it was gone.

Of course, Avrik thought, the realization dawning with painful clarity. *This was Karye's trap all along. She never lost control of her emotions when she attacked. It was all a ploy to see how well I can use my gift, and now she knows.*

The two guards, Dragon Keepers dressed in silver and gold, disarmed and restrained him easily, pushing him down to his knees. When they'd subdued him, they released his arms and stepped back, gloating, and shoved Lo down beside him. The girl trembled in her rags, the rain drenching her, but she glared at her enemies with unrestrained fury.

His chance was gone. Shame coiled through his belly like a snake.

Know your enemy. Those were the words he'd read in old texts about fighting and strategy, ones said to have been penned by the very generals who had helped win the war against Alrenor. He'd memorized them, dedicated himself to them, long before he'd ever fought a real battle or known a true enemy. And now his enemy was using that strategy against him. She knew him better than he knew her.

Karye sneered. The rain was coming down in sheets, plastering her yellow hair to her cheeks and running in rivulets down her face. "Not quite as powerful as Eldon, are you?" She sheathed her dagger and stalked toward him, clearly relishing his place at her feet. "Your threats are empty."

Avrik swallowed back the panic growing inside of him. His leverage was slipping away, as was his mask of confidence.

Life-Giver, show me how to use this gift, he prayed frantically, but it remained out of reach.

"You watched me defeat your dragon," he said, meeting her gaze steadily. "You know the power of my gift, or you wouldn't have been so shaken by it. And you know I'm not afraid to use it, not even if it means destroying your entire empire as I do it."

Karye laughed, but this time it came out sounding shaky. Her smile slipped just enough for him to know that doubt was taking hold. "You wouldn't threaten that many lives. Vionn and I know everything about you."

The muscles in his shoulders bunched up, but he didn't look away. Warm rain soaked through his shirt until it clung to his back, and he knelt in a growing patch of mud. The scent of wet earth mingled with distant smoke from the party torches, a strange mixture of sweet and acrid.

"Did you think after your display against my dragon, I would not have my advisor study you?" Karye continued, her arrogance returning. Her smile broadened. "I know about your dear mother and the way she suffered until she died. I know how your father shut you out for days afterward, barely speaking to you in his grief and anger.

He broke things. He shouted at the sky and wept alone in his bed at night, and you heard it all. It terrified you, didn't it? You were so young and alone."

Avrik steadied his breathing, trying to dispel the dark emotions and memories her words conjured.

"I know how horrified you were when you took a man's life to save your friend, the princess. And I know the dark path your father took, and how in the end, you turned your back on him. He bargained with the king regent for *your* sake, let others die for you, and you let him hang." Karye shrugged. "I know you. You're not a killer. You don't have it in you."

Raindrops caught in his lashes, blurring his vision as he glared at Karye. He thought of that dark night in Evren before his father's execution, when he'd bent over his bow, restringing it with shaking hands as he'd tried to steel himself for whatever would come in the morning. *Will you hurt an innocent man to help your guilty father escape?* he'd asked himself.

His voice was grating, like a blade scraping against its sheath. "Tell your guards to let me go. Face me in a real fight and find out if you're right."

Karye laughed. "Right," she said. "Who needs diplomacy when you can just murder each other?"

But Avrik was unfazed. "Maybe not kill each other. We're both more valuable to one another alive." He shrugged. "You like games. Maybe it's my turn to propose one. You win the fight, and you can have your way: marry me, enslave me, whatever you want so you can use my gift. Only let my friends go free. But if I win, my friends and I go free and your Dragon Keepers go to war against the nestrae with us."

Beside him, one of the Keepers stiffened.

Raising an eyebrow, Karye tilted her head, studying him curiously. "Why would I do that?"

"I don't think you can resist a challenge, and I suspect we're both too proud to make vows we wouldn't keep. According to proud Alrenian tradition, an empress's word should mean something. In Misroth, a soldier's word is unbreakable." Avrik drew himself to his feet, and the Keepers didn't try to stop him. He tried not to let her see just how desperate he was for her to accept, how much he longed to fight a battle he knew he could win. "Alrenor and Misroth were never meant to compromise. Let's settle it right here, right now. All or nothing. In a duel that would make your Alrenian emperors and empresses of old proud."

"You know it can never be that simple. Alrenor never accepts *nothing*." Karye's smile turned feral. "I have a different game in mind."

Led by Karye, the Dragon Keepers dragged Lo and Avrik down the muddy path and back toward the pavilion. It was empty now of all but a few slaves cleaning up platters of food and bottles of wine, empty plates and glasses, table linens and discarded items—earrings, sashes, a pair of sandals—left forgotten by their owners.

Without preamble, Karye drew her dagger and seized the first slave she neared, a young man who startled, his eyes wide. She pulled him toward her in an iron grip before spinning him around so Avrik found himself staring straight into the man's terrified gaze. The man's chest rose and fell evenly, trying to conceal the alarm pooling in his dark eyes. Orange torchlight reflected on his face, making his skin glow like he was burning from within.

All around them, the slaves stilled. Muscles tensed and faces taut with fear, they looked like statues gathered about the pavilion, some still clutching plates or trays of food. Perhaps they thought if they could only stop breathing, the empress would ignore them.

Avrik's chest tightened as Karye pressed her blade to the man's neck.

"For your sentimental heart, even a lowly slave will do," she sneered, "but I can summon your friends next. Surrender your gift to me, or these slaves die."

Avrik's voice was raw. "If you touch them, I'll—"

"You'll what?" Karye cut in, laughing. Without missing a beat, she slid the blade across the man's throat. A burst of blood splattered down her hand and on the front of her dress as she dropped him, where he lay in a growing pool of his own blood, gurgling and grasping at his neck. She was still laughing when the life faded from the man's eyes. "You can't stop me. If you want them to stop dying, surrender your gift to me. *I'll* wield it with the power you cannot."

Avrik struggled uselessly against the Keepers, who shoved him back to his knees and looked on impassively as Karye sauntered toward her next victim. Avrik couldn't feign confidence now, not when he tried to reach for his protection gift and found only emptiness. His breath came in ragged gasps. The blood pooling in front of him triggered a memory of Ellyse, killed because of his father's choices. But the guilt was his own, just as it was now. It felt like *he* had slit the Forwyn man's throat.

Sweat beaded on his forehead. Maybe he could stop Karye from slaughtering more of her slaves and then his friends, but at what cost? His power in her hands would be deadly. Karye could use it to protect Alrenor from any possibility of a nestred invasion while sealing the Misrothians inside their own tomb, left to a fate as nightmarish as what Toryn had faced.

But how could he choose between the innocent people dying before him now and his kingdom? It was cruel. Wrong. Impossible.

"Say the words and you can end this," Karye said. She clutched a Forwyn woman by the arm, who snarled and fought back. But Karye was strong, skilled, and ruthlessly methodical. She twisted the woman's arm until there was a sickening crack and the woman screamed in agony. The slave collapsed weakly in the empress's arms, while her arm hung limply at her side, twisted at an unnatural angle.

Wrenching the woman toward her, Karye turned back to Avrik again. Her pale eyes glinted with a feverish light.

Avrik's lungs burned, and his tongue was lead in his mouth. *Stop!* He wanted to shout the word. Every muscle in his body trembled with rage and horror. The scent of blood was thick in the air, a metallic tang so strong he could taste it. Squeezing his eyes shut, he forced himself to concentrate. *Life-Giver…*

The wet thud of another body hitting the ground shattered his focus. His eyes snapped open to see Karye already reaching for her next victim as the woman's lifeblood spilled out. Avrik ground his teeth together until his jaw ached.

"How many must die, Avrik?" Karye asked, her voice low and threatening.

Avrik shivered as an icy wave swept through him, reminding him of Nesrelle's deathly touch. He had the unpleasant sensation that she was watching, hovering somewhere behind him in the shadows. The slaves' terror and pain was like a cloud enveloping the space, as tangible as the smoke trailing into the sky from the torches or the storm clouds dispersing overhead. Maybe the Queen of Death followed Karye around, relishing in the bloodshed and pain the empress left in her tracks. He could imagine Nesrelle's chilling smile as her power grew in the presence of this despair and death.

Tell her to stop, a part of him pleaded. *Surrender the gift and save them.* But another part of him thought of home, of the nestrae storming into Evren and burning homes and farms. Of the forest bursting into flame and his childhood friends being tortured until they became sacrifices on a pyre. Of Evren Garden swirling in smoke and darkness, until that sacred place vanished forever in a mound of ash and char.

His mouth was dry. He opened his eyes and looked straight into the bright, angry gaze of Lo, trapped again in Karye's deadly embrace.

No matter what he did, his guilt would be unbearable.

Karye smiled at him wickedly. "This little girl too? What do you choose: does she live or die?"

Lo's eyes didn't leave Avrik's. Even in the empress's grasp, her body looked poised and graceful. The fire in her eyes and the determined, brave slant of her mouth reminded him of Jennah and her warrior's spirit. If Lo was afraid, she would not give any of the

Alrenians surrounding her the pleasure of seeing it.

There was a roaring in his ears, the blood rushing and pounding in his head. His pulse was a drum beating out the final seconds of Lo's life. The sound built louder and stronger, overcoming every other noise until it was all he could hear, almost all he could think about.

As blood began to trickle from the girl's neck, Avrik opened his mouth and unleashed a roar, a visceral sound that seemed to tear the world in half.

CHAPTER TWENTY-NINE

THE RAIN THAT HAD BEEN threatening with the approaching storm came in a downpour. It was warm but violent, the raindrops stinging my skin and quickly forming puddles on the garden path. My sandals slipped and stuck in the mud as I walked. The torches tucked within the shelter of the pavilion flickered steadily, guiding my path with their light even as I ventured further from it.

Rounding a bend in the path, I nearly ran straight into Vionn, who stood letting the rain soak him. No doubt waiting for me. As usual, his face was concealed within the shadow of his hood. Before I could step back, he reached out with a gloved hand and clutched at my arm, his fingers digging in painfully.

"I've seen the truth," he hissed, leaning in so close to me that I could feel his hot breath brush against my face. He smelled of fried fish from the party, with an underlying sickly-sweet scent that reminded me of dead things. His voice was barely louder than the rainfall, and I had to strain my ears to hear. "Your friend Avrik barely has control over his gift," he continued. "He's weak. Easily…manipulated. And your plans with that slave girl? You had to know I would see them. But I suppose it's easy to forget about my power when you let your own truth gift be taken from you."

Instead of frightening me, his words had the opposite effect. Perhaps the curse the Life-Giver had placed on him had weakened his gift somehow, because it was clear he didn't know everything. If he had, Karye would have never dared to send me away. "You're cursed for misusing your gift," I snapped. "Why would I feel threatened by anything you say?"

He squeezed his bony fingers more tightly on my arm. "Maybe it's time you see the truth about your beloved ancestor, so you can understand the weakness running through your veins."

Immediately, I was immersed in a vision Vionn shared with me. Tamelle and Eldon stood alone under a night sky, the stars concealed behind a thick blanket of clouds. It must have been a cool night, or perhaps they were just trying to go unrecognized, because they were draped in cloaks, their hoods pulled up so that I almost couldn't see their shadowed faces. They walked together on a grassy hillside. Below them, nestled against the hill, stretched an army's camp, the rows of tents extending far beyond what I could see.

Tamelle lifted trembling arms, squeezing her eyes shut in concentration. "I don't have the control, El," she whispered, frustration making her voice sound ragged and breathless. She spoke in Alrenian, but with Vionn's truth gift fueling the vision, I didn't have to try to translate her words in my head. Instead, an understanding flowed through me effortlessly. "I—I know nothing of these Alrenian gifts," Tamelle stammered. "I can't form a barrier large enough to protect them. I don't know how." When she turned to look at Eldon, tears sparkled in her bright eyes.

Eldon's eyes softened as he reached out to grasp her hands in his. When a tear rolled down Tamelle's cheek, he brushed it away with tender fingers. "You don't have to bear this burden alone," he said, his voice low. "You could give your gift to me and I could wield it for you."

Tamelle swallowed, her forehead crinkling with uncertainty as she searched his face. "Would you be able to?" she asked.

He glanced up at the sky thoughtfully, watching the clouds swirl overhead. Wind whispered through the grass and made his shoulder-length blond hair ripple around his face. "I think so," he said at last. "I grew up surrounded by Alrenian gifts, and I've learned how to wield my own. I'm sure I could learn to use yours."

Tamelle settled her mouth into a determined line. "All right," she said. "It's yours."

The vision changed. I was back under a blue sky with Eldon kneeling and praying to the Life-Giver to form the barrier that had sealed Alrenor and Toryn away from the rest of the world, protecting Misroth for two centuries. He sliced his palm and let his blood drip to the ground as a group of soldiers and guards looked on. Nearby, standing beside a white steed, Tamelle buried her hand in the folds of her cloak to hide the freshly bleeding wound that had appeared on her own palm, matching her husband's. Her face looked pale, her eyes dim and shadowed by dark circles, but she didn't let the other Misrothians see her uncertainty or pain.

Eldon turned to face the gathering. "We are safe!" he cried. One of the men stepped forward to bandage the king's cut while others cheered and bowed.

"Your gift is a miraculous blessing from the Life-Giver, Your Majesty," a soldier murmured from where he kneeled in the grass.

As soon as his hand was bandaged, Eldon waved the others away and strode toward his queen. "How are you?"

The muscles around Tamelle's mouth tightened. When he reached for her hand, which she'd already bandaged herself, she pulled back. "I told you this was wrong," she said, her voice tense. Anger flared in her eyes. "How could you ignore me and use *my* gift for this? The Toryn are our allies. They've begged for our help, and instead, you've ignored them. We've as good as sentenced them to death. And now you want to lie to all the people who've opposed you and claim you've only closed the borders, not sealed up the old Alrenian Empire." She straightened her shoulders. "Maybe I should show everyone the gift is mine."

"Who would believe you?" Eldon asked. His voice sounded gentle, but it didn't soften the blow of his words. "You cannot wield it. And even if you knew how, you've given the gift to me."

The pain of betrayal flashed across Tamelle's face for an instant before she settled her face into a mask of stern distance.

"A gift does not return to someone who has permanently surrendered it," Eldon went on, glancing down at his bandaged hand. "All I've done, I've done to protect us. I left *my* people to protect and serve *yours*."

But Tamelle turned away, ignoring his words. Maybe she'd heard them before.

As the vision melted away, leaving me staring at the hooded figure in front of me, my stomach twisted into uncomfortable knots. King Eldon, my ancestor, the hero of so many Misorthian histories and legends, hadn't even been blessed with the famous protection gift. He'd used Tamelle to wield it, thrusting himself into a position of power over her and her people. No matter what his motivation might have been in the beginning, no matter the ways in which he may have defended and saved the Misrothian people, he'd manipulated his own wife. Just as my father had done to my mother.

My head spun. It was sickening to think that my hero, my ancestor, could have been as calculating and power-hungry as my father. In my first vision back in Toryn, I'd only seen enough to believe he had been acting in what he thought was Misroth's best interests, shedding his own blood to form the barrier that would keep us safe. But instead, he'd used his wife's gift against her will and then begun the work of concealing the truth so his people would never know he'd turned his back on his Toryn allies.

The blood running through my veins seemed more poisonous than ever. I was descended from a long line of greedy tyrants.

I growled in rage, but I knew what to do. Pulling away from Vionn's grip, I broke free and pushed him off balance. He stumbled backward as his hood slipped down to reveal his face.

I tensed, resisting the urge to recoil. Without the cover of shadow, I could see the source of the stench surrounding him: the curse the

Life-Giver had inflicted. *The truths you hold back from the empress will eat away at you,* the Life-Giver had told Vionn. *They will be your end.*

Vionn's face was a seeping mass of discolored, rotting flesh. Blackened, withered skin surrounded his filmy eyes, and his misshapen mouth hung slack. Part of his nose was missing, and over all his skin were open sores that oozed blood and pus. In the rain, which had already slowed to a drizzle, the blood mixed with water and flowed down his chin, staining his cloak.

With trembling gloved hands, he pulled his hood up to conceal his face again. "You've already lost," he said, his voice still strong and unwavering.

I smiled at him, one full of teeth and a deadly threat. "We'll see."

Karye's games would end tonight.

Over Vionn's shoulder, I saw Narek, Jennah, and Gillen running toward us. Narek clutched an Alrenian dagger, and the front of his shirt was stained with blood that was not his own. I met Jennah's gaze, and with a grin of understanding, she leapt lightly down from the pavilion to seize Vionn's arm.

He startled. "Wh—what?" Only his eyes were visible, but they simmered with anger. "I suppose you think you are strong and clever, but all you've done is capture a dead man. The *amara* will put a stop to you."

I sneered at him. "Let's see if you live long enough to find out." I glanced toward my companions. "Follow me."

"The plan?" Narek asked, scanning the garden, probably for Lo and Avrik.

I nodded. "Slightly revised."

My friends on my heels, I traced my way toward the Keep. Jennah marched alongside me, keeping a tight grip on Vionn's arm. The burnished gold shimmered over her dark skin in the torchlight. Narek, still clutching the dagger, brought up the rear, with Gillen close at his side. When I spared a glance over my shoulder, I found his eyes bright, his cheeks flushed, like he had been involved in whatever fight Narek had claimed his weapon in. He looked alive and energized.

The rain soon stopped, and the night became eerily still and quiet in the wake of the storm. Flashes of light in the distance heralded its arrival somewhere deeper within Alrenor, while the clouds overhead swirled and broke apart into thin wisps that allowed starlight to bathe the palace grounds. My heart pounded with resolve, and Jennah's steady presence beside me made my courage rise.

When we arrived at the yawning mouth of the Keep, Narek tried to hand over his dagger, but I waved it away.

"Wait here," I said, slipping into the Keep.

As before, there were no guards posted at the mouth of the tunnel. Since many of the Keepers had attended the party, the tunnels were mostly empty and quiet as I crept through the same route Lo and I had walked for the past several nights. Not wanting to waste time, I didn't pause to gather dragon scale armor or a saddle. When I opened the door to Reyva's quarters, the dragon snorted in greeting and nuzzled me with her nose.

"It's time to ride," I murmured in Alrenian, then continued to repeat the word, turning it into a command. Slowly, I grasped hold of Reyva's back and pulled myself up. For an instant, she grunted and tensed beneath me like she had in the past, her muscles rippling beneath my hands. Then, slowly, she eased herself lower to the ground, allowing me to climb onto her back and swing my legs over her sides.

The first time she launched forward, my heart gave a lurch, partly of fear but mostly from the thrill. She leapt through the entrance and swept through the tunnels, her heavy footfalls thundering in my ears. Through every twist and turn, the torchlight flashed along her scales and her wings fluttered gently behind her, never fully unfolding from her back but twitching in anticipation. Slaves in our path screamed and threw themselves out of the way.

"Don't hurt them," I commanded in Alrenian, but my words weren't needed.

Perhaps she was too focused on escaping from the Keep and

stretching her wings, or maybe she somehow sensed my wishes. Whatever the reason, Reyva never spared the slaves a glance.

When we plunged back out into the damp night air, my friends wasted no time gathering around Reyva and me.

"Friends," I told Reyva in Alrenian, and the dragon lowered her head to let them touch her.

With a carefree laugh, Jennah brushed her fingers over the dragon's snout. Her eyes sparkled with wonder when she looked from the dragon and then to me. "You did it," she murmured.

Gillen ran his fingers along Reyva's side, his eyes shining. He looked up and beamed at me. "I told you that you're my hero."

I bit back a smile. "Climb on," I urged. "We need to hurry."

My friends climbed up behind me. Narek and Jennah settled Vionn between them, where he quaked in fear.

Reyva didn't waste a second. Unfurling her wings to their enormous breadth, she let out a feral cry that sounded joyful and free. And then, in one massive leap, we were air bound. My heart hurled into my throat and my entire body seemed weightless. Wind whipped through my damp hair, snarling it into hopeless tangles that half-blinded me. Jennah folded her arms around my waist, her own racing pulse hammering against my back while she whooped and laughed in triumph. Despite my worry for Avrik, I couldn't contain my own elation.

We swept over the gardens until we noticed the figures standing outside the pavilion. My stomach dropped when I recognized Karye's gold-bright hair glowing in the torchlight, and across from her, Avrik flanked by two Dragon Keepers.

As we drew nearer, I shouted over the wind in Alrenian. "*Vorre!*" I cried.

Reyva circled lower until the small figures below grew larger. Everyone looked up, their eyes widening at the sight of my friends and me upon the empress's dragon. When we landed, Reyva crushed shrubbery beneath her claws with a creak and a shudder.

From his place kneeling on the ground, Avrik stared at me, but it wasn't surprise on his face…he was consumed by other emotions. Rage and pain darkened his eyes. Damp locks of hair clung to his forehead and his mouth was set in a determined line. The aura of power I'd sensed around him when he'd first revealed his gift seemed diminished.

I snapped my gaze to Karye, who stared back at me, pale and furious. A terrifying gleam shone in her eyes, magnified tenfold by the flickering torchlight surrounding her. Cast in the orange glow, even her hair looked like an inferno cascading down her back.

The horror of the situation became immediately clear when I saw the blood splattered across her face and the dripping dagger she clutched in her hand. In her arms, standing still and expressionless as Karye pointed the bloody dagger at her neck, was Lo. The two of them were encircled by the bodies of other slaves, their throats sliced open and their eyes staring lifelessly up at a night they could not see.

Fury thundered through me.

Karye flashed me a wicked smile that looked more like a snarl. "Avrik can stop the death any time he wants, as soon as he surrenders his gift to me." She pressed the blade tip into Lo's neck, making the girl's eyes widen ever so slightly as a thin trickle of blood dripped onto her dress collar. "Even with Reyva, you can't stop me without also killing this slave, and I know you. You can't do that. You can't handle a single loss." She sneered at me and then flicked her gaze to the Keepers flanking Avrik. "And then Reyva will return to us."

I coiled my hands into fists. Karye was trusting in the fact that her dragon would respond to the vylae on her armor, but I knew she was wrong. "If you kill Lo," I said, my voice low and even but with an edge of wrath, "you'll die instantly. You won't live long enough to see if your dragon responds to you."

Lo met my gaze, and I was amazed by the courage shimmering in her dark eyes. Spine straight, body rigid, she faced her own end with grace beyond her youth. At the same time, I felt sick: this is what a lifetime of suffering and loss had forged her into. She had lived out all her years in the shadow of death, growing used to its threat, so what new fear could it bring to her?

Karye laughed, low and guttural, but I caught the uncertain tremble of her mouth, a brief crack in her confident mask. My riding in on her dragon had unnerved her. With a feral growl, she tightened her grip on her dagger, preparing to slash it across Lo's neck.

My heart stuttered. Behind me, Jennah cried out sharply. Gillen had already crumpled to the ground, moaning and clutching his head, fighting unseen demons that the real one facing us had brought back to life. Narek made a movement as if to control the Keepers standing across from Karye, but I knew they were too far away.

The dagger angled toward Lo's throat and bounced off, as if striking an invisible shield. *Avrik.* Before Karye could finish her cry of rage, Lo took advantage of the empress's shock and tore the dagger from her grip. Twisting in Karye's arms, Lo slashed the blade across the woman's throat. With a strangled, choking sound, the empress of Alrenor clutched in vain for her Forwyn slave and the weapon in her hands, and collapsed in a pool of her own blood, surrounded by her victims.

CHAPTER THIRTY

Avrik

AS SOON AS THE EMPRESS fell, Avrik's gift flared stronger, along with a surge of other strengths: a rush of courage from Jennah and a spark from Narek's war gift. They united to make his own feel more powerful, and his control sharpened. Focusing, he pushed his gift to spread further. The two Keepers at his side crumpled to the ground as if struck by an invisible force. He leapt to his feet as the few slaves who still lived, a man and woman who'd earlier shrunk back in fear, rushed toward the fallen Keepers.

Avrik could tell instantly that Narek's gift was helping their movements. They wrested the Keepers' weapons away with strength and skill they couldn't have possessed on their own. By the time Narek reached them, the Keepers already lay dead at the slaves' feet.

Eyes sparking with anger, blood still trailing down her neck, Lo stalked toward Vionn. She extended her bloody dagger, making a fearsome figure despite the way her voice trembled. "You," she began, but it seemed she couldn't manage anything more. Her body shook with emotion.

It didn't matter. Vionn turned and fled, screaming as he ran. "Murder! The empress! Guards!"

What happened next was a blur of violence and bloodshed, the moment a mighty empire began to crumble into chaos. Avrik plucked a dagger from one of the Keeper's bodies and followed Narek and Jennah as they chased after Vionn. Guards descended upon them, coming from seemingly every direction at once, but Avrik's gift flowed freely through his veins, pushing aside every blade or arrow sent their way. For every guard they encountered, there were also slaves who felt Narek's and Jennah's gifts emboldening them. They stole weapons from bodies or took hold of torches and attacked the guards. Soon Avrik was in the midst of a wild fray of tangled bodies, experienced warriors and inexperienced slaves fighting with terrible ferocity in the rain-slick night.

And the Alrenians were losing.

At some point, Halia and Gillen mounted the dragon again. Its wings pulsed like drumbeats as the beast bellowed and swooped low to clutch guards in its talons and then rise into the air to drop them, screaming and thrashing, from deadly heights.

At last, the remaining Alrenian guards, hopelessly outnumbered, surrendered. Nobles peered out through windows of the palace, their eyes wide and faces pale as the party that had been moved inside stopped altogether. The remaining Dragon Keepers stormed out in a fury of flashing armor and blazing eyes, but as soon as Halia landed the dragon in front of them, their procession halted.

"Your *amara* is dead," she declared. "And your dragons will now submit to us. If you want to live, surrender."

Avrik couldn't help but stare at her. The very air around her crackled with her commanding presence, in the confidence she'd found when she'd faced overwhelming odds and survived anyway. Though he'd never admit it to her, he could see that even her father's training had served her well in the way she made her face a mask, showing no fear or doubt. Her mouth was an unyielding line, her jaw sharp, and her eyes like fiery emeralds, beautiful but hard. This was the fierceness that he'd once seen, buried and nearly lost within the mute girl he'd befriended years ago, finally unleashed in the woman who would now be queen.

At first, the arrogant captain of the Keepers tried to sneer and protest, but Halia was right. Their eyes darted around to the bodies littering the palace grounds and then to the superior numbers surrounding them. All were protected by Avrik's gift and fueled by Jennah's and Narek's.

The captain glared at Avrik.

"You..." he snarled, but his threat died on his lips. There wasn't anything he could do to harm Avrik while he was in control of his gift, keeping the invisible shield he'd formed around himself and his allies. The captain's arms shook with repressed fury.

Avrik flashed him a bold grin. "I understand. I often leave people speechless."

The Forwyn set to work, binding the Alrenians with cords of rope. A few arrived with the empress's daughter, Jaliana, in custody, so all of Karye's people could see that their hope of resistance was gone—for now. Around Lo's age, Jaliana was the mirror image of the empress, but pale and trembling. Blue eyes shining with tears, she asked what had happened to her mother.

"We will not hurt the girl," a Forwyn man reassured Halia. "She is our chance to train up a new kind of Alrenian leader—one who could bring peace between the Forwyn and Alrenians."

Others surrounded Lo, bolstering her. Tears trailed down the girl's cheeks, mingling with the blood at her throat. But when Jennah stepped forward, unstringing golden ribbons from her hair until her curls fell free, the others seemed to understand and gave her room. Humming softly, she braided the ribbons together and tied them about the girl's neck.

Lo dried her eyes and stared ahead, her gaze distant and empty. "I thought killing her would make it hurt less," she said. "I avenged my brother. Why does it still..." She choked back a sob.

Inwardly, Avrik cringed, his own grief sweeping through him in response to the girl's loss painted so starkly across her face.

"Nothing will take the pain away," Jennah murmured. Her hands were gentle as she laid them on the girl's shoulders. "But let this braid be a reminder of him, and your memory of today, when you had the courage to fight for your people. Let that ease your pain."

Avrik turned away.

Enemy bodies were everywhere, the scents of blood and dragon smoke heavy in the air. Every muscle in his body ached with exhaustion. The cold that coursed through his veins, reminding him of Nesrelle's claim on his life, made the balmy air feel harsh. As a night breeze ruffled through his rain-damp hair, he repressed a shiver.

The remaining Keepers and guards were led to the palace dungeons, and the members of Karye's court who'd attended the party became captives in the palace, unable to leave until the Forwyn people decided what they would do next.

Forwyn power over the capital was tentative. They had the dragons and the future empress in their possession, but they did not command Alrenor's armies. As soon as word spread of the Forwyn uprising, resistance around the empire would begin. Avrik listened to them discuss this quietly as they reentered the palace. They made quick work of choosing representatives to speak with Halia.

How quickly violence turned to politics.

Avrik retreated to his old room in the palace to bathe and change. It was strange to walk the halls and hear the muttered curses of the nobles bound and locked in rooms, to see the halls empty of Alrenian guards and filled instead with armed Forwyn walking proud and free.

As the morning sun kissed the horizon, a knock sounded on Avrik's door. He opened it to see Halia standing in the hallway, with her hair braided and her face scrubbed clean. It looked like she'd only spared a moment to throw on a tunic and leggings and shove a dagger into the belt at her waist.

Though her eyes shone with an inner fire, her expression was schooled into a careful mask.

Avrik cringed inwardly. Despite the way they'd fallen back into familiar friendship, the awkward tension hadn't fully disappeared either.

Because you haven't told her, he told himself fiercely. Not how he felt. Not what Nesrelle had done to him. The secrets were a weight, heavy and unnatural between them.

"We're leaving," she said. "The Forwyn are letting us take three dragons to Misroth. It's all they dare offer, but I never anticipated a true alliance with Karye anyway. At least this way we'll be in Misroth soon." She drew a deep breath. "And…I think, maybe, even three dragons can make a difference for us in battle."

Avrik noticed the bag slung over her shoulder and assumed the Forwyn had also provided some provisions. Since he had no possessions left of his own, he had nothing to pack. Stepping into the hall, he followed her through the palace's endless passages. Now that the danger from Karye was gone and all of their time didn't have to be consumed with plans to stop her, his urge to speak to Halia—*really* speak to her—was overwhelming.

"Halia—" he began.

They rounded a corner and encountered two former slaves carrying trays of food. As soon as the girls noticed them, they burst into curtseys and words of gratitude. Avrik forced himself to smile back, despite his frustration at the interruption.

"Now that the Forwyn know how to tame the dragons more effectively than the Alrenians, they will have more power than they ever dreamed they could," Halia explained.

In every courtyard they passed, Forywn men, women, and children were gathered, patrolling with weapons even as they sang and laughed, rejoicing in their new freedom. Each time they saw Avrik and Halia, they greeted them with the reverence due royalty and the enthusiasm given to old friends. Halia nodded gracefully each time someone bowed or curtseyed before her, but Avrik was totally at a loss. His usual easy smile abandoned him. Instead, he blinked uncomfortably. The Forywn didn't seem to mind.

At last, they exited the palace and wound through the gardens, leaving the noise and crowds behind.

"Halia," Avrik ground out.

She pretended she hadn't heard him and went on with her speech. Maybe she knew what he was going to say and was trying to stop him. Maybe he was about to ruin everything between himself and his best friend. Maybe he was crazy for not letting her stop him. "Eventually," she said breathlessly, "the Forwyn hope to let Karye's daughter Jaliana rule, after she has lived among Forwyn and with their influence in the palace. They hope this way—"

Avrik caught her wrist and spun her around to face him. Halia's mask fell away as her eyes widened.

Taking both of her hands gently in his, Avrik stepped closer until he could feel the heat of her body countering the chill inside of him. Until he could feel her breath mingling with his own.

"Just friendship between us isn't enough, Halia," he blurted out, before he could lose his nerve like he had a thousand times before. "But I was terrified I could never be enough for you. I'm still terrified. You've always been…just out of reach. Even when you weren't royalty, I felt like I was always begging for your attention."

A crease formed between Halia's eyebrows. "You were always flirting with other girls."

Nerves and desire danced low in his stomach. "At first, I thought I only wanted your friendship, but when I pursued other girls…I realized they weren't what I wanted. I only continued to flirt with other girls because I was a fool, trying to get your attention and make you jealous. Those other girls…" He shook his head. "It never meant anything, because they weren't *you*. Many were just desperate to be noticed. But *you*…you are everything they could never be to me: beautiful and strong and fierce and brave."

Halia blinked, and Avrik drew a deep breath. How could he dare believe she truly wanted him?

"I'm afraid I could never deserve you, but I want to." His breath caught in his chest, making him feel equal parts weak and daring all at once. "You overwhelmed me as Elena, but as Halia? As princess, maybe queen?" He forced out a nervous laugh. "You are as unreachable as the sun. I haven't a hope in the world to deserve you. You're a *queen*. I'm no one. But I want to be someone, for you."

He drew closer, until their foreheads touched and the growing smile on Halia's face was all he could see. His heart thundered in his chest. Every one of his words sounded clumsy in his ears, but mirrored on Halia's face was the same wild hope that danced through his veins. In that moment he could read her more clearly than he ever had, and in her joy, she was radiant.

Her laughter bubbled up, carefree and musical. "You're a fool," she whispered, tugging her hands from his and encircling her arms about his neck. "I'm right here. It's always been you and me."

He tangled his fingers in her hair, drawing her face toward his. When he kissed her, she tasted like rain and salt and smoke. The deathly chill in his blood thawed.

For an instant, he could see their past and present and future all joining into something filled with hope. The images rushed through his mind: Halia laughing and racing him along the windswept countryside of Evren, under an endless blue sky. He envisioned her now, strong and unyielding and bright, leaning into his embrace and deepening their kiss. And he imagined the dream he'd held onto for so long: a future at her side, a world in which they held each other together, no matter how broken life made them. Hope swelled within him, almost blotting out the fear and despair that had been growing in the back of his mind lately.

And then Nesrelle's chill returned, along with searing pain that spread like lightning from his heart to the rest of his body. With a muffled groan, he stumbled back, pulling away from Halia.

Her hands reached for empty air. "Avrik?" she asked, uncertainty leaking into her voice.

Nesrelle's icy fingers grasped Avrik's shoulders, and her cool breath brushed the back of his neck. "You forget that you're mine," she whispered. "You have no future."

The pain nearly made his knees buckle. His insides were freezing over, organs ceasing to function, blood slowing to a crawl. His heart stuttered as he choked for air.

Halia caught him, her warm arms competing with the ice spreading through him.

Then, just as quickly, the pain was gone and the coldness receded. Avrik drew in a long, shuddering breath.

He peered up at Halia's face, watching the growing daylight paint strands of gold in her dark hair. But there was a shadow cast across her face and growing worry lines on her forehead. "What's wrong?" she demanded.

Forcing himself to his feet, Avrik shook the weak sensation off and tried to smile. His bravado didn't fool her. With birdsong and the scent of flowers heavy on the breeze, Nesrelle's darkness seemed distant, surreal. But the echo of pain was real, as was the growing fear shattering the hope he'd felt earlier.

His smile faded. "Nesrelle marked me," he said hoarsely, forcing himself to meet Halia's frightened gaze. "I'm dying."

CHAPTER THIRTY-ONE

A VRIK'S WORDS REPEATED ENDLESSLY IN my head: *I'm dying, I'm dying, I'm dying.*

But there was no time to ask questions. Lo and a few of the other former slaves approached to lead us to the Dragon Keep, where Gillen and my friends waited near the entrance. The Forwyn let us each choose our own dragon scale armor. I plucked a set of black pieces that appeared to be close to my size and slipped them over my clothes as my friends did the same. Finally, we slipped on our helmets, selected our saddles, and approached the two new dragons my friends would be riding. Just like my experience with Reyva, they submitted willingly when approached as equals, rather than drugged and forced. Narek saddled a vibrant green and black dragon named Kova, and Avrik and Jennah shared Jozek, whose ivory and sapphire scales flashed bright in the early morning sunlight.

As we prepared to leave, the Forwyn bidding us farewell with heartfelt blessings, I turned to Lo. "You could still come with us," I offered, as I had before when we'd first made our plan to escape.

Her smile carried all the hope and fierceness of her people, but she shook her head. "You gave us a fighting chance. Now it's left to us to use it and finally make Alrenor our home." She kissed her fingertips and pressed them to her heart in a traditional Forwyn gesture. "May Elhani hold you in his hands and the guidespirits lead you home." She bowed her head. "Thank you for all you have done for us, *melhona*. I hope your people win their war."

I nodded, though my smile was tight. "Thank you. If we do…your people will always have allies in Misroth."

Gillen rode behind me on Reyva, who was clearly a queen among the dragons. She took the lead in our flight, her wings thunder in a sky of gold. As the dragons ascended, so high that we brushed through wispy clouds, the capital and surrounding Alrenian landscape fell away to insignificant smears of color and shapes below us.

At first, I tried to track our progress by landmarks, but they were almost indistinguishable, and the speed at which the dragons flew was dizzying. Wisps of hair tugged free of my braid and whipped in front of my eyes. Even with the helmet I wore, the wind rushed in my ears and stung my eyes.

Using the commands Lo had taught me, I directed Reyva northward. We flew at a rate that seemed impossibly fast, and by late morning, when I guided Reyva to descend and search for a place to land, I recognized the land we'd traversed after fleeing the Aremakkin Temple. After months of trekking across Toryn and Alrenor, we would be home by the end of the day.

We landed near a hill in empty countryside, with nothing to see but livestock and farmland for miles in any direction. My skin prickled at the thought of lingering at all in Alrenor, even though I knew no one this far from the capital could know about the empress's death already. And the Forwyn were in control of the palace and the Dragon Keep—for now.

I leapt from the saddle and turned to Reyva, brushing my fingers along her snout. The thrill of touching this fierce creature and staring her in the eyes was nearly overwhelming. At first I wasn't entirely sure the dragons would remain committed to any of our commands when we weren't present. They weren't controlled by drugs or even truly tamed. But when I looked at the dragon before me, I had a respect and understanding for this creature I never could have possessed before meeting and flying with her. There was something more powerful between us than the relationship between mistress and tamed beast: the understanding that we were each free creatures, joined together by mutual respect. When she took flight and the other dragons followed, no doubt to hunt, I no longer had qualms about it.

Jennah came up beside me to watch them soar overhead. Casting me a sidelong glance, she arched her eyebrow in a silent question.

"They'll return," I said.

"What are you planning?" Jennah asked. Dressed in pure ivory armor, she cut an intimidating figure. Her carefully knotted curls had fallen free when she'd removed her helmet, and now hung in wild disarray around her shoulders. With two Alrenian daggers secured on the belt slung over her hips, she looked like an Alrenian warrior of old.

On my other side, Gillen sat in the grass, wiping a weary hand across his face and sighing deeply. "Misroth City, Kelwed, and Argelon are all overrun," he said, his voice low and heavy. "The nestrae have shown me in their visions."

I glanced down at him and the way his shoulders drooped.

"I've seen it too," I said softly, and the others nodded along. Though to a lesser extent than Gillen, we all were haunted by nestred visions.

"Most of Misroth's army is in Argelon." Narek watched me levelly, his tone matter-of-fact. His stance was relaxed, but everything about the way his hand rested on the hilt of his newly acquired Alrenian sword told me otherwise. He was prepared to go to war. Even if it meant facing an entire demon army with only the five of us and our three dragons.

"We'll have to do whatever we can to form a new army then. And the dragons will be useful. The nestrae might not fear their fire, but they will learn to fear their teeth." I set my jaw and eyed each of my friends in turn. It hurt to look into Avrik's face, to see his shadowed eyes and see the evidence of what he'd told me. He was dying. "I have to believe that this wasn't all for nothing, that just as we gave the

Forwyn the fighting chance they needed, they gave us ours. I don't believe the enemy has spread into Evren yet, so we're going to fly there to plan and prepare until we're ready to take back the capital."

Jennah, Gillen, and Narek all nodded. At the mention of Evren, Avrik tensed and pain lashed across his face for the briefest instant.

As the others sat to drink from canteens and eat a quick meal of jerky, nuts, and oranges, I pulled Avrik aside.

"Is this all right?" I asked softly.

He blinked back at me. "Evren is your home." He shrugged. "Even if…maybe it isn't mine anymore. It's close to the capital but easily overlooked. It makes sense to go there."

I squeezed his arm, but he reached out and grasped my hand instead, threading his fingers through mine. When I stared into his face, his eyes were dark. I could almost see the shadowy thoughts racing through his mind, the way a storm churned and swirled in his gaze. He might have worn a mask for the rest of the world, but I could see through the smile he gave me.

"Avrik," I whispered. "We can fight this. We can find a way." My voice sounded pleading in my ears, and I hated it.

He squeezed my hand tighter. "Let's not talk about it now." He flashed me another smile, still brilliant, even if I could see the tension behind it. "We have a kingdom to save."

A journey that would have taken weeks by land and sea took mere hours by air. We turned westward to cross the sea, and soon, too soon, the waves gave way to landscape I recognized. Rolling green hills spread out before us and farmland stretched as far as I could see. Relief fluttered through me to see farmhouses and fields tucked safely away in this part of my kingdom. As our dragons circled low, I scanned Evren's town center, with unblemished shops lining the dirt roads, just as I remembered. Everything was comfortingly yet painfully familiar:

the dress shop where Lyanna and I spent more time purchasing fabric than being fitted for dresses, the bakery where Benja made perfect buttery, flaky pastries, and *Wanderer's Rest* where Avrik, Bren, and I liked to linger after school and enjoy some of Selna's famed stew.

Everywhere there were memories, physical places that had held pieces of my heart all this time I'd been away. Places I'd feared I would never see again. It was almost too much.

My heart swelled with longing and fear, joy and sorrow. What would Lyanna and Rev do when they saw me again? Could they forgive me for leaving without a goodbye, and for all the other mistakes I'd made since then? Would they treat me differently when they knew I was royalty, and I'd kept it a secret from them? Unshed tears burned my throat.

Our dragons quickly captured people's attention. It was late afternoon, and the town market was filled with farmers and vendors selling their wares and shoppers milling about. As the dragons' shadows fell over them, men and women pointed and cried out, while others drew weapons. Mothers clutched their children tightly to them. A few people fled into nearby stores for cover, but most lingered, staring in awe and uncertainty at the sight before them.

I landed Reyva right there in the square. Her feet struck ground with a thud and a cloud of upturned dust. The other two dragons followed, descending on either side of her.

Murmurs and whispers rose around us, questioning who we were and what we wanted, though no one dared speak directly to any of us.

Removing my helmet and passing it to Gillen, I climbed down just as my eyes landed on Lyanna and Rev, and everything else fell away. My eyes clouded. There they were, just as I remembered them, Lyanna's gentle face and soft blue eyes filled with awe as she clutched a basket of produce to her chest, squeezing it so tightly her fingers turned white. Rev ran a hand repeatedly through his greying hair, tousling it into a wild mess until he switched to fidgeting with his glasses instead.

A tense moment of doubt filled me. My hair had long fallen from its braid, hanging in loose tangles around my face, and I was clothed in Alrenian armor. Did they even recognize me?

And then tears filled Lyanna's eyes as she opened her arms wide. I choked back a sob and launched myself toward them. No one dared stand in my way as I ran, the crowd parting like water. Tears burned my eyes.

Lyanna's embrace was warm, filled with the scent of lavender. It was acceptance and love and a broken heart returning to life and hope. It was sunshine in her garden and freshly baked bread in the kitchen. It was waking from a nightmare only to find Lyanna grasping my hand and brushing the hair back from my face, making me realize I had never been alone. Never.

Home. I was home.

"Oh, my dear," Lyanna whispered through her tears. She stroked my hair even as her shoulders shook. "You've come back to us. You're all right. You've come back."

Slowly, she pulled back, letting Rev step forward, blinking fiercely. Behind his glasses, his eyes were already red and puffy. "Oh, El—" He paused suddenly, stiffening and clearing his throat. "I mean, Y-your Majesty…" he stammered.

As if they'd planned it, they both fell into awkward poses, each trying to bow and courtesy and show respect. The Evren citizens surrounding us caught on, and with a string of gasps and murmurs, men, women, and children all around me began to kneel. Behind me, my friends had descended their dragons, they alone standing tall in the marketplace. They, at least, had learned to stop behaving formally around me.

Wiping the tears from my cheeks, I stared at Rev and Lyanna. "What are you doing?"

"Word spread to Evren of the missing princess returning to overthrow her tyrant father," Rev said, shooting me a significant glance. "Messengers described you quite clearly. Between that and your letter, everything finally made sense. We just could hardly believe that all that time we'd been caring for the princess herself…" He dropped lower, deepening his bow.

I shook my head vigorously. "No, stand up. You don't bow to me."

They rose, blinking in surprise, and I pulled Rev into a fierce hug. He patted and rubbed my back soothingly as I sniffed back the last of my tears.

"We weren't sure…now that you have your home at the castle…if—if you would care to return to Evren again," he spluttered. "Princess Halia."

"Of course," I said. "And just call me Halia. *This* is home. If—if you'll still let me call it that."

"We wouldn't dream of anything else," Lyanna replied. "You'll always be a daughter to us."

I stepped back to look at them both: their sweet faces showing a few more wrinkles than when I'd last seen them, their hair a bit greyer, but their eyes shining with as much love and life as ever. They were kindness and safety. And most shocking of all, I could see their unwavering pride and belief in me, even though they must have wondered after my years of silence and secrets, and then again after they'd heard I'd left Misroth for Toryn.

"And you can speak," Lyanna burst out, laughing at perhaps how ridiculous it sounded compared to the miracle of being together again. How insignificant it was. They'd always heard me, even when I'd been voiceless. I could be mute Elena or Princess Halia riding into Evren on a dragon—it didn't change the way they saw or loved me. Perhaps they'd always seen this brave side of me, just as Avrik had, even when I had not.

I laughed along with her. "Yes," I said. Drawing a deep breath, I straightened. "But my friends and I need some help." I searched their faces, watching as shadows passed over them. "Misroth is in danger."

Turning to the people surrounding me, I raised my voice. "Please, rise. Don't stand on formality here. You all knew me once as Elena, and even though I may be Princess Halia now, you are still my neighbors." I glanced at my friends, my eyes lingering on Avrik, who was standing stiffly, his face still concealed beneath his helmet. For now, he waited unnoticed in his dragon's shadow, but I wondered how the people of Evren would react when they realized he'd returned. Did they hate him as much as he seemed to think they did?

Corin, the town Leader, stepped forward from the crowd with a welcoming nod in my direction. Returning the gesture, I addressed him. "I need your help. Enemies have invaded the capital and we need to prepare for war. And that means that we'll need a place to stay and plan." I turned again to the people, meeting some of their eyes, mentally weighing the strength of their will and courage. "And we'll need men and women willing to serve as soldiers. I'll explain further once we've gathered some recruits."

Though I knew the people in Evren wouldn't have any idea about the nestrae, since even the people living under their oppression were unaware of them, he didn't question my authority. With a smile, he nodded quickly. "Yes, Your Majesty. We'll start right away." He began calling to some of the town patrol guards as Lyanna tugged on my arm.

"My dear, I know you have much to do, but let Corin and his men begin the work while you and your friends take some time to rest. Before the sun sets," she finished, and from the shadows that dimmed her eyes, I could tell that nighttime had become Evren's nightmare. The sedwa attacks must have continued to grow worse in my absence. My heart gave a painful twinge at the thought.

"Yes," Rev said eagerly. "Come home."

I looked in their faces, bright with those endearing, familiar smiles, and I couldn't hold back my grin.

Home.

The scent of Lyanna's famous freshly baked honey lavender bread filled the kitchen with its tantalizing aroma. Clustered around the table, where Rev had crammed every extra dining chair and armchair he could find in the house, I couldn't shake how surreal this was. If I closed my eyes and only listened to the sound of Lyanna humming as she sliced and served the bread, or her giggles as Rev swept her into a twirling dance around the kitchen, I could pretend no time had passed since I'd last sat here. It was just another evening after dinner, enjoying a sweet treat before bed.

I took a bite of the slice I held, still warm and crispy on the outside, and my mouth watered at the familiar taste.

Then I opened my eyes to see Narek and Jennah seated across the table from me. The man who'd been one of the reasons I'd fled in fear to Evren in the first place, and the woman who had helped me face that fear. It was strange to see my two worlds collide here in this tiny home: Elena's simple life joining with Halia's complicated one. On one side of me, Gillen smiled and sweet-talked his way into Lyanna's and Rev's hearts, as if he were a dear old friend or another member of the family and not their Crown Prince.

On my other side, Avrik was uncharacteristically quiet. He slipped his hand under the table and threaded his fingers through mine before leaning toward me and flashing a dimpled smile. For a moment, the pain churning in his eyes was almost invisible. The reserved, uncertain way even Lyanna and Rev had greeted him hadn't escaped my notice. Their hospitality never wavered for anyone, but they hadn't showered him with it, either.

With some help from Gillen and Jennah, I'd relayed the events that had happened since I'd left Evren, leaving out dark and dangerous details that would only grieve Lyanna and Rev. Maybe another day they could hear the story in full. Lyanna dabbed her eyes even at my shortened version.

"I'm so sorry I left the way I did," I murmured, probably for the hundredth time.

"Everything is forgiven," Rev said, also likely for the hundredth time. "We love you, El…Halia." He cracked an uncertain smile when he used my new name. It sounded foreign in his mouth, but not in a bad way. "We always will."

"Now we have other serious matters to discuss," Lyanna said, gently swatting Rev away when he tried to pull her into another twirl around the kitchen, and returning to the table. She sat down and folded her hands in her lap, ignoring the bread on her own plate.

Rev joined us, seating himself beside Lyanna. He squeezed his wife's shoulder and sighed. "You're right."

His eyes flicked briefly to Avrik before his gaze settled back on me. "After you left…" He cleared his throat. "The sedwa attacks have become more violent. Instead of the occasional attack from one creature here and there, they've struck in groups every night."

Lyanna's blue eyes looked darker, sadder. "There have been deaths," she said tremulously. "Eliya, Hevro's wife, Selna's oldest son, Tyol and Korev and some of the other patrol guards, and Bre—" Her voice cracked and she looked away, tears shining in her eyes.

I set my jaw and blinked back my own tears. "Bren's sister Elysse. I know," I said, voice raspy.

A muscle worked in Rev's jaw, betraying his own grief.

Unexpectedly, Lyanna reached across the table and squeezed Avrik's hand, and he didn't pull away.

"But we've discovered the sedwa won't enter the sacred garden," Rev continued, "so the entire town takes refuge there every night before the sun goes down. During the day we try to live as normally as we can."

"How are there so many?" I asked. "The forest is large, but surely that many sedwa would run out of prey by now. We killed some…" I shook my head, thinking of the early fights in Evren Forest with Gare, Layk, Jennah, and Narek at my side.

"They live in the mountains, too," Rev said in a low voice. "We believe they must travel between the forest and mountains more than we'd realized, always moving in search of more prey. It's only recently…with the…hunting…that they grew brave enough to attack humans." He cleared his throat when Avrik tensed. "And with the barrier now broken, they must be crossing through the mountains from Toryn."

Lyanna's eyes darted to the windows, where the sun was drifting toward the western horizon. The dying light filled the cabin with an orange glow, one that used to be comforting, but one that now brought terror to the people of Evren.

"It's time," she said.

She and Rev rose, leaving the dishes for the next day, wrapping the bread in cloth, and filling packs with canteens and toiletry items. I fell into an easy rhythm as I helped them. In mere moments we were outside, prepared for the trek to Evren Garden. Overhead, Reyva circled, her silhouette so huge it cast the whole cabin in shadow.

"What about your dragon?" Rev asked me. I could tell from his wide eyes that he was still in awe of Reyva. But then, so was I. My heart soared with adrenaline at the mere sight of the creature and the sound of her beating wings.

"She and the others won't go far."

As we turned away from the cabin, Avrik grasped my arm. "I'll meet you in the garden later," he said under his breath.

Before I could protest, he slipped away soundlessly.

CHAPTER THIRTY-TWO

Avrik's skin prickled as he pushed open the creaking door. The air smelled stale and dusty inside, but everything lay untouched since he'd last been home. A pair of his father's mud-encrusted boots sat by the door. Maps Avrik had pored over before he'd left still lay scattered across the kitchen table.

He wasn't sure exactly what had led him here. The need for a final goodbye? He watched dust motes dance in the bronze light pooling from the windows as the ever-familiar chill of death brushed the back of his neck. Death had haunted this house for many long years now, stalking both him and his father, watching them from the shadows. It had left a nightmarish memory in the back of their minds, and an omnipresent hole in their lives.

Avrik swore he could still hear his mother moaning in pain. His ears filled with echoes from his father, pushing over furniture and screaming at the ceiling after Mother had passed. "I hate you!" he shouted, and at first young Avrik had been so confused he'd hidden under his bed. Did his father hate him? Was it his fault Mother had died? But in time Avrik had come to understand that his father was screaming at the Life-Giver, the god who had led Mother to the afterlife.

But Avrik had never blamed the Life-Giver for his own pain. The shadowy presence of death lingering at the edges of his vision was different, hostile. And deep down, he knew it wasn't death itself that had been the worst thing for his mother, but the painful illness that had destroyed her body in life.

Avrik had become an expert at blocking out the difficult memories. He pushed them away with hardly a thought; it was something he had practiced every day for years, after all. Instead of lingering in those terrible memories, he wandered to his mother's library and ran his fingers along the spines of books he'd once loaned to Halia, along with tomes filled with fighting techniques and histories of battle strategies he'd once studied religiously.

Happier memories of his mother reading to him floated through his mind. Her laughter. Her gentle smile. The floral scent he'd always associated with her.

When he wandered to his father's bedroom, conflicting emotions warred within Avrik. Everything was as Kyrin had left it before he'd been arrested. The necklace his wife had gifted him upon their marriage lay on the nightstand, along with the one he'd given her. They were both white gold: hers with a simple diamond pendant and his with a tree of entwined branches. Avrik's throat tightened as he lifted them and hung both around his neck, the cool metal tickling his skin. He had the urge to cling to them and throw them away all at once.

He could hear his father's voice as clearly as if he'd spoken to him yesterday: "You'll do great things someday." He'd nudged Avrik gently, lovingly, as they'd ridden into Kelwed upon their horse Billa's back. Avrik had never been to a city before that day. "You're meant for more than just Evren."

The memories were potent. His father teaching him to hunt. His father laughing with him as he corrected his stance and trained him to shoot a bow better than anyone else in Evren—until Halia had arrived. His father holding him as they'd both wept for Mother, standing over the simple stone they'd placed in the memorial field, the place that marked where they'd scattered her ashes.

"We still have each other, son," Kyrin had told Avrik countless times. "You'll never be alone, do you understand? I'll always love you. I'll always put you first."

Tears burned Avrik's eyes, but he refused to let them fall. He wasn't sure how he could forgive his father. He wasn't sure how he could *not* forgive him, either.

Kyrin's love for him couldn't undo the bloodshed he'd caused, couldn't change Avrik's mind about the wrongness of it all. And yet, deep down, he loved and mourned his father. He grieved Kyrin's choices as much as he grieved his death.

Avrik let out a long breath and squeezed his eyes shut. "I forgive you, Father," he whispered. Then, opening his eyes, he frowned. Even though he couldn't see Nesrelle, he continued to feel the heavy presence of death. *You won't win,* he thought fiercely.

But as he left his house, the door squeaking shut behind him, he heard her voice, as if carried on the breeze. *I already have.*

Guilt over his father's crimes drove him to the memorial field, where carved stones and altars honored Evren's dead. When he entered through the gate, he found a familiar figure standing in front of one of the stones. Bren's sandy hair looked golden in the light of the setting sun, his lanky form even taller than when Avrik had last seen him.

Avrik hesitated, but the creak of the gate had already given him away. Bren glanced over his shoulder, and his dark eyes, normally soft and friendly, narrowed.

Avrik's eyes darted past Bren, to the writing on the altar. *Elysse.* A bouquet of wildflowers lay burning and smoking on its top, a fresh offering. Horror and grief clawed their way up Avrik's throat, but his legs wouldn't move. Every muscle in his body went rigid.

"I'm so sorry," he choked out, but there were several yards between him and Bren, and his voice was strangled. He wasn't sure if

Bren could hear him. He wasn't sure Bren cared to.

His old friend turned back to the altar, watching the flames lick at the amber and white petals. For the longest moment, Avrik was immobile, unable to step forward or retreat. A breeze kissed his face. A forest of grass and wildflowers waved between him and Bren, and Avrik wondered if the distance was too great to ever cross again.

"Sorry?" Bren didn't turn, and his response was so delayed, his voice so low, that for a moment Avrik thought he was imagining the words. "Sorry won't bring her back, Avrik."

Avrik grit his teeth against the influx of pain. He had expected his best friend to be bitter, but that didn't change how much it hurt. Even worse was the guilt he carried over the other lives lost. His wild, emotionally charged decision to try to eradicate the sedwa had been foolhardy at best, and deadly at the worst.

But he hadn't come here to beg forgiveness of Bren, or of anyone. He'd only wanted a moment to face the consequences of his and Kyrin's decisions, his stark reminder that he owed the people of Evren—and all Misroth—whatever fight was left in him, until his last breath.

Avrik's glance darted westward. The sky was stained the color of blood, the last sliver of sunlight slipping beneath the horizon. He scanned the forest, which, even at this distance, was old and vast enough to be a huge blot of green to the east. Beneath the swaying trees, the shadows were lengthening into oppressive darkness. He had the terribly familiar feeling that they were being watched.

"Staying here until the sedwa take you too won't bring her back either," he said.

Bren rounded on him, his eyes shining with a dangerous light. A vein in his neck stood out as he coiled his fingers into fists. "Avrik the soldier. Avrik the hero," he snapped. "Did you come here to redeem yourself? Play the gallant soldier saving his old friend? Make up for..." –his voice cracked– "failing the first time?"

"No," Avrik began, but his voice was lost as Bren continued, storming closer to him.

"I don't want you here! I don't want to hear your apologies." His face was as red as the apples from the tree on his family farm. "I want..." He cut off sharply, staring Avrik full in the face with pure fury.

It was hard to see his friend this way. Gentle Bren, who had always been the calmer, more logical of the two of them. The friend who had balanced Avrik's impetuous nature, the quiet boy who had been content to observe rather than do the talking. He had been Avrik's steady, unchanging foundation, even when his world was upended after his mother had died and his father had withdrawn into a tangle of brooding emotions.

Even though he was guilty of many things, Avrik was finally starting to release himself from his guilt over Elysse's death. That death, at least, had been beyond his control. He knew that now. But it still surprised him when his own anger kindled and burst, rushing wild and hot in his veins.

"Do you want to fight me, Bren?" he snapped. "Is that what you want?" He smacked his own chest. "Go ahead. Punch me. Knock me down. That will bring Elysse back from—"

Bren slammed into him like a solid wall, bringing not only the full force of his fist into Avrik's face, but also all the weight in his well-muscled farmer's body. He leaned into the strike, all but leaping onto Avrik, and Avrik stumbled back. Blood rushed from his nose, the metallic taste filling his mouth. He brought up his arms to block Bren, but he didn't hit back as the boy unleashed a flurry of strikes.

"Hit me back! Hit me back!" Bren cried out, half-choking on sobs. His whole body heaved and trembled as they both collapsed in the grass. Bren pulled back, tears streaming down his face as he studied Avrik. "Why won't you hit me?" he demanded.

"I don't want to hit you!" Avrik said as he sat up. He could already feel his face swelling. He didn't think his nose was broken, but it was sore and bleeding, and his lip was split.

The anger had leeched out of him, leaving only emptiness and sadness. It was clear to him that the same was happening to Bren.

Wide-eyed, Bren sat back in the grass and swallowed hard, staring down at the blood on his knuckles. "I know it's not really your fault she's dead," he said after a long moment. He scrubbed his tears away on his shirtsleeve, leaving a smear of dirt on his cheek. "It's just…your father…after he betrayed all of us, it was hard for me to accept that you didn't know. You two were close. You were so angry that he'd been captured, and I understood that, but then Elysse…" His voice broke.

"What my father did was terrible," Avrik said in a steady voice. He wiped at the blood on his face with his own sleeve, but he was sure he'd only succeeded in smearing it.

Bren lifted his head and met his gaze. "It was easier to be angry than to be sad. And being angry with you, when you'd left and I felt so alone and hurt…" His voice trailed away. "I've tried to be strong for Mother and Father, tried to be strong for Meva and Tyll. But it's hard."

Avrik hesitated before tentatively resting a hand on Bren's shoulder. For a moment, Bren tensed, but he didn't move away. Slowly, he let out a sigh.

"You understand about grief," Bren continued, staring down at the grass.

"I do," Avrik said quietly.

Overhead, clouds slithered across the sky while the sun bled the last of its rays across the horizon. A lone bird fluttered toward the forest. The world was painfully and wonderfully normal around them.

Bren swallowed and finally turned to meet Avrik's gaze. "I—I'm sorry." He glanced down again at his bloody knuckles, looking a little ashamed. "I don't know what I thought. I just—had to punch someone."

"I know."

"I've missed you, Av," Bren admitted.

Despite the pain of his lip, Avrik smiled. "Of course you did. I'm the best friend you've ever had."

Bren rolled his eyes.

As they stood, they both glanced over to the east again, where the first stars were glistening in a pure sky.

"I know I can't take the pain away," Avrik said, "but…" He pulled his friend into a hug. Bren sniffled again and embraced him tightly. "I'm here."

"Thank you," Bren whispered as he pulled back. Then his mouth pulled taut. "I heard El…Princess Halia is recruiting soldiers. I want to fight. I want to keep Evren and the rest of my family safe."

Avrik nodded. They reached out and clasped hands, firm and resolute. When he looked into his friend's eyes again, he saw Bren's familiar openness. "I'm sorry about your face," Bren added as they started to leave the memorial field.

Avrik shrugged. "I know I'm still handsome underneath all this gore."

"And very humble too." A hint of mischief darted across Bren's face and he nudged Avrik in the ribcage. "So, a princess, huh?"

CHAPTER THIRTY-THREE

SEEING AVRIK RETURN, FACE BLOODIED, swollen, and discolored, arm-in-arm with Bren, made the weight on my heart ease the tiniest bit. Despite the state he was in, with a crumpled shirt stained with grass and blood, hair in wild disarray, and a black eye, Avrik still managed to smile his dimpled grin that always made the girls at school swoon. I could almost forget what he'd told me about Nesrelle claiming him, almost forget he was *dying*. That seemed impossible, when he was so full of life.

Perhaps because they could see that Bren had clearly forgiven Avrik, the rest of Evren was more forgiving too. Only a few muttered under their breath or narrowed their eyes when he approached. Lyanna and Rev's earlier awkwardness around him melted away. As soon as they saw the state he was in, they ran forward. Lyanna fussed over him, leading him out of the garden and toward Corin's sprawling home and ordering Rev to fetch wet cloths, bandages, aluera, and painkillers. As Lyanna led Avrik away, he shot me a glance over his shoulder, his eyebrows raised in mock alarm. I laughed.

Bren caught sight of me and smiled and waved before he trailed after his friend.

I couldn't leave the garden to follow them, not yet. With Jennah, Narek, and Gillen, I was assessing the men and women Corin had gathered so far. They stood in neat rows, their backs straight and their eyes staring ahead, as if we really were in a military training camp. Still, as much as they tried, they were untrained and undisciplined. One of the boys shifted on his feet and an older woman stirred to scratch her nose.

It hurt to walk before them, pretending I knew exactly what I was looking for, pretending I knew exactly what I was planning. It hurt to see men and women, girls and boys, that I had lived and laughed and learned with, lining up to fight a war we might not win. Selna, with her calloused hands and muscled arms from cooking and scrubbing all day long, stood proudly among the crowd. Beside her was her husband Ekrem, his hunting bow strapped across his back. I recognized Dienn, her dark hair in a braided crown around her head and her soft hazel eyes looking too delicate for war, and I wondered if Bren had finally told her how he felt. If he knew she was joining our forces. To my surprise, even my old schoolteacher Arra stood among them, flashing me an encouraging smile when I strode past.

"And you can count on my services too, Your Majesty," Corin was saying to me as he swept into a bow. I'd spent time earlier, before studying the recruits, to address them all together and describe the nestrae and the threat they posed.

Eyes still on the crowd, I gestured for Corin to stand. "No need for that. Here, I am just Halia."

Jennah's normally confident face was uncertain. She brushed an errant curl behind her ear and squeezed my shoulder, compelling me to stop and look into her eyes. There was grief there. I wondered if, close as we were to Misroth City, her worries for her family were growing. I could feel the way her fingers trembled against my arm. Though I didn't have children, my responsibility toward my people gave me the slightest idea of what she had to be feeling, knowing she was so close and yet so far. Was she upset I hadn't chosen to storm the capital right away?

"These people will be walking into a slaughter," she whispered.

"With your gifts and some training, I have to believe we have a chance," I said.

Close behind me, Narek nodded. His face was grim, but if he was feeling doubts, his eyes didn't betray them. "This isn't ideal, but we have nearly six weeks, and determined people can learn a lot in that time." I could tell by the shadow that crossed his face that he must have been remembering days of training among the Zare'forith.

Jennah couldn't conceal the tremor in her tone. "We're running out of time."

Gillen studied her gently. "I understand you have family in Misroth City?"

As if not trusting her voice this time, Jennah nodded.

Gillen's gaze grew distant. "I know how desperate you feel," he said softly. "But you have to trust in their strength now, until you can be with them again. If we don't go to them with a plan, we will be no help at all. Our only hope—*their* only hope—is that we take the time that is needed to do this correctly. Our attack must be as flawless as it can possibly be."

Jennah relaxed at his words. She nodded and smiled, just a little, as if giving herself permission to hold onto comfort.

I glanced at Narek. "What next?" I asked quietly.

Narek watched me levelly. "We will need to send scouts to learn how to infiltrate the city. We will need to formulate a plan, perfect it, and train our people until they can do more than walk to their deaths."

"And you can train them?" We'd already discussed this before Corin had brought the recruits, but I wanted to be sure Narek was confident. I knew his skills were impressive as a former member of the Zare'forith, and his war gift alongside Jennah's courage gift would certainly help, but I needed to know this ragtag group had a chance to become something akin to soldiers.

Narek studied them as carefully as I did, though he knew what to look for. He'd already told me to send five away, and that left us with only twenty-five. "Yes," he said. "But we need more."

Corin had only just begun his work, with the promise of reaching out to nearby towns, but the small number was still disheartening.

Biting back my sigh, I dismissed the new soldiers, ordering them to gather here in the garden again tomorrow morning to begin their training.

As they shuffled away in the growing dark to join their families and settle in for the night, I turned back to my friends. "I'm going to need your help, Gil," I said, unable to keep the weariness from my tone.

But my cousin was staring up at the darkening sky, eyes wide as sweat beaded his brow. "Take cover," he rasped, seizing my arm so tightly I grunted in pain. "*Now.*"

"Gillen, it isn't real," Jennah said, her voice somehow both soothing and commanding all at once. A mother's voice. She cupped his face in her hands and forced him to look at her. "Listen to me. Can you hear me? It isn't real."

Gillen took a deep, shuddering breath. I could tell Jennah was feeding him her courage gift when his body relaxed visibly. He loosened his grip on me and sighed. Blinking around in a daze, he asked, "W—what…?"

His voice trailed off. Before any of us could answer, a cry rang out. One of the sentries at the edge of the garden nocked an arrow to his bow.

Heart ramming into my ribcage at the thought of golden sedwa eyes, I raced toward the sentry, my friends and Gillen close at my heels. Beyond the edge of the garden, three shadowy figures were approaching. One was limping, but otherwise, it was difficult to distinguish anything else.

"Those aren't sedwa," I said. Had the nestrae sent some of their own to Evren at last?

Other voices filled the air as men and women clustered near the garden's edge, whispering fearfully about nestrae. Everyone was reaching for weapons or shoving loved ones back toward cover deeper in the garden.

The sentry, a bearded man I recognized as Evren's blacksmith, Hevro, glanced at me out of the corner of his eye. "Your Majesty, I'd stand back if I were you. We haven't found out yet if this garden keeps out those demons you just spoke about," he said gruffly.

I ignored his warning. My heart was trapped in my throat. *Condemned...* The nestrae's hissing whispers plagued me, along with the memory of their claws tearing at my skin, their flames burning my flesh. I hated how they could fill me with such raw terror.

Why send only a few? a more rational part of my brain asked. They weren't being discreet enough for scouts, unless they'd come to share a message.

Beside me, I could hear Gillen's shallow breaths. I worried he would pass out, so I reached out to squeeze his hand. He scarcely had the presence of mind to squeeze mine back.

"Who are you?" Hevro called into the darkness. "State your business here."

"Please!" came a familiar voice. "We mean no harm!"

"Who are you?" Hevro yelled again, but Corin had brought a torch, and when he lifted it up, we could see plainly enough.

A few yards away, two Toryn women and one man stumbled toward us. They were dressed in dirty, tattered clothing, and one of the women was limping. The girl in the center looked up and her piercing blue eyes met mine. Iyleth.

"Put down your weapons," I told Hevro and everyone else within hearing range. "I know them."

As Hevro lowered his bow, Iyleth broke into a run. Before I could speak, she fell to her knees, tears streaming down her face. "Princess," she said. It was the most formal she'd ever been around me. "Please. Avela and Jabek and I come seeking sanctuary."

Only graceful Iyleth could cry and beg in the dirt and still manage to look both beautiful and commanding.

Beside me, Hevro snorted. "You came to the wrong kingdom,

girl." Then he seemed to realize he'd spoken out of turn. "Forgive me."

I waved away his indiscretion.

"What do you mean?" I asked as Avela and Jabek approached to kneel on either side of Iyelth. For an instant, my gaze snagged on Avela, the well-muscled middle-aged woman who had once tried to feed my friends to the monstrous vilspen in Calidar. She didn't look hostile now, only humble and afraid. When her eyes met mine, she lowered her gaze, shame burning her cheeks. I turned back to Iyleth. "Stand up—you don't need to kneel in front of me, Iyleth."

Trembling and sniffling, she rose. But when I spoke her name, her eyes met mine and I could see the fire in them. The nestred runes scarring her shoulders were visible in the sleeveless tunic she wore, which was black to blend in with the shadows. She looked bruised, weary—and angry. The hardness I'd seen in her expression back in Toryn after her brother Haed had been tricked into killing their father, Captain Luiken, had only grown.

She stepped forward a little uncertainly before throwing her arms around me. "Halia," she whispered. Her limbs trembled. "Toryn has fallen. It's lost. It's all lost."

Iyleth pulled back and brushed the tears from her face.

"If you're here, then you already know the barrier is broken. You must know Misroth is being attacked by the nestrae. They've taken the capital."

Iyleth nodded solemnly. "We've come to serve you in whatever way possible. But we had to escape and find friends who would still willingly fight the demons alongside us. We had nowhere else to go." She shuddered visibly. "The other Toryn...all the survivors of Haemil...they convinced Haed and the rest of our people to join *them*."

"What are you talking about?" Jennah asked, stepping forward from where she'd hovered beside me.

Iyleth blinked at her for a moment, perhaps surprised to see her alive, but she refocused quickly. When she spoke, it was to me. "The Toryn thought that if the only deity showing any power still was

Nesrelle, that they needed to serve her. That she and the nestrae were punishing us because we weren't bowing to her wishes and worshipping her and her alone." She swallowed, and my head pounded as the vision I'd had about her in Toryn flickered through my brain. I could still recall the darkness in her brother's eyes as he'd asked Iyleth to call on Nesrelle. "They were sick of suffering, sick of me saying that the gods were silent," Iyleth continued. "So my brother said…" Her voice dropped to a horrified whisper. "He said Nesrelle *was* speaking—speaking to him—and rather than suffer any more he would listen to her. They quickly decided anyone who didn't join them threatened to bring more of Nesrelle's wrath upon Toryn, and they would be…punished." Tears welled in her eyes. "We weren't the only ones to stand against the madness, to refuse to serve Nesrelle and the nestrae. We were just the only ones who escaped."

CHAPTER THIRTY-FOUR

WHILE MOST OF THE EVREN people laid out bedrolls and blankets wherever they found available space inside Corin's sprawling old house or out in the garden, my friends and I gathered with the Toryn in Corin's library to discuss plans. Three of the walls were filled with floor-to-ceiling oak shelves, where Evren's most important leather-bound books, scrolls, and maps collected dust. Corin was a widower, and I supposed the responsibility of being Evren's Leader while living alone in this expansive house didn't give him much time to clean.

A wide window, covering most of the fourth wall, overlooked the garden stream, its path serpentine and lazy. The steady sound of water rushing and splashing over rocks was a soothing backdrop, punctuated by a chorus of chirping crickets. It was now full dark, but the night was alive with silver starlight and golden fireflies hovering among clusters of flowers: sapphire embyth, ruby lamirae, and snow-white sythrel. With the window thrown wide open, the familiar perfume of flowers mingled with the scent of warm earth, a balm to my homesick heart.

How I'd missed this. How a part of me longed to linger, to pretend I was Elena again and stay with Lyanna and Rev in the town that felt more like home than anywhere else. But that was a selfish, cowardly part of me, one that had once cost me in regret and guilt.

Now that I'd found my courage, I would never again let fear rule over me.

We all gathered in chairs around the huge table occupying the middle of the room. A map of Misroth was spread out alongside a detailed map of Misroth City, each street and market square carefully labeled. Gillen stayed close at my side, with Narek near him. On my opposite side, Jennah fidgeted in her seat, leaning back and looking out the window more than she looked at our maps. Her eyes had a faraway look: her heart was with her family in the capital. I couldn't blame her for her restlessness.

Across from me sat Iyleth, Avela, and Jabek. Despite her obvious weariness, Iyleth stood, her fiery eyes studying every inch of the maps as she drank in our conversation.

Relying on Narek's knowledge and Gillen's education on war strategy as Crown Prince, we began discussing a plan for training our new recruits and choosing scouts to scope out the capital.

"We'll never have great enough numbers and resources to lay siege," Gillen said, reminding me of what I already knew. "We'll have to rely on surprise and our knowledge of secret routes to get past the capital gates."

Jennah toyed with one of her Alrenian daggers. Its bejeweled hilt glittered like fire in the dancing candlelight. "The rebellion already knew a lot about secret routes and entrances," she said. Her eyes flicked briefly to Narek and then away. I still didn't know if she had fully forgiven him for everything he'd done to harm the rebellion: imprisoning, torturing, and killing her compatriots and friends. Leaving her with the scar that traced her cheek. But she seemed to have accepted him as a valuable ally.

Even two seats away, I could sense Narek's body stiffen, the memory of his crimes clearly fresh in his mind.

Gillen grinned. "You may very well know more about the secret entrances than me," he said. "I studied some routes that were created as escape passages for the royal family if they ever needed to evacuate the city. But it's not as if I ever had to actually use any."

Jennah brightened visibly. "Then I could be one of your scouts," she said.

Narek turned his inscrutable gaze on her. "Not a wise choice."

She pulled her mouth taut, trying to restrain herself.

"He's right," I cut in with a sigh. "Jennah, I'm sorry, but we need scouts who aren't tempted to go too far into the city and be caught or killed before they can return." I shot her a sympathetic look.

Jennah fell silent. She twirled her dagger, watching the candle flames reflect on its surface.

"What about us?" Iyleth asked in a low voice. "Avela, Jabek, and I know no one in the capital." She glanced at me. Her bare arms were more toned with muscle than they'd been when I first met her, and she held herself differently. She was still confident, but there was pain and fear tugging visibly at her shoulders. Whatever trials she had faced since I'd last seen her, they'd cut deep. But they hadn't defeated her.

I leaned back, considering. Gillen tapped his fingers on the table thoughtfully.

But Narek's brow furrowed, as if he were holding himself back from speaking.

He studied Iyleth, who had leaned over the table to trace a finger along a section of the map of Misroth City. Her dark hair fell in a glossy, straight curtain past her shoulders. One rebellious strand fell forward and hung near the corner of her mouth. From the way Narek's gaze kept turning back to her, I wondered if he was imagining what it would be like to brush it away.

When Iyleth glanced up, Narek looked back down at the map. It was the first time I'd ever seen him flustered. I held back my grin.

"You aren't trained," Narek said at last, his voice gruff. "Anyone else would do a better job than you."

Iyleth's cheeks flushed. "Give us some credit. We survived the Toryn countryside, same as you." She swallowed. "And worse."

Ever the suave Crown Prince, Gillen cut in. "I'm sure you have all learned to fight well and to survive just about anything," he said.

"The trouble is, you aren't fresh. You need time to rest and recover, while some of the guards already here in Evren could also do the job."

A light knock on the door made us all pause. Avrik pushed open the door, his face looking even more swollen than before. But he broke into a huge grin when his eyes landed on the maps on the table. "Battle strategy, my favorite," he said, his tone sounding too cheerful for all the tense feelings in the room. Some might assume he was oblivious, but I knew him well enough to understand it was his attempt at smoothing things over.

Iyleth, whose back had been to the door, turned at the sound of his voice. From where I sat, I couldn't see her expression.

"A-Avrik," she stammered. "You're alive."

Avrik's smile looked a little strained. "That seems to be the case."

Before anyone could say more, Lyanna pushed her way through the doorway and set a hand on her hip. "I've been led to understand the kingdom will fall to ruin if you don't starve yourselves and stay up all night poring over maps, but I refuse to let guests go tired and hungry." She shot me a pointed look. "I have some food in the kitchen, and then I think it's high time everyone gets some sleep."

There was no arguing with Lyanna, and I was weary myself. My entire body ached; my eyes burned. I hadn't slept in over a day, and I knew I wouldn't be able to force myself to go on much longer. "We can reconvene tomorrow," I agreed.

As we shuffled out of the library, I went to Avrik's side. We loitered in the doorway behind everyone else. "Are you all right?" I asked in a low voice.

Avrik chuckled softly. "Is my smile a little less charming now?" he teased.

I met his eyes and for an instant we froze. His teasing was familiar, comfortable even, a happy return to our old friendship. But the spark between us was new—or was it, if we'd both secretly felt this way all along?

Everything was different now. It was thrilling and terrifying, awkward and normal, new and old, all at once. The memory of our kiss was fresh, and the taste of his lips—like sweet country air, like home—still lingered on mine. As I thought about it, I couldn't help but let my eyes stray to his mouth.

His eyes glittered with mischief, his grin turning a little more crooked until his dimple was pronounced. "I guess not."

I pretended to elbow him in the side, but he caught my arm and spun me closer. My heartbeat thundered in my ears. For an instant, he seemed ready to pull me closer and kiss me again. I wanted him to. But then his eyes darted over my shoulder, widening in surprise and fear, and his smile fell away.

I glanced over my shoulder, but there was nothing amiss. "What is it?" I asked.

He shook his head and squeezed my arm gently instead. Maybe he thought it was reassuring, but right now, with his words ringing in my ears—*I'm dying*—nothing was. "Go eat and get some sleep," he murmured, scanning my face, where I was sure dark circles and a wan complexion gave away my exhaustion. "We can talk more tomorrow."

Frowning, I tried to ask more, but Lyanna's voice called from the kitchen. "El—Halia, come eat something more before bed. You look skinnier than you were before."

Despite how grim he'd been only a moment earlier, Avrik laughed. "You'd better eat a cookie and ease Lyanna's mind. We might die in a battle in a few weeks, but at least we won't die underfed."

"Halia, wake up." Avrik's voice pulled me from sleep.

I was on a bedroll in Corin's expansive living room, where the furniture had been pushed aside to allow several families space to sleep on the floor. Corin had tried to assign beds to Gillen and me, insisting royalty shouldn't sleep on his floor, but we'd refused. Instead, the beds that were available were left to those who truly needed them, such as the sick and injured, the elderly, and a pregnant woman. Gillen and I had gladly laid out bedrolls in a corner of the room near Lyanna and Rev. Narek, Jennah, and the three Toryn had found places in the room also, but Avrik had disappeared before I fell into a deep, much-needed sleep.

Now I blinked bleary eyes at him and glanced over at the window. I could make out soft grey light filtering through the curtains, assuring me dawn was not far off. I turned back to Avrik, my brain still half-asleep and trying to puzzle through what was happening.

His grin was as disarming as ever. "Get dressed and come with me."

I reached for my pack, shuffled past the many sleeping forms, and found one of several washrooms located in the grand house. The only other outfit I'd brought from Alrenor, other than my set of dragon scale armor, was a blue Alrenian tunic and black leggings. I pulled on the clothes and a pair of boots, braided my hair back, and, using the fresh water already waiting in a basin, washed my face. Then I dipped my finger into a jar of mint and baking soda paste and scrubbed and rinsed my teeth.

When I emerged, Avrik was waiting with a look of boyish anticipation on his face.

Nerves fluttered through my belly. Again, I was struck with how new this was. I laid my pack beside my empty bedroll and he took my hand, leading me out into the garden.

The grass was wet with morning dew, the air thick with birdsong and the promise of morning. To the east, the night sky was swiftly fading to grey and the stars were twinkling out. Some of the Evren families had camped under the stars last night, but I didn't notice anyone stirring this early.

It was as if the rest of the world had fallen away, leaving only Avrik and me here in this moment.

Then I remembered what we needed to talk about. Nesrelle. The invisible mark of death stealing Avrik's life away, even when he looked as healthy and strong and vibrant as ever. In this moment, even though my heart knew the truth, I could pretend the instant he'd collapsed in Alrenor had been a nightmare. That I'd dreamt the words he'd spoken to me: *I'm dying.*

"Avrik…" I began, but he shook his head and pulled me deeper into the garden.

Bushes covered in a blanket of golden roses hemmed us in while embyth lay like fallen stars at our feet. Overhead, a bird tittered on a nearby tree branch, sounding for all the world like a scolding mother.

Avrik continued to lead me further along one of the garden paths, this one heading steadily east. The eagerness had fallen from his face, replaced by a haunted look that should have been foreign on him, but was becoming frighteningly familiar. He sighed, his gaze turning to the stars above as if he could find answers there.

"Avrik," I said again.

He turned to me and searched my expression. "Is it selfish to spend time with you like this?" His voice was rough. "I don't want to hurt you. Not when I…"

"You couldn't keep me away from you," I said fiercely. "And you know…" I hesitated, fighting against the pain in my chest. "You know I'll hurt anyway…*if* anything happens to you. But we're going to fight this, Avrik."

He reached out and brushed my cheek. "I believe you," he whispered.

Savoring his touch, I leaned into him. "We'll fight this," I repeated, and I wasn't sure if I was saying it more to convince him or myself.

"But," he said softly, "sometimes…you lose the fight."

I knew he was thinking of his mother: how nothing had been able to heal her, and instead, he had been forced to watch her fade away.

"I want to live while I'm still alive, Halia," he finished, his voice low and urgent.

My chest was tight, my breaths shallow. That was all I wanted, too. To hold onto every moment with him and fully cherish it before all our moments ran out.

"I understand," I said.

We cast away the subject of death and wound our way to the stream. Along its bank grew willow trees, the nearest one with branches sweeping so low its leaves brushed the water. It provided a natural curtain that shut out the rest of the world, all except a view of the eastern sky, now rose-tinted with the approach of sunrise.

Removing our shoes, we dipped our feet in the stream. Although I wanted to enjoy the beauty of this moment, the way Avrik did, I couldn't stop the endless thoughts coursing through my head.

Avrik's face turned serious. "Remember when we were fifteen and I was seeing Natanya?" he asked earnestly.

Jerked from my stream of thoughts, I frowned at him. "I tried to forget."

Avrik leaned forward and clasped my hand. "No," he said. "I wanted to tell you why I stopped seeing her. When I kissed her, all I could think about was you. That was when I first started to realize...how I felt about you." He smiled, almost shyly.

His words settled between us, comfortable and easy. My earlier uncertainty about Avrik's feelings had been ridiculous. Sitting here in Evren garden beside my best friend, the boy I loved, was the most natural thing in the world.

I shoved him playfully. "That's how long it took you?" I teased. "I knew for so long it's hard to decide when it started. But I think it was around the time I found out I could outshoot you."

Avrik knew I was making fun of him, but instead of throwing another quip my way, he laughed with me. He pulled me close until our laughter fell away and our faces were so near our breath mingled. This kiss was better than the first: full of confidence and familiarity and promises of a future we couldn't keep.

We stayed there and watched the sunrise, avoiding the weight of every burden pressing down on us, avoiding the way our time was running out.

Pretending we had forever.

The sun was still low in the sky when the recruits gathered after breakfast. Overhead, the three dragons circled, scales flashing blindingly bright. Reyva swooped low once, emitting a guttural sound like a greeting. Then they were gone, likely in search of prey for their morning meal.

Gillen had woken that morning screaming and thrashing. A friendly Misrothian man had tried to run to him, only to be wrestled to the ground. Narek and Avrik had been forced to pry Gillen off the poor man.

"I'll tend to him," Lyanna had offered in a low voice.

I'd been uneasy at first, but Rev had given me a reassuring nod. Gillen appeared more subdued, whimpering and trembling in a corner of the room.

"You know she's stronger than she looks," Rev had told me with a wink. "I'll stay with her a little to help before I join you," he added. The idea of mild-mannered Rev fighting the nestrae terrified me, but when we needed every able-bodied person we could find, I'd known I couldn't turn away his offer to fight. I couldn't show favoritism when so many other fathers and sons were willing to sacrifice for their kingdom.

Now out in the garden, I surveyed our recruits with Avrik. Bren, Shilam, and Jaren approached Avrik and me, their smiles warm and welcoming. Apparently Avrik had found his other friends last night, sometime after he'd bidden me goodnight, and they'd all caught up. If there'd been any previous awkwardness between Avrik and them, it seemed smoothed over and forgotten in the way only the best of friends could seamlessly mend things.

Shilam came close to clap me on the back while Jaren offered a friendly nod.

"We heard we aren't to call you Your Majesty or do any bowing around you," Shilam said with a crooked smile and a chuckle.

"That's right," I agreed. "No formalities among friends."

Bren stepped close to embrace me. He smelled just like a farmer should: of warm earth, fresh air, and sunshine. Towering over me, it was clear he'd grown a lot in the months since I'd last seen him. His usually friendly smile turned down when he stepped back. "I'm sorry I beat up Avirk."

"Everything's forgiven, remember?" Avrik said lightly, nudging Bren's arm.

Jaren cleared his throat. "Anyway, we're here to fight for you," he told me. His gaze was steady and solemn. "And our families."

"Thank you," I said.

Bren noticed Dienn standing amongst the crowd and excused himself. With knowing smirks, Jaren and Shilam followed.

I spotted Jennah amongst the recruits nearby, but she didn't come closer, and I wondered if she was angry with me. I knew she had to understand the wisdom in my decision to wait to enter the capital, but it had to weigh on her heart. Her shoulders sagged visibly, as if her worry for her family was tugging her downward.

Then I noticed the Toryn: their pale skin standing out amongst the tanned Misrothians all dressed in homespun, earthy tones. Avela and Jabek were standoffish, but Iyleth came to hover near Avrik and me. Her dark hair was pulled back with a ribbon, and her worn and dirty Toryn clothing shimmered blue and purple. She glanced at Avrik and then back at me, saying softly, "I'm happy for you."

I blinked at her. During my time in Toryn, I'd been suspicious of her motives, uncertain about her attempts at friendship, and annoyed about the attention she'd given Avrik. But maybe her intentions really had been pure all along. Maybe she truly was a friend.

Before I could answer, Narek ordered everyone to begin our training with a run. I set out at a steady pace, pulse thrumming in my ears and muscles burning with life. We followed a path through the garden and out into the hills and fields of Evren. It was good to be running through the countryside again, fresh air in my lungs and Avrik and Iyleth at my sides.

Narek ran up and down our line of recruits, urging us onward. Whether due to his training or his war gift, he seemed inexhaustible. Jennah, quickly catching up to our trio with her long legs, noticed too. "If outrunning the nestrae is going to save Misroth," she puffed, "then I'm a dragon."

Iyleth giggled, quickly followed by a sharp gasp for air. She stumbled over some rocks on one of our downhill descents and crashed to the ground. Dust kicked up in her path as Avrik, Jennah, and I stopped beside her.

"I'm sorry," Jennah said, her forehead scrunched in concern, as if it were her fault.

Before any of us could reach Iyleth, Narek was there, slowing to a standstill above her. "Not everyone who volunteers is suited for this," he warned, holding out a hand to help her up.

Sweat matting strands of hair to her face, Iyleth glared up at him. "I get it," she snapped. "You don't think I pass the test. I'm not good enough. But too bad. I didn't survive the nestrae, the ichgor, and my own brother's attempt to murder me just to lounge in Misroth." Ignoring his hand, she stood. "You were friendlier in Toryn." Blood streamed from a tear in her leggings, but she started running again as if nothing had happened.

Avrik clapped Narek on the back. "Great work. You'll fuel all the recruits with so much anger and adrenaline, they'll make up for their lack of skill with their pure fury."

He and Jennah started running again, no doubt expecting the rest of us to follow.

I hung behind, studying Narek's surprised face. This time, he didn't try to mask his grimace.

"Do you really think she can't handle this?" I demanded.

"I don't want to see her hurt," he admitted.

Recalling how he'd lost Reylinn, I understood the fear lingering in his eyes, fear he couldn't disguise.

"Trust that she can handle herself. You said you trusted in her before, when we were in Alrenor and she was off in Toryn. Now that she's here with you, you can't become this overprotective...boar."

Narek raised his eyebrow at my insult, and we both broke into laughter.

"But really, Narek," I insisted, catching my breath and turning solemn again. "Have you considered being kind to her, and letting her know how you feel? I know you're afraid of losing her, but pushing her away isn't going to help. You know this as well as I do."

Narek shook his head. "She's Toryn's Intercessor and the daughter of our former Captain. Probably the rightful ruler of Toryn now, if her brother is truly as mad as he seems to be. She's meant for more—she deserves more than me."

I frowned, but rather than argue, I ran to catch up with Avrik.

Later, Narek wordlessly tended to Iyleth's scraped and bleeding leg himself. His hands were gentle, his eyes soft, but he frequently averted his gaze, as if he could scarcely stand to look at her.

"Thank you," Iyleth whispered, her expression uncertain as she tried to catch his eye. She reached out and brushed his arm, and he drew in a sharp breath.

"I need to go," he muttered, and retreated to speak with some of the other recruits.

For a long moment, Iyleth stared after him, pursing her lips. Puzzled. Frustrated.

Then, sighing, she stood and pulled me aside.

"Are you all right?" I asked. Was she going to ask me what was wrong with Narek? Was it my place to tell her?

Iyleth seemed quiet and contemplative, unlike herself. She blinked, her gaze turning faraway as she stared out at the countryside. Everything was bathed in the warm, golden glow of summer.

But Iyleth didn't bring Narek up. "The garden we're staying in…" she said. "It's been touched by—by your god." It wasn't a question, but I nodded anyway.

Seated in the grass beside her, I studied her face, wondering how she knew. Her blue eyes looked bright and clear in the sun, and I remembered how her father had explained her role. Intercessor for her people. According to Toryn tradition, her light eyes, among a people of dark ones, had marked her as someone who could speak to their gods on her people's behalf. Was she somehow able to sense sacred things?

"Why would your god give me anything?" she asked in a soft whisper. Her eyes finally darted back to me, and her gaze was so intent it seemed like she could see right through me. "My gods have never spoken to me, have never helped my people. Why would yours grant me a gift?"

Scrunching my forehead, I shook my head at her. "I don't understand."

"Your god…the Life-Giver?" she asked. At my nod, she continued. "Last night, I couldn't sleep. My nightmares…" She let her voice drift away. "For a while I wandered in your garden. It's so beautiful and soothing, I could almost forget…everything. Then a figure approached me. A man that smelled like pines from the mountains, like—like a traveler, clean but smelling of the outdoors. Not like a god at all." She laughed. "His eyes were kind and he seemed moved by my grief." Tears glittered in her eyes, sparkling like diamonds.

Awe swept through me, chased closely by envy. "You met the Life-Giver," I said, hoping my jealousy didn't taint my voice. While he was silent toward me, he was still speaking with others. First Avrik, and now Iyleth. The god that many used to claim didn't walk among humans anymore was making a lot of appearances. "What did he say about a gift?" I asked.

Iyleth glanced down at her hands as she considered. "He said I'm gifted with healing." One of her tears leaked down her cheek. "Me—the one who couldn't save her people. The one who's broken and needs healing." She sniffed. "I don't know what it means. I don't know how I could possibly heal anyone."

"Maybe that's why healing is your gift," I said. "Because you understand its importance more than most."

"My kingdom has fallen," Iyleth whispered. "Everyone I love is gone. All I care about now is helping make sure that doesn't happen to Misroth too. I want you to know that anything we Toryn can do for you, we will. We're in this together."

She smiled softly, almost uncertainly.

"Thank you."

Iyleth's smile turned radiant. "I knew we were meant to be friends."

CHAPTER THIRTY-FIVE

Avrik

EVENING HAD TURNED THE SKY velvet shades of blue and violet as Avrik hovered outside his childhood home. He closed his eyes to concentrate and beg the Life-Giver to help him. Again.

He imagined his power expanding, enveloping the entire cabin in an invisible barrier. Exhaling sharply, he lifted the rock he was holding and hurled it straight at the wall, but apparently his focus was so terrible that it affected his aim as well as his gift. The rock crashed through a window instead, shattered glass raining down inside the barren home. Though the daylight was dying, he could see some of the shards glittering on a floor that was gathering dust and shadows.

Avrik's heart wasn't unlike the shattered window.

It's only a window in an abandoned house, he thought fiercely, even though deep down he knew he was lying to himself. To him, the house was still much more than that, and always would be.

Maybe this was the wrong place to practice his gift. Maybe this house was too haunted by death. Maybe it distracted him too much with grief for him to be able to concentrate on conjuring any type of protection.

He started to turn away, only to come face to face with a silent figure waiting behind him. The sun had already slipped beneath the horizon, but her hair still shone like flames. Clothed in a dress of pure black with a sweeping train and lace detailing, she looked more like Avrik would have expected her to appear the first few times he'd met her. The Queen of Death.

Avrik twisted his mouth into a smile, even though his mouth tasted bitter. Better to pretend that death didn't terrify him, or that his pulse wasn't rushing wildly at the sight of her. "You can't stay away from me," he said, as if he were flirting with a normal Evren girl.

Nesrelle sneered. "You mortals aren't desirable. I see you more like…" She paused, as if considering. "Pawns on my game board."

Avrik exchanged one pretense for a new one, and his smile transformed into a glare. *What are you doing here?* he tried to snarl, but the words wouldn't move past his lips. His throat ached and his chest tightened. A chill rushed through his body and his muscles turned to water. Staggering, he tried to breathe, tried to keep himself on his feet, but failed at both.

He collapsed in the cool grass, facedown in earth and weeds. It didn't matter that dirt pressed against his mouth or that grass tickled his nose; both were useless anyway. His lungs burned, begging for air yet refusing to let it in.

This is how I'm going to die, he thought, panic setting in. Nesrelle had come to claim him. She was going to stop his heart and leave his body lying prostrate before her like an awestruck worshipper. Like the weak, vulnerable person he had become.

When she spoke, Nesrelle's voice was a nightmare, right before it turned from beautiful to sour. It was a dazzling thunderstorm just before the first lightning strike.

"I see you and your lovely queen are still going to fight me. Fools." If Avrik's blood wasn't already chilled, her laughter would have done the job. "Try all you want. You can feel the call of death, can't you? And you know that death comes for everyone, in the end. You can't escape it."

She vanished and the weight on Avrik's chest lifted. Life returned to his limbs and the coldness receded.

But he wasn't quite right. As he stood, his body trembled, and his throat remained tight. His lungs continued to ache and burn. He coughed and something dribbled down his lips.

When he wiped it away, his hand came away red.

CHAPTER THIRTY-SIX

THE DAYS IN EVREN FOLLOWED a deceptively comfortable rhythm, swiftly slipping into weeks. With a haven in the garden from the sedwa at night and our seclusion from other parts of Misroth, I could almost pretend my kingdom wasn't crumbling. But at night, nestred visions filled with havoc and death troubled me. I trusted their word that the throne wouldn't fall before my birthday, if only because I knew far too intimately how much they loved to watch people suffer. They and their goddess wanted me to be there to see what they unleashed.

They are miserable, filled with a nameless dread, Nesrelle explained in my sleep.

In my dreams, citizens would stop in the middle of whatever they were doing and curl in on themselves, whimpering or outright screaming. I knew what it was like to experience a nestred vision: so vivid it seemed alive, filled with everything that terrorized me most. My people were blinded to the nestrae's presence with their mind tricks, oblivious to the demons that walked among them, but they knew something was wrong by the fear that stalked them all.

Sometimes, though, the nestrae showed me the future. The horror they would unleash on my birthday. In these visions, huge pyres filled the market squares, where the demons threw screaming victims to the flames. So much smoke filled the air that it appeared as if the entire city was burning, while citizens choked on the fumes and despaired because they couldn't even see the sun.

Each day I woke determined to end my people's suffering. I reminded myself of everything Meli had taught me as I focused and tried to mentally reach for my gift. But each time, I grappled with emptiness. I wanted to beg the Life-Giver to return the gift that Nesrelle had stolen, but words failed me. I hadn't heard from him in so long, and I had a sickening suspicion it was because he'd given up on me. Nesrelle had stolen my gift so easily, like I wasn't worthy enough to possess it. And maybe I wasn't. Maybe the Life-Giver was silent toward me because he'd turned his back after I'd failed my people. I'd set out to help Misorth, and all I'd done was hurl it into further danger.

I worried that any effort to save Misroth City without my gift to see through the nestred visions would be futile. If we fell prey like everyone else in the capital already had, we would begin turning on each other. All the training and preparation in the world wouldn't matter if we did the nestrae's killing work for them.

Rather than give into despair, I threw myself into Narek's lessons. Jennah, Avrik, and I joined the Misrothian and Toryn recruits in all the training exercises Narek put them through: running through the gardens, sparring with practice swords, shooting arrows at targets, and practicing hand-to-hand combat. He taught us how and where to strike and kick, which moves would knock even a larger opponent to the ground, and how to kill with our bare hands.

Some days, Gillen joined us, but others, he was lost to the world, his gaze faraway as he shuddered and babbled to himself. The closer my birthday drew, the more he seemed to retreat into himself—or perhaps it was more accurate to say he was losing himself. Trapped in nestred visions, not even Lyanna's soothing voice and gentle coaxing could pull him out. The Evren Healer volunteered one of his herbal teas, which made Gillen drowsy until he calmed and fell into a deep slumber. Unfortunately, his sleep wasn't always an escape, but just another path into nestred-induced nightmares. I spent my spare time at his side, brushing back his hair and talking to him as he moved restlessly in his sleep. Even though I wasn't sure he could hear me, I poured my energy into talking about childhood memories, adventures and jokes we had shared, and stories his uncle had told us. And over and over, despite the fact that he'd insisted he'd already forgiven me, I told him how sorry I was.

"You know he can't fight with us," Narek told me one day as he pulled me away from the rest of the recruits. "Your cousin is unstable even when the nestrae aren't around. He's more likely to kill himself— or those around him—than the demons."

I swallowed. "I know," I said softly. "He does too. He told me himself, in one of his lucid moments."

Narek frowned at me. "Then why is he still training with the recruits? Hasn't he heard the whispers?"

"Everyone has heard about the Mad King," I said bitterly, "even if the people of Evren are too afraid to say it aloud. Gossip spreads fast in a small town—especially one trapped together in this garden every night. But think about it," I continued, "and what it would mean if Gillen didn't ever train alongside his own people. I know word is spreading that he is surrendering the throne to me, but officially, he is still Crown Prince. He survived my father throwing him into Toryn. He's the rightful heir, despite all my father did to try to stop his rule from ever happening. The people need to see him, even if it's only because he's a symbol of hope."

"And when the day comes to leave for the capital?" Narek asked. "How do we explain his disappearance? Where does he stay?"

I sighed, watching as some of the recruits sparred one another. Gillen was himself today, holding his own against Shilam in a mock battle with practice swords. "I'll handle that when the time comes."

That afternoon, after Narek dismissed the recruits, he, Avrik, Jennah, and I left the garden to train with the dragons.

"Let me come," Iyleth begged, darting down a garden path to join me. Her eyes were wide with longing. "Please."

I understood her eagerness to be closer to the majestic creatures. "Of course."

Ahead, I noticed Narek glance back, just once, before quickly turning away.

"We could teach you to ride," Jennah offered, her eyes sparkling with adventure. She paused, shooting me a significant smile. "Narek's dragon is probably the most easygoing, so we can ask him to take you for a ride."

Holding back my own grin, I nodded.

Iyleth scrunched her face uncertainly, but her excitement for the dragons won out. As we paused on a hillside, a warm breeze fluttering through the grass and the sun bright on our faces, I whistled to Reyva. The dragons were just blots high in the sky, circling overhead, but they never wandered far from us. With their keen hearing, they were always fast to come when we called to them.

They landed with Reyva in the lead, twitching their tails and fluttering their wings as if eager to be off again. Their scales flashed in the sun like jewels.

Iyleth couldn't hold back her gasp.

I beamed at her. "They're beautiful, aren't they?"

"And terrifying," she added, her eyes never leaving the creatures in front of her, soaking in their magnificence.

We showed Iyleth how to approach the dragons until they let her step close enough to run her fingers along Kova's black and green scales. As Narek strapped a saddle on Kova, Iyleth turned to him.

"Would you take me for a ride?" she asked. Her posture was tense, expecting his refusal, but her eyes burned with hope.

Narek's eyes shifted from me to Iyleth uncertainly. He nodded curtly and finished buckling the saddle into place.

When he offered his hand to help Iyleth up, she hesitated before accepting it. The way they danced around one another, actively avoiding touching one another and pretending they weren't each completely aware of the other's movements, was almost painful to watch.

As I turned to saddle Reyva, Narek spoke at last.

"How do you do it?" he asked quietly, and I knew he was speaking to Iyleth.

Iyleth's voice was soft, full of surprise. "Do what?"

"You've lost everything. You should be tucked away, hiding from the world. You should be angry or bitter or sad—something. How do you keep smiling?"

"I *am* angry," Iyleth said, her tone low, filled with the truth of her words. "And of course I'm sad. But the only way I've survived is by finding ways to smile."

I glanced back to see Narek leaning forward, helping fasten Iyleth into the saddle. His face was close to hers, but neither of them bothered to draw back, instead studying each other intently. The angry tension that had crackled between them earlier seemed replaced by an entirely different kind. He searched her eyes, hesitating, and she drew in a sharp breath.

"You're resilient," Narek said at last, his gruff tone turning gentle. It was a rare compliment from him, one that made Iyleth smile.

Narek drew back abruptly, his mask returning as he put distance between them again.

"Hold on tightly," he said, and climbed into the saddle behind her.

Iyleth did, her knuckles white as she gripped the saddle and the smile slipped off her face.

When my friends and I weren't training, we were planning our attack. We selected and sent scouts to begin surveying Misroth City. All returned with news that echoed my haunting visions: everything was eerily normal in the capital, but for the heaviness of fear and despair that hung like a cloud over the city. Sometimes the scouts saw the nestrae walking through the streets, unseen by the citizens, but the scouts couldn't get too close without falling prey to the nestred visions themselves. Every man and woman we sent out returned with a new sense of terror that none of the other Misrothians could understand without having experienced the nestrae's power for themselves.

As Corin sent messengers to nearby towns, volunteers filed into Evren, prepared to fight for their kingdom. Slowly, our numbers grew, but they were still small—so small. I prayed our gifts could counteract our size and inexperience and actually give us a fighting chance.

Every opportunity we had, my friends and I practiced with our gifts together. Jennah challenged herself to extend her courage gift to as many people as possible, soon finding she could heighten the morale of our entire group of recruits. Meanwhile, Narek learned more about how his war gift worked. He didn't have to know exactly what was happening to anyone he was sharing the gift with, but we did discover that he couldn't control more than ten other people at once. Still, the way he could help others fight as if they were seasoned warriors— swifter, stronger, and more graceful than they ever were on their own—was miraculous.

Iyleth spent most of her time studying her gift and practicing with Evren's healer. The healer wasn't supernaturally gifted, only skilled, but Iyleth still needed to know the basics of treating wounds, which our healer could teach. She learned to identify and mix herbs into medicines and creams, how to bandage injuries, how to treat broken bones, and much more. Often, she practiced by treating the bruises and scrapes the recruits received in training. That was also how she realized that, when she concentrated, she could help others' wounds heal faster with the touch of her hand.

"But does my touch help against mortal wounds?" she asked me once, her eyes wide. I wondered if she was picturing her dying father, wishing she'd known about her gift then, wishing she could have saved him. But maybe he'd been beyond saving. Maybe she hadn't even been gifted with healing until she'd spoken to the Life-Giver in Evren. I just smiled and told her I didn't know, hoping she realized she couldn't blame herself for anything in her past.

All the while, Avrik focused on using his protection gift to defend larger groups of people, stretching out his invisible barrier until he could, for limited amounts of time, repel anything directed toward a dozen recruits. Since we'd already seen the evidence of Tamelle's protection gift, we knew that wasn't the limit of his. "I can't imagine the focus it would take to extend a barrier around entire kingdoms," Avrik said one day, his voice filled with awe. At first we had tested his barriers with simple things—grass, twigs, or pebbles, but that day he'd been confident enough to let another recruit shoot an arrow toward him and the group he was protecting. I stood at his side as we watched the arrow ricochet off an invisible wall and fall to the earth.

"You've done it!" I exclaimed, throwing my arms around him and pulling him into an embrace.

His smile was off, though, not quite reaching his eyes. Though he constantly tried to ignore it and pretend everything was normal, I knew the threat of death was haunting him.

Lately, though he seemed as strong and healthy as he had ever been, I'd noticed that his touch was ice cold. Then his skin would feel normal and warm again, and I'd wonder if I'd imagined it.

Though we never spoke the thought aloud, I knew we'd both considered that perhaps the same deadline Nesrelle had issued for Misroth was true for Avrik as well. Maybe she planned to claim his life on my birthday, too.

Time was running out.

Gillen was the one to bring up the topic of fighting with the recruits to me. One night, as he shuddered and blinked himself out of a nestred vision, he caught my hand in his and turned to me with wild eyes.

"No one can trust me when we face the nestrae," he told me urgently. "They already control my thoughts—imagine what they could do with me when I'm near them again. I'll be dangerous."

I sat beside him on the settee in Corin's library, where we had a rare moment of privacy with an entire room to ourselves. "I know," I said gently. It hurt to admit the truth.

"But I don't want to be far," Gillen continued.

"You're a symbol of hope to everyone," I agreed. "You should train along with us as often as you can."

Gillen shook his head, and I was surprised to see a smile on his lips. "No, Lia. You're their symbol of hope. Even without an official announcement from me yet, it's clear you are the true leader. Misroth accepted you a long time ago. You overthrew your father and you faced Toryn to find me." He laughed outright. "You rode in on a *dragon*!"

I poked him in the ribs. "So did you!"

Gillen's smile faded a little, his forehead scrunching with a trace of sadness. "It wasn't the same. They've seen…" He shook his head and gestured to himself. "Well, me. Or what has become of me."

"But it's still good for them to see you," I insisted, nudging his shoulder.

Gillen nodded. "Especially as a reminder that you succeeded. Again." He beamed at me. "I'm so proud of you. I see the way they all look at you."

I tried to smile, but it wasn't always easy to take Gillen's compliments. To me, they were only reminders of what he could no longer be for his people.

He sighed. "I know I can't go with you into Misroth City, but I want to be close when the fighting begins. I *need* to be." His voice was urgent, eyes intense.

"Of course you do. You want to see Misroth safe again."

"And I'm hoping my intercession gift can be encouraging," Gillen continued. "I hope I can be useful, somehow." He glanced down at his hands. "Even if it can't be with a sword."

"You can travel with us to the outskirts of the city and be involved in the training and planning until the very end. It's only right. And…Gil?"

He met my eyes.

"If…if we survive, and I'm to rule, I'll still need you by my side. I'm going to depend on all your wisdom."

I grinned at him, and he flashed me a smile.

Gillen pulled me into a hug. "I wouldn't leave you to face it all alone. I'll be with you every step of the way, Little Lia."

"He hates me," Iyleth said, hands on her hips as she stared out the window to where Narek and Avrik were sparring outside. As if we hadn't spent hours today practicing already.

Iyleth and I stood in Lyanna's kitchen while I baked bread for dinner. Lyanna and Rev were outside, harvesting tomatoes and cucumbers from the garden, and Gillen was seated by the fire, staring into its depths while a book lay untouched in his lap. He seemed composed, but not quite present either, as if at any moment he would slip away into another waking nightmare.

Jennah had joined Lyanna and Rev, too restless to stay indoors, or perhaps avoiding me. We hadn't had much time to speak lately.

I paused, using my forearm to brush the hair out of my face. "Narek?" I asked, raising an eyebrow at Iyleth. "You think he hates you?"

The tension between them had continued to simmer during our practice that day, although Iyleth mostly stayed near Avela and Jabek. Even though Jabek had once been one of Iyleth's suitors, there didn't appear to be any romantic connection between them. I wondered if he was one Iyleth's father had selected for her, and if Jabek had only viewed her as a way to achieve a higher social status.

Iyleth crossed her arms, silently fuming. "He was kind to me when we were in Toryn," she continued. Her voice was tremulous, more upset than angry.

I opened the oven to lift out a loaf of golden, crusty bread. Other than Jennah, I wasn't used to having a girl for a friend. Did Iyleth care about Narek like he cared about her? I suspected she did. Was I supposed to ask her about her feelings, or wait for her to talk about them?

"Are you all right?" I asked. "Do you...want him to like you?"

Iyleth shrugged, but her cheeks were tinged pink. "I just...we were good friends before," she spluttered. "Or I thought so. What's wrong with him?" Her eyes watched his every movement through the window, even as she frowned in frustration.

I tried to keep my focus on the bread to conceal my smile. "Avrik and I were good friends," I said softly.

Iyleth's eyes widened in alarm. "No," she said quickly. "Not like...I mean, he *is* handsome, but..." Her voice trailed off. "I really did like Avrik," she said after a long moment. She turned to me, her expression apologetic.

Unfazed, I nodded as I set the bread aside to cool. "I gathered that. You liked him, moved on, and now you like someone else."

Iyleth pursed her lips. "I've spent so long feeling alone. On our way to Misroth, I kept thinking about you, hoping you were all right. That you'd rescued Avrik and Jennah." She sighed. "I knew Avrik was...well, yours. I kept focusing on Narek, how he'd spent all that time with me, explaining the ways of the Zare'forith and never seeming to get tired of all my questions. The way he'd found it in himself to care about both Toryn and Misroth, just as I had. He told me about Misroth and—and he listened to me." She shrugged. "Maybe I was desperate for *any* friendly company back then, when almost everyone else seemed to want something from me. I'm just angry he's distant with me now. It's like he doesn't believe in me anymore. Did I do something...? Is it because of the threat my brother made to him?

Does he not trust me anymore?"

I shook my head. "What Haed said when we left the Toryn behind has nothing to do with how Narek feels about you." I bit my cheek, wondering if I'd said too much. Narek's feelings weren't mine to disclose.

Before Iyleth responded, Narek and Avrik set down their practice swords and entered the cabin.

Gillen jumped in his seat at the creak of the door's hinges. "Oh— Avrik. Captain Narek. Hello," he said, blinking up at them as if he'd just woken from a nap.

"Gillen," Avrik said with a warm smile. Narek saluted him, the picture of a proper guard before his king.

Smirking, Avrik stepped close to me, only to brush his fingers across my forehead. Flour fell away and I couldn't help but laugh with him.

Iyleth met Narek's gaze. "Teach me what you were showing Avrik just now," she said firmly.

Narek blinked at her. "I've shown you during training and I'll show you more tomorrow."

She lifted her chin. "You don't think I'm good enough to fight. So help me. Show me now."

For a long moment, they assessed one another, neither speaking, neither blinking, as if each weighing the other's stubbornness. Narek worked his jaw, as if about to say something, then stopped himself. "All right," he said at last.

They walked outside. Exchanging a glance with Avrik—who looked like he was holding back laughter—and Gillen, who rolled his eyes, we followed.

"Are they just too obstinate to admit they have feelings for each other?" Gillen muttered. He looked so at ease and like himself, it was hard to reconcile the young man standing next to me with the one who'd been seated inside only moments before. "It's obvious to everyone else."

We didn't answer, too intent on watching Narek and Iyleth circle one another, gripping their practice swords as fiercely as if they were real weapons. Their movements were graceful—Iyleth with her effortless poise and fluid motion, and Narek with his polished style and easy strength.

Anger threatening in her eyes like blue flame, Iyleth charged impatiently, slamming her stick at Narek's chest. Narek blocked her attacks without reacting. If I hadn't known him better, I would have assumed he was bored.

This only stoked Iyleth's temper. Her steps grew sloppy, her breathing ragged. Her chest heaved as she swung—this time too wildly. She missed her aim, without Narek even needing to step out of the way. He returned with a strike of his own that Iyleth swept aside angrily.

"Don't go easy on me!" Iyleth snapped, leaping forward with renewed energy.

Their sticks struck together with such force I thought they would snap.

"Why do you assume I'm going easy on you?" Narek asked, his breathing even, his tone measured.

"Because you think I'm not good enough," Iyleth said. "Because you think I'm *weak*" -she punctuated each word with a vicious swing- "and *vulnerable* and *incapable*." Her eyes shone with unshed tears.

Narek's eyebrows lifted ever so slightly in surprise. "I never said any of those things."

"Then prove you didn't think them about me. Stop going easy on me!"

Narek pressed forward, initiating the offense this time. Iyleth had to stumble backward as she parried his first strike. He laid into her with a series of swings, his motions all but a blur to me as she ducked, sidestepped, and then whirled away. Their sparring match looked more like a well-coordinated dance, and suddenly I was embarrassed to be watching, as if it were too intimate. The way they watched one another, eyes bright and intense, made it seem so.

For the first time, Narek's cool demeanor crumpled in a fight and transformed into anger. "Did you ever consider that maybe I don't want something to happen to you?" he demanded, his voice rough.

Iyleth paused, glaring up at him. She blinked fiercely, but one of her tears escaped and trickled down her cheek. "You're not the only one who's lost everyone!"

Narek froze, his practice sword poised in midair. Iyleth had already lowered hers, not even bothering to pretend she was focused on the fight anymore.

Her voice turned to a fierce whisper. "I've also lost everything. You know that. But if you're too afraid of loss to *live*, to care about anyone ever again, then they've already wo—"

Narek threw down the practice sword and pulled her to him before she could finish. Hands tangled in her hair, he kissed her. Almost as if, deep down, she'd been expecting it, she threw her arms around him and kissed him back.

"Finally," Gillen said, one corner of his mouth curling into a smile.

He, Avrik, and I started to turn away, when Lyanna, Rev, and Jennah came around from the back garden, each carrying baskets laden with fresh vegetables. "I'll just make a salad and then dinner—" Lyanna began. Her eyes fell on Narek and Iyleth and she smiled, a knowing twinkle in her eyes. "Well, I suppose we could wait a while to eat."

Narek and Iyleth sprang apart self-consciously. Cheeks flushed and body trembling, Iyleth wiped away her tears and laughed lightly. Even Narek's face looked a little pink.

"No, that's all right. We were just…sparring," Iyleth said.

Lyanna grinned again as she and Rev strode toward the doorway.

Rev threaded his hand through hers and nudged her playfully. "Why didn't we think to spar before dinner? That would work up an appetite."

CHAPTER THIRTY-SEVEN

AVRIK FELT LIKE A THIEF, stealing precious moments before he ran out of time to take. The more experience with death he'd had, the more he'd loved life. Though he'd grown up imagining the joy he'd feel when he met his mother again in the afterlife, those thoughts hadn't taken away his desire to embrace life wholeheartedly. If anything, they'd increased his need to capture each second and hold on dearly before death snatched it all away. He wanted to make his mother proud and achieve things that she had never been able to. He wanted to see the world, taste all its delicacies, hear all its languages, and experience all its adventures. He'd wanted to explore every land and swim in all the seas and even the far-off ocean. When grief made him ache and death followed him like a specter, he worked all the harder to laugh louder, smile broader, and rejoice more.

Now that he could see his time running out, just as he could imagine the future he and Halia could have shared together, he was more desperate. Whenever he was with her, he watched her like he could memorize her: every expression on her face, every color in her eyes, and every tone of her voice. He touched her like he could, too—as if he could perfectly remember the taste of her lips and the soft brush of her skin in the afterlife and that would be enough. But he knew it wouldn't be.

Even tonight, as they picked flowers in the garden and splashed through the stream, he could hear Nesrelle's voice whispering in the back of his mind. His chest was tight, and he wasn't sure if it was because of his fear or because of whatever Nesrelle was doing to him.

He and Halia strolled back toward the house, both exhausted and in need of sleep, even if they were reluctant. Every moment apart was another one of their precious few moments lost forever.

"You're…quiet," Halia said hesitantly, as if afraid to say what she was really thinking aloud. Avrik imagined what she was wondering anyway: *Do you feel her presence? Are you getting weaker?*

Avrik flung a deceitfully carefree smile in her direction, but he could tell immediately that it didn't fool her. None of his masks ever did. Relenting, he sighed and stared up at the stars. Constellations that had been glistening earlier, like a beautiful secret only he and Halia shared, now looked cold and distant.

"I'm not sure…I think she means for it to be soon," he said in a low voice. He hadn't told her about how Nesrelle had confronted him outside his home or how she'd left him lying in the dirt, half-suffocated and alone.

Halia turned to him, her posture stiffening and her eyes flaring with determination. And wasn't that one of the things he loved so much about her? She never gave up, not even when death stared her down. Avrik bit back a smile. Of everyone he knew, only she could look into death's eyes and make death turn away first.

But not this time.

"Avrik," Halia began, her voice surprisingly soft for the hard expression on her face. "Have you—"

A terrifyingly familiar shriek shredded the calm night air, jolting their gazes upward. Circling overhead, just out of the garden's range, was a huge black shape that blotted out the stars. The sound of thunderous wingbeats pounded against their ears, nearly as loud as the sound of their dragons' flight. But the dragons weren't nocturnal creatures, and the form above was different. And that shriek…

"Ichgor," Avrik said. Instead of fear, he was overcome with anger at the reminder of all the terrors they'd faced in Toryn. Against all odds, they'd survived—only for Nesrelle to claim him as a pawn in her deadly game.

At the edge of the garden, the sentries cried out in alarm. Avrik and Halia rushed toward the nearest man, who, despite his shaking arms, had his bow aimed carefully at the circling creature. It was Hevro the blacksmith, though Avrik hardly recognized him at first—he'd never seen the man look so afraid.

"Wh—what is that?" Hevro stammered.

"A nightmare," Avrik said.

He watched the beast intently. Even in the sky, the ichgor never crossed the invisible line where ordinary Evren gave way to the magnificence of its garden. Whatever blessing the Life-Giver had bestowed upon their town to create the garden, its protection clearly blocked out more than sedwa.

Hevro seemed to have noticed too. Exhaling slowly, he lowered his weapon. "Eldon's crown, but that is the most…" He shook his head, at a loss for words. "I've never seen such a creature."

"We're safe here," Avrik said. "Why don't you get some rest? I can take over your watch."

Though Hevro's eyes were shadowed with dark circles and his whole body stooped with weariness, the man studied Avrik uncertainly for a minute. It made Avrik second guess himself: maybe the effects of Nesrelle's curse were more visible to others than he had believed. Could Hevro see the weakness on Avrik's face?

But Hevro nodded slowly. "All right. Thank you." He offered Avrik a rare friendly smile. "Whatever your father…" He stopped and cleared his throat awkwardly. "You're a good young man." He shuffled away without making eye contact again.

When Avrik glanced to Halia, she was frowning at him. "You need to rest too," she said. "How do you expect—"

Avrik clasped her hands gently in his own, and she cut herself off with a sharp intake of breath. He couldn't help the flirtatious smile that flickered across his mouth. "I don't even have to kiss you to make you swoon. Just one look at this face, huh?" He winked and Halia rolled her eyes.

"You'll never see me swoon," she insisted, and he laughed.

"I couldn't sleep anyway," he said earnestly. "And even though the garden seems to be protecting us, I want to feel like I'm being useful." He shrugged. "It's better than sleeping...and the nightmares."

Halia swallowed and nodded, as if not trusting herself with words.

"But you need rest," he continued. He could tell she wanted to protest, but even she couldn't argue the fact that she was exhausted. "We need you to lead us, Your Majesty."

Pushing away the pain on her face, Halia forced a smile. "Never call me that again."

"Well then, feel free to call *me* that whenever you'd like," Avrik teased before leaning in to kiss her. "Goodnight."

Halia hadn't been gone long before Avrik sensed someone else approaching. He stood up from where he'd been leaning against a tree trunk.

Gillen stood behind him, his hands shoved deep into his pockets.

Avrik offered him a nod in greeting. "Your Majesty," he said.

"I heard..." Gillen's voice trailed off. He seemed lucid, and despite the obvious fear in his darting eyes, he was more composed than usual. His brow scrunched in an uncertain frown. "Or was it only in my head?"

The ichgor had disappeared...for now, but Avrik expected it might circle back. Or maybe it had found a nearby town full of vulnerable people. Although many had arrived from other towns to take refuge in Evren's garden, there were plenty of other towns further away that didn't know about the sanctuary. A chill snaked down his back.

"You didn't imagine it," Avrik said in a low voice.

Gillen nodded slowly, looking out at the stars. "It's hard to know what's real sometimes. I get so lost in my head—in the nightmares, waking and asleep, and their whispers." He shuddered, and then his gaze snapped to Avrik. "I haven't thanked you properly yet. You were the one who helped Halia after she had to flee the palace. You…" He smiled slowly. "You cared for her, as a friend and companion when she had so few others. And as more now, I see."

Something in Avrik's heart clenched painfully. All this time, he'd known whatever he and Halia had couldn't last, and so he hadn't considered what others would think. Did Gillen look at him and see an unremarkable commoner, unworthy of standing beside royalty?

"Do you…approve?" he asked haltingly.

Gillen's formal expression melted into a friendly laugh. "Approve? Avrik, I could never repay you for what you've done for Halia. Or what you faced beside her to help rescue me." He shrugged. "And I've seen the way she looks at you. She deserves someone who makes her smile like that."

A new kind of pain tore inside Avrik. Would Halia find someone else to make her happy when he was gone? He hoped she would.

"It used to be me." A hint of sadness tinged Gillen's smile. "Growing up, she was like my sister. My best friend. It's not like we were able to leave the palace much, and when we did meet anyone our age, it was usually some daughter or son of some important so-and-so one of us would probably be married off to."

Avrik tried to imagine growing up that way, isolated and set apart from any possible friends. He'd spent all his free time with Bren, Shilam, and Jaren, finding healing from his grief in their competitive antics and brotherly affection. As he'd grown older, he'd found happiness, however fleeting, in making his schoolmates burst into smiles or outright laughter with his jokes, and he'd found pleasure in the way he could coax a blush out of a pretty girl with some casual flirting. Even if most of his classmates still whispered behind his back about his father and him now, it seemed better than years of loneliness.

Gillen settled himself on the ground in the shadow of a nearby maple tree and stared up at the sky. Avrik sat beside him.

"Do you mind if I keep you company?" Gillen asked after a quiet moment.

"Not at all," Avrik said. He studied Gillen's face, relieved to see him so coherent and at ease. "I hear them too," he added after a minute. He didn't clarify that he heard Nesrelle more than the nestrae now; what was one demon from another? "Whispering. Taunting."

"Reminding you of what they marked you with," Gillen finished softly. He stared down at the grass, watching a breeze flutter through the blades in front of him. "I think my rune says *Mad King*." He smiled ruefully. "I was never as strong as even my own father wanted me to be, when it came to swordplay or anything physical. Everyone called me artistic and intelligent and a kind-hearted dreamer." He shrugged. "Gentle words for a gentle prince. People loved me, but I always feared I was lacking and wouldn't be enough as king. I often feel powerless, weak. And now…now I'm weak in mind too, and I won't ever be king."

"Are you sure? Time might help," Avrik said slowly. "Halia could help you rule."

He met Gillen's bright blue eyes, which were clear and focused and entirely certain. "I am. In my heart, I think Halia was always meant to rule."

As the night wore on, Avrik shared what his own rune meant, and opened up about his father's mistakes. His own mistakes. He could see why Halia had appreciated growing up beside her cousin, who could sit and listen and understand, even when words failed Avrik. Gillen did have a gentle presence about him, but not in a powerless way. When Avrik sat beside the would-be king, he never doubted he was sitting with royalty. Gillen had a commanding aura, perhaps only made more powerful for his quiet voice and mild manners.

"I'm not sure what use I can be to anyone—my own people, Halia…" Gillen said after discussing his gift for intercession. His frustration showed in his knotted brow. "But I know I'll do anything I can to keep her safe."

"I will too," Avrik vowed. He thought of his protection gift, and remembered, with a sinking heart, that it would die with him. He wasn't strong enough to build a barrier as Eldon had and ask the Life-Giver to sustain it long after his death. Even if he had been, it was too late to place a barrier around Misroth—the threat was already within their kingdom. All he could hope was that he'd live long enough to protect the Misrothians as they fought against the nestrae.

"I know," Gillen said with a wink. "It's why I approve of you with her."

CHAPTER THIRTY-EIGHT

MY GIFT HADN'T RETURNED, AND we were out of time. Since we had too few dragons for everyone to ride, we had to leave today in order to arrive in Misroth City by my birthday. Before the nestrae revealed themselves to the people they were tormenting, took the throne, and began shedding my people's blood.

When I rose that morning, I plaited my hair into a braid and pulled on an old pair of riding leggings and tunic from my days living in Evren. The material clung a little more than it used to around the muscles in my arms and legs. First, I gathered my new quiver and bow, prepared just for me in Evren for this fight. Then I slung a belt around my waist and strapped on the blade Hevro had forged for me: a light but deadly sharp weapon with a small rendering of Vehgar wrought on the hilt.

Strength, beauty, and light, I thought, and in my mind I saw the way Reyva's muscles coiled beneath her scales and her body flashed in the sunlight. Dragons like Reyva represented what Alrenor prided itself in and Misroth had stolen from her. And Misroth's sigil of the dragon constellation was my reminder of what I fought for.

People had gathered in the kitchen or seated themselves outside on the grass under the early morning sun. They ate breakfast and spoke in hushed tones. I noticed Iyleth and Narek clustered close together, and not far away, Lyanna and Rev spoke with Bren, Shilam, and Jaren.

Dienn leaned familiarly against Bren's side, and he had his arm wrapped around her. Avrik was nowhere in sight.

When I approached Lyanna and Rev, I found the latter dressed for travel and armed with weapons. It was strange to see gentle Rev, with his spectacles and his hands that were so frequently ink-stained from his bookkeeping work at the bank, dressed to fight. Growing up, he'd always been a stronghold for me, but his strength had seemed to be of a very different kind from that of a typical warrior. Looking at him now, a lump formed in my throat as I imagined what the nestrae could do to him. To any of my remaining loved ones.

Lyanna threw her arms around me, nearly suffocating me against her. "This time we'll have a proper goodbye," she whispered, and then her shoulders began to shake as she cried against me. "Come back to me again," she begged. "Come back, my sweet, dear girl. My brave and wonderful daughter."

I couldn't stop my own tears as I squeezed her back, inhaling the sweet scent of lavender. It seemed I'd only been home a moment, and to leave a second time was nearly unbearable. Whether we won or lost this fight against the nestrae, I couldn't even begin to guess when I'd be able to return to Evren again. The thought left me feeling empty.

It took a long time for us to release one another so Lyanna could return to helping serve the recruits breakfast and pack bags of supplies for the journey. Even though we would travel and fight together, I hugged Rev too, unable to shake my fear that this could be the last time we truly were able to spend time with one another.

Clearly at a loss for words, he stroked my hair and continued to murmur, "It'll be all right," until I finally stepped back and left him to eat his breakfast.

Not feeling hungry, I bypassed the crowds and started toward the edge of the garden, thinking to seek Reyva's reassuring presence. I rounded some shrubs and startled when I almost collided with Jennah.

Her haggard face made guilt prickle through me. I knew she hadn't been sleeping well lately, too worried about what her family must be suffering without her. It had taken everything within my friend to linger here in Evren to train and prepare, rather than rush ahead to be with her loved ones.

"Jennah!" I said.

Her gold-brown eyes widened, taking me in. She too was dressed for travel in a homespun tunic and leggings made by some of the Evren women, and with two Alrenian daggers on her hips. She'd braided her hair back, but stray curls had already escaped to ring her face.

"Halia," she said, discomfort evident in her expression. "I'm…" She swallowed and hugged herself tightly. The summer air was too warm, even this early, for her to be cold. "I'm sorry," she said softly, not quite meeting my eyes.

I didn't need to ask her what she was sorry for. My friend had been distant for days, and I knew exactly what she was struggling with.

"I forgive you," I said softly. "I know you have been suffering, and I'm sorry for it."

"Not me," Jennah said, her eyes dark with sorrow, her voice tremulous with her gathering tears. "My daughters. My husband. My mother." She drew in a deep breath and lifted her gaze to meet mine. "But it's not your fault. It's just…I can't help regretting…" She fidgeted with the hilt of one of her daggers. "The nestred voices have only grown stronger lately. All I can hear is them telling me I'm inadequate, and they show me horrible visions of what they are doing and still plan to do to my family." A tear slipped down her scarred cheek.

I stepped forward and seized Jennah's free hand. It was cold in mine. "Not for long," I said firmly. "We're going to save them, Jennah."

Jennah watched me for a long, silent moment, as if considering my words. Because how could I make a promise like that? How could I know anyone would be safe from the nestrae in three days' time?

"Even if I don't have my gift," I said quietly, "I still can't lie. Just thinking about it is painful for me, and I never could lie when I repressed my gift years ago either." I sighed. "I may not know the future, but I'm not giving you empty words. I believe what I'm saying."

Finally, Jennah nodded. Straightening her back, she pulled her hand from mine and wiped away her tears. "Of course," she said softly. She offered me a tremulous smile. "We are Misrothians. We don't bow to anyone else. We're Dragon Tamers, Empire-Breakers, and Demon Slayers." And with that, she laughed, and I could see a spark of defiance and hope growing in her eyes.

Instead of searching for Reyva, I walked straight to Avrik's cabin, knowing in my bones that he would be there. As I approached, the first golden rays of morning reflected off the windowpanes, drawing my eye to a shattered one. Shards of glass sparkled in the grass below it. Otherwise, the home was still and quiet and looked just as I remembered it.

Heart heavy in my chest, I stepped up to the door. I could almost imagine Kyrin on the other side, chatting with Avrik or fondly ruffling his hair. My hand trembled when I knocked, but the door hadn't been latched. At my touch, it swung inward with a soft creak.

The door opened to the living room and kitchen, where Avrik, Bren, and I had once taken turns practicing our dancing before Evren's Great Feast. Though the summer air was soft and warm, the house's interior was shadowed and cold. Dust motes lingered in the beams of sunlight pushing their way through the dimness.

In the kitchen, everything still appeared to be in its place: table and chairs ready and waiting, like they'd always been when I'd joined Avrik and his father for dinner. The counters were dusty, but the familiar jars of flour and sugar, salt and pepper, and various other herbs waited near the kitchen window. The shelves were filled with dried vegetables, garlic, and onions. A faint smell of rot lingered in the air, relieved by the fresh breeze stirring through the broken window.

Avrik didn't seem to notice or care about the dirt and decay gathering around him. Shoulders slumped, eyes shadowed, and face wan, he sat at the kitchen table, looking as if he hadn't slept all night.

"It's only a matter of time," he said. His voice was low and hoarse, and when his eyes met mine, I could see the despair he could no longer hide.

"Avrik," I said, his name like a plea on my lips. I'd never felt so helpless or afraid in my life. "Tell me how I can help."

He shook his head, staring down at the maps and books strewn across the table. We'd once spent hours studying them and dreaming of what it would be like to explore all those kingdoms ourselves. My chest tightened at the memory. We'd been innocent and naïve then, even with our painful pasts. We had no idea what other horrors laid in wait.

"It's getting worse," Avrik said. His warm brown eyes, normally shining with mirth, now shone with tears. "I'm feeling weaker, colder. I hear her voice all the time."

"There has to be a way to fight it." I stepped closer to him, trying to break the distance that yawned between us. He couldn't be slipping away from me. Not now. "Misroth needs you—and your gift. *I* need you."

Avrik stood and wrapped me in his arms. Despite what he'd said about being cold, he still felt warm to me. Like home.

"The Life-Giver…he gave you that gift for a reason," I insisted. "Surely that means he can spare your life too."

Avrik pulled back to look down at me, and his smile was strained. "Death can't be defied all the time. Sometimes it has to win."

I could hardly breathe. Images spun through my mind's eye: my mother's blood coating my hands as she drew her last breath. My uncle, choking and spasming and foaming at the mouth. Gare's lifeless form, looking too small and empty after all the life and laughter and strength he'd radiated. Layk disappearing behind a wall of fire, his pained screams echoing in my ears.

You will not be so easily broken, my mother had said.

But I was breaking now.

"Nesrelle can't win," I bit out. "She *can't.*"

Avrik cradled my face in his hands. Tears glistened in his eyes, despite how fiercely he tried to blink them away. "She won't win," he said firmly. "In the end, the afterlife waits for me. My mother is there, maybe even…" His voice drifted before he spoke the word *father.* "Death is not the worst thing."

Of course he would say that here, in this cabin filled with echoes of moments spent with his parents. He'd probably helped his mother cook in this kitchen; he'd sat at this table with his father and discussed hunting trips and travel plans to trade goods in other cities. This was a place of ghosts and loss, betrayal and darkness.

Anger flared in my chest, hot and piercing. How could he pretend it would be all right? How could he resign himself to death and leave me behind? "Is that you or your grief speaking?" I demanded.

Avrik's lips thinned to a firm line. "I'm not *giving up.*"

I pulled back and shoved my hands against his chest to push him away. "It sounds like giving up to me!" I cried. My voice sounded unnaturally high-pitched in my ears, strained and wild. My body trembled with a fierce energy and I longed to hit, to kick, to fight something. Anything. I was furious with Nesrelle, with the world, with the Life-Giver, and with Avrik.

This angry person wasn't me. Or was it?

Was this what happened to a person when they broke into a thousand pieces?

Avrik's eyes flashed with a flurry of emotions: fury, hurt, fear, and sadness. "Do you think I *want* to die?" he demanded. "That I rolled over like a submissive dog when Nesrelle came after me?"

I clenched my jaw, trying to hold back everything building inside of me. I was sure I'd break down and either weep or scream.

Avrik snagged my hands in his again, warm and firm. "I want to *live.* To explore the whole world, to fight for Misroth, to have a future with you. To love you."

It was the first time either of us had admitted this aloud, and even my fevered brain was able to pause and linger over the word. We stared at one another, wide-eyed and gasping. The air was thick, heavy and electric with every emotion between us.

Avrik cupped my face in his hands, brushing back stray wisps of hair.

"Then keep fighting," I snapped.

The barest ghost of Avrik's familiar, flirtatious smile darted across his face. Teardrops clung to his eyelashes. "I will fight until my last breath," he said, and he kissed me.

This wasn't like the kisses we'd shared before, when we pretended we had forever. Now it was all too clear we were running out of time. This kiss was a fevered, futile rebellion against time. It was every declaration of love and every touch we would never share again. It was a bittersweet, tearful goodbye.

Avrik's lips were warm and desperate and angry against mine. He tangled one hand in my hair, tugging it free until it spilled over my shoulders, and cupped the other around my waist. I threw my arms around his neck and pulled him close to me, trying to memorize the way he felt. The way he always smelled of the sun-drenched grass and sweet countryside air I associated with Evren, with home.

The approaching wing beats of our dragons drew us reluctantly apart. For a moment, we stood close, catching our breath and drinking each other in. Then Avrik strode to the far wall, where his sword and bow leaned, and began strapping them on. I retrieved my ribbon from the floor and pulled my hair back again.

Without another word, we stepped out of Avrik's cabin to meet our friends and fellow recruits, already making their way in a long, winding path toward the forest.

CHAPTER THIRTY-NINE

RUNNING MY FINGERS ALONG REYVA'S shimmering scales, feeling their reassuring strength, I squeezed my eyes shut and tried to focus for the millionth time on my truth gift. Nothing but a gaping hole awaited me. The emptiness left an ache in my chest almost as intense as grief.

As if trying to reassure me, Reyva pressed toward me, gently butting her forehead against mine. A low rumble rolled through her chest, drawing the eyes of some of the recruits trying to settle down in the camp.

Our dragons encircled a clearing in Evren Forest, an easy barrier to block out the sedwa lurking at night. All day, Avrik, Jennah, Narek, Iyleth, Gillen, and I had ridden the beasts, forcing them to fly as slowly as possible and then circling back as needed while the recruits marched beneath us. We wouldn't reach the outskirts of Misroth City until the third day. My birthday.

My chest was tight with worry. But stronger than my fear was my anger, as steady and sustaining as my thrumming heartbeat in my ears.

"You have no right," I said under my breath, into the gathering darkness. Leaves rustled and boughs creaked overhead. Something scurried through the undergrowth as a distant owl hooted. "No right to my gift." Though my voice trembled, I clenched my hands into fists and searched the shadows. Surely Nesrelle was out there, watching and waiting. Hadn't she said herself she wanted to witness my despair as

Misroth fell? "No right to *him*."

"I have every right," came a familiar voice, soft as a dream.

I found her form among the trees and glared, feeling the urge to draw my bow. Casting a glance back at the camp, my gaze fastened on Avrik, taking in his widening eyes and sharpening expression. Perhaps he'd heard her too. Everyone else was murmuring and laughing together around the fires and tents scattered throughout the clearing, oblivious to Nesrelle's presence. When Avrik started to stand, I gave him a single shake of my head, though I knew there was no chance he would obey and let me face Nesrelle alone.

Reyva stirred, sensing how tense I was. I laid a calming hand on her side, murmuring reassurances to her, and then pressed into the forest. Branches scratched my bare arms and snagged on my tunic as I wound my way toward Nesrelle.

She waited calmly, her face as pale as moonlight in the shadows. Her blue eyes were so bright they hurt to look at; her lips full and blood-red. She was clothed in a dress of midnight blue, overlaid with silver lace and intricate detailing that looked like shimmering galaxies. It reminded me of the gown my mother had been wearing the day she'd died. Of the sort of gowns Misrothian royalty wore to give tribute to our sigil constellation, Vehgar, along with our other admired cluster of stars: Shyla the archer. On her head rested either the Misrothian queen's crown, or a startlingly exact replica.

I was light-headed with fury. The Queen of Death was mocking me, reminding me that she was about to tear Misroth from my grasp.

And that death would take more of my loved ones.

Rage sparked so fiercely I almost couldn't see straight. *I'll cut her and see if she bleeds, demon goddess or not,* I thought. But that wasn't a fight I could win, not now. That wouldn't save my people. Would it?

Flashing a deceptively sweet smile, Nesrelle splayed out her hands and gestured to herself. "You summoned me?" she asked, as if she didn't already know what I wanted.

There was no sign of her unnaturally long teeth or claws for the moment. I resisted reaching for one of my weapons. Sucking in a deep breath, I forced myself to at least pretend I was calm. "Return my gift," I said through gritted teeth.

Nesrelle raised her red eyebrows as if surprised. "Oh, dear," she said in mock concern. She tapped a white finger against her chin and studied me. "I'm afraid I'm not able to give gifts." A slow snarl revealed all her perfect, glistening teeth. "That is your Life-Giver's area of expertise."

I swallowed thickly. "You took it from me," I snapped, "so give back what you stole."

She smirked. "I can only take, dear. Haven't you noticed?" She twirled a hand elegantly, like a little girl pretending to be a grand lady. "Death steals," she continued, stalking toward me. Her dress whispered across the forest floor and fluttered around her bare feet. "Fear steals." She leaned toward me, her breath brushing my face. Her gaze was black now, her blue eyes replaced by the same endless, yawning pits for eyes that her nestred servants had. Her teeth were long and sharp; her skin so translucent I could discern the shape of her skull and see blue veins mapped across her temple. "I'm a thief."

My hands twitched, ready to seize my sword and attack her. But her mouth flipped into another smile, as if just realizing something. Her appearance returned to the deceptively beautiful mask she usually wore.

"He won't return it to you, will he?" Nesrelle giggled gleefully. The sound skittered eerily off the trees, surrounding me. Her eyes snapped to me and pain shot through my body. "Pathetic."

"You're spying on us, telling your demons exactly what we've planned, aren't you?" I said, my stomach clenching. What a fool I'd been to think there'd ever been an element of surprise in anything my friends and I did. "They know where we are and what we've been doing all along, and they've been sitting back and waiting for us." Though the night air was cool, my cheeks were flushed, like I was boiling from within. "They're toying with us."

Nesrelle shrugged and stared down at her fingernails. "Did you summon me only to remind me of how little hope you have?" She smirked. "And to try to demand a gift that your Life-Giver refuses you?"

I drew myself to my full height. "I know something *you* won't refuse."

Nesrelle raised her eyebrows, her red lips curving into a smile.

"A challenge to fight me on my birthday," I went on. "A duel just between you and me."

Mischievous light gleamed in Nesrelle's bright eyes. "A fight to the death with the future Queen of Misroth? You're right. I can't refuse."

A twig snapped behind me and Avrik launched himself between Nesrelle and me, his sword tip pointed in Nesrelle's face. "Get back!" he snarled.

Nesrelle rolled her eyes. "And what are you going to do?" She gave a careless wave of her hand and Avrik dropped the blade. Collapsing to his knees, he pressed his hands over his heart and choked for air. "Did you forget you're *dying*?"

I dropped to Avrik's side, squeezing his shoulders as if I could offer him some of my strength. I stared into his wide eyes. "It's all right," I said frantically, nonsensically. Of course it wasn't all right. His chest was rising, but each breath he sucked in was a heaving gasp of pain. He was pale and shaking, and a part of me was terrified his heart would burst right here.

I glared at Nesrelle. "Enough," I ground out. "Stop this."

Nesrelle sighed, but relief spread across Avrik's wan face. His breaths grew even as color returned to his cheeks.

"All in good time," she told him with a nasty smile. Her eyes darted back to me. "I'll see you soon."

Just as suddenly as she'd appeared within the forest, she was gone.

"Don't do this," Avrik said. His eyes were dark and intense as he searched my face. "How do you plan to kill an immortal?"

I stared up past the forest ceiling, where I could catch glimpses of the stars beyond the swaying leaves. "It's not about winning," I said softly. "It's about distracting Nesrelle from leading the nestrae. It's about trying to give our people any advantage I can."

"Halia…" Avrik said, desperation in the lines of his brow. The dark circles beneath his eyes looked deeper than before, like bruises standing out starkly against his skin. He seemed about to say more, but he stopped himself. Instead, he drew in a deep breath and grasped my hands in his. Leaning forward until our foreheads touched, he wrapped his arms around me.

We stood like that for a long time, soaking in one another's company and pretending we could shut out the world. Pretending we could stop the inevitable.

CHAPTER FORTY

Avrik

THE FIRST RAYS OF DAWN glistened golden and bright through the forest leaves, awakening the world to vibrant color and life in the way only a summer morning could.

But all Avrik could feel was death's shadow hovering over him.

As the camp ate a hasty breakfast and packed up their supplies, preparing for their third and final day of travel, Avrik slipped away into the forest. He hadn't told anyone but Halia about Nesrelle's death claim on him. Each day he'd walked and joked with Bren, Shilam, and Jaren as if everything was as it had been before he'd left Evren. His friends, though concerned and afraid of the battle that lay ahead, had no sense of the heavy despair that hung over him. They hadn't lived through the terrors of Toryn or experienced nestred torture. They had no idea what the nestrae or even the ichgor were truly like, and that meant they couldn't quite fathom how hopeless their efforts were. They might speak of their group's small numbers and inexperience, but without having experienced what Avrik had, their terror wasn't real yet.

Leaning back against a tree, Avrik sucked in a breath and balled his hands into fists. "I'm not ready," he hissed under his breath.

Lack of sleep made the world around him look fuzzy, almost surreal. In the early light, the tree trunks and leaves appeared gilded, too stunning to be real. He didn't want to let go of this beautiful world or the future he'd hoped for, not yet. Everything within him strained toward fighting for survival, for life. But this wasn't a real battle. There were no counterstrikes he could plan, no strategies that would let him outsmart his enemy. Not this time.

Avrik sank to a fallen log. There was no outmaneuvering death.

"What do I do?" he muttered. "Why give me this gift if I won't live long enough to use it?"

"It's not about how long your life is, but how worthwhile you make it," a voice said.

Avrik startled, blinking up at the man standing before him. The Life-Giver was clothed in his usual travel-stained cloak, his hood thrown back to reveal his care-lined face. Though he didn't appear old, he wasn't exactly young either: his brown eyes were gentle and kind, yet they bore an unearthly wisdom that knew no age. His beard was fuller than the last time Avrik had seen him, back in his Alrenian prison cell before he'd known what his gift was.

Now that Avrik knew how the Forwyn people were treated in the Alrenian Empire, the Life-Giver's dark Forwyn skin stood out sharply to him. How willfully ignorant the Alrenians had to be, to pretend the Forwyn were less than them and that the Life-Giver had blessed only Alrenor as his Chosen. Stranger still was the fact that this supernatural being looked more like a humble slave and not an Alrenian warrior.

"Is it my time?" Avrik asked, his voice sounding thick in his own ears. He didn't feel like he was dying, but how could he be sure? Many times in recent days he'd gone from feeling healthy and strong to sensing Nesrelle stealing the life out of him. "Have you come to take me?"

The Life-Giver shook his head gently. "Not yet."

Avrik stood, studying the man before him uncertainly. "Is…is there a way to stop it?"

"I'm sorry," the Life-Giver said, and his crinkled brow and shining eyes made him look sincerely pained. "But death still has a place in your world."

Though even thinking about leaving Halia behind gave him physical pain, Avrik nodded. He was intimately acquainted with death, and though many times it had been his enemy, in some ways he also could imagine it as a friend. A cold embrace, wrapping him up in darkness and rest. After that he knew there would be light and life beyond, where his mother waited for him in a place where she felt no pain. He'd imagined it often enough that a part of him longed for it, even if he still ached to live. For his mother. For Halia. For himself.

He could almost see his mother beckoning to him. "Soon, my dearest son," she said. "We'll be together soon."

"What's it like?" Avrik asked the man. "Is she waiting for me? Is…he?" Avrik didn't need to explain that he meant his mother and father; it was obvious the Life-Giver knew whom he was thinking about.

The man stepped closer and laid a comforting hand on Avrik's shoulder. It was warm and calloused, as real as any human touch. Avrik blinked, once again taken by surprise. But hadn't Halia spoken of the Life-Giver holding her in his arms and weeping over her when she'd almost died?

"The afterlife is too much for me to simply explain it to you," the Life-Giver said gently. "I have to show you."

Avrik's chest was tight as he pictured his mother's face. "Right," he said softly, nodding. "Then I'll know soon enough." He closed his eyes and inhaled deeply through his nose, trying to quell the emotions threatening to drown him: fear, sorrow, regret…acceptance.

"Nesrelle can't win," the Life-Giver explained, his voice deep and reassuring. "In the end, death only gives way to another life. Death itself has an end." He squeezed Avrik's arm before stepping back. "Look for me then."

Drawing a deep breath, Avrik tried to respond, but the man was already gone.

CHAPTER FORTY-ONE

THERE WAS NO CONCEALING OUR approach toward Misroth City, no need even for hidden entrances or sending our dragons away to hide while we infiltrated the capital. Not when Nesrelle was able to watch and report on our every move and conversation.

The nestrae knew we were coming, and they were doing nothing to stop us. No, they were *welcoming* us.

When we arrived at the edge of Evren Forest, we scanned the surrounding countryside to find no nestrae, and no Misrothians either. The road leading up toward the gates was empty, though the afternoon was still young, and none of the homes nestled along the road or Emrell River showed any signs of life. An unnatural quiet lay over the land.

I glanced toward the capital, where the gates were flung wide open. A chill ran down my spine.

"The nestrae are waiting for us," I said.

Beside me, Narek's jaw was tight, his stance rigid. Just like my other friends and me, he was clothed in the dragon scale armor we'd brought from Alrenor. His gleamed green and silver, contrasting with his dark hair and eyes. "I don't like this," he said gruffly. He cast a sidelong glance my way. "We could try to plan a different strategy, but…"

"We're out of time," I said, not moving my stare from the open gates and the empty road leading into the city's heart. "And Nesrelle will know."

Avrik grasped my hand.

Behind me, Jennah said, "We have no other choice. We can't sit back while they start to kill…everyone." Her voice cracked.

"Jennah's right," I agreed, forcing my words to sound steady and firm. "Our only choice is to face them head on."

The recruits at our backs gathered around us, muttering worriedly under their breath and stirring restlessly. "It's suicide," was repeated over and over. Word had already gotten around in the past two days that the nestrae already knew of our plans, but seeing the truth before us, how confident our enemies were to simply sit back and lure us in, was terrifying. Even for men and women who didn't fully understand yet what the nestrae were capable of.

I spun toward them and lifted up my voice. "People of Misroth! You must remember why we fight." As I said the words, my mind flitted back to the horrors of Toryn, to Layk's measured voice saying the very same thing. "We didn't come here today because we were assured victory. We are here because our kingdom is dying, and our people—mothers and fathers, husbands and sons, wives and daughters, brothers and sisters—are under attack. If we turn our backs on our capital, can we call ourselves true Misrothians? Can we call ourselves heirs of King Eldon and his rebels?"

Avrik threaded his fingers through mine and Iyleth shot me a look of encouragement. I wished that my friend whose words were so naturally full of hope could speak for me, but I knew this message had to come from me. Gradually, the recruits' mutterings died away and their expressions turned determined. In the crowd, Rev met my eyes with a gentle smile. Emotion tightened my throat, but I pressed on.

"If we turn back today, we let Misroth as we know it die. We let our people die. And in the end, the nestrae will still come to our towns' borders and to our homes." The recruits shuffled restlessly, their hands shifting toward hilts and grasping for bows. Their eyes shone with fervor and courage, the same fire that was burning in my own chest. "So yes, this may be dangerous," I shouted. "This may be our last stand. But this is our choice: to flee and die as defeated cowards, or to face the demons who have invaded our land and fight with all we have left. And if we die, we die as courageous, dragon-hearted Misrothians!"

Men and women erupted into cheers.

"For Misroth!" I screamed, and my people took up the chant.

"For Misroth!"

Our numbers were impossibly few, but our shouts seemed to shake the earth and sway the tree branches. To announce to our waiting enemy that we were not afraid.

With the threat of defeat hovering over us, recruits turned to friends and loved ones, embracing each other and offering words of encouragement and blessing. I was surprised to see Jennah standing before me with tear-filled eyes, pulling me into a strong embrace. "Every moment I have served you and Misroth has been an honor." She drew an uneven breath. "I am proud to fight alongside you, my queen."

The title sent a jolt through me, but not in the same way it once had. I refused to flinch from my responsibility now. "It's been an honor to have you as a friend," I answered.

Pulling away, she spoke in Alrenian. The same words I'd heard her speak in my nightmarish nestred vision in Toryn, back when I'd thought the demons had executed her right before my eyes. "*Ivanah meryk.* Eternal peace." She smiled. "Those were the words of the old Alrenian warriors, before they became corrupt. Their reminder to one another of what awaited them, even in defeat and death: the eternal peace of the afterlife. I don't know how far my gift can reach, but may the Life-Giver grant you courage."

My eyes widened. I hadn't told anyone of my plans—only Avrik even knew about my challenge to Nesrelle.

"How did you know I was going somewhere else in the battle?" I asked.

She winked. "You have…a look. I can tell you have a plan."

As she turned to Avrik to bid him good luck, Narek clapped a hand on my shoulder. "I…" He hesitated, shaking his head. "I once said you were like your father," he said at last, his eyes dark, his forehead pinched with regret. "The truth is, you are only everything that was good in your father. You have his strength and determination. And you are so much more than he was. This fight is *not* your fault. You have been the leader Misroth needs, and your people's blood is not on your hands. Never blame yourself for this, or for what your forefathers did. You are better than them."

I pulled Narek into a hug. "Thank you."

Iyleth hugged me next. Marked by nestred runes she didn't try to hide, dressed in a tunic of chainmail—one of many Hevro had worked tirelessly to help prepare for the recruits—she looked fierce. Ready for whatever this day would bring. Slung over her shoulders, she carried various medical supplies, while a sword hung at her hip. She was prepared to do whatever it took on the battlefield to save lives. "You bring hope to more than just Misroth," she said as she pulled back. "Whatever happens here will make a difference for our world. If anyone can defeat these monsters, it's you."

She turned to embrace Narek, leaving Gillen to pull me aside.

"Halia," he said fervently. His fingers grasped his sword hilt, his hand trembling slightly. Even though he wouldn't be joining us in the fight, he was still dressed in gold dragon scale armor, a sword at his side. To me, he looked exactly like the king he should have been. "I wish I could fight at your side, but…" He shook his head and smiled slowly. "None of that matters." He kissed my forehead. "Find my mother."

I nodded.

Gillen squeezed my hands in his firm, calloused grip. "I'm proud of you. You're not so little now, Lia." His chuckle was low and rumbling.

"You would have made a great king," I said, stubbornly holding back my tears.

His eyes glittered with pride. "I'm proud to serve Misroth alongside you. I know this isn't the best birthday…" He smiled wryly. "But I'll make it up to you when this is over."

I smirked. "Stargazing on the north turret." I let my smile grow wider and more mischievous. "Oh, and a portrait of me covering an entire wall in your sitting room. So you always remember your favorite cousin."

Gillen laughed outright. "Maybe I should take the crown back. It's going to your head."

I rolled my eyes and he hugged me. "I love you, Lia," he said.

Swallowing, I squeezed him tighter. "I love you too, Gil."

As my cousin stepped back, I locked eyes with Avrik over his shoulder. A thousand silent words passed between us in a single glance, all the words it hurt too much to say. Before I could step closer, Rev crushed me in his arms.

"I'm proud of you, daughter," he whispered, his voice cracking on the words.

I couldn't speak, only cling to him tightly as I choked back my own tears.

"Whatever happens…" Rev said after a long moment, "to me, to anyone… You are loved. And if…" He cleared his throat. "If anything happens to me, tell your mother I love her too."

"No," I said, shaking my head fiercely, even though I was still pressed against his chest. "You will tell her yourself."

He released me, nodding and wiping away his tears. "Giver willing," he said softly, and turned to his fellow Evren people to wish them well.

For a long moment, I could only stare at Avrik. It seemed that if we never drew closer, never embraced or said the words, we wouldn't have to watch this moment end.

"If I can stop Nesrelle," I said slowly, "I can save you."

Avrik smiled, but it didn't reach his eyes. He stepped forward to tuck a loose strand of hair behind my ear. The rest was gathered into thick braids knotted together at the nape of my neck, thanks to Iyleth, who had told me that morning that I should look both queenly and fierce in battle. In the pure black dragon scale armor I'd brought with me from Alrenor, I already knew I cut an imposing figure, like the Alrenian warriors of old. I hadn't had the heart to remind Iyleth that my armor also came with a helmet that would cover the braids.

Now Avrik studied my face silently, as if at a loss for words.

"You make a great queen," he said at last, leaning forward until our foreheads touched.

I hated the way he spoke, like he was trying to share words I could carry with me when he was no longer there. "Avrik…" I started, but he shook his head and wrapped his arms around me, holding me close.

My protests died in my throat. It felt unfair to say goodbye, when we'd finally righted the wrongs between us, and our future was only beginning. But if he and I knew anything of death, it was that it was a force as strong as the life flowing in us now. It couldn't be stopped, not forever.

If by some miracle death didn't come for Avrik today, it would come another day. Just as it had come for his parents, for mine, for Layk and Gare, and for everyone else we had lost along the way. Death was inevitable, which meant that even if by some miracle we were given countless years together, our time would still eventually end. In goodbye.

Our kiss tasted like desperation and bitter tears, though neither of us was crying. Not anymore.

"You're strong," Avrik said at last, pulling back just enough to look in my eyes. "You'll find a way to save Misroth." A half-smile tugged at his lips. "And when you do, you'll make this kingdom into something so much greater than it ever was before, because you know what lies beyond our borders. You'll build alliances and form a greater future for Misroth. And you'll travel the rest of the world to see all the sights we've dreamed about."

I nodded, unable to speak.

"Keep living," Avrik said. "Keep fighting. Keep dreaming. I'll be waiting for you in the afterlife, where you can tell me about all of your adventures."

"I will," I vowed, forcing my voice to be strong.

We pulled apart, and there was nothing left but to approach the capital and face our enemies. I crept toward the edge of the forest and drew a deep breath. When I glanced back at my recruits behind me, I didn't see a ragtag group of farmers and bookkeepers, blacksmiths and shop owners, hunters and traders, family members and friends. I saw armed Misrothians with fierce hearts, prepared to defend their kingdom and their freedom at any cost.

"For Misroth!" I shouted again, unstrapping my bow from my back.

Behind me, metal rang out as swords were drawn and my people answered. "For Misroth!"

We left the shelter of the forest and marched out into the open, joining the road that led straight to the unguarded gates. Overhead, Reyva and the other dragons circled protectively, awaiting our commands. The tension in the air was palpable, fear and uncertainty radiating off everyone around me in waves. But the goodbyes I'd shared had unleashed something else within me.

Rage coiled inside me like a snake.

I'm coming for you, Nesrelle.

Even if she was my undoing, even if she and her demons burned all of Misroth to the ground, I would make her taste my anger first. It was not for nothing that Narek, or even my mother, had seen similarities between my father and me. Where he had shown strength of purpose and ferocity only for himself, I would show my enemies my unbreakable will to save the people and land I loved.

My mother's voice echoed in my ears. *You will not be easily broken.*

Misroth's gates yawned wide before us, the city streets seemingly deserted. Wariness prickled up my spine as I studied the buildings, their empty windows staring back at us. A hint of smoke tinged the air, burning the back of my throat.

Then a line of nestrae materialized, almost as if they were shadows come to life. They emerged from the buildings, from alleys, and even dropped from rooftops. Together, they set themselves aflame and began chanting, rushing toward us like an overwhelming wave. Already, their numbers were terrifying compared to ours, and my heart slammed hard into my chest.

"Avrik," I said, but when I tossed him a quick glance, I could tell from the set of his shoulders that he was already concentrating on his protection gift.

Then, without a single command from me to Reyva, she dove, taking the lead. The two other dragons flanked her, each with their claws extended as they emitted a chorus of earsplitting roars. Before the line of nestrae reached us, the three dragons collided with the demons, tearing through their ranks like they were a child's toys. With a handful of struggling nestrae clutched in their claws, the dragons launched themselves back into the air, circling high over the city's rooftops before releasing the demons, letting them plummet to the ground far below.

By the time I led my people through the gates, the dragons had cleared a path for us. When the remaining nestrae swung their blades, they bounced off Avrik's invisible shield. I shot two before they could move out of range. Hope bloomed in my chest, and I could hear the rallying cries of my troops behind me as their morale lifted.

But now that we were within the city limits, I had somewhere else to be. "Lead them in," I told Narek as he sliced his sword through a nestred throat.

Narek kicked the dead nestred away from his path and saluted me.

At my other side, Avrik grasped my hand. He cast me a sidelong glance as we entered the shadow of Misroth City's gate. His bright smile was a little shocking even to me, who had been familiar with his unwavering strength for years. It was remarkable how he could look his own death in the eyes and grin.

"I don't know if my gift will reach you. But if anyone can bring the Queen of Death to her knees, it's you."

I smirked. "Are you finally admitting I'm a better fighter than you?"

Avrik laughed. "Never. Maybe a better shooter, but fighter?" He shook his head playfully, before his face turned serious again.

"I'll be waiting," he finished softly, as I released his hand and whistled to Reyva.

The dragon landed before me, and I attached my bow and quiver to the saddle strapped on her back. As I swung onto Reyva, I found Avrik's gaze one last time. The words seemed feeble, a flimsy offering for him to carry into the afterlife and cling to when we'd be apart for a lifetime, but I said them anyway. "I love you."

Before he could respond, I commanded Reyva into the sky. She leapt and launched toward the clouds that hung low over the city, a foreboding mass that reminded me of curling smoke from nestred fires. Even up here, where fresh air stung my eyes, I could taste ash and smoke on my tongue.

As Reyva swept over the city, I spotted more movement. The other streets that had been empty and quiet before erupted into chaos as the nestrae unleashed their powers on the citizens. In fact, the nestrae weren't even fighting my Misrothian troops anymore. My stomach lurched. Instead, men, women, and children rushed through the streets, their screams and shouts loud enough to reach my ears. Just as in my nestred visions, the Misrothians attacked each other, slaying their own, and then turned toward my soldiers. Fires flared to life, sending up plumes of smoke, and the nestrae began to drag the bodies of both the living and dead toward their flames.

Despite the daylight, the shrieks of ichgor rent the air as their huge shapes appeared on the horizon, flying straight toward the capital. My heart stuttered in my throat. Perhaps it was through Nesrelle's unnatural power that the creatures were flying in the day. They'd never fought alongside the nestrae before, but now they swooped toward the city as if obeying a call only they could hear.

They outnumbered our dragons, and I could only pray that our forces could hold against them.

My fingers trembled with horror and rage as I clung to Reyva's back. "Faster," I muttered, knowing she didn't understand my speech in the New Language. I gritted my teeth as the castle loomed closer.

We climbed high in the air to scale the cliff. The sea's briny scent permeated the air as we circled over the Alrenian. My eyes snagged on the golden beach below the castle, where Gillen and I had spent hours horseback riding and swimming. The depths beneath the cliff brought flashes of my first near-death experience to mind, but the sea didn't hold the same terrors for me anymore. Closer at hand were the castle grounds, where statues of past kings and queens gazed upon me solemnly and the vibrant hues of the summer garden contrasted sharply with the destruction happening down in the city.

As we drew near the main courtyard, a thick cloud of smoke mingled with shouts filling the air. Even more terrifying were the noises of the nestrae: their stomping boots and hissing voices rose in a thunderous beat and taunting chant that made my skin crawl. My heart lodged in my throat as I thought of my aunt surrounded by the demons.

"*Vella*," I whispered, and my dragon instantly hovered quietly over the ramparts encircling the courtyard. She seemed to understand the need for caution on an instinctual level, not only dropping soundlessly to the parapet, but also tucking in her wings and coiling her tail against her body. Sinking against the grey stone, she made herself as small as a beast her size possibly could, while still giving me a perfect view of the courtyard below.

The scene below was horrifying. Nestrae swarmed the courtyard like rats infesting a ship, their dark, grotesque bodies hulking over the terrified forms of servants, nobles, and the Royal Councilmen and their families. Huge bonfires roared throughout the space, filling the courtyard with flickering orange light and oppressive heat. Some of the nestrae were dragging screaming figures toward the fires and striking down anyone who fought to free their loved ones. Bodies littered the cobblestones, blood pooling around them.

In the center of it all stood Nesrelle, dressed in a blindingly white dress, pure save for the blood soaking the hem and staining her bare feet. She was unarmed but every inch the terrifying Queen of Death and Despair, from the cold light in her eyes to the cutting smile on her blood-red mouth.

As I watched her face, she didn't turn toward me. She was focused on the veiled figure standing across from her, chin lifted in defiance. My heart lurched. That woman, clad in shades of black and grey and wearing a veil of lace, was my aunt. I recognized her poise and the flash of auburn hair gleaming in the firelight. Behind her veil, her expression was inscrutable.

Two nestrae shoved my aunt, forcing her painfully to her knees. Others stomped and chanted around her: "Death, death, death."

"It's a shame you insist on being difficult," Nesrelle said in her melodic voice. She curled her fingers until they resembled claws, her true nature beginning to show. "All you have to do is surrender the throne to me, and you can live. I don't need you to die—not yet. You have plenty of despair already, enough to feed my nestrae and me for a long time to come."

Velaire raised her head, meeting Nesrelle's gaze unflinchingly. "The threat of death holds no power over me."

Nesrelle snarled, pouncing toward my aunt.

But I was already in the courtyard, Reyva coiled reluctantly in one shadowy corner as I stepped forward alone. "Stop!" I shouted. Despite the nestred chants, the people's terrified cries, and the roaring flames, my voice rang out clearly. Everyone froze as all eyes turned toward me, though I knew my foreign armor and helmet concealed my identity to all but Nesrelle herself. "I'm who you want. Princess Halia, heir to the throne."

Nesrelle pulled back from my aunt, whose face was scratched and bleeding from the demon queen's claws. Slowly, Nesrelle turned to face me, a wicked smile twisting her mouth. "You came," she said softly, sweeping toward me like a mother greeting her lost child. Her feet stepped gracefully across the blood-slick stones and unceremoniously over bodies, never slipping or stumbling.

"Halia," my aunt whispered, her eyes wide with mingled relief and fear.

Nesrelle transformed directly in front of me. Her dress rustled and shifted into shimmering white armor wrought in a similar fashion to that of the Misrothian Royal Guards' ceremonial suits. Across her chest, the constellation Vehgar glittered like diamonds. A mockery against me, against Misroth.

And yet…all I could think of was Shyla facing down Vehgar in the night sky, eternally defying the dragon. Or the meaning of the sigil, chosen by King Eldon and the rebellion that had turned Alrenor's dragons against them and laughed in the empire's face. It represented not the strength, beauty, and light of the Alrenians or their dragons, but all those aspects of the independent Misrothian kingdom and its people.

It reminded me of all the ways I could still defy her before I died.

My bow and quiver were strapped to Reyva's saddle, useless to me in this close combat. Instead I drew the sword that Evren's blacksmith, Hevro, had forged for me. It was lightweight and simple, something he'd insisted wasn't worthy of a queen, but I thought it was perfect.

One of Nesrelle's demon followers held up its black-bladed sword toward her reverently, and with a nasty smirk, she lifted it and pointed it toward my neck. Behind me, Reyva growled ominously from the shadows. Without glancing over my shoulder, I lifted a hand toward her, commanding her to stay back.

Nesrelle's blue eyes flashed. "A fight to the death." She licked her lips at the word, like she was tasting it.

"You cannot die," I said. The flames lit by the nestrae were climbing higher, but beneath my dragon scale armor, I did not feel their heat.

"Very true. A fight to *your* death," she crooned.

"Possibly," I conceded. "Or until you surrender."

Nesrelle chuckled lightly, the tinkling noise sending shivers down my back. Her eyes turned sharp and dangerous. "Unlikely." She cocked her head to the side, studying me closely. Perhaps she could see through my façade—or maybe she could feel my fear, since she fed off it. "You're afraid."

I didn't waver. "Yes," I said, my voice rising over the roar of the flames in my ears, above the sound of the nestrae as they began chanting once more. "*Iyg kurik vouren. Iyg kurik nestryk.*" I stared straight into Nesrelle's ice-blue eyes. "I'm terrified. But I'm not ashamed of my fear, and I will not give in to it. I will not cower before you. I can admit to my fear and face it anyway."

"Many say such things," Nesrelle said, "until they face their end."

And she slammed her blade against mine.

CHAPTER FORTY-TWO

Avrik

IT SEEMED AS IF THE whole world was nothing but flame and ash, blood and death. Screams rent the air, mingling with the clash of weapons and the chants of the nestrae.

As Avrik pressed deeper into the city, striding alongside Narek, he honed all his concentration into his gift, blanketing as many of the recruits as he could in an invisible shield of protection. He could sense it tingling through his veins and humming in the air around him. As long as he lived, he could keep them—or at least most of them—safe.

But the chaos in the streets made him hesitate. Even impassive Narek, as accustomed to death as he was, paused for one terrible moment. Flames licked at buildings on either side of them, but there were no nestrae here. The demons had vanished quickly after the dragons had cleared a path into the city, and Misrothian citizens had emerged from the buildings to take the nestrae's place. Now the citizens, armed with torches, weapons, or whatever they could get their hands on—axes, scissors, sticks—attacked one another in the streets, maiming and murdering or fleeing in fear. Every one of them had wide, glassy eyes, all trapped in the false visions the nestrae were forcing them to experience, all blind to the fact that they were slaying their own. One man leapt upon another and strangled him, shouting hysterically until his victim collapsed, utterly still. Another, swinging an axe, failed to fend off a woman who stabbed him in the eye with a fire poker.

"Giver of Life," Jennah breathed behind Avrik, her voice full of horror. "What have they done?"

Tears streamed down Iyleth's face. "There are children," she whispered. "We can't fight children."

Narek set his jaw. "Fend them off, keep them from hurting each other." He cast a glance toward Avrik. "They can't hurt us. We'll try to stop as many as we can."

But Avrik could hardly hear over the roaring of fire in his ears. Nestred voices hissed in his mind: *Failure. You cannot hold us back. You cannot stop us. Embrace death.*

Avrik grit his teeth, struggling to keep his hold on his barrier as he stepped forward. His sword hilt was slick in his palm.

On the road ahead, a screaming little girl stumbled away from a woman swinging a kitchen knife. Jennah leapt forward and scooped the girl out of the path of the woman, who raced down a side road, doubtless looking for a new victim. Clutching the girl tightly, Jennah sighed with relief, but the girl bit down hard on her hand, drawing blood. With a surprised cry, Jennah dropped her and the girl disappeared.

A Misrothian guard tore down the street, racing straight for Avrik and the recruits. Lifting his bow, the man shot an arrow straight toward Avrik's heart. Avrik sensed the barrier quiver as the arrow struck it, stopping midair and falling against the cobblestones. The next arrow soared toward a hapless woman down the street, who stood stock-still amidst the chaos, covering her ears and screaming. Tears of horror streamed down her face. Avrik swung his sword, knocking the arrow off course.

But the action broke his concentration, just for a moment. A burly man, clothes soaked in blood and eyes frenetic and bloodshot, broke through the barrier and slammed into Iyelth, knocking her sword from her grasp. With a cry, she crashed to the ground, pinned beneath the man. He seized her neck and began to squeeze as Iyleth flailed, trying in vain to shove the man away.

Torn between pausing to rebuild the barrier and running to Iyleth's aid, Avrik stumbled. Guilt seared him as two more citizens surrounded Bren, swinging axes. Avrik pushed all his thoughts toward envisioning a wall forming around the recruits and himself, shielding them from the onslaught of wild, angry citizens storming toward them.

Nestred words tangled with his thoughts, their hissing voices slithering like serpents through his mind. *You're nothing but a failure*, they reminded him. The twisting nested rune on his forearm burned hot, like flames searing his skin. Pain mingled with his humiliation. They were right. He couldn't concentrate. His gift slipped away from him, just out of reach. Taunting.

All around him, there was nothing but roaring: the cries of men, women, and children, the rushing flames growing ever larger, the shriek of metal against metal, and the distant thudding of nestred boots marching across the cobblestones. Avrik watched those around him like he was separate from it all, disconnected from the tumult. He tried to lift his sword, to step forward, but he was frozen, trapped in his own body.

Though it was daylight, an ichgor screeched overhead, its shadow falling over the street. Citizens screamed in horror as the creature swooped low, snatching up struggling people in its claws. More flooded the sky, filling the air with their horrible cries. The dragons Kova and Jozek were outnumbered and surrounded by ichgor circling them.

The creatures clashed in the air in a flurry of flame and claws and shrieks, but the dragons couldn't stop all of the numerous ichgor from ravaging the city.

As Avrik struggled to regain control, to rally his strength and reach for his sword, he spotted new terrors. Sedwa were pouring into the streets, springing from rooftops to attack unsuspecting citizens or slinking into the shadows to ambush them. Their golden eyes glowed in the swirling smoke and ash, while their black scales flashed red as they reflected the devouring flames.

This is your end—and theirs, Nesrelle said calmly in Avrik's head, her tone soft and melodic, reminiscent of his own mother's voice when she'd whispered stories to him to help him drift to sleep.

Thick smoke curled through the street, a stifling cloud that stung his nose and eyes. Nearby, Jaren stumbled, an ugly gash in his arm bleeding as he staved off a man's attacks. Rev was shouting, trying to help someone up from the ground, but the body was motionless. Dead. Jennah fought like a woman possessed, but tears trailed down her cheeks—the child she'd tried to help no doubt reminded her of her own daughters. Beneath her attacker, Iyleth began to still, a vein in her temple pulsing, her eyes glazed, her lips blue. With a roar, Narek reached for her attacker and snapped his neck. The man collapsed limply on top of Iyleth, but Narek kicked him away.

For one horrible moment, his face pale and drawn, Narek stared down at the dead man. His fists trembled at his sides. The corpse was just one more innocent Misrothian in a long string that Narek had slain, and if not for the nestrae's influence, the man never would have attacked soldiers pledged to help Misroth. The guilt on Narek's face was unmistakable. Then he turned to Iyleth, who, coughing and gasping, was already on her feet.

Down the street, nestrae marched toward them, chanting and scraping their weapons of black steel together.

Someone slammed into Avrik's shoulder, knocking him to the blood-slicked road. The blood was still warm, coating his skin and filling his nostrils with its rusty tang until he thought he would heave. An arrow soared overhead, just where he'd been standing less than a second ago.

"Avrik!"

It was Bren's voice, Bren's hand outstretched toward him. Avrik found he could move again, though there was a ringing in his ears and he was unnaturally cold. When he turned, Bren's expression was wild, his face splattered with ash and blood.

"You have to put the barrier back up!" Bren shouted.

Bren's lips continued to move, but the nestred voices were louder in Avrik's ears, rising until he could hear nothing else. "Powerless," they chanted. "Death, death, death."

"It's time," Nesrelle hissed, and it was as if she was bending over him, her cold breath in his ear.

Darkness fluttered at the corners of Avrik's vision.

"No," Avrik said through gritted teeth. "Not yet."

Pulling himself up, he staggered to his feet. Blood dripped from his fingertips and stained the front of his armor. *It's not my time yet,* he thought, imagining the barrier reforming around the recruits. *Give me time, Life-Giver.*

He didn't wait to wonder if his plea would be answered. As the nestrae marched nearer, he stepped forward. Past Narek and Iyleth, standing back to back as they fended off attacking Misrothians. Past Rev, who had collapsed in the street, with Jaren hovering over him, shouting something incoherent. Past the piling bodies of Misrothians who had fought and killed one another.

Avrik stopped between his people and the approaching demons. Holding out his bloody hands, he summoned every ounce of his strength and willpower into this one final task. *Keep them safe,* he thought, even as men and women continued to scream and die around him.

Flames licked nearer, until at last they faltered, unable to burn past the invisible barrier Avrik had formed around the recruits. An arrow shrieked through the air, only to stop dead and fall. The marching nestrae halted in front of Avrik, snarling and hissing.

Avrik stared into the depthless eyes of the centermost demon. "You can't hurt them," he said.

"Fool. Your gift will die with you," it snarled. "You're powerless."

He thought of Halia facing Nesrelle, and he dared to smile. "Maybe they won't need my gift to fend you off much longer."

The nestred reached out its grotesque hand, sharp claws extended toward Avrik. "Your time has come."

Avrik reached for his bow, only to discover it had fallen from his back at some point. Perhaps when he'd collapsed. *But it doesn't matter anymore*, he thought numbly. Maybe the time for fighting was over.

And he couldn't take weapons where he was going.

CHAPTER FORTY-THREE

NESRELLE'S FIRST STRIKE SLAMMED INTO my sword so forcefully that I could feel the blow reverberate through my arm. For such a wispy creature, sometimes almost phantom-like, her strength was unexpected. Still, my anger was a fire in my blood that made it easy for me to match her force. Together, we stepped around bodies and danced through flames that could not burn us. Ash and blood coated her white armor until she no longer looked like a shimmering angel, but the nightmare she truly was.

I could feel more than see my aunt's anxious eyes tracking my every movement. Crouching and shivering, the Royal Councilors watched me too, and in the corner of the courtyard, Reyva's eager energy to fend off my attacker was palpable in the very air I breathed. But nothing they could do or hope would change my fate.

It was only us now: the Goddess of Death and the Death-Defier.

"The fear in this city is making me stronger," Nesrelle taunted, licking her lips again as if she could taste the terror on her tongue.

I narrowed my eyes and swiped my blade low, toward her stomach. "And our courage will make you weak."

She parried the attack easily and chuckled. "There's no room for courage when your worst fears are coming true." With a vicious grin, her eyes darkened, and suddenly I was weightless, frozen, trapped in her gaze. In her eyes, I saw a reflection of Avrik standing amongst clouds of smoke and screaming Misrothians. Blood covered the front of his armor and his face was pale. He staggered weakly toward the nestrae marching for him, and behind him—behind him… Rev lay still and bleeding in the street.

Anger ripped through me as the vision faded and Nesrelle swung her sword at me again. Screaming, I slammed my blade into hers and drove toward her, launching a series of strikes and kicks. She merely laughed and flicked her wrist at me.

Pain seared through my lower back where my nestred rune was. It swept through my body until every one of my muscles shook in agony.

"You will fail," came the hissing voices of the nestrae all around me. Or were they speaking in my mind?

Black spots danced before my eyes. Clenching my teeth together, I forced my legs to keep working, to keep holding me up so I could stand. By sheer force of will, I squeezed my hand tightly enough that my sword hilt didn't fall from my grasp.

Just as suddenly, the pain disappeared, leaving me empty and hollow. Nesrelle tossed her sword away.

"There are more entertaining ways to play," she said.

I lifted my sword arm again, but she was too fast. Another flick of her wrist, and the bone in my leg snapped and shattered where her demons had broken it in their Toryn fortress. I couldn't hold back my cry as I collapsed to my knees.

My vision swam and my consciousness faded, my body going liquid. I teetered on my knees. My sword fell with a clatter to the cobblestones.

More pain radiated from my stomach to my back, reminding me of the searing agony I'd experienced the day I'd nearly been executed in front of my people. The day one of my father's men had stabbed me and only the Life-Giver's power had saved me.

Nesrelle stepped forward and ripped my helmet from my head, tossing it away.

Mirothians muttered. Velaire's sharp intake of breath rang out as loudly as the hiss of a knife being drawn.

I clawed feebly for my sword until Nesrelle lifted my chin and stared at me. Her skin looked pallid and grey-toned, while her eyes were black as chasms as I fell into another one of her visions. Eldon was using his wife Tamelle for her gift, even when she tearfully begged him not to turn his back on Toryn. I watched him fall to the allure of power and fame, allowing the Misothian people to honor him for gifts and deeds that were never his.

In another instant, I saw the grandmother I had never known, a bitter woman who cut my father down with her words. *You'll never amount to anything. You'll never be what Reylon is,* she sneered, slapping him across the face and punishing him by sending him away from the family whenever he fell short in his lessons.

Last of all, Nesrelle showed me my father on the day I'd been born. While my mother cried out and the midwife told her to breathe, my father argued with my grandmother on a balcony overlooking the castle grounds far below. One push was all it took…

"There's been a terrible accident!" Zarev cried out to the guards, sobbing into his hands. "My mother! She's fallen!"

Shuddering, I blinked and found myself staring back at Nesrelle again. The nestrae were chanting and the scars on my back burned in a terrible reminder. My mouth tasted sour. I'd known my father was a murderer, but these were new revelations. Corruption ran deep in my lineage. The nestrae were right. Nesrelle was right. I was guilty.

You'll never win, her voice hissed in my ears. *Your line is poisoned. The blood that runs through your veins is the same blood that ran through weak and cruel kings.*

She pulled me into another vision, reminding me of all the deaths I was responsible for. Rebels my father had slain when I'd hidden away in Evren. Gare and Layk, laying down their lives for a cause they'd believed in—for a leader they had believed in. Toryn people who had lost their haven in Calidar when I'd managed to lead the nestrae to them. And countless Misrothians, falling even now in this bloody, burning city, because I had failed to keep the barrier secure and prevent this demon army from invading.

Tears pricked my eyes. As everything she'd shown me faded away, Nesrelle raised her hand. "I could strike you down now, with a flick of my wrist," she spat, disgust thick in her voice.

Before I could move, she stole my breath. Though I could still see the courtyard and Nesrelle's face, tinged red in the firelight, I could also hear the rushing waves of a tumultuous sea. The cold, dark deep overtook me. My lungs burned and terror clawed up my spine. At the corners of my vision, the growing sparks from the fire surrounding me mingled with the descending darkness clouding my brain.

I was thirteen again, and I was drowning. Was this how I was meant to die all along?

"You should have been mine," Nesrelle breathed. Her hand trembled with her fury, while her eyes shone with a fierce, terrifying light. My terror and pain were feeding her strength. I could feel her drawing the life from me.

I'd cheated death when the sea had nearly taken me, but that wasn't the day she spoke of. No, I had been meant to die a different time, years later.

I closed my eyes, remembering when I'd bled out before a crowd of my own people, on the day my own father had declared I should die. I remembered the power of my gift flooding through me and the longing I'd had for my people to see the truth and be free of oppression. And I remembered the hands that had held me and the tears that had fallen, all from a stranger I'd met in the woods.

A stranger who had given me the powerful gift that had helped save my people.

A gift that was still mine.

The truth settled through me, deep in my bones. Nesrelle could not take my gift from me. Only I could—when years ago, I'd wished it and my very ability to speak away. Or recently, when I'd succumbed to the lies the nestrae and their queen had fed me. When I'd thought I had failed my people and wasn't worthy of my gift.

Nesrelle had never stolen my gift. She'd only convinced me to stifle it.

And all at once, the truth returned to me. I could feel it burning inside my chest, warming me where I'd been hollow all this time. It was easy to breathe now, to recognize the lie Nesrelle had been feeding me for what it was. I was not drowning. My leg wasn't broken, either. The pain and shortness of breath had all been part of an illusion. The roar of the sea in my ears faded away, the pressure lifted, and I was able to breathe again.

Looking up, I met Nesrelle's wide eyes and smiled.

Before she could react, visions flashed before my eyes so rapidly I almost couldn't see them, but in my heart, I knew what they were telling me.

Somewhere in the city, Narek was pouring every ounce of strength into sharing his war gift, and I could feel it inside me. He turned and squeezed Iyleth's free hand, sharing a wordless glance as they faced the incoming horde of nestrae tearing down the street. Iyleth fought with power and grace, her movements those of a seasoned warrior due to Narek's influence. And she had a different gift, one that flowed through those around her, staving off wounds that should have been much worse. It poured through me too, dulling my pain until it was numb and distant.

Somewhere else, distant from the battle, I could sense Gillen using his gift for interceding, sending encouragement through the ranks of our soldiers, sending wishes even to me. *Be strong, Lia. You aren't alone.*

My vision showed me Jennah racing through the streets, half-frantic with worry as she sought out her family. She found the rebel home they had been staying in and bit back her cry. The door had been kicked down and shattered furniture and dishes crowded the entrance. The other family's bodies were strewn throughout each room Jennah entered, making even her gift of courage waver in her horror and fear.

"Mama! Mama!" It was her littlest daughter screaming. Jennah tore into the last room of the house, where a blood-soaked man towered over her daughters and the unconscious bodies of her husband and mother. Jennah's gift did not fail her as she struck the man down. Her daughters collapsed sobbing into her arms.

Tears pricked my eyes, yet Jennah's gift burned through me. Courage despite the terror and loss. Courage despite staring death in the face.

And alongside the other gifts, there was one more that hadn't fully faded yet—Avrik's gift of protection hovered around me. Maybe it could last long enough for me to help Misroth, even if Nesrelle killed me in the end.

All I needed to do was give my people a fighting chance.

CHAPTER FORTY-FOUR

Avrik

AVRIK'S PULSE THUDDED DULLY IN his ears as he stumbled forward. The real world faded in and out, replaced by otherworldly images. Shadows swirled like living things while flames encircled him, snapping tongues of red and yellow in his direction. There was no pain, but he wasn't sure if that was due to his dragon scale armor's protection, his lingering gift, or the fact that half of what he saw wasn't even real.

"Avrik," someone whispered, and he blinked in confusion, turning toward the voice. His mother stood in the street, wrapped in the same robe she'd worn the day she died.

Heart in his throat, Avrik hesitated, unsure whether to run to her or flee. Surely it was a trick. Just beyond her, he could still see the nestrae, now impossibly distant. The leader extended its hideous hand toward him, beckoning him onward. "*Powerless,*" it hissed.

"Don't be afraid," she continued. Her eyes burned with the fervor of hope and love, everything she'd clung to in the end, when she'd had nothing else left. "You've made me proud. So proud."

Avrik's eyes already burned from the smoke in the air, but now his grief swallowed him whole. The Life-Giver had assured him that more would be waiting on the other side. As much as he hated to leave Halia behind, to leave Misroth to an uncertain fate, maybe this was what was meant to happen after all.

Let my gift live on after me, he thought. *Life-Giver, before you guide me to the afterlife, please grant my last wish and protect my kingdom. Protect Halia.*

A chill crept along the back of his neck and down his spine, like Nesrelle herself was standing behind him and breathing on him.

Just ahead, the nestrae leered at him, saliva dripping from their yellow fangs. Blood oozed from the leader's claws. Bodies both new and old lay in growing puddles of blood on the street: Gare and Layk, his father and Bren's little sister, and the Misrothian Royal Guard from years ago—Avrik's first kill. And all the while, the flames grew higher and closer. Smoke hung heavily in the air until Avrik coughed and gasped for breath.

He squeezed his eyes shut for a moment, wondering what it would be like to make the final step into death. He could tell by his slowing heartbeat and the icy grip on his body that he was already succumbing to whatever death-hold Nesrelle had on him. Would the Life-Giver be standing there as he fell? Would he open his eyes to a new, bright world? Would both his mother and father be waiting to greet him when he crossed over? Would the Life-Giver grant his last request and save his friends from the same fate?

He dared to believe so as he opened his eyes. Maybe he would be right, or maybe he would be disappointed. But that was the blessing and the curse of his unwavering optimism: he could hope for anything, even here, on the edge of death.

Avrik paused directly in front of the nestrae and stared into their empty eyes. It was chilling, how deep and dark their gazes were. They threatened to draw him down into blackness, into hell itself. But that wouldn't be his ending, no matter what Nesrelle wanted.

Death stared hungrily down at him, and he smiled widely back.

"In the end," Avrik said, gazing at the demons, "I only lose my life. But you will lose everything. Me. This battle. Misroth. It's not yours."

He took the nestred's clawed hand, and his heart stopped beating.

CHAPTER FORTY-FIVE

THE INSTANT AVRIK'S PROTECTION GIFT vanished, I felt its absence as keenly as if a piece of my heart had been ripped from my chest.

Nesrelle's horror melted into growing satisfaction. She threw her head back and spread out her arms, like an overjoyed child catching snowflakes on the tip of her tongue. When she lowered her chin and opened her eyes to look at me again, her gaze was piercing. Her blue eyes nearly glowed with power.

"His death—" she began, but this time, I was faster. Shock and grief wouldn't hold me back now.

Shrieking like a wild animal, I threw myself at her, my sword already clutched in my hand. Nesrelle recovered quickly, but not quickly enough. The first swing of my blade sliced a cut on her arm— small, hardly worth noticing. And yet it sparked furious hope within me.

The goddess of demons and death could be harmed. I had made her bleed.

I flashed a toothy smile at her, every warrior instinct overtaking me. This was no heroic swordfight like Avrik and I had imagined and practiced on sunny days in Evren. This was an ugly battle of pain and anger, my final defiance against all the evil that raged against my people, against all the loss and grief that had taken hold of my life. It was the lonely, last effort of a lost and aching girl in an unwinnable war.

Swinging again and again, I advanced wildly on Nesrelle, stepping closer than I'd dared to before. Sweat clung to my forehead and strands of hair untangled from my braid and fell across my face. Nesrelle gestured toward me, slamming very real pain through my body, but my adrenaline and fury numbed me to most of it. I was strangely disconnected now, like an onlooker commanding my limbs to move, but feeling nothing they did. Perhaps part of it was also Iyleth's gift, though I wasn't sure how much of my friends' gifts touched me anymore. With Avrik's gone, the others seemed to be wavering in strength, as if the final loss of his protection was pulling their focus away. Or maybe they were hurt and dying too.

At last, I moved in so close to Nesrelle that she reached out and touched me. Her hand was like ice, and the pain she brought rolled through my entire body, making my muscles spasm. Blood trickled from my lips and nose. Even more streamed from a gash on my forehead and ran into my eyes, stinging and blurring my vision. But even that pain did not last. One instant I screamed, and the next the spots receded from my eyes and there was only my anger and my bloodlust. If I could just make her bleed more, just make her taste a bit of her own pain…

There wasn't room in my heart for fear anymore. What grip did death hold over me if so many of my loved ones waited for me on the other side?

"I'm not afraid to die," I snarled, swinging toward Nesrelle again. "Not anymore."

She dodged my blade and slammed her fist into my face. I staggered backward, ears ringing, stars sparking before my eyes.

"No matter," Nesrelle breathed, knocking the sword from my grasp and seizing my neck with one bony hand.

I struggled and choked, kicking at the ground as Nesrelle lifted me into the air. This time it was no illusion I could break. She spun me to face the line of Misrothians, all surrounded by demons and waiting beside the growing flames that would take their lives. Among the tearful, horrified faces, my aunt continued to kneel. Her lips were moving as if in prayer, or a silent plea for me to keep fighting.

"Their fear is enough," Nesrelle said.

With one final bruising squeeze, she hurled me to the ground, directly in front of one of the nestred pyres. There was a sickening pop as my left wrist slammed onto the stones, pressed awkwardly beneath my body. I gasped for air and choked on soot and smoke.

Give me time, I prayed. The first real prayer I'd dared to speak toward my god in far too long. Now was his moment to prove himself: was he the distant, formal Giver of Life the Misrothian priests had taught me about throughout my childhood? Or was he the man from the woods who had healed me and filled me with purpose?

Was the God of Life still there when the Goddess of Death reigned over my people?

Protect my people, I pled.

"Behold your broken queen," Nesrelle sneered to the terrified Misrothians watching me. "Let her be the sacrifice that steals the last of your hope for your foul, bloody kingdom."

Stomping and chanting in their hideous language, two hulking nestrae leered over me, prepared to lift me onto their pyre. I rolled away before they could reach me and leapt to my feet, springing toward my sword. I had my blade in my hand and was lunging toward her before the demon queen could attack. She stepped back before my sword could slice clean through her neck.

With one effortless swing of her hand, Nesrelle sent a shock of pain through my sword arm, and I dropped my weapon. She slammed into me, knocking me to the ground and attacking with her clawed hands. She scratched bloody, burning trails down my cheeks, moving with the frenzy of an angered beast. I slammed my fists at her nose, her neck, her jaw, all while blocking her as best as I could. Shoving against her, I rolled until I was on top, smashing my armored forearm into her bloodied face, but my strength was hardly a match against hers. She had me pinned again in an instant, her eyes shimmering with an otherworldly light as she extended her knife-like claws toward my neck. I grasped her arms, every muscle in my body trembling as I tried to hold her back. I knew this was the moment when she would slice open my throat.

I squeezed my eyes shut and caught a glimpse of grassy, rolling hills and sunlit fields. A forest of dappled sunlight and shadow, welcoming and free of stalking sedwa. Nearby was a garden, more vibrant and colorful even than Evren's, with my mother walking and laughing, the most carefree I'd ever seen her. Beside her walked my uncle, healthy and whole. Beyond the garden, in an open field beside a winding stream, Gare and Layk were teasing one another and sparring. Their old wounds and scars were gone, their eyes full of life and light.

My throat ached with unshed tears. Was this one last cruel nestred trick?

No, I realized. That was the afterlife, a glimpse into a world where even the demons couldn't touch us. Where there was hope, even for the ones Nesrelle took. For every one of my people she had slain. For Avrik.

"In the end, you lose," I ground out, and the truth of my words swept through me with fiery conviction. "I am not afraid, and my people will not live in fear forever either."

Despite the strain on my arms, my voice didn't waver when I lifted it to address the Misrothians witnessing this fight. Whether I lived or died, I couldn't let hope and truth die with me.

"The nestrae are showing you lies!" I cried out. "They use tricks to fool and defeat you, but you are stronger than that. *We* are stronger." Narrowing my eyes, I turned back to the demon goddess hovering over me. "Our courage is stronger than the fear you inflict, and our hope is greater than the despair. And both our courage and hope are already stealing your strength." I laughed in her face. "I feel it. Do you?"

Nesrelle leaned back, her eyes wide with fury. Her claws were gone, and she stared at her trembling hands. All around her, the nestrae were hissing and shifting restlessly, their pyre and their victims forgotten. Men and women were weeping openly—not in fear this time, but in relief, as if they were waking from long nightmares. The nestred visions were breaking.

Gasping, Nesrelle's face turned pallid, until her shimmering form was no longer solid and vibrant, but fading…nearly translucent. She looked more deathly than deadly, more ghost than goddess. Her beauty leeched away as her flawless skin tinged a grey, sickly pallor. Dark circles grew beneath her eyes, while her face turned gaunt and her teeth yellowed and sharp. Though the wound I'd struck no longer bled, she didn't appear corporeal enough to strike her own blows either.

Her eyes, now black and hollow-looking, locked on me. My heart froze beneath her empty gaze. It was like staring at a corpse, only to find it staring back.

"I cannot be defeated," Nesrelle hissed. "I'm immortal."

"But you can be sent away," I snapped. "I know the truth. You are nothing, only full of lies and illusions. You can't take anything from me—not really."

Nesrelle barked out an ugly laugh, grating painfully against my ears. "Your loved ones are all dead or about to die!" Her eyes flicked up toward an ichgor circling overhead, listening for its next victim amid the chaos and noise of the burning city. "Your city is crumbling. You're haunted by your fears and your time among my nestrae. I've taken everything."

I held onto the vision I'd had of Layk and Gare, of my mother and uncle. And I hoped that it was true for the others who had fallen today as well. I had to believe it was. "No," I said, despite the tears that burned my eyes. "Everyone I've ever loved—they're still with me. Their words echo in my mind. Their choices still affect my own choices. Their love is not dead. Their legacy is alive." Standing, I towered over her and threw all the authority I could muster into my next words. "As queen, under the authority of the Giver of Life and my people, I command you to leave my kingdom."

Nesrelle hissed and threw herself at me, but her form disappeared before she reached me, like smoke on the wind. The nestrae dropped their weapons and let out inhuman howls that sent shivers down my spine.

And my people were waiting.

Servants and nobles, young and old, men and women, took their chance and seized the nestred weapons. Turning on their captors, they began to add demon bodies to the piles of corpses in the courtyard.

I signaled to Reyva and she sprang into the fray, effortlessly tearing through the nestrae's armored bodies with her claws and fangs. Lifting my blade, I threw myself into the fight, slicing my sword straight through a nestred neck. Its head, helmet and all, fell with a wet thud at my feet. Rather than disgust, I felt elation. Though my body was racked with weakness from the pain Nesrelle had inflicted, and my mind felt numb, I knew there was hope for my people.

The other Misrothians seemed to notice this as well. Even as they continued to fall and bleed, they began to cry out and chant in hope.

"For Misroth!"

"Victory!"

"For Queen Halia!"

Above the carnage, Reyva swooped low around me, attacking any nestrae who tried to step past my defenses.

Ripples of anger and fear stormed through the demons. They shrieked and shuddered, showing fear for the first time as they realized their goddess was no longer leading them and their own were beginning to fall. Some charged for the gate, desperate to retreat. But the way was narrow and easy for Reyva to fill. She plowed down the nestrae, sending some toward the switchback path far below, or even all the way to the distant city streets. Others she cut down at the gate, until the bloody bodies began to pile up and nestrae were climbing over their own dead and dying just for a chance to get out.

Trapped between an angry dragon and a mob of desperate, armed Misrothians, the nestrae struggled to fill our heads with visions that would turn us against one another and make us easy prey. But now that I owned my gift in a way I hadn't before—not even when I'd faced my father—I could easily detect the differences between their lies and the truth. Just as I'd started to do aboard the nestred ship months ago. Their illusions flickered, dim and ghostlike, across my sight, but they didn't fool me.

However, they could still trick my people. A Misrothian nobleman dropped his weapon and screamed, tearing back toward the courtyard and the flames waiting within. His shrieks were drowned out by the men and women crying out around me, turning on one another with weapons raised and crazed terror in their eyes.

"They're lying to you!" I shouted, fighting to be heard over the tumult. "These are illusions! Ignore them!"

My gift held power over those who could hear me, but not everyone did. Though we outnumbered the nestrae, the Misrothians turning on us made it harder. More Misrothians fell, at the hands of demons and men alike.

I searched the crowd frantically for my aunt, praying she was still alive. There was no sign of her. A woman charged me, waving an axe, and I sidestepped before hitting her over the head with the blunt side of my sword, knocking her unconscious. Before I could turn toward him, Councilor Emren punched me in the jaw. "Stop!" I cried. "It's a nestred trick!"

Blinking dazedly, he staggered back.

"Pick up your sword and fight the enemy," I ordered, shoving him toward the weapon he'd dropped behind him.

I turned in time to see the final nestred fall, gurgling on its own blood at the top of the pile of demon bodies. Smoke curled around the crowd as they came to, crying out or weeping as they realized what they'd done under the influence of the nestred illusions. Both demon and human blood made the stone floor slick beneath our feet. It stained our weapons and clothes and hands. Its scent permeated the air. It was everywhere.

Ahead, my aunt emerged from the press of people. She looked awkward wielding a heavy nestred blade, when in all my childhood memories she had always been the picture of an elegant lady. Yet here she was, blood-splattered and fierce. The woman who had held my kingdom together as best as she could while I was away. The woman who had survived the loss of her husband, the betrayal of a tyrant regent king, and the disappearance of a beloved son.

Racing to her, I threw my arms around her neck.

"Halia," she breathed, squeezing me tightly. "Thank god." Tears tracked down her dirty cheeks, and I knew she was seeing a mirror image on my own face. My eyes burned with the pain and happiness mingling in my chest.

"Aunt Velaire," I began, but an unearthly ichgor screech interrupted us.

Pulling back, Velaire's eyes narrowed as she surveyed the monster swooping overhead, diving toward the city. Her eyes fastened on me.

"We have work to do."

CHAPTER FORTY-SIX

Avrik

AVRIK STUMBLED FORWARD, FINDING HIMSELF on a cliff's edge, staring down into a pit. The world was submerged in darkness except for the dancing flames of a pyre far below. Everything about the city around him was wrong and distorted: buildings were skeletal structures splattered in blood, gates were crumbling ruins, and the shadows spilling from every alley moved and whispered like wraiths. Behind Avrik, corpses stood and strode purposefully toward him, their eyes dark and empty.

Nestrae circled within the fiery pit below, whispering and beckoning to him.

Somehow, Avrik wasn't quite dead yet. He could feel his heartbeat, an erratic rhythm in his ears. He was caught between the living world and the next, trapped in a grotesque, nightmarish spirit world. Or perhaps it was all a horrific nestred illusion.

In the living world, was he crumpled in the street somewhere as his heart slowed and the nestrae marched toward his friends? Hovering on the cliffside, he grit his teeth. He was helpless to save them now. He was helpless to save even himself.

"It's our time," the corpse of a man told Avrik in a hollow voice. He stood at his side, though he didn't meet Avrik's eyes. The dead man was focused on the flames far below. "Time to burn," he whispered. "Time to move on."

The man stepped off the edge and tumbled down, down, until he crashed into the fire. He made no sound as his body disappeared, consumed in the pyre.

Avrik shuddered as more bodies stepped off the ledge.

And yet, the same pull that drew them was tugging on him too. *Time.*

Nesrelle's cold breath brushed against his cheek. He blinked and she was standing there, reaching out a pale hand. Her eyes sparkled like those of an old friend welcoming him after a long time apart, but when he looked closer, he could see the flames reflected in her gaze.

He closed his eyes for a moment and pictured Halia. *I'm not ready,* he thought.

But it wasn't his choice. Not anymore. His body was surrendering. His blood was sluggish; his heartbeat slow.

He hoped somewhere on the other side, the Life-Giver was waiting to take him away from this nightmare.

Avrik stepped off the edge.

Gillen

Gillen couldn't quite understand what drew him toward the battle. Despite the risk of losing himself to nestred influence, when the screams of his people reached his ears, he knew hiding in the forest wouldn't be his fate. His gift burned within him, calling out to be used in a more tangible way.

He yanked his sword from a dead sedwa to find the blade coated in slick black blood. The monsters had crowded around him as he'd kneeled and called out to the Life-Giver to protect his friends and save his people. Though he knew them to be nocturnal creatures, just like the terrifying ichgor circling over the capital, something must have stirred them.

Nesrelle and her demons' power was growing.

He'd drawn his sword and put his years of training to work, fending off as many of the beasts as he could, but most were uninterested in him and managed to slip past him and into the city. He was shocked by their numbers—there were too many to be coming from Evren Forest alone. Some must have traveled from Toryn to join the fight.

But now, as he wiped his sword clean in the grass, Gillen knew he was needed in the city. Maybe it was another layer to his gift that let him not only share messages to his friends but also receive them directly from the Life-Giver. All he knew was that despite the risk, he had to go.

Sword clenched in his hand, he sprinted into the capital and through the city streets, cutting down nestrae and sedwa alike. His rune burned and the nestrae hissed in his ears, but he grit his teeth and kept going.

Find Avrik, said a voice in his mind. It rang out stronger than the whispering taunts of the nestrae and the horrors they tried to fill his mind with. *Find Avrik*. The purpose those words gave him filled him with strength and courage. What he needed to do once he found Avrik, he didn't know yet, but he didn't doubt the message or its urgency.

It didn't take him long to find the boy. Dropping to his knees beside Avrik's body, Gillen ignored the nestred shrieks around him. After haunting his sleeping and waking thoughts for months, they could hold no new horrors over him today. He nudged Avrik's shoulder, but the boy lay unnervingly still, his face pale and smeared with blood. Even worse, he was already cold to the touch.

Despite the tumult of battle, a memory from his childhood swept over Gillen, clear as yesterday.

"You haven't smiled much in weeks, Lia," he'd said, frowning at his younger cousin across the table. She was practicing sitting up like a lady, a stack of books

resting atop her head.

"I wish my parents were like yours," she muttered, lowering her head just enough so that the books tumbled into her lap. "Curse this!" she snapped.

Gillen stopped himself mid-chuckle to glance up at Halia sharply. "Uncle Zarev and Aunt Ryn love you," he said.

Halia shrugged despondently. "Your mother and father show they love you and are proud of you no matter what you do. Mine seem to only want me to be better." She gestured toward the books. "More ladylike. Stronger. Prouder. Better." She glanced over at the pieces Gillen was moving about on his war map, strategizing for an imaginary war. "Does Uncle Reylon tell you often that he loves you?"

Gillen paused, setting an opposing piece—gold for Alrenor—back down on the board. "Often enough."

Halia plopped the books down on the table and stared vacantly out the window on the other side of the room. Though she didn't say it aloud, Gillen could almost see the thought flit across her face: I wish I knew what that was like.

Now, Gillen swallowed back the lump in his throat and concentrated on his gift. Intercession for others. The ability that had allowed him to call across the miles to Halia in times of need, to encourage her when she needed it most. The ability that allowed him to plead for the lives and safety of those around him and, sometimes, to hear the Life-Giver answer back: *I will help.* Could it help now, to pluck someone from the edge of death?

Gillen had seen the painful goodbye that had passed between his cousin and Avrik. He'd seen the bond they'd shared, the things they'd fought and survived together. And though he also knew that Avrik had a powerful gift that could help Misroth, he couldn't deny that deep down, he desperately wanted to see his little cousin happy. After all the pain she and the rest of their family had suffered, couldn't Gillen do one small thing to prevent more grief?

Avrik's eyes darted beneath his lids and for the barest instant, his body twitched uneasily. If possible, he grew even colder.

And Gillen knew. He'd lived with those nightmares long enough to know who influenced them.

Let me intercede, he thought, reaching out to squeeze Avik's shoulder and closing his eyes.

When he opened them, he was in a dim, shadowy world, standing on a cliff that overlooked Misroth City. The city was crumbling and blood-soaked, empty of all signs of life. Bodies littered the streets and smoke and ash swirled on the wind.

Gillen turned to see Avrik standing on the cliff's edge, firelight from below dancing across his face. Beside him, Nesrelle leered and stretched out her hand.

"Avrik!" Gillen called out, but Avrik didn't seem to hear him.

Gillen's heart pounded wildly in his ears.

If Avrik died, his gift died with him.

If his protection gift died, so did Misroth's hope.

The choice was instant, almost as if it had been made for him. Had his gift always been meant for this?

Avrik stepped off the edge, but Gillen was there, snatching his arm before he could tumble into the waiting pyre. Avrik's arm wrenched painfully and Gillen thought that if they hadn't been in this otherly world, it would be out of joint. As it was, Avrik still gasped in pain as he glanced up at Gillen. His eyes were shadowed with circles like bruises, his gaze haunted like someone already resigned to death.

"I have no choice," Avrik explained. "Nesrelle claimed me. It can't be undone."

"I know," Gillen said, tugging until he'd drawn Avrik back onto the ledge with him.

Avrik lay there cringing for a moment, cradling his arm as if it really were hurt. An illusion of pain.

"Someone has to die to satisfy Nesrelle's claim," Gillen continued, gazing down into the flames. The nestrae were still calling Avrik's name.

"What?" Avrik asked sharply. He sat up quickly, realizing Gillen's intent. "Gillen—Your Majesty…"

"Intercession," Gillen whispered. "It's my gift. It can be more than just praying when someone needs me. I can take your place."

"Gillen, no!" Avrik jumped to his feet.

"It has to be me." A smile played across his lips. "Maybe they can remember me as something other than the Mad King." He glanced back at Avrik. "You have to use your gift to save them, Avrik. I know you can. They need you. Halia needs you."

Before Avrik could move, Gillen leapt.

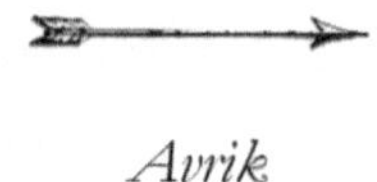

Avrik

Avrik jolted awake. The street was thick with smoke and screams and nestred voices, and rank with the scent of ash and blood and death. His heart was beating steadily in his chest. His body was warm and alive again.

Beside him lay Gillen's body.

CHAPTER FORTY-SEVEN

THE TIDE OF BATTLE CHANGED swiftly. Without Nesrelle near to lead them, without the heavy presence of fear swirling through the city like a fog, the nestrae began to retreat. As I shared my truth gift with the people, shattering the nestred illusions imprisoning them, the number of fleeing demons grew. Without the power of their lies and their queen, without potent fear and despair to feed and strengthen them, they were vulnerable.

Wherever my aunt and I went within the city, guards and soliders and citizens alike rushed to our sides. "Her Majesty has returned!" became their rallying cry of hope, soon intermingled with shouts for "Queen Halia!" Without knowing the fate of their Crown Prince, the people had chosen and accepted me long ago. And deep within my bones, though it ached to admit it, I realized that maybe Gillen had been right all along. Maybe this was what I was meant to do.

Still, death was not done with my people. With each nestred I slew, I was reminded of the fact that nothing could bring back what—and whom—I had lost. I was angry, and no amount of demon blood or bodies could quench that anger. No amount of death or battles won against them could bring back what they'd taken.

While I raced through the city streets, cutting down my enemies, oblivious to the pain and exhaustion tracing its way through my body, I knew what else I was doing. I knew I was looking for him, searching for where Avrik had taken his final breath. I both dreaded and longed for a chance to see his body and say my goodbye.

The dragons circled overhead, Reyva always staying close so she could see me. Without Nesrelle's power to influence them, the ichgor had long since fled to find cover from the daylight. Now the dragons focused on diving and attacking the nestrae, their fangs and claws making short work of several at once. Flames continued to roar through the streets, sending plumes of smoke that a blessed wind tugged seaward before they could stifle us. Ashes fell like snow. Bloody bodies, demon and Misrothian, filled the streets.

As the din around me quieted, and I realized that I'd lost my aunt somewhere in the fray and there were no longer any living nestrae nearby, the grief within me began to unspool. Sighing, I leaned against an old, abandoned shop for support, the bricks cool and rough against my skin. The sensation kept me rooted in the present when my emotion, exhaustion, and pain threatened to make me collapse right there in a dank alleyway. Tears blurred my vision. When I wiped my sweaty face, I found my hand covered in smeared blood—nestred and my own, mingling red and black. My entire body ached, and the old wounds Nesrelle had made me relive were hurting again. Even though it was not broken, a fiery, shooting pain darted up my leg, reminding me of when a nestred mace had once shattered bone. The places where a sword had once pierced my back and stomach burned, and my nestred rune was raw and painful beneath my armor. My cheeks ached too, from where Nesrelle had sank her claws into my skin, and my left wrist throbbed, likely broken.

In the state I was in, it seemed beyond belief that my people had been crying out my name in hope. I choked back a sorrowful laugh. I must have looked terrifying.

The sound of footsteps cleared my head from my haze of weariness. I looked up to see a familiar figure, cloaked and hooded, a sword at his side. He walked slowly among the bodies lying in the street, not seeming to notice or care about the blood that stained his clothes and hands as he kneeled beside them, whispering words in another language. Forwyn.

As if hearing my thoughts, he glanced over his shoulder at me. His dark eyes were ageless and full of sorrow. Though he was leading the dead to the afterlife, he stopped and grieved each person's death first.

I stepped into the street, kneeling next to him to look down at the dead woman he lingered beside. Laying a hand on her head, he murmured words in his soft, rumbling voice. Though I didn't understand the words themselves, I could understand their meaning. Sorrow and hope. Death and life.

I couldn't see the moment the woman's soul passed on, couldn't know exactly how it transpired, but a sliver of peace filled me and I knew she was gone.

"So many of my people are dead," I said numbly, staring at the bodies in the street, thinking of my loved ones. I feared who I would find among these dead. I could hardly bear to look at these strangers' faces and know what they had given.

"It took many sacrifices to stop Nesrelle," the Life-Giver said quietly.

I thought about the old stories of how the Life-Giver had shed his own blood to unlock the gates to the afterlife so mortals could pass through. He knew about sacrifice, and he knew the pain and loss I'd borne and even wept alongside me. In that moment, I understood that all those times I'd felt alone, it had been my own doing. I'd let Nesrelle convince me I was guilty and unworthy of my gift, so I'd let her take it from me. And I'd convinced myself that the Giver of Life had abandoned me, so I hadn't seen or heard from him. But he'd been there, in my gift and my friends' gifts, fighting for both the Forwyn people—his first chosen people—and for my people all along.

I reached forward to close the woman's eyes. She looked young and peaceful, almost like she was asleep, if I didn't look too closely at the wound in her chest. "I thought death fed the demons and made them strong."

"Only the fear of death. You already know it was your people's courage that weakened them and drove them away. The courage to lay down a life for others—that only weakens the nestrae."

"But they'll return?" I asked, thinking of Nesrelle's relentless eyes, her endless greed.

The Life-Giver settled a calloused hand on my shoulder, and my pain and grief eased. "Maybe not in your lifetime," he said.

Raindrops started to fall, gently at first, but quickly turning to a steady rain. They were a blessing and a curse, a way to quench the flames burning throughout the city and a way to make the work of finding and healing the wounded more difficult.

I rose hurriedly to my feet. "Have you taken him…?" I began, but choked on my words and shook my head, avoiding his eyes. I didn't want to see the sorrow in them when I asked if he'd carried Avrik to the afterlife yet. I didn't want to think about it, even as I knew I was rushing away only to say goodbye. "I must go."

The city was eerily quiet as I raced through the streets. It wasn't silent by any means, but the soft sounds of the living searching through the bodies, weeping over the lost or tending to the wounded, were nothing compared to the roar of battle. The fires were smoldering; the buildings that had burned lay silent and still. Reyva and the other dragons were no longer circling the city, but pursuing the nestrae that had fled toward their ships at sea or stumbled into the surrounding countryside. Many would never make it out of Misroth alive.

At last, I turned a corner and found a lone figure racing through the streets like I was. It took me several wild, confused moments to understand. Dressed in the same dark dragon scale armor, coated in ash and blood, his body was hunched with grief and weariness. He seemed as ragged and desperate as me.

He looked up and saw me the same instant that I recognized him.

I didn't ask questions, not yet. I sprinted toward him like I'd once raced across Evren fields with him, and, despite the limp in his gait, he matched my speed. We crashed together, almost knocking one another off balance. Between gasps for air, we laughed and cried. He held me close, spinning me around like we were just children playing in the Evren garden again. Like we weren't on a battlefield, like we hadn't faced death and nearly lost.

We'd been friends and competitors and enemies. We'd been grievers and survivors, and we'd been warriors and leaders.

But in that moment, we were just Avrik and Halia.

CHAPTER FORTY-EIGHT

THE WIND CARRIED THE TANG of the sea and the now ever-present odor of ash as it whipped through our cloaks. Overhead, the sky was a merciless shade of blue, pure and bright and entirely heedless of the somber proceedings below.

I stood tall and motionless, knowing that I needed to show strength on this day. Even though my heart was hollow, my people needed to see a leader they could trust. A chance for hope in the wake of so much loss and horror.

Only a few days had passed since Misroth had forced Nesrelle and her demons off our shores. Only a few days since my cousin had laid down his life to protect his people. For me, it seemed like both a lifetime and no time at all had passed.

Ahead, the priest intoned the old funeral rites, words that held little meaning for me now. I'd spoken with the Life-Giver, had even glimpsed what the afterlife was like. I didn't need to hear these dry proceedings, nor did I want to. All I wanted was to curl up somewhere quiet with my grief and memories, and try to imagine Gillen somewhere safe and happy and far away from here. In a place with no more nestred nightmares.

Nearby, the Councilors murmured to one another, their eyes flicking toward me repeatedly. Did they see a queen? I knew I'd changed in their eyes from the moment they'd seen me fly into the castle courtyard on a dragon's back and challenge Nesrelle. They knew they didn't have a chance to control or change me.

"We commit your soul to the hands of the one who gave it life, and we ask him to guide you safely to the afterlife," the priest announced, kneeling before the stone altar that already bore Gillen's name.

King Gillen of Misroth,
Son of King Reylon and Queen Velaire.
Born Year 182.
Perished Year 201.

At my side, Velaire grasped my arm, the first sign of her grief she'd shown this entire time. Just a second to steady herself and cast a glance at me, her face weary beneath the red veil she wore. I would have thought she'd worn it to conceal her tears, except that she hadn't wept at all. Not today.

As we knelt in the rustling grass, everyone around us followed our lead. I glanced around and caught Avrik's gaze, steady and reassuring, before he bowed his head in a moment of silence. He was dressed in Royal Guard colors, with a smart new cloak and boots, and an elegant sword in his belt. Though the Royal Council and remaining guards had fiercely questioned my decision, one quick demonstration of his sword fighting and shooting abilities had removed their doubts. Avrik, a so-called nobody from a small, half-forgotten town, was fully capable of leading the guard as my new captain. Especially when they realized that it had been his gift that had settled a barrier over our kingdom after the battle, one unlike Eldon's in that it only kept out the nestrae and the other creatures that had sought to destroy us. For good or bad, our kingdom's borders would be open to all others, from the kingdoms across the sea to our neighbors, Alrenor and Toryn.

"It's not as strong as Eldon's was. It won't last forever," Avrik had explained to me, sinking to the sand in weariness as he gazed out over the sea. The nestred ships had long since vanished, the survivors either fleeing back to Toryn or to their home in the Wastelands. Messengers from both Kelwed and Argelon had already arrived with reports of mysterious demons who'd descended upon their city seemingly out of nowhere, only to retreat soon afterward. Their information was reassuring; neither city had been besieged by numbers as great as Misroth City had faced, and though both had sustained damage and casualties, they were rebuilding and recovering.

"But now we know we're capable of fighting them," I told him. "Your barrier doesn't have to last forever. It's enough to protect us now while we rebuild our strength."

"Strange, isn't it?" he asked after a long moment. "I thought creating a barrier this size would be impossible, but that was when Nesrelle was haunting me. When she made me feel weak, I doubted myself and my gift. I didn't think I was strong enough. Now I'm almost as powerful as Eldon was. But if our gifts depended on our own strengths and abilities to function, they wouldn't be called gifts, would they?"

I smiled at him, thinking of my truth gift and how I'd long doubted my worthiness to wield it. "No," I agreed, "they wouldn't."

Now, further back in the crowd, Narek and Iyleth stayed close together, heroes of Misroth and yet strangers among the people. They'd already shared their wish to return to Toryn someday and try to save whatever was left of their kingdom. They hadn't given up hope, not yet. Though many of the Misrothians still eyed Narek with suspicion and even hate, others were beginning to see what I claimed: that he was a friend and ally, and that he had fought bravely to save our kingdom. He was dressed in Misrothian red and blue, clothed in the uniform of a Royal Guard. With so many guards distrustful of him, and with his plans to eventually leave Misroth, it had made sense for Avrik to take his place as captain. But it hadn't made sense to strip him of a position among the guard. I told him that as long as I had the throne, he would hold that honor. In my eyes, he'd done more for Misroth than most could lay claim to.

Iyleth wore a simple gown, looking like the foreign leader she was—perhaps the last living heir to rule Toryn. She didn't know what had become of her brother after his betrayal. Her eyes were weary and sad, but her jaw was sharp, reminding me of the unexpected strength she carried. She was no stranger to surviving grief. "I wish I could heal hearts too," she'd told me gently when she'd found me in the street, weeping over Gillen's body. "But that is a kind of healing one has to search for and find all on their own."

Today, my wandering eyes settled on Jennah, clustered together with her husband Marke, her mother Kam, her two daughters, and Layk's siblings—young Dalen and Fia. It warmed my heart to see them safe and together at last. Breaking the news to Dalen and Fia had been crushing, but Jennah's heart was big enough to welcome them into her family with open arms. Though the children's eyes were red-rimmed and shadowed with sorrow, I could tell by the way they leaned in toward Marke and Jennah that they felt safe and cared for. They had a home again.

Finally, I found Rev gazing back at me, his eyes full of sadness and understanding and love. He smiled gently at me. Though he stood a little stiffly, hunched over from the pain of broken ribs, he looked proud and strong.

Other familiar faces were in the crowd too: Benor and his wife; Gare's wife, son, and new daughter-in-law; other rebels that I'd worked alongside to stop my father and his loyalists; and surviving servants and nobles that had been staying in the castle. Some citizens from Evren were there, like Bren, with his arm in a sling, or Corin, his bearded face bearing a new scar. Others were too injured to be present, and some had been among the countless bodies we'd burned and sent to the afterlife. Shilam had fallen in the fighting, as well as Hevro the blacksmith, Selna the innkeeper, and others from Evren I hadn't been close to, but had lived alongside. People I'd purchased goods from, passed as they worked in their fields, or chatted with on feast days or during visits to *Wanderer's Rest*. I'd closed countless familiar eyes, some too old to have been fighting, and some far too young.

The grief was unending. Mothers holding their children in their arms and weeping. Wives crying our for their husbands, and husbands collapsing at the sight of their dead wives. Fathers failing to hold back tears as they watched the flames flicker over their children's bodies.

There had been so many that we'd been forced to hold a mass funeral, building a great pyre outside the city gates that the demons themselves would have been proud to call theirs. Any the nestrae hadn't burnt in their sacrifices, we laid out in rows and burned until we were able to scatter the ashes across Misrothian ground. Ground the dead had paid dearly to keep free and safe for those they loved.

Kneeling now for my cousin, I thought about how Gillen would have protested. I could hear his voice in my mind as if he were still alive, or as if he was using his gift to speak across the endless distance between us. *My memorial should be no greater than my people's. They gave their lives for Misroth too.*

As the priest stood to light the flames, I helped Velaire to her feet and we stood, arm in arm, watching the fire consume Gillen's body. Avrik had recounted how he'd nearly succumbed to Nesrelle's curse and how Gillen had appeared in time to save him. He'd been shocked at first to find Gillen's body lying still and unharmed in the street beside him. When I'd first seen Gillen, I hadn't believed my cousin was dead either. He was unwounded, eyes closed and face composed as if he were enjoying the first peaceful sleep he'd had in countless months.

But he hadn't responded to my cries, and when I'd touched him, his body had been stiff and cold as ice. Claimed by Nesrelle.

That is what the Life-Giver had been telling me about sacrifice, I remembered now. *He was telling me that Gillen's sacrifice had been one of the greatest acts of courage that had weakened the nestrae.*

And it was what had kept Avrik alive to use his gift and keep Misroth safe now.

The flames leapt higher, dancing toward the bright sky. Smoke stung my eyes and my throat ached, yet I refused to shed a tear. My heart was broken, but I couldn't let my people see that, not today.

This is not a day I feel strong, I thought, remembering the words my cousin had spoken to me years ago at his own father's funeral. *Oh, Gil, I wish you were here to teach me how to be strong for them. How to lead them.*

We bid Gillen a final farewell before turning to begin our winding path down into the city, toward the very same square in which my father had been crowned. Wind tugged through my hair, and I knew despite the crown of braids Jennah had used to tame my locks, they would look wild by the time the ceremony began. My dress was blood red for mourning, matching my sythrel-marked armband and rustling behind me in a long train. In the days following the battle for Misroth, the Royal Seamstress had worked tirelessly on a new wardrobe for me, beginning with this, my gown that served as both my mourning attire and my coronation outfit. To me, it seemed empty and petty after everything my kingdom had suffered, but to the seamstress, it was imperative I looked queenly on this day.

"Send a message to the people," she'd murmured to me as she showed me the sketch she'd made. The flowing gown was embroidered with gold stars, the constellations of both Vehgar and the archer Shyla facing one another on the bodice. Strength and beauty and light. The courage to defy a greater power. They were important symbols to Misroth, even if they were set on a backdrop the color of mourning and blood and sacrificial flame. "You're Misroth's first ruling queen. Remind them you are a hero, a powerful warrior and leader, and their symbol of hope."

My tongue cleaved to my dry mouth and my nestred rune still ached. I felt like none of those things, but I'd nodded. I would do this for my people. For Gillen.

Despite the possibility of later protests from the nobility and Councilors present, Avrik and my friends walked close to me as we marched into the city. Rev strode behind me, placing a sturdy hand on my shoulder for an instant to whisper in my ear, "I wish your mother could see you now." My heavy heart lifted. Lyanna, my true mother. The thrill of knowing she and Rev loved me and were proud of me, that they thought of me as their own daughter, would never grow old.

The streets were lined with people waving ribbons and wearing armbands, their cheers of hope and tears of grief mingling together in one tumultuous cry. Everything reeked of smoke and ash, and there was no concealing the skeletons of half-burned shops and pubs, inns and bakeries, homes and sanctuaries. Though many of my people had dressed in the finest clothes they owned, plenty more were homeless, with nothing but the dirty, faded clothes on their backs. Rebuilding our city and our lives would take time.

Despite the grief that seized the city, signs of hope had sprung up again. This was a time of celebration as much as it was a time of mourning. Children laughed and played, chasing one another through the crowds. Banners proclaiming victory streamed from windows or over the doors of businesses. The tantalizing scent of fresh apple cinnamon pastries and steaming mugs of tea and cider filled the air as vendors passed out treats. Boys and girls sold bouquets of wildflowers they'd gathered outside the city and tied together with twine for a drae apiece. Now and then the three dragons, soaring overhead and racing one another through the skies, would swoop low. As soon as one of their great shadows fell across the street, the citizens would pause and gasp and point. Some cringed or cowered, still terrified of the beasts, but others smiled or clapped their hands in awe.

Avrik slipped his hand in mine, squeezing it reassuringly.

"I don't think it would be considered proper for the Captain of the Guard to hold the queen's hand at her coronation," I whispered with a smile.

Avrik raised his eyebrows in mock surprise. "Oh, you're worried about being proper now?" he teased.

He started to withdraw his hand, but I laughed and squeezed his back before he could move away. We both knew our relationship would be frowned upon, but we also knew, whether I was queen or not, no one would tell me what I could or couldn't do. Not anymore.

When I halted in the square, waiting in the shadow of Eldon's statue, I remembered what my visions had shown me about my ancestor's flaws. I lifted my head and drew a deep breath, squaring my shoulders. The priest was already waiting, the crown clasped in his hands.

I will not live in the shadow of my ancestors and their mistakes, I thought. Eldon's and my father's blood flowed through my veins, but I wasn't them. I would be stronger, better, braver.

The priest lifted his voice in the customary song:

> *"O bren valt hali,*
> *O bren valt mis.*
> *Mari, O emba l'val…"*

My aunt patted my arm as the priest finished and beckoned me forward. The air hung quiet and still as everyone watched the priest lift the crown over my head. The same silver crown that had once rested upon my father's head, my uncle's head, and my ancestor Eldon's head. Today it would go to a woman for the first time in Misrothian history.

When I glanced at the Councilmen, their heads were bowed, their eyes lowered to the ground. Perhaps my fight against Nesrelle had won their respect at last.

"I vow to protect my kingdom with my own blood…" the priest began, and I repeated the words after him.

In the crowd, I found Jennah, who smiled and winked at me. Narek offered me a salute. Not far away, Rev was trying to wipe his eyes discreetly.

"…and, if circumstances demand it," I finished, "to give my own life for Misroth."

The priest set the crown on my head and turned me to face my people, who were already kneeling, pressing their fists to their hearts and bowing their heads. "I present to you Queen Halia of Misroth!"

"Long live the queen!" someone called out, and the people took up the cry.

Avrik caught my gaze and grinned. For the first time that day, I found myself able to smile too.

"All hail Queen Halia the Unbroken!" he shouted, and the citizens echoed the new cry.

Unbroken. It was true for all of us. We would have difficult days ahead, but we were survivors.

Undefeated, unafraid, and unbroken.

EPILOGUE

TRACING GILLEN'S PAINTED CONSTELLATIONS WITH my fingertips, I closed my eyes, keeping the tears at bay. A memory from after Uncle Reylon had passed stirred in my mind, the night before everything had gone wrong in my life. Before retreating to his chambers, Gillen had hugged me tightly, as if he worried that *I* needed comforting more than him, when he'd been the one to lose his father. *It's never goodbye forever,* he'd whispered in my ear, *when it's someone you love.*

"It feels like forever," I murmured bitterly to the empty room. Unlived in, it felt cold and dismal. The light that Gillen had carried with him was snuffed out, and everything he'd left behind, while comforting, was also hollow. Memories were a poor substitute for a life.

But the warmth of my truth gift stirred inside me, filling my bones that ached with grief and reminding me of the vision I'd seen of my lost loved ones on the other side. The afterlife had seemed just a breath away then, bright and golden and joyful. The ones I grieved weren't so distant after all; their presence lingered in my heart, in my soul. I'd live for those who no longer could and honor their memories, and someday I'd be with them again.

My palm landed on the silver stars Gillen had painted to create Vehgar. *Strength and beauty and light.*

"Halia?" Iyleth's soft voice broke through my thoughts as she stepped through the doorway.

When she noticed me hovering by Gillen's paintings, she didn't waste time asking questions. She crossed the room silently and wrapped me in a warm embrace.

"I'll be all right," I said, relaxing into her hug. The truth gift flowing through me confirmed that this wasn't a lie. "I'll be ready to leave soon."

With a gentle smile, Iyleth squeezed my hand. "We'll meet you soon then."

I lingered a moment longer after Iyleth left, studying this room that had once been so familiar. Then I strode through the castle halls toward the training room for the Royal Guard. A vast, circular space lined with weapons and old suits of armor, its stone walls stretched toward a balcony where spectators could view those sparring or training below. Set at intervals rising all the way along the walls toward the high ceiling, numerous windows allowed plenty of natural light into the room. Despite the fact that even now most were open wide to the fresh autumn breeze, the air still smelled of stale sweat and blood.

When I entered, Avrik and Jaren were the only guards present, laughingly taunting one another as they sparred with practice swords. Their training clothes, also in Misrothian red and blue like their uniforms, were rumpled and sweaty.

While all the other recruits from Evren and the surrounding towns, including Rev and Bren, had long since returned home, Jaren had chosen a different path. Not long after I'd named Avrik Captain of the Royal Guard, Jaren had approached us both.

"I want to join the guard," he said. His eyes had been shadowed, his shoulders hunched with the unending grief and weariness that plagued us all after the battle. "I want you to train me, Avrik." He drew a deep breath. "Bren has his farm he'll inherit. Shilam is…gone. Going back won't be the same anymore. I want to serve Misroth and help my friends." His gaze shifted between Avrik and me. "Please."

Avrik had been happy to welcome a friend into his ranks. We were all grieving Shilam, and it was true that Bren belonged in Evren. Having another member of our friend group close to us in the capital was a comfort. Especially when everything was even more unfamiliar and challenging for Avrik than it was for me. He had new customs and etiquette to learn, guards older than him to convince of his worthiness to lead, and nobles and Royal Councilors forever sneering at him for being a commoner. They accused him of not deserving his position of power and of using his relationship with me to gain it.

Now, I lifted an eyebrow at my friends and set my hands on my hips. Still, I couldn't avoid the grin tugging at the corners of my mouth. It was heartening to see my old friends laughing and joking. "This doesn't look like preparing to leave," I said.

Straightening, Avrik and Jaren sprinted to the wall to discard their practice swords before crossing back toward me. "We'll be ready in ten minutes," Jaren promised.

"Oh really?" I said skeptically.

"Really," Avrik said, leaning in close, wrapping me in his arms, and kissing me firmly on my mouth. I blinked in surprise before melting into him and deepening the kiss.

Jaren rolled his eyes dramatically. "You're disgusting."

Laughing, I pulled back, but Avrik only smirked at his friend's complaint and kissed me again, harder.

"I'm leaving now," Jaren announced loudly, walking backwards toward the door as he pretended to glare at us. "Since you seem to have forgotten I'm here anyway."

"We should go too," I said, seizing Avrik's hand and tugging him toward the hall.

Outside, Councilor Veren swept by in his bright, perfectly pressed attire and narrowed his eyes at the sight of Avrik and me walking hand-in-hand.

"They can complain about us all they want and insist I marry a foreign king to 'strengthen alliances,'" I muttered as soon as Veren was out of earshot. "But they can't rush me into marriage or choose my husband.”

As soon as the words left my mouth, I froze, embarrassed. Avrik and I might have spoken of forever when we'd thought he was dying, but we'd never talked about it in a world in which he was safe, in which it was a true possibility. In the months since the battle, we'd been endlessly busy with rebuilding and with the responsibilities of our new roles. My coronation had occurred almost immediately, sweeping me into the world of politics again, and Avrik had numerous responsibilities to juggle as my new Captain of the Guard. Our time together consisted of stolen moments like this one.

Avrik turned to me, stepping closer until I was backed against the wall. A mischievous glint sparkled in his brown eyes. "Is that another proposal?"

I smacked his shoulder playfully, but Avrik's grin disappeared, his expression sobering to something earnest. Intense. He reached up and brushed a strand of hair back from my face, resting his calloused palm against my cheek.

"Possibly. Eventually. The Royal Council might insist you become king and share responsibilities with me," I said quickly. "Or they might refuse you entirely and—"

Avrik cupped my face in both of his hands. His eyes burned into mine, his expression so full of joy and longing that my breath caught in my throat.

"I've thought about it. A lot," Avrik added with a smile. "I'm willing to learn to rule alongside you if that's what I must do. And I'm willing to remain only the Captain of the Guard. I don't care about titles, but I care about Misroth and I care about you. I'll do or be whatever it takes to share a life with you." He pressed his lips to my forehead. "Whenever you're ready." His eyes dropped briefly to the red armband on my bicep, the accessory it seemed I'd be wearing forever these days, and I knew he understood what I needed. "Take your time to grieve, to lead and rebuild Misroth, to build a new life. I'll wait for you."

Entering Evren would always feel like coming home. I could finally breathe freely. Standing under the open Evren sky, studying the farmland with crops ready for harvest, the rolling hills with grazing livestock, and the cozy homes tucked throughout the countryside, I closed my eyes and drew a deep, cleansing breath. The smell of freshly fallen leaves and chimney smoke gave the autumn breeze a warm, homey scent.

"The air does smell cleaner out here, doesn't it?" Avrik said. We'd ridden our dragons to the edge of the forest, where we'd dismounted to walk the rest of the way. Overhead, the beasts circled one another, soaring and diving through the air as if they too rejoiced in the sweet country air.

I grinned at Avrik. He was clothed in his attire as Captain of the Royal Guard, with the sigil of Vehgar stitched on his shoulder. The vivid shades of blue and red suited him. With his old habit of carrying around a bow everywhere he went in Evren, always having a sword at his side seemed to keep him at ease. When he looked at me, his warm brown eyes danced with happiness. It was like we shared a secret each time we glanced at one another. *Forever.* We had the promise of forever.

"Fresh air?" On Avrik's other side, Jaren raised his eyebrows skeptically. "Smells like good old Farmer Erron fertilized his garden again."

Avrik glanced back at Evren Forest, still a somewhat ominous feature in the landscape with its tangled, ancient trees and shadowy undergrowth. When he'd used his gift to create a barrier around our kingdom to keep the nestrae out, he'd created others to encircle the forest and mountains and prevent the sedwa from leaving. I'd seen the visible weight it had lifted from Avrik's shoulders to know the people of Evren were safe at last, to know that he could release the guilt he'd carried for so long.

Even if Misroth City was our official home these days, there was no replacing Evren in our hearts. It was reassuring to know the little town rested safe even when we were miles away.

Now, at last, we all had an opportunity to break free from the endless work of rebuilding the capital. It was comforting, even if our reason to be back in Evren this soon was not. Jennah, her family, Narek, and Iyleth had joined us. It was time to officially honor the sacrifices the recruits and their surviving families had made by holding a memorial service here.

But first, I returned home.

Lyanna was running out the door, Rev on her heels, almost as soon as our group drew within sight of the house.

"Halia!" she cried, throwing her arms around me. "It's so good to see you. You're staying here until you leave, of course? Avrik, Jaren! Oh, look at your uniforms, so dashing!" She crushed the boys in another embrace as Rev stepped forward to hug me. He'd recovered and left for Evren soon after my coronation service.

"It's always good to see you," he murmured.

After we all settled inside, Lyanna served tea and sandwiches. As happy as she was to see me, she hovered around Jennah and Marke a lot so she could dote on their daughters, Laydin and Avalee, and Layk's young siblings, Dalen and Fia. "Would you like some cookies?" she asked with a wink, patting Avalee on the head.

Laydin nodded eagerly.

Jennah beamed. "Getting spoiled, I see," she said. Seated beside her, Marke chuckled and patted her hand. Months after our return and the two remained inseparable, as if making up for lost time.

Then again, Avrik and I were the same. It was hard enough to find time to be together, and we rarely were alone. When we worked together to clean up the city, clearing rubble or overseeing construction of new buildings or handing out food and water to struggling families, we'd find any excuse we could to stand close or sneak a moment to hold hands.

"I wish we were here for a happier reason," I said at last.

My eyes met Iyleth's from across the table. Ever since the battle, she'd had constant dark circles under her eyes from the long hours she worked to heal the injured. The healing gift had only manifested in a few others, meaning that they were in frequent demand and often exhausted beyond their means. Even now, when most had either succumbed to their wounds or healed since the fight, many families in the city were homeless, living crowded together in empty rooms in the castle, in vacant buildings, and in tents throughout the city, and they'd begun falling prey to illness. Iyleth's work, it seemed, was never-ending.

Narek had been there to support her in any way he could, holding her when she wept over the ones she couldn't save. Sharing his hopes for saving Toryn and building something from the fallen kingdom they both loved so much. Reminding her that every time she managed to smile as she spoke words of hope over suffering Misrothians she was showing her strength.

They'd both done so much for my kingdom. Every evening, they, Avrik, Jaren, and Jennah and her family, who had moved into the castle, shared dinner with Velaire and me. Having my friends close had made the capital feel a little more like home. I knew I'd miss Narek and Iyleth dearly whenever they decided it was time to leave and brave Toryn.

Having this group of close-knit friends here in Evren reminded me once again how important they were to me. How much I relied on their support as I began the work of learning how to rule a kingdom.

As if sensing my melancholy thoughts, Avrik leaned closer to me and took my hands in his own. His warm, reassuring presence grounded me.

"I wish you were here for a happier reason too," Lyanna sighed, "but the families will all be so grateful for the honor of your visit." Her bright eyes scanned the room, settling on each of us. "And I don't just mean Halia, but all of you. You have contributed to serving and protecting Misroth in countless ways." She looked at Narek and smiled, startling a grin out of him. "You're all heroes to me and the people of this town."

We visited homes, hugging mothers and fathers, sisters and brothers, daughters and sons. We spoke of selfless sacrifices and immense courage, of love and hope and a new beginning for our kingdom. Whenever I struggled to find the words, Avrik or Iyleth had a ready supply of encouraging things to say.

We shook hands with Corin and walked through Evren Garden, a sanctuary of warmth and life despite the deepening cold of autumn. We visited Wanderer's Rest and comforted Selna's husband and surviving son, who despite everything, insisted on offering us drinks and food and thanking us for our presence. We held a service for the dead in the memorial field, burning sacrifices of flowers and singing songs for those gone ahead to the afterlife.

At long last, our weary business was done, and it was time to bid Evren goodbye.

My friends and I lingered outside of Lyanna and Rev's house, not ready to leave. Not yet.

"Take care of her," Rev said, his voice gruff with suppressed tears as he hugged Avrik.

"Always," Avrik promised.

Rev and Lyanna turned to the others, thanking Jennah, Narek, Iyleth, and Jaren endlessly for all they did and all the ways they supported me. They waited to approach me last, when I was already blinking away tears.

"Oh, my dear," Lyanna sighed, wiping her own tears from her cheeks. "It always seemed like you were too good to be true. A wonderful blessing sent by the Life-Giver, but never meant to stay forever."

I shook my head fiercely. "Just because my home is in Misroth City now, doesn't mean that you aren't still family."

"I know," she said, sniffling. "I hope you visit any chance you get."

"Lyanna. Rev," I said firmly. "I know your home is here in Evren, but couldn't you consider staying with me, in the castle?"

Rev's eyes widened. "Would the people—the Royal Council—your aunt—would that be acceptable?" he stammered.

A smile tugged at my lips, a laugh almost bubbling from my throat despite the tears still clinging to my eyelashes.

At my side again, Avrik wrapped an arm around me, pulling me to him. "She's the queen," he said with a smirk. "Everyone kind of has to accept what she decides." He winked at me. "Even deciding on a commoner like me."

Lyanna drew a deep breath, a smile blossoming on her face. "Really?" she breathed.

"You don't have to live there year-round. I know you love your home and your garden and Evren, and I think if we kept it, it would be a good place for us to stay whenever I have a chance to get away," I went on hurriedly.

Lyanna pulled me in for a hug so fierce she yanked me right out of Avrik's grasp. We all fell into laughter.

"Of course we would love to!" she said.

"Yes," Rev agreed, joining our hug.

"I feel left out," Avrik complained, until Lyanna laughed and pulled him into the embrace.

Giggling, the children dashed forward to cling to our legs, much to Jennah and Marke's entertainment.

"As one of her guards," Jaren chimed in, crossing his arms but smiling in spite of himself, "I think I need to intervene. I don't want to go back to Misroth with a message about how the queen was crushed to death."

Narek smirked as Iyleth leaned into him. "And as one of her other guards," he countered, "I think she'll survive this just fine."

I laughed aloud and squeezed Lyanna and Rev tighter.

Misroth had many more uncertainties and difficulties left to face. Maybe even more grief and pain and danger. Perhaps the nestrae would never threaten us again in our lifetimes, or maybe we only had a few years of peace ahead of us. Alrenor and its instability could prove a threat, or the survivors in Toryn could choose to rally together and continue what the nestrae had started. As queen, I had much to learn and many new burdens to carry.

But, surrounded by the ones I loved, I knew I could face anything.

THE END

CAN'T GET ENOUGH?

Read the complete *Cursed Empire* series, set in the same world as the *Silent Kingdom* series!

You can also sign up for my newsletter to read four exclusive prequel chapters introducing you to the characters in *Cursed Empire*, including both Lo and Jalie, Empress Karye's daughter.

These bonus chapters aren't available anywhere else, and they are the perfect bridge between the *Silent Kingdom* trilogy and the *Cursed Empire* series!

ACKNOWLEDGEMENTS

First of all, I want to extend a huge THANK YOU to anyone who has joined me on this journey. In some ways, this was as grueling and transformative for me as it was for Halia and her friends. The concept for the first book of *Silent Kingdom* was born in late 2012, though it was a pathetically underdeveloped short story, and now here we are, at the end at last, 8 years later. In those years I've grown and changed, lost loved ones, faced difficulties, wrestled doubts, found love, and moved way more often than anyone should ever move. Without a doubt, my personal experiences helped shape these books.

But no author is truly alone. Just as in my real life, I couldn't have made it through the challenge of writing this series without some dear friends and an amazing team along the way.

As always, I thank author David Estes for his support and guidance in my publishing adventure.

I'd also like to thank Julienne Calhoun and Sheree Whitelock, my dear friends and critique partners, who let me vent to them about my books, who agree to read and reread my books to analyze and overanalyze the plot and characters with me, and who always offer me encouragement and support throughout every stage of the writing process. If I were Halia (we all know I'm not cool enough to be Halia), you'd be the Jennah and Narek to my life. You two can fight over who gets to be whom. ;)

Special thanks to all the other family and friends who have offered an encouraging word, purchased and read my books—even if they're outside of your typical genre, and cheered me on. And of course, thank you to my husband, who believes in me and gives me the space and support I need to work. Even if your non-fiction reading habits mean you never finish reading this series, you've had a part in bringing them to life. Thanks for helping me achieve my dreams and for celebrating my little victories.

Of course, I owe my beta reader team my immense gratitude as well. This story is so much better because of your thoughtful feedback and advice. So thank you, thank you, Tricia Ghent, Kate Hausladen, Rebecca Isley, Julie Janis, and Monica Khan!

To the One who gave me the ability to write and put these stories in my heart: thank You for this gift. Thank You for the incredible, beautiful way in which words can inspire and heal, transform and motivate, captivate and encourage. I'm forever in awe that we live in a world filled with the power and beauty of words and the magic of stories—and that I have the privilege of contributing some of my own.

Last but not least, I want to thank all my readers who have read these books and stuck with me throughout this wild ride. Thanks for your support, for your reviews, for your sweet messages, for your beautiful photos of my books, and for all those times you've shared my books with your friends and family! You are incredible!

ABOUT THE AUTHOR

Rachel L. Schade was born on the first day of summer in a small town in Michigan, only to end up in another small town in Ohio. She attended The Ohio State University to learn how to write obnoxiously long papers, cite people who use big words, and discuss her passion: books. She has a great love for the color blue, sunshine, chocolate, and not folding her laundry. Currently she lives with her husband and surrounds herself with books, coffee, and furry creatures on a regular basis.

You can email Rachel at rachelschade@gmail.com, or find her on Facebook and Goodreads: Rachel L. Schade, and on Instagram and TikTok: @rachelschadeauthor.

www.rachelschadeauthor.com